Simply Love

Catherine Anderson

Simply Love

WHEELER
PUBLISHING, INC.
ROCKLAND, MA

★ AN AMERICAN COMPANY ★

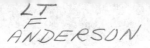

Published in Large Print by arrangement with Avon Books, a division of The Hearst Corporation, in the United States and Canada

Wheeler Large Print Book Series.

Set in 16 pt Plantin.

Library of Congress Cataloging-in-Publication Data

Anderson, Catherine (Adeline Catherine)
  Simply love / Catherine Anderson.
      p. (large print) cm.(Wheeler large print book series)
  ISBN 1-56895-641-X (softcover)
  1. Large type books. I. Title. II. Series
[PS3551.N34557S5 1999]
813'.54—dc21
                                                                    99-011185
                                                                         CIP

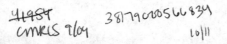

Simply Love

PROLOGUE

Black Jack, Colorado
August 1887

৯৯ Alone inside the church, Cassandra Zerek scooted on her knees across the floor, rubbing industriously at the squares of oak within her reach until they shone like polished agate. Anemic afternoon sunlight came through the stained glass windows, casting a rainbow of colors across the empty pews, all of which gleamed with the fresh coat of beeswax she'd just applied. Mingling with the scent of the wax were lingering traces of incense from Mass that morning and the acrid smell of smoke from the flickering votive candles that burned near the altar.

Sitting back on her heels to catch her breath, Cassandra swiped a tendril of curly, sable hair from her eyes and puffed air past her lips to cool her cheeks. Perspiration ran in rivulets from under her breasts and trickled over her ribs, the sensation making her itch under the heavy wool of her blue dress. Dratted dress, anyhow. No matter how many layers of underclothing she wore, the coarse weave always managed to irritate her skin.

Eyeing the distance she still had to cover before she would be finished with the floor, Cassandra nearly groaned. It was another twenty feet up the center aisle to the doors. Considering the fact that the aisle was four tiles across, each a foot square, and she was the only person there to buff each one, that was no short distance. Her arms already felt like aching lumps hanging off her shoulders, and her back hurt. Her eighteen years felt like a hundred.

Waxing the church floor was a big job for one person to tackle, and three-quarters of the way through, she always wondered why she'd ever promised to do it. The answer was simple, of course. Because she couldn't afford to give money to the church as other people did, she made a gift of her time instead, helping the nuns over at the convent and orphanage every weekday afternoon, laundering Father Tully's vestments, and cleaning the church from top to bottom twice a month.

Today was her day to clean....

Resuming the task with renewed vigor, Cassandra refolded her buffing cloth to leave a fresh side out, then bent to resume her rubbing. Suffering, she reminded herself, helped to build character, and since she truly wanted to become a nun, she needed all the character she could get.

To make the time go faster while she worked, she decided to make some personal intentions, short prayers she said almost daily asking God for special help. Heaven knew she needed divine intercession if she meant to enter the convent any time soon.

Please, God, help me become more practical. The next time I start wishing for frivolities, like those patent leather slippers in Miss Dryden's dress shop window, help me to pray, instead, for the poor, that they may have food aplenty and warm blankets.

Finishing one section of floor, Cassandra scooted forward to begin buffing another.

And, please, when I stop by the convent later today, don't let me stare at the good sisters and wonder what their heads look like shaved. To become a Bride of Christ, I'll happily part with my hair. I promise, I will. And I'll never mourn the loss.

Even as she made the vow, Cassandra cringed. Her thick sable hair was the only pretty thing about her, and of all the sacrifices she'd have to make to take holy orders, she dreaded having to shave her head the most.

And, please, Father, in Your immense goodness, help me not to get angry today. Bless my dear mama's soul, but the Irish temper I got from her isn't at all the thing for an aspiring nun.

A sudden noise interrupted Cassandra's train of thought. She froze to listen and heard the outside door to the vestibule open and close. If it was someone coming in off the street who hadn't thought to wipe his feet, she'd have his head.

Prepared for battle, she watched the closed double doors that separated the vestibule from the interior of the church. *Nothing.* Cocking an ear, she heard footsteps, followed by a crackle of paper and a muffled thump. *The poor box?* It sounded to her as if someone had just opened it. Probably just some good-hearted soul leaving a donation.

3

Unless, of course, it was a thief.

The thought made her pulse race. Where there was one thief, there could be a half dozen. What if it was an entire band, and they'd come to pilfer and vandalize St. Mary's?

She made a quick sign of the cross, praying for courage. If a band of hooligans had entered the church, it would be up to her to protect the Holy Eucharist that Father Tully always kept in the tabernacle.

It was one of Cassandra's favorite daydreams, to one day be required to sacrifice her life for the faith. Preferably in such a heart-wrenching fashion that everyone who heard of her courage would weep and cross themselves at the mention of her name. *Saint Cassandra.*

Ruffians storming into the sanctuary would be *perfect*, especially if they were determined to desecrate the sacrament. In true saintly fashion, she would drape herself over the tabernacle to protect its sacred contents, her body a bleeding shield. When Father Tully, the parish priest, found her afterward, she would be near death, and with her last breath, she'd whisper, "It is nothing, Father. Do not weep. I have given of myself for Jesus, and I die with a glad heart."

She flung down her cleaning rag and pushed to her feet, determined to face her fate as bravely as Joan of Arc or Saint Catherine, who'd chosen a horrible death by torture to preserve her chastity. Well…neither of them had anything over Cassandra Zerek. She would die for God, and do so gladly.

All she needed was an opportunity.

Creeping toward the double doors, Cassandra steeled herself for the worst. Carefully turning the knob, she pushed the portal open a crack and peered into the vestibule. She glimpsed a man standing at the poor box, a very tall man in an expensive gray topcoat. Intent on counting out money to put in an envelope, he seemed unaware he was being watched.

Not a robber.

For a moment, Cassandra felt keen disappointment. But then, beneath the man's smartly tipped, felt fedora hat, she saw neatly trimmed, tawny-colored hair. Only one man in Black Jack, Colorado, had hair that color.

Her heart kicked against her ribs. *Luke Taggart.* And he was right here in St. Mary's? Cassandra couldn't quite believe it. Oh, she'd seen him on the street plenty of times, but never from up this close.

He was the most important individual in Black Jack, barring none. The man owned nearly the whole town, including most of the producing gold mines. He even owned the mine where her papa and older brother, Ambrose, were employed. For the first time in Cassandra's memory, her papa and brother had to work only six days a week, their shifts a mere ten hours long instead of the customary fourteen, and they still had enough money to buy food and pay the rent each month. As a result, Luke Taggart's name was almost a prayer upon all the Zereks' lips.

But few people in Black Jack shared her family's high opinion of Mr. Taggart. He was rumored to be a harsh, godless man who

5

engaged in all manner of wicked activities. Cassandra wasn't quite sure what kinds of wicked activities, only that she'd heard her papa say Mr. Taggart consorted with "shabby women," showing no preference for any particular one. In Cassandra's opinion, that was further proof of the man's altruistic character, for he was extremely rich. If he chose, he could consort only with ladies as wealthy and well-dressed as he was.

Even now, observing Luke Taggart through a cracked door, she felt in awe of him. A funny, fluttery feeling in the pit of her stomach made her pulse quicken. His topcoat was unbuttoned, revealing a pale gray silk vest over a crisp white shirt and darker gray trousers, the sharp creases in the legs drawn smooth by the bunched muscles in his thighs.

Hair the color of burnished oak framed his sun-darkened features, which were so well-defined they might have been chiseled from granite. His jaw was angular. An aquiline nose jutted from between tawny, winged brows. A full yet firm mouth was bracketed by deep creases that offset the stubborn thrust of his squared chin. It was a beautiful face, classically masculine, its planes weathered by the elements, the skin etched with tiny crow's-feet.

Free to study him closely for the first time, Cassandra couldn't help but notice that his expression seemed at odds with the strength he emanated. A lost, confused look dominated his features, like that of a little boy wandering the streets who'd forgotten his way home a long time ago and had no hope of finding it again.

Tapping the fat envelope against his palm, he gazed at the poor box, clearly troubled and undecided about whether or not he should make a donation. Then, with a determined briskness, he thrust the envelope back inside his jacket and strode to the door. Once there, he stood with his back to Cassandra, one hand resting on the doorknob, his shoulders rigid. At any second, she expected him to leave. Instead, he heaved a sigh that conveyed soul-deep weariness, then spun back around to descend on the poor box again, his manner so filled with frustration that she wasn't sure if he meant to make a donation or dismantle the box.

As he stood there, wrestling with emotions she couldn't define, he suddenly seemed to sense that someone was staring at him. He jerked his head up, his preoccupied, unguarded expression turning wary, his stance taking on a sudden tension that electrified the air. His reaction was like that of a man who'd been caught red-handed in an act of thievery or some other equally iniquitous wrongdoing, which made no sense at all.

Cassandra caught her breath against the impact of his startled, piercing gaze. His eyes were the color of whiskey shot through with firelight, the glinting amber irises ringed with black. She'd noticed them before, of course. Lots of times when she had passed him on the streets of Black Jack, but she'd never felt the full force of them leveled directly at her.

As fierce and golden as a tiger's, his gaze turned her skin hot, seeming to strip her bare. Held transfixed, she felt a sudden rush of fear as inexplicable as it was paralyzing. *Nonsense*, her practical side scoffed. But another part of her felt completely unnerved, and she wanted to run. Insolent and bold, his gaze slid over her, lingering for an endless moment on her breasts before continuing downward, then sweeping back up to her face.

The silence in the otherwise empty church seemed deafening, driving home to her how vulnerable she was. Even if she screamed her very loudest, no one was likely to hear.

As if he guessed her thoughts, he cocked a tawny eyebrow, one corner of his mouth twitching with a suppressed smile. Tapping the envelope against his palm again, he said, "It would seem I've been found out."

His voice curled around her like warm smoke, the wispy tendrils holding her fast. She tried to think of something to say, but her mind had gone stupidly blank.

He quickly closed the envelope, then thrust it into the poor box. Bringing his gaze back to her, he tipped his hat. "I trust this will remain our secret? I'd just as soon no one knows."

Before Cassandra could think of a response, he turned and exited the church.

Silence swamped the vestibule after his departure—a heavy, echoing silence that seemed to press against her eardrums. She stared at the poor box for several seconds, then began moving slowly toward it, curiosity outweighing her hesitancy. Lifting the lid of the box, she withdrew the envelope he had left. Scrawled across its face was one word: *orphanage*.

A smile touched Cassandra's mouth. A few weeks back, she'd heard the good sisters of St. Mary's wondering aloud about the anonymous benefactor who had made a sizable donation to the orphanage. Now the mystery was solved. The do-gooder had been none other than the scandalous, godless, and wicked Luke Taggart.

Cassandra returned the envelope to the box, her heart catching as she recalled the confused, lost look she'd seen in his eyes before he realized anyone was watching him. Wickedness? For reasons beyond her, he apparently wanted everyone to believe that of him. He might even believe it himself.

But for a few brief seconds, she'd glimpsed the man behind the mask, and somehow she knew that Luke Taggart was many things, but wicked wasn't one of them.

ONE

It was the devil's own afternoon. Black clouds gathered over the teeth-sharp peaks of the Rocky Mountains, and an angry wind from the north drove gusts against the buildings. Locked into his own thoughts, Luke Taggart stood by the window in the Golden Slipper's best upstairs room and watched the sun drift behind a patch of thunderous gray. Heralding the approach of winter, September was coming in with a vengeance. Unless he missed his guess, there would be one hell of a rainstorm before nightfall.

The warm glow of the gaslights placed strategically around the red and gold bedchamber did little to offset the gloom. Oblivious to the opulence he'd once admired, he listened with half an ear to the sibilant hiss of the gas jets, his heart striking two muted beats to every click of the pendulum.

From beyond the windowpane he heard a hoarse shout, followed by a stream of curses. *Another barroom brawl in the offing?* he wondered without much interest. Leaning a hip against the sill, he gazed morosely through the glass at the cobblestone sidewalks two stories below him. Townsfolk scurried past the Golden Slipper to patronize shops farther up the way. As the ladies walked by the gambling house, they stepped clear off the curb and into the street, their noses lifted in disdain, their fancy skirts drawn close around their ankles, as if the very air might be contaminated.

Anger burned low in Luke's gut like a smoldering coal buried under a thick layer of ash, the fire inside him always there but carefully banked. Snobbish bitches. Let them risk life and limb if that pleased their condescending sense of morality. It was no skin off his nose if one of them got run over by a passing conveyance.

Running a hand inside his unbuttoned shirt, Luke rubbed his chest, his fingertips tracing the hard bulges of muscle under his sweat-moistened skin. God, he felt tired, the kind of tiredness that ran bone-deep and far beyond the physical.

"Luke, baby. Come back to bed."

Gloria's purring demand raked down his spine like a fingernail over a blackboard. In spite of its pretension to elegance, the room carried the subtle odor of fish that always seemed to accompany sex. As was his habit after he'd finished with a woman, he'd scrubbed all trace of her from his person, but the faint smell that lingered in the air and clung to the satin sheets still made him feel unclean.

Christ, what in the hell was wrong with him these days? He should be snuggled into the soft feather mattress of the fancy bed behind him instead of scowling out the window like a restless prisoner. Gloria was a gorgeous woman, with a mane of silky blond hair, skin like cream, and pink-tipped breasts the size of melons. She was also willing to do almost anything for a price, and Luke had an endless store of money to accommodate her. Six months ago, he would have kept her busy until well after midnight. Then, if he'd gotten bored, he might have called in another girl to spice things up. There was nothing like two women in one bed to whet a man's sexual appetite.

Feeling a mild interest stirring, he toyed with the idea of doing just that. Two women—hell, maybe even three. With a bottle of expensive scotch to numb his senses, he could sink back on the downy mattress and give himself up to their ministrations. He was rich, for God's sake. Anything he wanted

11

was his for the asking. All he had to do was snap his fingers.

He'd done it plenty of times before. He could do it again.

So, why didn't he?

That was the question that had lured him from the bed to the window, the question that had his belly knotted and his mind running in dark circles. Not that he was unhappy, exactly. How could he be when he had damned near everything he'd ever wanted? And yet he'd come to realize over the past few weeks that his life reminded him of a glass of ale left out overnight—flat, with all the fizz gone.

Making more money didn't help.

Nor did the women he bedded. Blondes, redheads, brunettes…each more beautiful than the last. They didn't seem to make a difference. Flat ale was flat ale, and no matter how much salt you added, sometimes it wouldn't come to a head.

"Luke, love. Come make Gloria a happy girl, hmm?" The bed ropes creaked as she shifted her weight. He heard the covers rustle and guessed she was kicking them aside, the better to tantalize him. "Just look at what I've got for you."

His throat tight with a sense of revulsion he couldn't understand, Luke glanced over his shoulder. Gloria lay on the bed, her nude body seductively arranged to thrill and entice. Her dark lashes swept low over her sultry brown eyes as she cupped her large breasts, thrusting the twin mounds of flesh high and toying with her nipples. Luke watched the rosy

12

peaks grow turgid as she tweaked and rubbed them.

He felt nothing…absolutely nothing. Except an urgent need to escape.

"Come do this for me," she pleaded with a pretty pout. When he made no move to accept the invitation, she lifted her slender hips and spread her knees. "Or I can do this while you play elsewhere." She caught the rigid peak of one nipple between her fingers, rolling the sensitive flesh and shuddering delicately. "Please, Luke. I need you, love. It's lonely over here without you."

Moving from the window, Luke began to button his shirt. As he thrust the tails into the waistband of his trousers and fastened the fly, he forced a smile. "Not today, sweetheart. For some reason, I'm just not feeling up to snuff."

Gloria ceased the self-titillation, huffed with indignation, and jerked the bedcovers back over herself. "Anymore, you always say that. 'Not now, Gloria. I just don't feel up to it.'" She sat erect, holding the sheet to her breasts, her brown eyes snapping. "If you're tired of me, Luke, just come right out and say so. I'm a big girl, and I'd rather that than have to endure this infernal beating around the bush."

Luke sighed and raked the fingers of one hand through his hair. "I'm not tired of you, Gloria. Don't be silly." He stepped to the bed and bent to brush a kiss over her forehead. "You're beautiful. How could any man in his right mind not want you?"

Looking mollified, she smiled slightly. Luke turned quickly away, grabbing up one boot and searching the floor for the other one. *Jesus*. What he'd just told her was true, absolutely true. She was beautiful, and only a madman would turn his back on the offer she'd just made him. In the past, Luke had been able to go for hours, exhausting his bedmate long before his own store of energy and sexual desire flagged. Lately, though, he seemed to be good for only one round. Then, almost immediately afterward, he felt this inexplicable weariness and an urgency to leave. To breathe clean air. To sink neck-deep into a bathtub of hot water.

He sat in a nearby chair to thrust his feet into his boots. As he bent to work the laces, he heard Gloria slip from the bed. Relief flooded through him when she stepped to the sideboard to pour herself some whiskey. He didn't want to further offend her by pushing her away. He just wanted—

What? What, exactly, did he want?

Over the last year he'd developed a hankering—a nameless, indefinable craving he couldn't appease. It had started out slowly, a subtle restlessness. Then it had gradually gotten worse, until recently nothing seemed to satisfy him.

Always before when Luke had begun to feel this way, he'd sought new and more exciting diversions. But at this point in his life, he'd already done it all. Women of all colors, shapes, and sizes. Deviant sex. Adventuresome investments. What else was there? Nowadays, he no longer even got much thrill from winning big at the gambling tables.

14

His life was lacking something, only he wasn't sure what. Saloons, gambling every night, the tawdry trappings of the brothels. He was bored with everything—sick-to-death bored.

It was crazy, but sometimes Luke found himself thinking about getting married, about fathering children. The only problem was, there wasn't a woman on earth he'd tie himself to for a lifetime. Not Luke Taggart. He enjoyed them until he grew bored with them, then moved on to new pursuits. He wanted to keep it that way.

Pushing to his feet, Luke hooked his jacket off the back of the chair. As he shoved his arms into the sleeves and shrugged the garment onto his shoulders, he met Gloria's troubled gaze. God only knew why, but he felt obligated to explain himself, to assuage her bruised feelings. "Gloria, this has nothing to do with you," he said softly. "I swear it."

She stood there, completely comfortable in her nudity, one slender leg slightly bent, her nipples peeking out at him through curtains of flaxen hair. Raising the glass, she gave him a mock toast. "I've heard that one before. It always ends the same, with me getting the boot." She took a mouthful of whiskey and tossed back her head to swallow. Then, with a wave of her hand, she said, "But that's all right. It's not as if you're my only customer. And nobody else seems to have any complaints."

Luke straightened the gray lapels of his jacket, then tugged at the cuffs of his silk shirt until a precise inch of white showed beyond

15

the edge of each coat sleeve. "You're taking this too seriously. Men have bad days, you know, just like women. Tell me you enjoy having sex every single time, that your heart is always in it."

She gave an elegant little shrug. "It's different for me. You're the buyer, I'm the seller. Sometimes, when you come to see me, you're the tenth in line. I'm not always as enthusiastic as I pretend to be, I admit. After ten times, who would be?"

Tenth in line? The words hung in Luke's brain like slimy stalactites. Muttering something—he wasn't sure what—by way of farewell, he let himself out of the room. Once in the hall, he hastened toward the landing, his one thought to get downstairs and outdoors as quickly as possible. *Tenth in line? Just another piece of meat slapping into her.* No wonder the room smelled bad.

A year ago, the thought of sharing a woman with ten other men wouldn't have bothered Luke—hell, it was expected in a brothel, especially the good ones—so he wasn't sure why it should bother him now. The girls he patronized were free of disease and kept themselves reasonably clean. Until now, that was all that had ever mattered to him.

Once outside on the street, Luke leaned a shoulder against a lamppost and hauled in a deep, cleansing breath. The crisp Rocky Mountain air carried with it the scents of early autumn—of fallen leaves, of fields gone fallow for the winter, of forthcoming snow. He filled his lungs, once, then twice, exhaling slowly.

As he cleared the scents of tobacco smoke and stale air from his nostrils, he looked up the street, his gaze fixed on a man and woman walking together on the opposite sidewalk. *Mr. and Mrs. Prim and Proper,* he thought scathingly. The woman had that buttoned-to-the-chin, "don't touch me" look that some ladies worked so hard to cultivate, and the man carried himself with an air of superiority that made Luke grind his teeth. Why, then, did he feel a sense of loss when the pair stopped to admire a display in a shop window? The woman spoke and smiled up at her husband. Whatever she said made the man laugh, and he rocked back on his heels, shaking his head.

Luke imagined them walking home together. There would be a fire burning in their hearth and children sitting in the parlor, heads bent over their schoolbooks. The woman would remove the fitted jacket of her wool walking suit and slip on an apron to prepare the evening meal, which she'd serve later in a cozy dining room, the man holding court at the head of the table, king of all he surveyed.

Luke closed his eyes, trying to imagine himself seated at the head of that table, with a woman seated opposite him, her gaze filled with affection as he measured out servings on their children's plates. A sturdy, mischievous boy with his eyes, a little girl with rosy cheeks and golden curls. A swaddled baby in a cradle he'd made with his own hands.

Madness, Luke thought with a hard scowl. He wasn't the marrying kind, never had been

17

and never would be. Yet, suddenly, with an intensity that stunned him, he wanted that picture in his mind to become a reality.

Pushing away from the lamppost, Luke struck off up the street. Not for the first time over the last few weeks, he found himself wondering if taking a live-in mistress might not be the answer to his dilemma. Such an arrangement would give him exclusive rights to the woman's favors, as though he'd taken her to wife, but it would leave him with the option of getting rid of her once the new wore off, a far safer proposition than legally binding himself to anyone.

Only who? He took a fast mental trip through the list of his female acquaintances. The prostitutes he patronized were beautiful, certainly, and experienced at how to entertain a man behind closed doors. But they lacked that certain something he yearned for—wholesomeness, for want of a better word.

A virginal young miss would be more to his taste. Someone who at least looked sweet and innocent. Not that he believed, even for an instant, that such traits actually existed in the female gender. In his estimation, all women were born calculating and manipulative. It was simply that the prim-and-proper types were more adept at concealing their true natures. Like a velvet sheath over an ice pick.

"You little guttersnipe!"

The angry roar of a man's voice cut into Luke's thoughts like a well-honed knife through softened butter. He spun to scan

18

the street. His gaze came skidding to a stop at the front of the general store. The store-keeper, Elmer Myrick, stood on the side-walk next to a potato barrel, to which was affixed a sloppily printed sign advertising a spud sale, the paper flapping in the wind. Caught by the scruff of his neck in Elmer's brutal grasp, a skinny boy of about ten twisted and kicked, trying frantically to escape.

"Steal my spuds, will you, you little bastard?" Elmer gave the child a hard shake. "We'll see how enthused y'are about stealing while coolin' your heels in the hoosegow!"

"No, mister, please!" the kid cried. "I wasn't gonna steal 'em, I swear. I was just admirin' them. Honest!"

Luke cut quickly across the street, dodging a speeding wagon en route. As he gained the opposite curb, an irrational anger surged up inside him. Idiot. Couldn't Myrick see that the boy was half starved? Under a tattered, filthy shirt that was more holes than cloth, the youth was little more than skin stretched over bone, the ladder of his ribs pathetically visible.

Just as Luke reached the struggling pair, Myrick drew back his arm to backhand the kid. Luke snaked out a hand to grab the stout man's wrist. "Don't do that, Elmer. I'd hate to have to stomp your ass."

Keeping a firm grip on the child, Elmer whipped around to see who'd had the effrontery to interfere. When he saw Luke, his angry red face went suddenly pale. "Mr. Taggart, sir."

Because Luke held the mortgage on the storekeeper's business and could foreclose any time the mood struck, Myrick's expression went from angry to ingratiatingly respectful in a flash. The man released the boy with an unexpectedness that sent the kid reeling. Luke reached out to clamp a hand over the starving mite's shoulder to prevent him from escaping. His guts lurched with a wave of nausea when he felt nothing but sharp bones and stringy muscles beneath his palm.

Releasing Myrick's wrist, Luke dove a hand into his pocket, fished out a dollar, and stuffed it into the storekeeper's shirt pocket. "That should cover your potatoes, you stingy son of a bitch."

Elmer fell back a step. "You've no call to say that, Mr. Taggart. The boy has been stealing me blind. Every time I put a display out here, he sneaks by to help himself. Yesterday, he took apples! The day before, carrots. How can a man make any profit?"

Luke cut a scathing glance at the storekeeper's fat belly. Then he curled his hand over three large potatoes, lifted them from the barrel, and thrust them at the child. Hugging the unwashed vegetables to his chest as if they were gold, the boy clutched one in his grubby fist and began to eat it ravenously, clumps of dirt and all.

Drawing the child into a walk, all the while keeping a firm hold on his shoulder, Luke headed toward a nearby alley. Once there, he drew to a stop next to a reeking trash barrel, watching as the street urchin tore at the raw potato meat with teeth gone yellow from malnutrition and lack of brushing. Wind whistling down the alley whipped the scrawny youth's brown hair. Between swallows, he darted wary looks up at Luke, but he was clearly so hungry, fear took a second seat to clawing need.

Finally, the boy seemed to have eaten enough to stave off the hunger pains, for he lowered the spud from his mud-ringed mouth and regarded Luke with suspicious green eyes. "You gonna have me tossed in the hoosegow?"

Suddenly aware that he towered over the kid, Luke hunkered down in the hope that he might seem a tad less intimidating. After gazing toward the street for a moment, he turned back to regard his prisoner. "You're going about that all wrong, you know. It's little wonder Elmer Myrick caught you."

Bewilderment flashed across the boy's dirty face. Luke bit back a smile. "You got a name, son?"

"Tigger is what folks call me."

"Well, Tigger, when you're going to steal, you need a distraction," Luke advised with a chuckle he couldn't quite suppress. "Though I don't recommend a life of crime, because you *will* eventually wind up in jail, let me give you a couple of pointers, just in case you have to steal again out of necessity. Do you know anyplace where you can catch rats?"

The boy nodded and gestured at the alley with a toss of his head. "There's lots of 'em right through here."

Luke had already guessed that the trash-lined lane was crawling with rodents. "You catch one of the buggers. A nice fat one. Hide it, if you can. Some old newspaper will work if you don't have a blanket. Take care it doesn't bite you, and then stand on the sidewalk, watching that store until mid-morning, when all the fancy ladies are out and about to do their daily shopping. When there are a bunch of them inside, you sneak in and turn the rat loose. Do it at the back of the store, so the rat can't make a quick getaway. I guarantee you, every woman in the place will go berserk. While they're screaming and trying to climb the shelves, you load up on food and hide it under whatever you had the rat wrapped in." Luke inclined his head at the half-eaten potato. "Get something decent to eat, while you're about it. Raw spuds? You've got no class, kid. If you're going to steal, steal something worth your while."

The child regarded Luke with traces of fear still in his eyes. "You're Mr. Luke Taggart, ain'tcha? The rich bloke."

"I haven't always been rich." Luke smiled slightly and reached up to ruffle the kid's grimy hair, which he felt fairly certain was crawling with lice and undoubtedly a few fleas from those rats he probably slept with. "Where are your folks, son?"

"My ma died this winter past, and my pa skedaddled. I took my little brother and sister over to them nuns at the orph'nage, but I didn't want to stay. I'm too old to be recitin' Bible verses and prayin' on them beads. There ain't no such thing as God, anyhow, so why learn all that tripe?"

Luke shared the sentiment and completely understood the youth's abhorrence of winding up a charity case in a nunnery. "You did the right thing, taking your brother and sister to the nuns," he said. "It's too rough out here on the streets for little kids. Now we just have to figure out what should be done with you."

"I ain't goin' to no orph'nage," the boy stated.

Luke nodded. "I understand that." He studied the kid, making a great show of sizing him up. "You look old enough and strong enough to turn your hand to honest work. Have you tried to find a job?"

"Ain't nobody hirin'."

"I was just wondering," Luke said thoughtfully, "because I've been looking for a good man. You probably wouldn't be interested, though."

"Yes, I would!"

Luke narrowed an eye and shook his head. "Nah. It's probably not what you're looking for. It'd be really boring work for an adventurous young fellow like you. Just a position as night watchman at my offices. There's a cot, of course, in the back room, and a place to wash up if you've a mind. Nothing fancy. And all you'd have to do is sleep there, keeping one ear open for intruders. Definitely not exciting employment."

"It sounds grand!" the kid asserted eagerly.

Luke kept his expression carefully blank.

Then, after a moment, he reached inside his jacket for one of his calling cards and his fountain pen. He jotted a brief note on the back of the paper, then handed it to the child. "You know where my offices are, those brick buildings midway down Diamond Street?"

"Yessir!"

"You take that card to my man of affairs, Mr. Brummel. He's a tough nut to crack, so look smart while he interviews you. He does all my office hiring."

"I can look smart," the boy assured him. Then a worried frown pleated his brow. "I'm sorta dirty, though."

Luke grinned. "Brummel will judge you on your character, not the fact that you need a bath. I put in a good word for you on the card."

In actuality, Luke had only written, "Take care of this." As the boy scurried away, still hugging his potatoes, Luke gazed after him, the ever-present loneliness that ate at his gut held at bay for a moment.

The rich bloke, the boy had called him. *If only you knew, kid,* Luke thought glumly. *God, if only you knew.*

TWO

As Luke resumed his walk toward the church, his gaze shifted to the spired rooftop of St. Mary's, and he recalled the envelope he'd slipped into the breast pocket of his jacket that morning before leaving for his office. Why he felt compelled to make another orphanage donation, he wasn't certain. He'd already made his second one just a little over two weeks ago, and even that had been uncharacteristic of him. Benevolent, he definitely wasn't. Yet he had this urge to make a third contribution.

It made no sense. But, then, lots of things he'd been doing and thinking the last few weeks failed to make sense. He only knew this was something he had to do, part and parcel with the strange restlessness that had come over him six months ago and been growing increasingly worse ever since.

Coming to the corner of Diamond Street, Luke took a right on Gambler's Way, his thoughts shifting to the young woman he'd encountered in the church the last time he'd been there. He hoped she wasn't lurking around again today. Getting weird urges to make contributions to the orphanage was one thing; having others witness his actions was quite another. As things stood, people in Black Jack felt intimidated by Luke. If word got out that he was a bleeding-heart do-gooder, he'd lose that edge.

Not that he expected her to be there. A young woman that age probably had far better things to do than hang around a church. Though too strong of feature to be pretty in a conventional way, she was a striking little minx with an amazing wealth of sable hair and big blue eyes. She undoubtedly had a number of young men sniffing at her skirts and vying for her favor.

He smiled slightly, recalling the way she'd

stared at him. A visit from the devil himself couldn't have elicited a more startled or wary reaction. Clearly, he wasn't an individual people expected to encounter in what they deemed a "holy place."

Luke had seen the girl around Black Jack several times before, usually in the company of Milo Zerek or his son Ambrose. Both men worked in the Taggart Mine. Because of the family resemblance, Luke guessed she was probably Milo Zerek's daughter. That would explain the threadbare condition of her dress. The combined earnings of Zerek and his son probably provided only enough for the family to scrape by, with little left over for anything else.

Luke refused to feel guilty about that. He paid a better hourly rate to his employees than any mine owner in Colorado, and though he hadn't checked, he suspected the prices in his company store were the most reasonable in the state as well. That and providing safe working conditions for his men was the best he felt he could do for the poor bastards. Given the fact that few other mine owners did as much, Luke was lauded for his munificence, which increased his workers' productivity and made Luke money—more than enough to compensate for the above-standard wages he paid.

Once at the church, Luke made fast work of dropping the orphanage donation into the poor box. Determined not to question his action or to analyze his reason for doing it, he turned his thoughts to hurrying home, taking

26

a long hot bath, and spending the evening toasting before a fire with a good bottle of scotch near his elbow. But as he exited the building, a cold gust of wind swept across the porch, carrying with it the faint, almost musical sound of a woman's laughter.

Coming to a stop, Luke cocked his head to listen, drawn to that sound in a way he couldn't understand. *An angel laughing,* he thought, then scowled. But instead of walking on, he found himself heading down the church steps and around the corner of the building.

Just a glimpse, he promised himself. To satisfy his curiosity.

A cobbled walkway, separating the rectory from the church, ran the length of the two brick buildings and led to the gate of the orphanage playground, which was boxed in on three sides by the rectory, the rear of the church, and the three-story convent. Roses and shrubbery grew in untamed profusion along the narrow pathway, giving Luke the feeling he was in a tunnel of greenery that led to another world. Judging by the sounds of merriment coming from the playground, which grew louder with every step he took, perhaps it did. A world far different from his own, at any rate. Luke couldn't recall the last time he'd heard anyone laugh with such complete abandon.

At the white gate, Luke stopped and folded his arms atop the pickets, his gaze fixed on the young woman whose laughter had lured him there. Evidently oblivious to the chill afternoon wind and the ominous threat of rain, she sat on the grass, surrounded by a dozen or more

27

children. She wore the same blue wool dress she'd been wearing two weeks ago when he'd seen her inside the church, a pathetic, threadbare garment. Yet she still managed to look so lovely that his breath caught.

His reaction took him by surprise as few other things had. As figures went, hers wasn't the most fetching he'd ever seen. A little too buxom for a woman of her slight frame, she would have been best described as milkmaid-plump, or perhaps voluptuous. He preferred a more slender build. Her features were irregular, the nose a trifle too large, the mouth a bit too generous, her cheekbones cut a shade too sharply. Yet, taken as a whole, those features blended together to create a face so fascinating, he couldn't look away.

Even from a distance of twenty feet, Luke was mesmerized by her eyes, which he hadn't been able to see as clearly inside the dimly lighted church vestibule. A rare shade of dark cobalt blue, they were uncommonly large, wide set, and lined with thick sable lashes. *The kind of eyes a man could get lost in,* he thought, then immediately chided himself for being ridiculous. Even so, he couldn't deny his sudden urge to smile or the feeling of warmth that came over him, almost as if the sun had broken through a cloud and was spilling over his shoulders.

In the middle of telling a story to the children, the girl appeared unaware of Luke's presence, and since he had nothing pressing to do, he decided to linger there for the sheer pleasure of watching her. Hands in motion. Eyes sparkling.

Her face animated. Her voice enriched with the faintest trace of an Irish brogue. She was, quite simply, a delight to behold.

The tale she told was about a young boy and girl who were being held captive by a wicked old witch in a large house in the woods. *A silly children's story*, Luke told himself, but he was captivated. Soon he was leaning slightly forward over the pickets and cursing the wind, which made it difficult to hear her.

"Would you care to join us, Mr. Taggart, sir?"

Luke jerked and straightened. The Zerek girl's gaze was pinned right on him.

"I...um..." He tugged on the lapels of his jacket, then shrugged his shoulders. "I'm sorry to interrupt. I came to see one of the nuns. When I heard voices back here, I thought—"

She lifted an elegantly drawn eyebrow. "Oh? And which one might that be?"

"Which one what?"

Her cheek dimpled in a smile. "Which sister? I can have one of the children run to fetch her, if you'll only give me her name."

"Actually, I don't believe she ever gave me her name." He held out a hand to measure off the fictitious nun's height. "A little woman with dark hair?"

The Zerek girl looked bemused. "You're sure she was a nun?"

"Absolutely." Luke lifted the corners of his mouth in a forced smile. "I take it the description doesn't ring any bells."

She shook her head, her gaze never leaving his. "None of the nuns I've met has hair."

Realizing his mistake, Luke quickly back-tracked. "Well, no. Of course not. I was going by her eyebrows." He made a slashing motion at his forehead. "Very dark, bushy eyebrows. A big nose. Brown eyes."

She shook her head again. Then she graced him with another smile. "I'm sorry. I don't recognize her by the description. Was your business with her important?"

"Not really. Nothing that can't wait, at any rate."

The children around her had begun to squirm. One dark-headed little boy who could very well be Tigger's brother, judging by his looks, tugged on the pigtails of one little girl. The resultant squeal had Luke retreating a step. "Well, I'd better leave you to your storytelling. I didn't mean to interrupt."

"Peter!" The Zerek girl leaned around to grab the recalcitrant boy by his wrist. "No hair-pulling. How many times must I remind you?"

"It was only a itty-bitty tug!" Peter cried.

"Nuh-uh," his victim wailed. "It hurts, Cassandra! He near yanked my hair out!"

So, her name was Cassandra. Luke smiled to himself as he watched her corral the children with a gentleness of hand that only a woman could master. When all was quiet again, she looked back up at him. "Please, won't you join us?" She patted the ground beside her. "We've plenty of seating room, as you can see. You might enjoy yourself."

Luke had no doubt he would. More amazing was that she had extended the invitation.

Given his reputation, which even he had to admit was well-deserved, most of the so-called "decent" young women in Black Jack avoided him. To be seen being friendly with Luke Taggart was to scotch all hope of wangling a marriage proposal from a "respectable" young man.

Without making a conscious decision to do so, Luke pushed open the gate, strode across the patchy lawn, and lowered himself to the ground beside her before he could think better of it. Dimpling her cheek in another radiant smile, she resumed telling the story. Within seconds, Luke was leaning forward again, as enthralled by the story as the children were.

Magic and fairy tales. Looking into Cassandra Zerek's cobalt eyes, even Luke could almost believe in such things. Superficial though he knew it must be, there was a glow about her—an innocent sweetness in her smile, a guileless look in her lovely eyes. Sitting near her like this made him feel as if he'd just entered a well-heated room after being outdoors on a chill winter day.

In actuality, dark storm clouds still gathered overhead, and the cold wind bit through his jacket. It was crazy, sitting here on the damp grass in his expensive, tailored clothing. Crazy, yet utterly irresistible.

Quite simply, Cassandra Zerek was the most delightful creature he'd ever met. Her mane of sable hair was tied back with a bright red ribbon, at odds with her otherwise drab attire. Just below her prim little collar rested

31

a gaudy paste brooch, the fake jewels lusterless, the gold-colored setting worn away in spots. Despite that, the girl herself seemed to sparkle.

Sweet. It was a word he'd never associated with a woman, but Cassandra struck him as being that and more. She reminded him of a box of gaily wrapped confections, each nuance of her a mystery, yet promising to be delicious.

When she finished the story, the children began to clamor for another. "Not today. You've chores to do in the convent, remember. I promised Sister Rachel that I wouldn't keep you out here past four."

"Oh, hang it," Peter grumbled.

Cassandra ruffled his dark hair. "Go on. Away with all of you. I'll be back tomorrow, and I'll tell you another story then." She pushed to her feet and bent to swipe bits of grass from her long skirt. As the children scampered away, she turned a twinkling gaze on Luke, her expression quizzical. "I hope you'll come again as well, Mr. Taggart. I think the children enjoyed having you with us."

Luke pushed to his feet beside her, surprised to discover she barely cleared his shoulder. Yet, gazing down at her, he couldn't honestly say he still found her too well rounded for her height. Taken as a whole, Cassandra Zerek was too uniquely lovely to be measured against the usual standards.

"And you, Cassandra? Did you enjoy my company as well?"

Two bright spots of color flagged her cheeks, and her eyes went suddenly dark.

Glancing away, she toyed with the brooch, the nervous flutter of her fingertips a dead giveaway. Luke recognized the signs. For all her angelic behavior, she wasn't unaffected by him.

"I, um..." She drew her gaze back to his. "Yes, I enjoyed your company very much."

Luke took her hand and bent over it in the most courtly fashion. As his lips brushed the back of her wrist, a feeling very like hunger clawed at his middle, and it took all his self-control not to let the polite gesture turn into a full-blown kiss. If he once tasted that ivory skin, he feared he might try to devour her, much as Tigger had the potato earlier. "In that case, Miss Zerek, perhaps I'll accept your invitation and come again sometime."

"I hope you will."

Even as she spoke, Luke saw the sudden wariness in her eyes. Did she sense what he was thinking, or his intense neediness?

Need for what? Luke asked himself as he released her hand. The question eddied like a black riptide inside him.

He smiled slightly as he turned away and strode back to the gate. Miss Zerek's instincts served her well. Less than an hour ago, he'd been going through his list of female acquaintances, searching his mind for just one woman who might be remotely suitable as his paid companion. Someone pleasing to the male eye, who still managed to look sweet and seem innocent. Someone whose company he'd find entertaining. Cassandra Zerek was exactly what he'd been looking for.

Oh, yes...she had every reason to be wary of him.

Luke Taggart had just found his live-in mistress.

Luke never hesitated once he set his mind on a goal. So instead of going directly home after leaving the church, as he had originally planned, he retraced his steps to the Golden Slipper. As he strode at a rapid clip along the familiar streets, he discovered that his mood had changed from gloomy to expectant. As he walked, he settled a plan in his mind.

Workers at the mine changed shifts at six sharp every evening. Milo Zerek, who worked days, would be getting off in an hour and ten minutes, and when he exited the mining tunnel, Luke intended to be waiting outside to intercept him. He had a proposition to make to the older man, a very generous proposition, and he didn't intend to take no for an answer.

To pass the time until six, Luke decided to play some high-stakes poker. He rarely made a mistake or a bad decision; the fortune he'd amassed and the power he wielded gave testimony to that. But he soon discovered that his thoughts weren't on the game. Since spending those few minutes with Cassandra Zerek in the churchyard, he couldn't get her out of his mind. Instead of the cards, he kept seeing a laughing angel with a wind-tousled halo of sable hair and the body of a temptress.

His gaze settled thoughtfully on a group of men gathered around a set of scales at the bar, where Harvey, the barkeep, measured out gold dust as viable tender to finance his customers' evening festivities. Not really seeing what he was looking at, Luke conjured a picture of Cassandra's face. She was lovely and wholesome-looking, just the kind of woman he'd been thinking about hiring as a paid companion, and he couldn't stop imagining her in his bed, those lovely cobalt eyes filled with sultry yearnings.

"Hey, Mr. Taggart, you gonna play?"

Luke thumbed the Liberty head on a ten-dollar gold piece, commonly known as an eagle for the bird imprinted on its reverse side, and tossed in the coin to ante up. "Sorry, gentlemen. I'm a little distracted this evening." He smiled slightly. "I ran across something I never expected to see today—a young woman from the miners' district who seemed to be a virginal innocent."

The mismatched group around the table, well-groomed businessmen and grimy miners out for a little gaming before they started their night shift, all looked up. One, a whiskery rock-buster named Fred, snorted loudly. "What was she—a twelve-year-old?"

"Somewhere between eighteen and twenty would be my guess," Luke replied.

One of the younger miners laughed. "Mr. Taggart, no disrespect intended, but maybe you're needin' spectacles. There ain't a girl over twelve in the whole of shantytown what's still got a cherry. I get me a little pert'near every mornin' comin' in from the mine. The girls linger there at the far end of miners' row, just waitin' for us gents, all of 'em eager to lift their skirts for the bits of dust we can brush off our shirtsleeves."

No stranger to miners' row himself, nor oblivious to the girls who plied their wares there, Luke arched an eyebrow. "I have to admit, this girl's looks bewildered me. She seemed to"—he hesitated, not wanting to sound the fool—"I don't know. There was this sort of glow about her."

"Probably from all the gold dust that's rubbed off on her," another man said with a chuckle. "You find a gal over twelve with a cherry in the mining district, and I'll give you a hundred bucks to have first whack at it!"

Cherry or no, Luke had no intention of divulging Cassandra Zerek's name. Tossing down his cards, he decided these fellows were probably right; he needed his eyesight checked. No young woman her age could have grown up in shantytown without lifting her skirts to help feed her family a time or two. That fact reaffirmed, Luke felt more convinced than ever that she was fair game. "I have to fold, gentlemen. I've got an appointment."

Luke left the Golden Slipper lighter in the pockets, but no less determined to have Cassandra Zerek as his mistress.

As he climbed the steep incline to the Taggart Mine, he was utterly confident that he would ultimately achieve his latest goal. Though she might demur at first, Cassandra would eventually accept his offer. There hadn't yet been a female born who couldn't be bought. The question in Luke's mind wasn't *if* he could buy Cassandra Zerek, but how much she might cost him.

The one stumbling block, as Luke saw it, would probably be her father. A short, stocky little Greek with twinkling blue eyes, Milo Zerek struck Luke as the type who took fatherhood seriously. He was protective of his son Ambrose, always insisting that the younger man be assigned to work with him, ever watchful for unsafe conditions in the tunnels. If Milo was as protective of Cassandra, he might get his nose out of joint when Luke spoke to him. It was one thing for a man to let his girl earn a little gold dust by lifting her skirts on the sly and quite another for her to become a rich man's plaything, with everyone in town privy to the fact.

Nonetheless, because Cassandra hadn't yet reached her majority, Luke hoped to get Milo's blessing—not because he feared any legal repercussions, for he was pretty much above the law in this town, but because it would be simplest that way. Although Luke hated to play hardball with anyone, he wouldn't hesitate if Zerek proved difficult.

In truth, however, he didn't really expect to encounter any hurdles he couldn't overcome. Once, he'd had a hunger for money and power. He understood the tug of desperate need and the lengths to which a man would go to fill that need.

Zerek was a poor man. His needs might be different than Luke's had been, but they'd be no less pressing, for all that. Unless Zerek proved to be a very rare individual, he would be easily tempted, and just as easily bought.

When the whistle blew for shift change, Luke was sitting on a large boulder outside the mine, ready to intercept Milo when he appeared at the mouth of the tunnel. The Rocky Mountain air grew several degrees colder with the setting of the sun, and within seconds after sitting down, Luke began to feel the chill even through his thick wool jacket.

The shudder that gripped him made him thankful he wasn't down inside the mine. There was no cold that ran so deep as that inside a tunnel. It seeped clear to the marrow of your bones and stayed with you for hours, even on hot summer nights.

Above him on a promontory, the silhouettes of scraggly spruce and cedar trees jutted against the dusky sky, a few long roots their only anchor in the rocky earth. Damp with a fine mist of rain, the crisp air smelled of evergreen and the chimney smoke from houses scattered farther down the mountain. Though it wasn't yet quite dark, the faint glow of lantern light illuminated the windows of those dwellings, the glow lending a cheery radiance to the drab gray of the early autumn mist.

Soon, bobbing miner lights began to appear in the yawning blackness of the tunnel entrance. Luke squinted against the glare, trying to see the faces behind the bright yellow beams.

"Hello, Mr. Taggart!"

"Howdy, Mr. Taggart."

The surprised greetings came again and again

38

as the tired, grimy workers emerged from the blackness, dousing their headlamps as they spoke. Luke exchanged greetings with them all, doing his best to address each man by name. If there was one thing Luke had learned as a mining magnate, it was how to inspire loyalty in his men. The crew foremen couldn't be everywhere at once, and if Luke's workers thought of him as some rich son of a bitch who treated them like dirt, they'd be slackers every chance they got.

A few of the men stopped to exchange pleasantries. Though polite, Luke was careful to maintain a certain distance, not wishing to seem unfriendly, yet not wanting his men to forget, even for a moment, that he was their boss.

Finally, Milo Zerek emerged from the tunnel. A squat little fellow bundled in slicker trousers and a wool coat so thick it made him resemble a bear, Zerek looked startled to encounter Luke. "Mr. Taggart," he said, inclining his head with a polite nod. "Good to see you."

As he pushed up off the rock, Luke glanced at Zerek's son Ambrose, who was just emerging from the digs. Taller than his father by half a head and built like a young bull, he was a handsome youth with a shock of sable hair, strong features, and cobalt eyes like Cassandra's.

"Mr. Zerek," Luke said, extending his hand. "You're just the man I've been waiting to see. I'd like a word with you, if you can spare me a few minutes."

Zerek rubbed his palm on his coat to remove the grime, then reached out to shake hands. Even in the dusky light, Luke could see the imprint of a headlamp across the man's brow. Jet hair tufted in a rooster tail at his thinning crown where he'd jerked the band from his head. Gripped in his left hand, Zerek's light and lunch pail clanked as he pumped Luke's arm up and down.

"What're you wantin' to speak with me about?" Zerek asked. "Not my job performance, I hope."

"No, nothing like that." Luke reached past the older man to shake hands with Ambrose. "You fellows are two of my best men. I just have a proposition for you, Milo. One that I'd like to discuss privately, if you wouldn't mind." With an apologetic smile at Ambrose, Luke glanced back at Milo and added, "I thought, perhaps, you'd let me buy you a drink down at the Golden Slipper."

Zerek glanced over his shoulder at his son. "The boy and me usually put in a few hours each night at our own dig before we call it a day. I reckon we can take a night off, though, if you've got something important to discuss with me."

"It's important," Luke assured him. He directed a pointed look at Ambrose. "I apologize for excluding you, Ambrose, but the matter I need to talk with your father about is of a personal nature."

Ambrose shrugged a muscular shoulder. "Don't make me no never mind." He gave his father a broad wink. "I'll just head home and have a nice big bowl of Cassie's stew. There's worse things than spending an evening toasting my toes before the fire."

Cassie's stew. Picturing the girl standing at a hot stove, with a rosy glow on her sculpted cheeks and lantern light creating a halo around her dark hair, Luke felt a yearning that ran so deep, it stymied him. To go home every night and find her there. To see her smile. To feel that odd warmth she emanated surrounding him. He wanted that, he realized with some startlement, even more than he wanted her body, which was to a considerable degree.

As Ambrose Zerek walked off, Luke clapped Milo on the shoulder. "Well, now that that's settled, how's about we go get that drink?"

Milo smiled and fell into step beside Luke. In places, the path was so steep and narrow, Luke hung back to walk single file. With every step they took, the darkness became thicker. By the time they gained the bottom of the hill, they could no longer clearly see Ambrose, who walked some distance ahead of them.

"So, you do a little prospecting on the side, do you?" Luke asked as they reached more level ground.

Milo shifted his light and lunch pail from one hand to the other. "Isn't no rule against that, is there?"

Luke chuckled. "Hell, no. As long as I get a full day's work for a day's wages, I don't care what you do on your own time. Found any color yet?"

"Only a sniff," Milo admitted. "But I have

a gut feeling. There's gold in that hole, mark my words."

It was a familiar refrain around Black Jack. Unlike Luke, who'd struck a rich vein, most prospectors spent their entire lives chasing a dream, with nothing to show for it but a bent back and calluses on their palms. Lady Luck, their elusive mistress, usually got the last laugh.

"Well, I wish you well," Luke said, sincerely meaning it. "There's nothing quite like hitting pay dirt that first time."

"I hope I get to find out for myself," Milo replied.

Luke gazed ahead, searching for a good way to broach the subject he wished to discuss. As they gained the cobblestone sidewalk on Diamond, the main street of town, they angled right toward the Golden Slipper, the third gambling establishment on the opposite side of the thoroughfare. Piano music drifted to them, and occasionally Luke heard bursts of laughter. With the setting of the sun, things began to get lively at the various saloons around Black Jack. The miners, off work for the day, had a few hours to play, and the sporting girls, ever eager to turn a trick, began to drift downstairs to entertain them.

"I ran into your daughter today," Luke began, "over in the churchyard. She was telling the orphans stories, and I lingered for a few minutes to listen."

Milo nodded. "That's my Cassie. She loves the children, that she does. Seems to me the girl oughta be thinking about getting married and havin' some of her own."

42

Luke leaped at the opening. "Eventually, yes. She's a lovely girl, and someday she'll make some man a fine wife."

"Yeah, well...tell her that." Milo shook his head. "Damned fool girl. Got her head full of nonsense, make no mistake. Thinks she wants to be a nun."

Luke was incredulous. "A *nun*?"

"You heard me. Soon as my youngest boy, Khristos, is old enough to take care of himself, she plans to enter a convent." Milo gave his head another shake, light and lunch pail clattering as he lumbered along. "Don't misunderstand me. Even though I grew up Greek Orthodox, I raised my children to be devout Roman Catholics. It was a promise I made to my Mary Margaret, you see, God rest her sweet soul." He quickly crossed himself and blew a kiss off the backs of his grimy knuckles. "Never a dearer woman breathed, I'll tell you that. And I have no regrets raisin' our kids in the church, for that was her dying wish. To be honest, I don't have a quarrel with one of my children taking up the cloth. It's a fine calling, being a priest or a nun. It's just that in Cassandra's case, it strikes me as being a terrible mistake."

Luke nearly said "Amen." If he'd been a praying man, he might have. "I agree. She doesn't strike me as the sort to become a nun."

Milo made a disgruntled sound at the back of his throat. "She isn't, and that's a fact. Likes her pretties too much. I keep tellin' her so, but she's got the temperament of a little Missouri

43

mule, just like her mama." He crossed himself and blew another kiss into the darkness. "God rest her."

Luke hauled in a deep breath, his thoughts in a sudden tangle. A nun? *Jesus Christ.*

"You know, Milo, a girl like Cassandra has a few more options than getting married or going into a convent. That's why I asked to speak with you tonight. I have a proposition to make to you, as I said, and it involves your daughter."

Milo shot him a curious look. "What kind of proposition?"

Luke swallowed. "Well…first of all, I'd like to point out that—" He broke off, not at all sure how to put this delicately. Beating around the bush had never been his style. "You know, Milo, even if you convince Cassandra not to enter the convent and to get married instead, she's likely to wind up with some poor sot as her husband, and six hungry kids clinging to her skirts. It's not very often that a girl from the mining district gets an opportunity to marry well, or to better herself financially. The offer I'm about to make will give your daughter that chance. If you give your blessing, she'll be a very wealthy woman, after all is said and done, and she'll never want for anything again. Neither will you, for that matter."

Zerek's expression had gone from curious to wary. "Why do I have a feelin' the proposition you're about to make has something indecent hangin' on the tail of it?"

Luke flashed a grin. "Indecent? I guess it's all in how you look at it. To put it frankly,

I'm very taken with your daughter. With your permission, I'd like to offer her a position of employment."

Milo swung to a sudden stop. Light from the saloon behind Luke fell across the shorter man's dirt-streaked face. "What kind of employment?"

Judging by Milo's expression, Luke had the feeling this wasn't going at all well. He shrugged away the concern. When all else failed, he'd let money do his talking, and all the convincing. "Please don't get the impression that I'm making this offer lightly. This is the first time—the only time—I've ever been so smitten by a young lady that I've considered a long-term arrangement."

Milo narrowed an eye. "A long-term arrangement?"

Luke smiled. "Cassandra would live in my home, and for the duration of our contract, she would be treated with all the respect of a wife. She wouldn't be required to turn her hand to any kind of work, and in return, I'd pay her a phenomenal wage, buy her beautiful clothing, and surround her with every luxury."

Milo narrowed both eyes. "Are you askin' me to give you my permission to make a whore of my daughter?"

"That's a rather crass way of putting it."

Milo rocked forward on his toes, and though he was nearly a head shorter than Luke, he did a commendable job of standing nose to nose with him. "You cocky little son of a bitch. I oughta knock those pearly white teeth of yours straight down your throat."

Considering the fact that he outweighed Zerek by a good seventy-five pounds and was at least twenty years younger, Luke didn't feel he was in any imminent peril. On the other hand, though, he'd seen enraged men do some amazing things, including kicking the shit out of opponents twice their size. "Now, Milo. Let's keep this civilized."

"Civilized? You call askin' to make my girl a whore 'civilized'? There isn't enough money on God's green earth, young man."

"I mean no offense."

"Well, I'm offended! The answer is no." Zerek leveled a finger at Luke's face. "And you stay away from my daughter. You understand? I don't give a rat's ass who you are, my boss or no, I'll kill you if you touch one hair on her head. That's a promise, boyo."

Zerek swung away and strode angrily back down the street toward the miners' district. Luke gazed after him a moment, stunned that the conversation had taken such an unexpected turn. He was offering Cassandra Zerek the opportunity of a lifetime. Didn't the ornery old cuss understand that?

"Mr. Zerek, wait!"

As the older man came to a stop, Luke broke into a loose jog to catch up to him. Drawing to a halt, he rubbed the back of a hand over his mouth, no longer quite so certain money would do all his talking for him.

"Look, Mr. Zerek, you're taking this all wrong," he began. "I hold your daughter in highest esteem." That sounded lame, even to Luke. He decided the blunt truth might serve him better. "She...um..." He hauled in a jagged breath, decided one lungful wasn't enough, and grabbed for more air. "You know, it's the strangest thing. Until I saw her in the churchyard, I didn't really think she was all that pretty, but—"

"Who's askin' your opinion?" Zerek glanced around as if looking for the idiot who'd solicited it. "Sure as hell not me. And if she's so lacking in looks, why the hell are you makin' this fine proposition of yours?"

Luke winced. That definitely hadn't been the right thing to say. "She's not lacking in looks. That's just it." He clamped down hard on his back teeth. After a moment, he said, "Not after you're around her for about two seconds. Then she's beautiful. I've never met anyone else quite like her."

Zerek tipped back on his boot heels, his expression going from enraged to slightly mollified. Through the gloom, he studied Luke, his brow pleated in a thoughtful frown. "I'll be damned," he finally muttered. "You really are smitten, aren't you?"

Luke gave a humorless laugh. "Would I be here if I weren't? Your daughter is lovely, Milo. And she'd make any man a delightful companion. I mean no offense by making this offer. Truly. I've never felt strongly enough about any other young woman to go talk to her father, you can bet your ass on that."

Milo hauled in a deep breath, then rubbed his nose. With a chuckle, he said, "My daughter isn't for sale, Mr. Taggart. No how, no way. I know it might be hard for you to conceive, but there are some things your money can't buy. My little girl is one of them."

No longer exhibiting anger, Zerek turned and walked away. After taking only a few steps, though, he drew to a stop and glanced back. "If it's any consolation, I felt poleaxed the first time I saw my Mary Margaret, too." He made a quick sign of the cross. "God rest her, but she was so pretty, I near went blind just looking at her." A reminiscent smile spread across his craggy features. He shook his head. "But, son, women like that—they're for marryin', not for taking as mistresses."

Luke folded his arms. "I'm not the marrying kind, Mr. Zerek."

"Well, then, you're not my Cassie's kind." He flashed another kindly smile. "And just for the record, no man's the marryin' kind until he runs across the right woman. Let me give you a little advice. If you really want my daughter, pay court to her. After getting to know her a little better, you might think marriage sounds a hair more appealing."

Somehow, Luke doubted that. "You're making a mistake," he said softly. "Cassandra will never get another chance like this. In a year, maybe two, you could all relocate to another town. No one would ever know about her past, and you'd have money beyond your wildest imaginings. Enough to live well for the rest of your lives. You think about that."

"No need. There are some things more important than money. If you offered her a million dollars, Mr. Taggart, it wouldn't be enough."

48

"That's absurd."

Milo lifted a shoulder. "Maybe so, but that's the way it is. If I see you around my daughter, Mr. Taggart, you'd best be packin' flowers in one hand and a passel of respect in the other. You understand me? It's a wedding ring or nothin' with that girl."

That said, Milo Zerek ambled away into the darkness. Long after he disappeared, Luke could hear the muted clank and clatter of his light and lunch pail.

For a long while, he stood in the moon-swathed shadows, his gaze fixed on nothing. Courtship? He'd never danced attendance on a woman in his life, and he had no intention of starting now. As for Cassandra Zerek's becoming a nun? That would happen over Luke's dead body. He *wanted* that girl. Wanted her in a way he couldn't define— a deep, insatiable yearning that made him feel almost desperate. *Christ.* He was so upset his hands were shaking.

Taking a deep breath, Luke chalked off his discussion with Milo as a bad move. But there was always more than one way to skin a cat. A man only had to find it. He would have Cassandra Zerek in his bed. It was a given.

What Luke Taggart wanted, Luke Taggart got.

THREE

Several nights later, Cassandra was cooking the evening meal and listening to her eight-year-old brother, Khristos, recite his sums

49

when Ambrose threw open the front door of the one-room cabin. As he bent to set his lunch pail and headlamp under the coat pegs next to the door, he waved a paper at her, his handsome face split in a broad grin, his blue eyes dancing.

"Guess who you're lookin' at!" he cried.

Putting the lid back on the kettle, Cassandra asked, "Ambrose Zerek?"

"More than just Ambrose Zerek," he said, slapping the paper with the backs of his knuckles. "You're looking at a soon-to-be rich man, Cassie girl. Papa and I decided to go in partners with that fellow, Peter Hirsch! We signed the contracts when we got off shift tonight."

After tossing the paper onto the table next to the lighted lantern, he caught Cassandra at the waist and twirled around the room with her. In the process, he sent one of the five-gallon buckets that served as a kitchen chair flying. "In four hours, we found more color at his dig than we ever did at ours! There's a vein in there, Cassie, love. I feel it in my bones. We're gonna be filthy rich!"

Lessons forgotten, Khristos jumped up from the table, his blue eyes alight. "Whoo-ee!" he yelled, nearly rattling the thin walls. "When you get rich, what're ya gonna buy me, Ambrose?"

Awakened by all the loud voices, Lycodomes, Cassandra's dog, crawled out from under the table and began to bark. A huge beast with shaggy yellow and white fur and a bald patch along one side, Lycodomes was too large for the small house. Cassandra was afraid Ambrose might accidentally tromp on her beloved pet's toes.

"Go lie down, Lycodomes," she managed to gasp out between giggles. "Ambrose, stop it! If you don't break your own fool neck, you'll wind up breaking mine."

"Ambro-oo-ose!" Khristos wailed. "What're you gonna buy me if you get rich?"

"Anything you want!" Ambrose said with a deep laugh. "The sky'll be the limit, little brother. Just you watch and see."

Breathless from the pressure of her big brother's arm around her waist, Cassandra thumped his strong shoulder with the heel of her hand. "Put me down, you great oaf, before you crush my ribs!"

Ambrose gave her one more twirl for good measure, then set her gently on her feet. Cassandra drew back, still laughing as she tried to smooth her hair. She was pleased to see Ambrose so excited. Usually when he came home at night, his feet were dragging, and he had a distant, hopeless look in his eyes. Unlike her papa, Ambrose had never really caught the gold fever. He worked in the mines with Papa because their family needed the additional income, but Cassandra knew his heart wasn't in it.

After patting Lycodomes on the head and shooing him back under the table, Cassandra said, "So...it's decided, then. You and Papa and Mr. Hirsch are partners?" She reached back to retie the strings of her apron. "I thought Papa said he wanted to think about it for a few more days."

51

The twinkle of excitement in Ambrose's eyes sent a tingle up Cassandra's spine. "Hirsch made it sound so good, I guess Papa changed his mind."

Peter Hirsch was a new hire at the Taggart Mine, and for the last few days, he'd been all that Cassandra's papa and brother could talk about. Like most new hires, Hirsch had been assigned to work under Milo as a trainee, and ever since his first day on the job, he had been regaling the Zerek men with fantastic tales about the amount of gold he'd already found in his dig. All he needed, he'd told them, was a couple of partners with strong backs who could help him chip the rock.

"So where is Papa?" Cassandra asked Ambrose. "Is he still with Mr. Hirsch?"

Ambrose grinned and nodded. "I was so anxious to tell you the news, I headed home before he did. He'll be along."

Ever conscious that her father and brother got little enough sleep without having to wait for their evening meal, she said, "Then I'd best be getting supper dished up." She poured water from the teapot on the stove into a basin so she might rinse her hands. As dearly as she loved Lycodomes, he was stinky, and she'd soiled her fingers petting him. "I'll bet you and Papa are starving. You're running a little late tonight."

"Starving isn't the half of it," Ambrose admitted. "I feel like my belly button is fastened to my backbone. This business of working until ten with no supper break between shifts isn't easy, I'll tell you. And now

52

that we've gone in partners with Peter Hirsch, Papa is talking about working every night until eleven. Can you believe it? He's just that excited."

With a touch of sarcasm in her voice, Cassandra asked, "And while you were working Hirsch's dig, did you find any nuggets the size of marbles just lying about on top of the ground, like he said you might?"

"None yet." Ambrose peeled off his jacket and hung it on one of the coat pegs. "But the light was poor, Cassie. There's nothing to say we won't find some nuggets eventually. There's gold in there. I feel it in my bones." He flashed another broad grin. "You know me. Papa's always getting excited, but I hardly ever do."

That was true. Ambrose was the proverbial doubting Thomas when it came to prospecting. The fact that he seemed to think this particular dig might actually have gold had to be a good sign.

"Wouldn't it be something if you and Papa really did strike it rich?" She drew four soup bowls off the cupboard shelf. "If any man on earth deserves a streak of luck, it's Papa. He's worked so long and so hard..." Her voice trailed away. In her mind's eye, she tried to imagine what it would be like to live in a big, fancy house and have all the money they needed. An image of the patent leather shoes in the dress shop window flashed into her mind, and she felt a flurry of excitement. "Oh, Ambrose, I do hope the two of you are onto something this time, that Papa doesn't get disappointed again."

"Me, too!" Khristos chimed in. "I want me a shotgun of my very own. I ain't never had me a real gun."

"Haven't, not ain't," Cassandra corrected, turning to ruffle her little brother's hair. "A shotgun, you say? I didn't know you were hankering for a real gun."

"I'm comin' on to bein' grown, Papa says," Khristos reminded her. "Only babies play with toy guns."

She gave Ambrose a conspiratorial wink. "Growing up before our very eyes, that you are. I've had to let your pants down twice in the last three months. Next payday, if there's any way we can, we need to buy you some britches and shoes."

"Maybe I can work a few extra hours," Ambrose mused aloud. "The night shift foreman is always needing an extra man to fill in for someone who doesn't show."

"Don't you even think about it." Cassandra picked up the wooden spoon to ladle stew. "You work enough as it is. Besides, if Peter Hirsch is telling the truth about his claim, who's to say you'll need to work any extra hours? We may be rich by next payday."

Ambrose chuckled. "Well...that might be expecting a bit much. But if all goes well, I may have a few gold flakes to cash in. Those would bring plenty enough to buy britches and shoes for Khristos." Planting his hands on his hips, he leaned his head back and closed his eyes for a moment. "Ah, Cassie...wouldn't it be grand? I can hardly believe he asked us to go in partners with him. A rich dig like that!

Maybe things are finally going to take a turn for the better."

Angling a glance over her shoulder, Cassandra asked, "Is that the partnership agreement you tossed on the table? It might get stew spilled on it."

Grabbing up the paper and carefully refolding it, Ambrose placed it on the knickknack shelf for safekeeping. Then, hooking a foot around the bucket he'd displaced earlier, he drew it back to the table and sat down. Cassandra didn't have the heart to remind him to wash up. After working such long hours, her papa and Ambrose were always exhausted when they finally got home.

She placed bowls of stew before both her brothers, then turned back to the stove to fill bowls for Papa and herself. Milo walked in just then, weariness etched into the seams of his face, his eyes rimmed with pink from the strain of squinting against the harsh glare of the miners' lanterns for hours on end.

"Ah, Cassie, girl. You are a blessing. Hot food always waitin', and a fire roarin' to warm my old bones."

Cassandra went up on her tiptoes to brush a kiss across her father's whiskery cheek. He'd brought the smells of the night in with him—chill wind, autumn leaves, and the crisp scent of evergreen. "Sit down, Papa. I know you must be tired."

After setting aside his miner's light and lunch pail, Milo stripped off his heavy wool jacket, then wiggled out of his slicker pants. He sat on his cot, which was situated under the front window, to tug the trouser cuffs off over his boots. "Amazingly enough, I don't feel tired at all tonight. Fact is, I think we should celebrate." He winked at Ambrose as he rose and walked to the table. "What'd ya say, son? Will you share a little ol' nippee with your da?"

"Can I have a taste this time?" Khristos asked as Milo took a seat at the head of the table.

"Eight-year-old boys don't get tastes of whiskey," Ambrose informed him. "Liquor stunts your growth."

"Nuh-uh," Khristos cried. "Cassandra gives it to me when I'm sick, and it ain't never stunted me yet."

Cassandra placed a bowl of stew before her father, then turned to set the kettle in the middle of the table so everyone could refill their bowls whenever they wished. As she nudged the lantern out of the way, she shot Ambrose a warning glance. "How's about if I make you a 'toddy,' Khristos?" The toddies she occasionally fixed for her little brother contained only a trace of whiskey. "You like those, and we've a bit of milk still left in the jug."

"You spoil him, Cassandra," Ambrose grumbled.

She raised an eyebrow. "I spoil you, too, and I never hear you complaining. Besides, as Papa says, it's a night to celebrate, and Khristos is as much a part of our family as anyone else. He should get a wee nippee, too."

Khristos grinned, displaying huge gaps

56

where he'd lost front teeth. "Can I have a dash of cinnamon?" he asked hopefully.

"I'm out of cinnamon, but there's nutmeg aplenty."

"Are you gonna have a toddy, too?" Khristos asked her.

"I'm planning to be a nun, Khristos. Nuns don't drink toddies."

"How do you know?"

"I just do, that's all. Maybe I'll have a bit of hot milk spiced with nutmeg, though. Will that make you happy?"

Holding her own bowl of stew cupped in her hands, Cassandra lowered herself onto an overturned bucket beside her little brother. "Ambrose says the Hirsch claim has lots of color, Papa." The smell of lantern fuel blended with the spicy scent of the stew as she took her first bite of supper. "Do you think this'll be your lucky strike?"

Cheek bulging with a lump of venison, Milo nodded and swallowed. "More color than I've ever run across." His blue eyes fairly danced. "I'm telling you, Cassandra, when Peter Hirsch came to work at the Taggart Mine, it was our lucky day. Imagine, having a rich claim like that, and no one to help him work it." Milo smiled, clearly incredulous about their good fortune. "He needed partners. We needed a decent claim. It's an arrangement that will feather all our nests, make no mistake."

"Oh, Papa, I hope so!" she said. "You've worked so hard, for all of us. It's time you had a bit of comfort and ease."

Khristos fastened big blue eyes on his father. "If you get rich, I want a shotgun, Papa. I'm old enough now, ain't I?"

"Pert'near it. You're growing like a weed, and that's a fact."

"I'd like one of them there flutes, too, like what we saw in the catalog," the child added. "If you get rich, can I have one of them, too, Papa?"

"You can have a half dozen!" Milo promised. Turning his gaze to Cassandra, he added, "And, you, young lady, will have so many pretty new dresses, they won't fit in your closet."

At the moment, Cassandra didn't have her own sleeping area, let alone a closet. The one-room house provided only enough space for the stove, the table, and their cots. What little clothing they owned hung on a rod in the corner. "I don't need that many dresses, Papa. One or two would do me."

But, oh, it would be nice, a small voice sighed inside her head. To feel fine lawn and satin against her skin instead of the coarse cotton of the flour sacks she'd turned into a chemise or the rough wool of hand-me-down dresses.

Ambrose propped his elbows on the makeshift table, constructed from two sawhorses and some salvaged wood. "You know what I'd like? One of those fancy box cameras and a felt fedora hat."

"Don't be forgettin' I want a shotgun!" Khristos reminded him.

"I think you're still a bit too young for a shotgun, Khristos," Ambrose told him. "You

58

may have to wait a few more years. One good kick from a twelve-gauge, and you'd be knocked flat."

Under cover of the table, Cassandra thumped her older brother on the shin with the toe of her shoe. Ambrose jumped. "Ouch!"

She slipped an arm around Khristos, who appeared about to cry. "Don't you believe him for a minute, Khristos. I'll start feeding you up, and by the time Papa strikes it rich, you'll be plenty big enough to handle a shotgun."

It was a promise Cassandra felt fairly safe in making. Even if the Hirsch mine was chock full of gold, it could still be a very long while before her papa struck it rich. With only three men to chip at the rock, working a dig was slow going.

"I'll get you a shotgun," Milo assured his youngest child. "Don't you worry. Pretty soon, we'll all have everything we ever wanted."

Cassandra sighed dreamily as she took another bite of stew. It was fun to contemplate all the things she'd like to have. "You know what I'd like, Papa? More than dresses, even? An indoor *twa-let*."

"You mean a toilet?" Ambrose asked.

"Don't be vulgar."

"What's vulgar about saying 'toilet'?"

"It's an uncouth word, that's all. *Twa-let* is the French way of saying it."

"Yeah, well, we aren't French."

Holding her spoon like a pencil, Cassandra drew little figure eights in the grease that had risen to the top of her stew. "Wouldn't it be grand, Papa? Having an indoor *twa-let*? No more shivering all the way to the necessary on winter nights. There are folks right here in Black Jack who have them, you know."

Milo looked amazed. "You don't say. Right here in Black Jack?"

Cassandra nodded. "A girl down at the mercantile was telling me all about them."

"Cassandra," her father said with a scolding note, "I thought I made it clear I don't want you talking with strangers. Straight to the church or the convent, remember? No dallying in between."

"I only stopped in to make a quick purchase, Papa," Cassandra explained. "And Zelda isn't a stranger. She helps out over at the convent. Not as often as I do, mind. But she's a good Catholic girl, and we only just visited at the mercantile for a minute."

Looking mollified, her father said, "Just you mind what I say, hmm? No lingering in the shops or hanging about outside to look at the pretties on display too long. This town is full of scoundrels who wouldn't hesitate to take advantage of you, if given half a chance."

Not entirely certain what "take advantage" meant, Cassandra only nodded. She'd long since become reconciled to her father's rules and seldom questioned his reasons. Papa was a very wise man, and she knew he had only her best interests at heart, even though his mandates were sometimes difficult to obey. Educated by nuns, her schooling sporadic because there hadn't been sisters in every mining town in which they'd lived, Cassandra knew that her own knowledge of the world was sorely lacking. Her father had intended it to be that way.

"I promised your mama I'd raise you to be a lady," he always reminded her when she complained. *"And you won't be a lady if I let you attend regular school and wander the streets in these mining towns. The commonness of the people in places like this rubs off on a person. It's different for your brothers. One day they'll have to work in the mines, and there's no keeping them from it. But your mama wanted better for her daughter, and God as my witness, I'll carry out her wishes."*

"I always mind what you say, Papa," Cassandra said softly, looking her father directly in the eye. "You know I do."

"I know you *try*," he corrected with a wink. "You're a good, sweet lass. But sometimes you slip a bit." Flashing a smile, he said, "I'm sorry for interrupting. Where were we?"

"She was tellin' us about *twa-lets*," Khristos reminded them. "Tell us more, Cassie!"

Trying to regather her thoughts, Cassandra frowned. "Well...Zelda says they've got little chains hanging from the water tanks above. When you pull the chain, the tank empties, and everything in the *twa-let* runs outside."

Khristos wrinkled his nose. "Where does all the puckey go?"

Cassandra considered for a moment. "In a hole, I guess."

"Yuck. I wouldn't wanna fall in!"

Ambrose chuckled. "Let's see if Cassie is still saying *'twa-let'* after she falls in!" He scooted back on his bucket, avoiding the toe of Cassandra's shoe before it connected with his shin again. "What's the matter, Stump? Legs too short?"

"I told you, Ambrose, don't call me 'Stump.' I'm not *that* short."

"You barely reach my chin, even with your shoes on."

"Now, children," Milo interrupted. "Tonight is no time for quarreling. We should be happy." He patted the breast pocket of his red-checkered shirt. "I've got a contract here that gives me legal one-third interest in a rich mining claim. Ambrose has another third. That gives the Zereks two-thirds interest, which means two-thirds of all the profits. That's what we should all be thinking about."

Distracted from the argument by the gleam of excitement in her father's eyes, Cassandra asked, "Where is this claim, Papa? Will it be very far for you and Ambrose to walk every night after you get off work?"

"That's the greatest part," Ambrose inserted. "It's just over the ridge from the Taggart Mine, on the back side of Taggart Mountain." Lantern light bathing his features, he leaned forward over the table, his gaze clinging to hers. "Just think, Cassandra. We'll be hauling ore out of the same mountain that has made Luke Taggart a rich man!"

It was an exciting prospect, Cassandra had to admit. "How come Mr. Taggart is allowing people to file claims on the back side of his mountain?"

Ambrose shrugged and smiled. "Beats me!

62

Papa and I thought he'd filed on every inch of it himself. But Peter Hirsch has papers, all legally filed and stamped with an official seal. Papa and I even double-checked the boundaries to make sure he hadn't made a mistake. It's all on the up-and-up, legal as can be."

Taggart Mountain was full of gold; everyone in town knew that. She turned an incredulous gaze on her father. "Oh, Papa! I'm so happy for you. After all your years of hard work, it may really happen for you."

"For all of us, darlin', not just for me." Milo winked at her. "I found color tonight. Not a lot, mind you, but more than I would've found at our dig if I'd worked it for weeks." He clucked his tongue. "She's in there. Mark my words, honey, she's in there, just waitin' for us to find her."

A claim on Taggart Mountain. Cassandra closed her eyes for a second, scarcely able to believe it.

Abandoning her stew, she pushed up from the table and did a waltz step around the table, taking care not to kick over any of the pans that were strategically placed to catch leaks from the roof.

"Oh, Papa. What if you really do strike it rich?" She swung to a stop. "Wouldn't it be wonderful?"

Milo chuckled. "Now you see why I'm wantin' to celebrate." He motioned at Ambrose. "Fetch my whiskey, son."

Cassandra hugged her waist. "And I guess I'd better be fixing your lunches for tomorrow.

Extra-big ones so your energy doesn't flag while you're working over at the Hirsch Mine tomorrow night."

"It ain't the Hirsch Mine no more," her papa corrected as he sloshed measures of whiskey into two coffee mugs. "From here on out, it's the Zerek Mine as well." He lifted his cup in a toast, swinging his arm to encompass them all. "Mark my words, we're going to be one of the richest families in this whole state."

Milo felt like a boy again, with hot blood racing through his veins and dreams of all he would soon be able to do for his family spinning like a top in his head.

After a lifetime of wanting and trying, he was on the brink of doing, really doing. Cassie and the boys would finally live the good life he'd promised his darlin' Mary Margaret, God rest her sainted soul.

Not that he wasn't willing to work for it, he hastily reminded himself as he took up his pick. A few feet away, Ambrose was brushing away the debris of an hour's labor, looking for the telltale glint of gold in the quartz. At the mouth of the new tunnel, Peter Hirsch was adjusting the wick in his light. The three of them made a good team. Willing to work hard for what they got. Honest men, doing honest labor.

For two evenings running, the three of them had dug for five long hours in this tunnel, and excitement was still high. At eleven o'clock each night, when Milo and Ambrose dragged their tired bodies home, Cassandra was waiting up for them, a hot meal warming on the stove.

Suddenly Milo heard voices at the entrance to the tunnel. When he left Ambrose to go investigate, he saw torches bobbing in the darkness.

"Who goes there?" he called out. "Do we have visitors, Peter?"

No answer.

Milo was about to advance a few more steps when a torch swung up close to his face. Throwing up an arm to cover his eyes, he said, "Peter, is that you, son?"

A deep voice replied, "No, Mr. Zerek. It's Marshal Sizemore."

Squinting to see, Milo eased his arm down a bit. "Marshal Sizemore? What on earth are you doin' here?"

"Now ain't that a coincidence. I was about to ask you that same question."

Milo waved at the light. "Would you mind getting that out of my eyes?"

The marshal moved the torch to one side. As Milo's vision readjusted, he saw the shadow of another man behind the lawman. After a moment, he recognized Luke Taggart. Behind Taggart stood a half dozen deputies, all of them packing side irons.

A tingling, uneasy sensation inched up Milo's spine. Something was amiss here. Exactly what, he didn't know, but he figured he was about to find out.

"Mr. Taggart? Good evenin' to you."

Taggart inclined his head. "Mr. Zerek."

Just then, Ambrose came ambling out.

Coming to a stop slightly behind his father, he swept off his headlamp and politely greeted all their visitors. Neither Taggart nor any of the lawmen responded in kind.

Milo rubbed the sleeve of his coat over his mouth. "Is there a problem?" he asked, sensing that there was, yet still unable to determine what it might be. "Can we help you with somethin'?"

Marshal Sizemore sighed and shifted his weight. "What are you doing in here, Mr. Zerek? Surely you know Mr. Taggart can't let you get away with this. If he overlooks one claim jumper, he'll be overrun by them."

"Claim jumper?" Milo bristled. "I ain't no claim jumper. We got legal right to be here." He eased up on his toes, trying to see past the group of men. "Peter? Show yourself, son. It seems we've got a bit of a misunderstanding here."

Peter Hirsch didn't respond to Milo's call. Thinking that the younger man might have gone to pay nature a visit, Milo drew his copy of the partnership contract from his pocket. "Peter Hirsch filed on this claim, all legal and proper. He needed partners, so we went in thirds with him." He shoved the paper out. "Read for yourself."

The marshal took the contract and shined the light from his torch on it. After glancing over the terms, he passed it to Taggart. A heavy silence fell. Then the lawman said, "That contract isn't worth the paper it's written on. This is Mr. Taggart's mountain,

66

every square inch of it. No one can file on any of the claims up here. He has them all tied up."

"But Peter Hirsch had claim papers. I saw them." Milo looked at Taggart. "You remember Hirsch. He's the new hire you put on shift with me and Ambrose. He was here just a minute ago. I'm sure he'll be back shortly. He'll be able to set this straight."

Luke crumpled the contract in his fist. "I don't know what you're talking about, Mr. Zerek. I've never heard of a man named Peter Hirsch."

Milo felt his stomach drop. Mouth slack with shock and scarcely able to credit his ears, all he could do was stare at Taggart. How could the man stand there and say he'd never heard of Hirsch, one of his very own employees?

The marshal shook his head. "You and your son are under arrest, Mr. Zerek." He cupped his hand over the holstered revolver that rode on his hip. "If you're smart, you'll come along peaceably."

"Arrest?" Ambrose repeated. "But we haven't done anything wrong. Hirsch has legal papers. And we checked the maps. This is his claim, not Mr. Taggart's."

Milo simply stood there, his gaze fixed on Luke Taggart's eyes. The other night, Milo had seen only the yearning and loneliness in the younger man's gaze. Now, when it was too late, he also saw the ruthlessness.

He'd been had, Milo realized. This entire situation had been contrived, Peter Hirsch hired by Luke Taggart to lure Milo and Ambrose into a trap. That explained why Hirsch had lingered near the entrance to the mine tonight, pretending to fuss with his light. He'd been watching for the marshal's approach so he could do a quick vanishing act. Now, caught red-handed in the act of claim jumping, both Milo and Ambrose would go to jail, which would leave Cassandra with no adult male relatives to protect her.

Cold fear shot through Milo as he continued to stare into Luke Taggart's unreadable gaze. The bastard had planned this, no question about it. With both Milo and Ambrose behind bars, Cassie would be Taggart's for the taking. As innocent as she was, she wouldn't realize the danger this man represented until it was far too late.

FOUR

When her father and brother didn't return at a reasonable hour, Cassandra began to worry. By the time the clock struck midnight and they still weren't home, she was biting her lip and pacing. Never in her recollection had her papa stayed out this late—especially on a day when he'd been hard at work since before sunup.

A shaft of fear shot through her. Had there been an accident at their dig? A cave-in, possibly? Were Papa and Ambrose even now lying buried under a pile of rubble?

Please, God, she prayed silently, *don't take my papa and brother.*

After lifting the stew kettle from the stove and moving it to the warming shelf so the contents wouldn't scorch, she stepped over to the window and rubbed the glass so she might peer out. Beyond the fogged pane, the night looked dark and forbidding with only a half-moon to light the landscape. The other miners' shacks were also dark, the inhabitants long since abed.

A good sign, she told herself firmly. Surely, if there had been a cave-in, other miners up on Taggart Mountain would have heard the rumble, and the town would be swarming with men attempting a rescue. Someone would have come for her as well. That was the way of things in a mining town.

So why weren't they home?

Perhaps they'd found a rich vein and didn't want to leave it, she thought as she circled the room. At this very moment, maybe they were hurrying home to tell her the good news.

Glancing toward the door, she held her breath, listening for the slosh of footsteps in the mud. Instead she heard the thudding of her own heart and the familiar hiss of the lantern. Not even the rhythmic sound of Khristos's breathing from the nearby cot calmed her nerves.

Still tense, she sat at the table, glad she had Lycodomes for company.

"What do you think, Lye-Lye?" she asked the dog, gently running her hands over his thick fur. "Are Papa and Ambrose all right? Or should I go looking for them?"

Lycodomes whined and licked her nose. Laughing softly, Cassandra bent to hug him, burying her face against his ruff. Three years old, going on four, the dog seldom left her side, and only then to watch after Khristos. The devotion was mutual, for Cassandra loved her pet nearly as much as she did the members of her family. Lycodomes, her friend and trusted confidant. Just looking into his liquid brown eyes made her feel better.

"I guess I'm being silly," she told him. "Even if there's been an accident, it's unlikely that both of them could be hurt. Right?"

Unless, of course, there'd been a cave-in. Entire crews of men could be buried alive if a tunnel collapsed.

Unable to get the thought of a cave-in out of her head, Cassandra couldn't bear to pace the floor and do nothing. Finally, in desperation, she awoke Khristos, bundled him up against the cold, and set off through the darkness toward Taggart Mountain with Lycodomes as their escort. Even if nothing was amiss, she knew her papa would understand why she'd chosen to break his rules this one time by going out after dark.

Uncertain where Peter Hirsch's claim was located, she ended up wandering over the back side of the mountain for nearly an hour. Soaked to the skin by a fine drizzle, she was chilled, worried to death about Khristos catching a cold, and completely lost by the time she decided to give up the search. Lycodomes saved them by guiding them back to town.

Once the three of them hit Diamond Street, some of Cassandra's panic began to abate. Khristos was a tough little nut, and even though he was soaked to the skin, it was highly unlikely he'd catch his death. As for her papa and brother, maybe they'd had a streak of good luck and stopped by one of the saloons for a celebratory drink. If they had, she'd snatch them bald-headed for worrying her.

"Likely they're fine," she told Khristos with a reassuring pat on the shoulder. "Still, it can't hurt to make sure."

The only way to do that, she determined after a moment's thought, was to take a peek through the windows of all the saloons to see if she could spot her father or brother. If she didn't find them at one of the drinking establishments, she would have no choice but to ask the marshal to send out a search party.

"Khristos, you and Lye-Lye wait for me down by the mercantile," she said, pulling her brother's knitted cap lower on his forehead. "Don't talk to anyone, and sing out if anyone tries to bother you."

"But, Cassie, them saloons are dangerous, especially with you bein' a girl and all. You know what Papa says. No dallyin' on the streets."

"Hush, now. This is a special circumstance, and I'll be careful. You take Lye-Lye and hurry on. I'll be with you soon."

Cassandra waited until her brother and Lycodomes disappeared into the shadows. Then, gathering her shawl more tightly around her, she turned her steps toward the section of Diamond Street where all the saloons were grouped together.

Engaged in another high-stakes poker game, Luke Taggart was about to match his

71

opponent's bet and raise him by a hundred dollars when he glanced up and saw Cassandra peeking in over the bat-wing doors. Luke forfeited his possible winnings by folding his hand, then pushed up from his chair.

"Excuse me, gents," he said as he pocketed his chips. "I just remembered a pressing matter of business."

As he headed toward the entrance, he saw Cassandra duck away. Respectable young women did not, under any circumstances, frequent the vicinity of establishments like the Golden Slipper. Luke could only suppose she was embarrassed to have been caught peeking inside. To him, that attitude went beyond silly, and he tamped down a spurt of impatience at the absurdities of Christian morality. Addlepated girl, anyway. As if he'd think less of her simply because she approached a saloon.

Pushing open the doors with a thrust of his shoulder, he stepped out onto the cobblestone sidewalk, his gaze routing through the shadows.

"Cassandra?" he called, half afraid she might have hidden between the buildings. "Cassandra, I know you're out here. Don't play foolish games."

Drunks were a penny a dozen along this part of Diamond Street, passed out on the shop steps, propped against lampposts, sleeping in the alleyways. It was no place for a young lady, especially late at night.

"Cassandra?"

Something moved in the shadows. A moment later, she materialized. When she stepped

72

into the illumination of the lamplight, he saw that her cream-colored wool shawl and old blue dress were soaked from the drizzling rain.

Her skirts clung to her legs, revealing the curve of her hips and the juncture of her thighs. Luke had difficulty looking away, and when he finally managed, he found himself staring at her bosom instead. Her saturated shawl had grown heavy, stretching the loosely knitted yarn and widening the holes in the weave. Through one enlarged opening, a nipple, hardened to erectness by the cold, thrust against the wet cloth of her dress.

Forcing his gaze to her pale face, Luke asked, "What in God's name are you doing out here at this hour?"

"It's my papa and brother," she told him in a quavery voice. "They never came home. I'm afraid something has happened to them." Shivering against the cold, she wrung her hands, her vulnerable mouth turning down at the corners. "I...um...I was hoping they might have stopped by the Golden Slipper for a drink. You haven't seen them, have you?"

As Luke took in the condition of her clothing, he knew she'd been traipsing all over Taggart Mountain looking for her father and brother. The hem of her skirts was black with mud, and every time she shifted her weight, he heard her shoes squish.

Christ.

Until this second, he had never stopped to think that she might grow alarmed when Milo and Ambrose failed to come home. The women

73

in his acquaintance wouldn't walk across the street out of concern for someone else, let alone climb the side of a mountain in the freezing rain. Luke knew as well as anyone how slick those steep slopes could get. It was a wonder she hadn't broken her fool neck.

Biting back a curse, he struggled against the urge to give her a good shake. Then he realized that if anyone needed shaking, it was him. He was responsible for her father and brother's not coming home, after all. If he'd been using his head, he would have anticipated her concern and taken measures to prevent it.

"Ah, honey, I'm sorry. I meant to stop by your place in the morning to tell you what happened."

Her huge eyes widened even more, luminous in the lamplight. "Are they all right?"

"Yes, they're fine. There's just been a spot of trouble, that's all. Nothing that can't be ironed out."

"Trouble?"

Luke bit the inside of his cheek. She looked so fragile standing there, her shoulders hunched, her body shuddering. He felt awful knowing he was responsible for her having gotten so wet and chilled. If there had been a way to avoid it, he would have delayed adding to her misery. Unfortunately, there wasn't. The Zereks were in jail, Luke had every intention of keeping them there, and someone had to tell her. He was the only someone available.

"Cassandra, I'm afraid your father and brother have been arrested for claim jumping."

Her eyes went wide, her lips slack with astonishment. "Claim jumping?" she repeated faintly. "Papa and Ambrose? There has to be a mistake. They'd never do such a thing."

Carefully choosing his words, Luke told her what had happened.

"No!" she cried. "It can't be. Not my papa. He'd never steal someone else's gold, especially not yours, Mr. Taggart. He thinks you're the most wonderful employer he's ever had."

Not anymore, he didn't. Luke gazed off up the street for a moment, recalling the fury and hatred he'd seen in Milo Zerek's eyes. When he swung his gaze back to Cassandra, he said, "I'm sorry, honey, but the marshal caught them red-handed. They were inside one of my tunnels, and it looked as if they'd been working the dig for several days. I accompanied the marshal, so I was present when they were arrested. I saw the evidence myself."

She made a quick sign of the cross, then pressed a trembling hand to her mouth. After a moment, she visibly groped for her self-control, raising her chin, squaring her shoulders, taking a deep breath. Her eyes were shimmering with tears when she met his gaze again.

"I'm sorry," he said softly. "I like your father and brother. Believe me when I say I hate to see them in jail. Especially since it involves one of my claims."

"I can only thank God it *was* on one of your claims, Mr. Taggart. Another mine owner might have shot them on the spot."

For reasons beyond Luke, he suddenly felt oddly uncomfortable. He'd never had anyone look at him in exactly the way Cassandra Zerek was, as if he'd single-handedly hung the moon.

As he struggled to shove aside his feelings of uneasiness, a drunk came weaving up the sidewalk. Watching the fellow, Luke once again realized that it wasn't safe for her to be out here alone after dark. Indeed, it was a miracle she hadn't been accosted. The thought made him feel weak at the knees.

In his memory, Luke had never been protective of anyone; given his plans for this girl, such inclinations were ludicrous in the extreme. It was like a wolf worrying that another dog in the pack might steal a taste of his bone. Nonetheless, he stepped closer, shielding her with his body as the drunk staggered past.

"Cassandra, do you realize what a foolish chance you've taken, wandering these streets without an escort? Don't you know what manner of men frequent places like the Golden Slipper?"

The words were no sooner out of Luke's mouth than he wanted to call them back. He was, after all, one of the Golden Slipper's most regular customers.

He grasped her by an elbow. "I really think it might be best if I see you home. We can settle the rest of this in the morning."

"Oh, Mr. Taggart, you needn't bother. I'm perfectly safe." She glanced up the street at the marshal's office. "Besides, I want to see my papa and brother before I go. There has to be more to this than meets the eye—some sort of mistake, surely. And the quicker I get to the bottom of it, the sooner they'll be released."

"Honey, there is no mistake." Luke could only wonder at the husky regret he heard in his voice. Maybe he'd missed his calling and should have been an actor. "Your father and brother were caught red-handed on my claim. As for your seeing them tonight, that's impossible. The marshal has already left for home."

"Maybe I can talk to them through their cell window. I really do need to see them, Mr. Taggart. Please, try to understand."

"I do understand. But talking to them through a window isn't possible either. By my special request, they've been assigned to inside cells. I didn't think windows were a good idea."

A troubled frown pleated her brow as Luke drew her into a walk. Faltering a step, she hung back, looking over her shoulder at the jail.

"Why did you request that? Papa will go crazy being locked in a cell with no window."

"Ah, but it's for his own safety." Tightening his grip on her arm, Luke steered her around an empty display rack a shopkeeper had left out on the sidewalk. "This is a mining town, remember. Most of the men who live here have mines of their own, and they have to leave their pieces of ground unattended while they're working for me. Claim jumpers aren't very well thought of. I was afraid some intoxicated miner might take the law into his own hands and try to punish your father and brother with the business end of a shotgun."

Cassandra grew even more pale—so pale, in fact, Luke feared she might faint. She stumbled, caught her balance, then fastened a frightened gaze on him. "My papa and brother are in very serious trouble, aren't they?"

"Grave trouble indeed," he admitted. "So much trouble that they should, by all rights, be kept in jail for a very long while." He softened that with a kindly smile. "I'm a fair man, though. Your father says they went in partners with some fellow named Peter Hirsch. Evidently the man misled them into believing they were chipping rock on a legally filed claim. Even though the story sounds farfetched, I'm inclined to believe it."

"I promise you, it's true," she rushed to assure him. "There *was* a man named Peter Hirsch. He's all Papa and Ambrose have been talking about for days, and I saw the partnership contracts they signed with my own eyes."

Luke nodded. "I saw one as well. Unfortunately, it wasn't valid." He pretended to mull the situation over. "Unless we can catch Peter Hirsch, I guess we'll never know the truth. The marshal has sent out a couple of deputies to try and track him down, but..." He let his voice trail away. "Well, you know as well as I do what their chances of success are. Hirsch probably isn't even the fellow's name, and the description your father gave of him was fairly nonspecific."

"I wish they'd find him. He deserves to

be punished for doing something so awful. My papa is a good man. He's never done anyone a bad turn in his whole life."

"I'm sorry this has happened. You'll never know just how sorry."

"It isn't your fault."

"No. But what happens from here on out will be."

"What do you mean?"

Luke looked down at her. "I can't allow claim jumpers to get off scot-free, Cassandra. If I do, every man in these mountains will get the idea I'm an easy mark."

She nodded solemnly. "I understand."

"Do you? I'm caught between a rock and a hard spot, and I have no choice but to press charges. If your father and brother truly are blameless, as they say, that means they'll be punished for something they didn't mean to do."

She caught her bottom lip between her teeth. After a moment, she said, "I'm just thankful it's you we're dealing with. At least we can trust you to be fair."

Luke heaved another sigh. "I'll try to be. God knows, I want to be. Otherwise, I don't know how I'll sleep nights."

"No matter what happens, you mustn't blame yourself," she said shakily. "My papa wouldn't want that, and neither do I. As I said, it isn't your fault."

"Then why do I feel so awful?"

She pulled to a stop and turned to look up at him, her movement forcing him to release his grip on her elbow. With trembling fingers, she lightly touched his jacket sleeve. "Oh, Mr. Taggart. In a way, this is nearly as terrible for you as it is for my papa and brother, isn't it?"

"Well, I'm not sure I'd say that." Luke cupped his hand over hers where it rested on his arm. Her fingers felt small and fragile against his palm. "I've been trying to think what to do all evening. The most obvious solution, of course, is to make them serve a short stint in jail and fine them for damages. The only problem is, I doubt your father has the extra money to pay a fine."

Cassandra shook her head, her gaze still frightened. "No, he doesn't. We do well just to keep food on the table and pay our rent."

Drawing her arm through his, Luke began to walk again, his hand still covering hers. "You know, until this second, I hadn't considered the fix you'll be in if your papa and brother are kept in jail for any length of time."

"You mustn't concern yourself with me. I'll manage somehow." She frowned, drawing her finely arched, dark eyebrows together. "My biggest worry is for Papa and Ambrose. Jail...I can't believe this has happened."

"Well, it has. What in God's name are you going to do, honey? In a town like Black Jack, there's little by way of employment for respectable young ladies. And as I recall, it's not just you at home, either. Don't you have a little brother as well?"

"Yes—Khristos. He's only eight."

Luke gazed pensively into the darkness. "I'll never forgive myself if the two of you are tossed out into the streets."

"The streets?" she echoed faintly.

He glanced down. She was staring ahead at the rain-washed cobblestone, obviously imagining how awful it would be if she were homeless. "That *is* what happens when you can't pay the rent, you know," he told her softly. "Landlords don't tend to be very understanding."

"Oh, my..." The corners of her mouth quivered, and he felt her hand tighten on his arm. "Oh, my...I hadn't thought of that. If Papa and Ambrose are kept in jail for very long, what will Khristos and I do?"

"I'm not trying to frighten you," he inserted gently. "And I promise you, Cassandra, if there's any way I can prevent such a thing from happening, I will. It's just that I can't think how." He grew silent for a moment. "As much as I'd like to, I can't very well lend you money. How would that look to all my employees? The first thing I knew, I'd have claim jumpers crawling over these mountains like a plague of insects."

Cassandra was beginning to feel truly frightened. Mr. Taggart was right. Absolutely right. There were no jobs for decent young ladies in Black Jack. She'd already tried to find one. If her papa and brother had to stay in jail, even for so much as a week, she and Khristos would run out of money.

Cassandra knew she could throw herself upon the mercy of the nuns and that somehow they'd make room for her and Khristos, but the orphanage already operated on a shoestring. She and Khristos would literally be taking food from children's mouths. And what of Lycodomes? He was only a dog and Cassandra knew it was ridiculous to worry over his fate when she had so many more important concerns, but she couldn't bear the thought of abandoning him.

There was always Father Tully, of course. He would help them in any way he could. But there again, money was scarce, and the kindly priest wouldn't be able to spare enough to keep the wolves from their door for any length of time.

Luke Taggart's hand flexed over hers, his grip warm and wonderfully strong. "Hey..." he said huskily. "I'm afraid I have frightened you, and that wasn't my aim. We'll work this out. Trust me on that. Somehow, we'll work it out."

"But how?" Cassandra heard the tremulous note in her voice and wanted to kick herself. She was a Zerek, not some lily-livered sniveler, and the Zereks were made of strong stock. Or so her papa said. Right now, she didn't feel very courageous.

"I'm not sure how," Luke admitted, "but I promise, I'll think of something."

He traced his thumb over the back of her hand, his touch like a feather moving on her skin. Cassandra got the strangest feeling, a tingly sensation that began where he caressed her and moved up her arm. It had the unsettling effect of making her forget what she was worried about. All she could think of was his thumb and how wonderful it felt, moving in those little circles, setting her nerve endings afire.

"I had planned to stop by your house in the morning to tell you what happened. Would you mind if I drop by anyway?"

"What?"

His firm mouth quirked at the corners, deepening the slashes in his cheeks. "Would you mind if I drop by to see you in the morning?" he repeated.

Cassandra lifted her gaze to his. Like one half of a broken china supper plate, the moon hung in the dark sky behind him. The illumination spilled across his broad shoulders and threaded his tawny hair with silver. Accustomed to the short, stocky men in her family, she couldn't help but feel in awe of his height and the strength that seemed to emanate from him. Recalling the evening that Ambrose had twirled her around the kitchen, she wondered how it might feel if Luke Taggart were to put his arm around her. At the thought, a funny, liquid heat swirled through her stomach, tendrils of warmth ribboning from there to the tips of her breasts.

The reaction shocked Cassandra. She planned to become a nun, after all, and she was fairly certain nuns didn't get these feelings. Considering the trouble her papa and brother were in, she felt guilty as well. How could she be getting the tingles over Luke Taggart when two of the people she loved most in the world were locked up in jail?

Gulping down a strange lump that had lodged in her throat, she finally managed to say, "Of course I don't mind if you drop by. But, Mr. Taggart, it's really not your concern what happens to me and Khristos. I wish you wouldn't trouble yourself."

"Don't be silly."

"No, really. It's enough that you're being so kind about Papa and Ambrose. You've been as grievously wronged as they have been—maybe even more so—and I—"

"Nonsense," he interrupted, patting her hand and then releasing his hold on her.

Glad to have her hand free so she could think, Cassandra moved the backs of her fingers over her skirt, trying to rub away the electrical sensation that still lingered there.

"This is all a terrible mess," he went on, "and because it happened, you and your little brother are going to need help. Strictly speaking, the families of my employees aren't my concern, I suppose, but I've never really looked at it that way. And I certainly can't in this instance, not believing as I do that your father and brother were hoodwinked."

"But I—"

"No buts," he said gently. "I'm making your welfare my concern, end of discussion." His amber eyes glowed like banked embers in the shadows. "If I request a favor of you, Cassandra, will you promise to try to do it for me?"

At that moment, Cassandra felt so indebted to him, she could have denied him nothing. "Yes, of course."

"Then I want you to promise you won't worry. I'll find a workable solution to everything. You have my word on it."

His dark face suddenly seemed to swim

84

in her vision, and she realized she was looking up at him through tears. Blinking furiously, she swiped at her cheeks, then glanced away, embarrassed to have so little control over her emotions. It was just—well, he was so incredibly kind. When she thought of all the mean and nasty things some of the people in this town said about him, it made her so angry, she wanted to wring their necks.

He caught her chin and brushed at the wetness on her cheeks. Once again, his touch was wonderfully light. Cassandra gazed up at his sharply carved features and the slight smile that kicked up one corner of his mouth. He was beautiful, she thought dreamily. In a very masculine sort of way, of course. Rather like she pictured one of God's archangels, incredibly strong and invincible, with a goldenness about him that gleamed in his hair and eyes.

"Will you be at home around ten in the morning?" he asked.

"I...well, yes. I can make it a point to be."

He nodded. "An idea has just occurred to me, but before I discuss it with you, I need to think it through and consult with my attorney."

"All right."

The soft, tremulous sound of her voice made something catch in Luke's chest. She was giving him that look again, as if he could slay dragons. For reasons beyond him, he didn't like the feeling it gave him. Didn't like it at all. Luke had never aspired to being anyone's hero, and he had no intention of starting now.

As he drew her back into a walk, he realized she was without the protection of her male relatives for the night. A slight smile settled on his mouth as he ran his gaze over her figure. She wasn't unaffected by him, he felt sure. He hadn't missed that telltale shiver that had coursed through her when he caressed her hand, or the sultry look in her eyes when she gazed up at him.

Christ, but she is lovely. Almost too lovely to be real. It had been a long while since Luke had felt such fire racing through his blood. There had been times over the last few months when he'd even entertained the notion that he might be losing his virility. Not so, he realized now.

Sweet Cassandra. When he got her delivered safely home, perhaps he would try his hand at courting Milo Zerek's daughter, after all.

Even as Luke toyed with that thought, a small boy and a huge yellow-and-white dog slipped from between the buildings to join him and Cassandra on the sidewalk.

"Khristos!" she cried. "You startled me. I'd nearly forgotten you were waiting here."

Soaked to the skin and shivering with cold, the child looked like a street urchin in his tattered clothing and worn-out boots. Luke couldn't help but notice that the boy's trousers were high-water short.

The dog wasn't in much better shape. A shaggy beast of oversized proportions, the animal sported mud clear to its belly and had lost all the fur along the left side of its body. It appeared to Luke that the dog had been burned or, God forbid, had a bad case of mange.

"I was startin' to think you weren't comin' back," the child said, reaching up to wipe his snotty nose with his ragged jacket sleeve.

Cassandra knelt down. "Of course I came back."

"Did you find Papa and Ambrose?"

"Yes, and they're safe and sound." She gave the boy a quick hug, then turned him toward Luke. "Mr. Taggart, this is my brother Khristos."

Khristos thrust out a thin arm. Sticky little fingers pressed into Luke's palm.

"Hello, Khristos. I'm pleased to meet you."

"You're my papa's boss, ain't ya?"

"Khristos, mind your manners," Cassandra chided. "What do you say to Mr. Taggart?"

"I'm pleased to meet you, Mr. Taggart," the boy mumbled.

Rubbing the stickiness from his hand onto his trousers, Luke forced himself to smile.

"And this," Cassandra said with a flourish of her hand toward the dog, "is Lycodomes." She reached out to scratch the huge animal behind its floppy ear.

"What happened to his side?" Luke couldn't resist asking.

"Kerosene, we think. When he was little more than a pup, he came home shaking and quivering, and he smelled of lantern fuel. Papa figured Lycodomes had made a pest of himself somewhere, and someone had doused him. It burned his skin, I guess. His hair fell out and never grew back." She pressed a quick kiss atop the dog's head. "Shake hands with Mr. Taggart, Lye-Lye."

Luke would have happily foregone the honor, but the canine obediently sat back on its haunches and thrust out a paw. A very large, muddy paw. So much for Luke's wiping his hand clean. Mentally cringing, he grasped the animal's foot and made a quick pumping motion. The strong odor of wet, unwashed dog drifted up to him. "I'm pleased to make your acquaintance, Lycodomes."

The dog gave a throaty snarl and bared all its teeth. His fangs were lethal looking.

"Lye-Lye!" Cassandra cried. "What on earth has gotten into you?"

Luke had no difficulty intepreting the canine's message and jerked his hand back. Dogs, he knew, weren't as easily fooled as people. Lycodomes obviously recognized a low-down toad when he saw one.

As Luke straightened, he made a mental note to get rid of the huge, mangy beast at the first opportunity. He didn't need or want the added frustration of a canine running inter-ference between him and Cassandra.

The dog growled again, more softly this time but no less threateningly. Luke shared the sen-timent. Silent war had been declared.

With an embarrassed little laugh, Cas-sandra said, "Well, as you can see, I'm not entirely without an escort."

Luke had noticed that, yes. Woe to the man who dared to accost her. Lycodomes would probably rip his balls off.

Pushing to her feet, Cassandra placed a hand

on Khristos's shoulder and extended her other to Luke. "We'll say good-bye to you here, Mr. Taggart. It really isn't necessary for you to walk us all the way home. In the miners' district, the streets aren't paved, you know, and there are no sidewalks. The mud might ruin your shoes."

Luke was well aware of the deplorable conditions in the miners' district. Yet Cassandra stood before him, extending her hand as if she wore silk and was the grandest of ladies.

"I couldn't care less about my shoes. But I do need to see my attorney, as I mentioned earlier, and the sooner I roust him out of his bed, the sooner I'll get home to my own." Grasping her slender fingers, he bent slightly at the waist. "Until tomorrow morning at ten, then?"

"Shall I give you directions? I wouldn't want you wandering about looking for our house."

Calling the place a house was an overstatement. Luke had already sent his man of affairs on a scouting mission to learn which shack the Zereks lived in. He knew for a fact that it was a tiny little structure with a roof that boasted more holes than shingles. "I'll have no problem finding you," he assured her.

As she started to turn away, Luke called her back. "You will remember your promise to me, won't you?"

Letting her brother and dog walk on a ways without her, she fixed a puzzled gaze on Luke. "Promise?"

"Not to worry," he reminded her. "About anything. You'll trust me to take care of everything?"

She flashed a smile radiant with gratitude. "Mr. Taggart, aside from my papa and brothers, I honestly can't think of a single person I trust more."

Luke gazed after the ragtag threesome as they walked away. Long after they faded into the darkness, he remained standing there, a slight smile touching his mouth. So she trusted him, did she? That was good.

That was very, very good.

FIVE

❦ Despite the chill of the September morning, a feeling of warmth hung over the unpaved street like a cozy quilt. As Luke strode along, head bent to watch for mud puddles in his path, he heard bees buzzing in and out of the nearby bushes and birds chirping on the tree limbs above him. Not to be outshone, some hens in a tumbledown chicken coop between two miners' shacks clucked and fluttered their wings every time the wind gusted.

Soon winter would embrace the mountains, but for now sunlight dappled the sodden earth, the patterns dancing in dizzying splendor. Luke took a deep breath, sorting out the smells that drifted to him: frying bacon, the faint odor of sewage, baking bread. In the distance, children laughed, and then a dog began to bark. This was Cassandra's world, he realized. He had no doubt she would thank him for taking her out of such squalor. A beautiful girl like her deserved to live in a mansion, surrounded by fine things.

A smile curved his lips as he anticipated her soft cries of gratitude. His body stirred as he thought of allowing her to express her gratitude between the silken sheets of his bed.

Sidestepping a puddle of dun-colored mud, he quickened his pace. Once he'd made up his mind to take action, he never allowed anything to stand in his way. And he had definitely made up his mind about Cassandra Zerek.

The Zerek house wasn't even a decent shack, Luke thought as he drew to a stop before it. Only about twelve feet square, the dwelling's roof sagged pitifully on each side of its peak, and the chimney pipe looked to be in perilous danger of falling through. He stood there staring, not quite able to believe his eyes. Things had been bad when he lived down here, but nothing quite as awful as this. Jim Briesen, the landlord of the mining district, ought to be shot for charging people rent for these structures. Hell, from what he'd heard, the man was all but gouging the lifeblood from his tenants.

Luke stepped up onto the porch—at least, what served as a porch. It was made from a few planks of low-grade lumber nailed to disintegrating joists. Making a fist, he rapped lightly on the door, half afraid it might fall off its hinges. From within the shanty, he heard something scrape the floor, followed by muted footsteps and the creak of floorboards giving under someone's weight. An instant later, the door swung open.

Cassandra. A vision in a brown wool dress every bit as ugly as her blue one, she stood with one hand pressed to her slender waist, the other clasping the door frame. This morning she wore her hair caught up at the crown with a red ribbon, the glossy sable curls tumbling in artless abandon. The style revealed the sweet curve of her slender neck and accented her oval face. Her eyes, more vivid a blue in contrast to the drab brown dress, seemed to dominate her features even as a radiant smile curved her lips.

"Mr. Taggart, won't you come in?" Her voice was low and rushed as she extended the invitation with all the elegance of a princess beckoning a guest into her palace.

"It looks as though you survived the night well enough," Luke observed.

"I remembered what you said and tried not to worry," she said softly. "It helped immensely, and I even managed to get a little sleep."

Luke stepped across the threshold, his gaze moving swiftly over the one-room shanty's interior. It was a pathetic sight. A makeshift table, with upended buckets serving as chairs. Water-soaked walls made of rough wood. A puncheon floor that had been patched with mismatched lengths of board. He cringed at the thought of her living like this. They had tried to cover the wide cracks in the walls with newspaper, but he could still see daylight. When winter came, the place would be freezing, with icy wind whistling through the gaps to assault her delicate skin.

"Do be careful, Mr. Taggart," she cautioned, gesturing at a pan of water on the floor. "The roof leaks a bit, I'm afraid."

A bit? As her voice trailed away, he heard a cacophony of dripping that sounded like an entire orchestra of off-key and slightly muted xylophones. As far as he could see, there were more leaks than there was roof, and given the fact it had stopped raining outside, he could only stare in amazement.

As if reading his thoughts, she glanced at the sagging ceiling boards. "The water seems to pool up in the attic. It, um, takes a while between storms for all of it to drip through."

"I see." More than she knew, he added silently.

Wiping her palms on her skirt, she hurried to the stove. "I hope you enjoy tea." Her voice had a high-pitched, quavery note, as if she were unbearably nervous. She glanced back at him. "I'd offer you coffee, but we're out."

"I like tea fine."

Luke stood there, feeling like a weevil in a flour sack. He wished he knew how to put her at ease.

"Cassandra," he began, then stopped. The smooth words he'd planned suddenly seemed wrong. He cleared his throat, searching for an alternative, but before he could speak, she whirled around, clapped a hand to her forehead, and rolled her eyes. "Heavens! I've totally forgotten my manners, not even taking your coat or offering you a chair."

As far as Luke could see, there wasn't a chair to offer. As for his jacket, he had no intention of staying long, and when he left, he hoped to take her with him. "I'm fine, Cassandra. Just tend to the tea and stop worrying."

She wrung her hands as he straddled a bucket and sat down. Luke angled a glance up at her and winked. "You know, it wasn't very long ago that I lived down here in the mining district. Just one row over, in fact. I've done my share of sitting on buckets, and my roof leaked a little, too."

"It did?" She looked vastly relieved. "For some reason, I pictured you always living at the other end of town in that big, beautiful, white house."

It *was* a beautiful house, and he was tempted to tell her now that she'd soon be living there with him. He shifted on the bucket, trying to get positioned so the sharp bottom rim didn't bite into his ass or, God forbid, something more essential.

As she turned back to the stove, he took the opportunity to study her home more closely. Despite the air of penury, the shack had been made livable, no doubt by Cassandra's clever hands. A chipped vase filled with greenery from the hillsides served as a centerpiece on the table. Lining the walls were four cots, each neatly made, with embroidered pillows tossed here and there to make them look less utilitarian. A fire crackled cheerfully in the rusted belly of the stove. He could almost picture the Zereks gathered at this table of an evening, the cozy glow of a lantern illuminating their faces.

Not what he had expected, he realized, then frowned as he tried to remember the image he'd carried in his head whenever he thought of the life Cassandra must lead. Relentless dreariness, he guessed.

Memories tried to slip through the dark curtains of his mind—memories he quickly shoved away. By the sweat of his brow and a streak of incredible luck, he'd become a rich man. Anything he wanted was his for the taking now, including this girl—and by God, he was going to have her.

He felt no trace of guilt. Although he would be taking her away from her family, he was doing her a definite favor. He would give her everything her heart desired—not only a lovely home to live in, but luxury beyond her dreams.

Finished setting out the tea, she placed the kettle on to boil, then turned to join him. As she took a seat across from him, she folded her small hands on the table, her gaze direct and guileless. Not that he believed, even for a moment, that any woman from this part of town could be that innocent.

Cassandra was, however, incredibly lovely, and he'd settle for that. Skin like cream. Thick, dark lashes. A full, rose-pink mouth that begged to be kissed. And eyes a man could get lost in. She had a countenance that was as eye-catching as it was unforgettable.

"Well," he finally said, "shall we get down to business?"

"Business?" she echoed.

Luke waved a hand. "A manner of speaking. As I told you last night, I have a plan, and after discussing it with my attorney, I've decided it may be workable. All that remains is for you to agree to it."

"What sort of plan?"

Sparing no words, Luke reminded Cassandra that her father and brother were in jail for an extremely serious offense. "As you said last night, claim jumpers are often shot where they stand or, if not that, sentenced to lengthy terms in prison. But given your father's story about the man named Peter Hirsch, I've decided to be lenient."

She closed her eyes for a moment. When she opened them again, that worshipful look he'd noticed last night was back in her gaze. "I never really doubted you would be, Mr. Taggart. You're just that kind of person."

Luke smiled slightly. So far, so good. "After consulting with the marshal and my attorney," he went on, "I've decided to fine your father and brother each in the amount of five hundred dollars. In addition, both of them will have to serve a three-month stint behind bars. Under the circumstances, I feel that is letting them off lightly. Very lightly."

Cassandra grew pale. Lips quivering at the corners, she averted her gaze, then finally looked back at him. "Mr. Taggart, please don't think I'm ungrateful, for I know you're being very lenient indeed. But you're talking about a thousand dollars, all totaled. To people like us, that's a staggering sum of money. There's no way my papa and brother can pay such an amount."

Luke held up a hand. "Please, just hear me out. As I said, I've got a plan. For the last few months, I've been searching for a paid companion. Now that I've gotten to know you, I've decided you would be ideal for the position."

"A 'paid companion'?" she questioned with a puzzled frown. "I'm not sure I understand what you mean."

Luke had expected her to be offended at first and possibly even to balk, so he wasn't unduly alarmed by her stricken expression. He flashed another smile. "Whether I hire you or end up hiring someone else, I'm prepared to offer a very generous wage, Cassandra, so I don't want you to think that this is a charitable gesture on my part. I'm willing to pay five hundred a month, plus board."

"Five *hundred*?" she repeated dazedly.

"Yes, five hundred. At the end of one year, when I and my paid companion part company, I will bestow a twenty-thousand-dollar settlement on her. If you agree to take the job, you'll be able to pay off your father's and brother's fines in only two months. For the remaining ten months of our agreement, you'll be able to keep the five hundred each payday, to save or spend as you wish."

"I see," she said faintly.

"If you're interested," he went on, "I will, of course, insist that you sign a contract that will bind you to the agreement for the period of one year." He shrugged. "I apologize for complicating the relationship with legal documents, but I don't have a lot of faith in verbal agreements. Experience has taught me that people seldom honor their promises unless they are bound to do so in writing. That is not to say you would break your word, mind you. I'll just feel more comfortable with all the terms spelled out in writing and signed by both of us."

Fully prepared for her to be outraged and to initially refuse his proposition, Luke fell silent, waiting for the storm to erupt. In the end, he would win. She would either agree to his terms, or her father and brother would be punished for claim jumping to the full extent of the law. He felt certain Cassandra would never allow that to happen.

She looked pensive and troubled but said nothing. Finally Luke could bear the silence no longer. "It's a very generous offer, Cassandra. Three months in jail is hardly any time at all, considering the alternatives."

More silence. She just sat there, staring at him, her blue eyes dark with shadows, her expression still stricken. Luke hadn't expected her to take it quite this badly.

Propping his arms on the table, he leaned slightly toward her. "Cassandra, is my offer really that awful?" he asked carefully. "Just think what the alternatives are. If your landlord evicts you, which he most certainly will when you don't pay the rent, this job could keep you off the streets."

Her eyes slowly filled with tears. "Oh, Mr. Taggart," she whispered shakily, "it's not that I don't appreciate the offer. It just breaks my heart that you feel it's necessary to make it."

Luke circled that for a moment, not entirely sure what she meant.

"When I used to see you on the streets, I always sensed you were lonely," she went on, "but I never dreamed you were *this* lonely. As much as I appreciate your being so kind to my papa and brother, I can't possibly take money for just being your friend. It would be like stealing." She reached across the table to press her hand over his. "Don't you see? It's not necessary to pay me to be your companion. I'll happily do it for free. We're going to have to come up with some other idea."

Luke felt as if the bucket beneath him had disappeared. Either this girl was the best actress he'd ever encountered, or she was pathetically dim-witted. He looked deeply into her eyes, which seemed to gleam with intelligence. He could detect no sign of artifice, just naivete and sweetness. Was it possible she truly didn't understand the nature of his offer?

For the first time in his life, Luke experienced a wave of pure and unadulterated guilt. He quickly shoved it away, assuring himself such feelings were absurd. No one raised in the squalor of mining towns, with coarse and uncouth individuals coming and going at every turn, could be as pure of heart as Cassandra Zerek pretended to be.

No, he decided, she was simply trying to raise the ante. And very cleverly so. Most men were willing to pay all they could afford for the privilege of deflowering a virgin, and she apparently hoped he was one of them. Unfortunately for her, Luke had never been so inclined. Besides, he'd already offered her an astronomical amount of money.

"Cassandra," he said with an edge of warning, "if this is your way of trying to haggle with me on the wage, I feel I'm already offering more than any man in his right mind would be willing to pay."

Looking totally bewildered, she said, "Why would I try to haggle when I don't think you should have to pay for companionship at all?"

He held her gaze for a long moment. "The position I'm hoping you will fill is going to be very demanding, and very much a job. Don't think for a moment it won't be. That's why I offered such a generous wage to begin with. I'm sure if you think about it, you'll agree it's more than fair."

"Frankly, I think it's way too much."

Luke sighed. He'd never been good at double-talk. "I like that word, frankly," he said softly. "So let me lay it out on the table for you, hmm? Long before I saw you in the churchyard the other afternoon, I'd been toying with the idea of taking a live-in companion. You suit my requirements in every way. To be blunt, I'm bored with the company I find in the saloons and gambling establishments. The women there are"—he shrugged—"otherwise occupied much of the time. I suppose you're right; I am lonely. At this point in my life, I'd like a lady friend who will devote herself exclusively to me. In return for monopolizing her time and energy—and I assure you, I will be very demanding—I am willing to pay a very generous wage.

"If you take the job, you'll be expected to make yourself available to me at odd hours, usually at night, to accommodate my schedule. That will necessitate your living in my home. If I have free time during the day, I'll expect you to cancel your own plans to facilitate mine. In short, if I require your services, I will expect you to drop everything and devote yourself entirely to me and my entertainment."

He reached inside his jacket and withdrew three documents: the contract in triplicate, which his attorney had drawn up last night, inequitably worded, of course, in Luke's behalf. If Cassandra signed it, she would be, to all intents and purposes, an object in his possession for the next twelve months, with no legal recourse. He slid the papers across the table to her.

"That said, perhaps you should look this over and decide if you're even interested," he said with an air of finality he was far from feeling.

"Of course I'm interested," she said softly. "I'm in no position not to be. With Papa and Ambrose in jail, Khristos and I are in a devil of a fix, and my chances of getting a job elsewhere are practically nil."

"You won't be in a fix if you accept my proposal," Luke reminded her.

She unfolded one of the documents and

began to read it aloud, skipping over parts of it, frowning at others. At some of the wording, Luke cringed, half expecting her to toss the contract back in his face, but she was seemingly oblivious to, or didn't understand, the legal jargon. In one section, she waived all custodial rights to any issue that might arise from their relationship. In another, she agreed to willingly and without complaint surrender her person to Luke in whatever manner pleased him.

The terminology was clearly above her head, for when she finished scanning the clauses, which stripped her of practically all personal rights, she had only two questions.

Fastening wide blue eyes on his, she said, "What will people think of my living in your house? And with my papa and brother in jail, who will take care of Khristos and Lycodomes?"

After his brief encounter with the dog last night, Luke wasn't thrilled at the prospect of having the slobbery mongrel in his home. But it would be a simple enough matter to get rid of the hairy beast later. As for Khristos, he was only one small boy, and Luke had a very large house and an entire staff of servants to look after him.

Flashing what he hoped was a benevolent smile, he reached across the table and took the contract from her slender hands. Pulling his fountain pen from his breast pocket, he quickly jotted an addendum, which he also appended to the other two copies. "There," he said smoothly. "Your brother and dog may reside with me until your father and brother are released from jail. You have my word on it in writing."

She took the contract when he pushed it back to her. After reading the clause he had just added, she glanced up. "Thank you, Mr. Taggart."

"Luke, please." He extended the fountain pen to her. "If you're going to sign that contract and become my companion for the next twelve months, I believe we should dispense with the formalities and begin addressing each other by first names. Don't you?"

If she had noticed that he'd been calling her by her Christian name since their first meeting, she gave no sign as she accepted the pen. His stomach knotted with tension when she nibbled on the end of the ink reservoir and then tapped it against her teeth. *Christ.* Why didn't she just sign the damned papers?

Luke sat there, alternately holding his breath, then inhaling deeply.

"I'm still a little worried about living in your house," she mused aloud. "People can be so peculiar sometimes. Just last month, tongues were buzzing about Hope Bowers, and all she did was let Henry Chadworth walk her home from church." She wrinkled her nose. "Papa says when a boy and girl are alone together after dark, folks with evil minds think the worst."

Luke struggled not to smile. "I've made that same observation myself a time or two."

She heaved a high-pitched sigh. "Anyway, you can see my concern. When Khristos turns

103

twelve, I plan to enter a convent. Because of that, I have to be very careful of my reputation."

"Are you willing to let evil-minded people dictate to you, Cassandra? What you do with your life—this job included—is no one's business but your own." He paused a moment to let that sink in. "Besides, as I understand it, nuns come from all walks of life. I'm no expert on the church, of course, but it seems to me that it will be your sincerity and devotion to serving God that will be questioned, not what kind of job you held before you decided to become a nun."

"I suppose that's true."

Luke's smile was so stiff, he felt as if he had drying egg white all over his face. "Under the circumstances, I think your residing in my home should be perfectly understandable to everyone in Black Jack. You and Khristos have no other relatives here in town. Your father and brother can't provide for you. I'm your father's former employer, and there's the matter of his and Ambrose's fines, which you'll be working to pay off. I'd venture a guess that people are going to think you're a very lucky young woman."

Luke leaned forward, holding her gaze with his. "Have you any idea exactly what I'm offering you? In exchange for one short year of your life, you'll not only be able to pay your papa's and brother's fines, but you'll be well set for the remainder of your days. Twenty thousand dollars is a fortune. Most people only dream of getting an opportunity like this."

She tapped the pen against her teeth again,

her expression pensive. "I think that before I make a final decision I really should talk to my papa."

"Cassandra, your papa is in jail."

"But surely I can go visit him."

"When I stopped by the jail this morning, the marshal told me only wives are allowed to visit the prisoners. Daughters and sisters aren't afforded those privileges."

It was yet another lie, of course. The jail had no such policy, but Luke had made special arrangements with the marshal in Cassandra's case. There were benefits to being the most powerful man in town. Luke had a political reach that stretched from Black Jack to Leadville, and then again to Denver. The marshal, like many of the other town officials, was in Luke's back pocket. Luke had made it clear, to the marshal and all his deputies, that Cassandra wasn't to speak with her father under any circumstances.

After letting her mull everything over for a moment, Luke decided to wield the emotional knife. "Cassandra, do you understand what may happen to your father and brother if you don't sign the contract?"

She fastened worried blue eyes on him.

Luke held up his hands. "I have to exact some sort of recompense for what they've done. I have no choice. The steep fines will satisfy all my other employees, giving them a sense that justice has been meted out. If you don't pay those fines…" He heaved a sigh. "Well, there's no telling how long your father and brother will be in jail. Even if you could find some other job, which is highly unlikely, how much money can you conceivably hope to make? And out of that wage, how much will you be able to spare for fines?"

"You mean they'll have to stay in jail until the fines are paid?" she asked in a strangled voice.

"That's usually the way of it. Even if I made arrangements otherwise, where would they work around here after their release? I can't very well hire them back. How would that look?" He shook his head. "They'd have to leave town, and I couldn't let them do that before they settled their obligations to me. Appearances are everything in a situation like this. It has to look as if they're getting their just punishment. Your taking the job as my paid companion will bring about a happy ending for everyone."

Her forehead knitted into another frown, and her amazing blue eyes narrowed in concentration. She looked over the contract again, during every second of which time Luke was in a sweat, thinking she would call him on some of the inequitable wording.

"I still feel funny about taking money for being your companion," she said faintly. "It doesn't seem right, somehow. Especially such a great deal of money."

"Don't be silly. I'm a wealthy man. The money means nothing to me."

Smoothing the document out on the table, she bent to sign. A swishing sound pulsated against Luke's eardrums as he watched her finish writing her last name. The instant she straightened, he reached out to retrieve the first signed document before she had time to think better of her decision. She signed the other two copies without hesitation.

"I'll keep your copy in my wall safe with my own," he said congenially as she slid the signed documents to him. Taking the pen, he added his signature to each of them as well. "My safe is even fireproof, so nothing will happen to your copy or mine that way."

Gazing across the table at her sweet countenance, Luke folded the papers and returned them to his breast pocket, scarcely able to believe how easy it had been. She belonged to him now. Every sweet, delectable inch of her was his, to do with as he pleased. He had a host of plans for her, which he would now be free to implement, and far sooner than he had dared to hope.

"I take it Khristos is at school?"

"Yes, until two o'clock."

"And where's...what's his name? The dog."

"Oh, Lycodomes. He's with Khristos. He always walks him to and from school. Lycodomes is very protective, you know."

Luke had noticed that.

"Sometimes he returns home to be with me until school is out, then goes back to walk Khristos home. Other times he just waits outside the school, and then the two of them meet me over at the orphanage when Khristos is finished for the day. Then we all walk home together."

Luke nodded. "I'll arrange to have a servant meet them over at the school and escort them to my place." He glanced around the shanty. "Can I help you gather your things?"

"Right now?"

Luke knew he was rushing her, but the truth was, he couldn't wait to have her ensconced in his home and at his disposal. Tonight she would be his.

"I'll make arrangements for your father's and brother's possessions to be stored," he told her. "All you need to worry about are your and Khristos's personal items."

He pushed up from the table, rubbing his hands together. "Just aim me in the right direction, and I'll help you pack."

She stood as well, glancing around as if she were in a daze. "It never occurred to me I'd be leaving so soon." The tea kettle chose that moment to whistle, and she leaped with a start. "It all seems to be happening so suddenly."

Not suddenly enough to suit Luke. He stepped around her to take the kettle off the heat. "Is there something specific you need to do before you leave?"

She shook her head. "It's just—" She gestured with her hand and flashed a wobbly smile. "Shall we go ahead and have tea?"

"I'll have the maid fix you tea at my house." To push the point, he withdrew his pocket watch. "I have some errands to run this afternoon." *An emergency trip to the dressmaker's,* he thought to himself, *to buy her some ready-made gowns and lingerie.* The awful blue dress and the drab brown rag she wore right now were destined for the burning barrel. "It's really best for me if we don't waste time."

"I could always start the job tomorrow," she offered.

Over his dead body. "If I send people down here to move everything into storage, where would you sleep tonight?"

She pressed the back of her wrist to her forehead. "Oh, my...well, I guess—" Her gaze snagged on the stove. "I need to put out the fire. I can't just walk off and leave that. Are you sure you'll be able to send someone to the school to collect Khristos? He'd be frightened if he came home to an empty house."

"I promise to have someone waiting outside the door for him at precisely two o'clock." Bending to open the stove door, he added, "I'll tend to the fire. Meanwhile, you gather your and Khristos's clothes. How's that sound?"

"All right."

He heard her dragging something out from under a bed as he rearranged the firewood with a poker. When he straightened, there was a satchel on one of the cots, and she was standing beside it, apparently finished packing.

"Is that it?" he asked incredulously.

She gave a slight nod. "Khristos has outgrown nearly all his clothes, and mine have mostly worn out. We have only enough to wear clean while the soiled are being laundered. Papa planned to take us shopping soon."

Soon. Luke had a feeling Milo Zerek was big on making promises but shy on execution. He stared down at the worn bag, trying to remember how it had felt to have all his worldly possessions stuffed into something so small.

The realization that the Zereks were so poverty-stricken banished any trace of guilt he might have been harboring. Lecherous though his plans for her were, this girl was going to be far better off in his care than she'd ever been in her father's.

If she played her cards right and devoted herself to pleasing him well, anything she wanted would be hers for the asking.

SIX

A picket fence bordered the velvet front lawn of Taggart Manor, which rose in a two-story display of splendid white over manicured rose gardens and sculptured shrubbery. Cassandra had admired the mansion many times from a distance, but she'd never been close enough to set foot on the grounds. As Luke held open the gate for her, she stood rooted, her lips slightly parted, her gaze moving from one impressive architectural feature to another: gables with curlicue wood sculptures supporting the eaves, balconies with ornamental railings, and, most incredible of all, four brick chimneys. Why on earth might a house need so many fireplaces? Surely it couldn't be that spacious inside or have that many rooms.

"Cassandra?"

She jerked at Luke's softly spoken summons and turned a stupefied gaze on him. "Yes?"

He arched a tawny eyebrow, his whiskey-colored eyes twinkling with suppressed laughter. "Are we going in, or would you prefer to stand and stare all day?"

"It's just so—" Cassandra broke off for lack of words. "Big and...and lovely."

He chuckled and gave her a light nudge with the satchel he held in his left hand. "It's just a house, honey. Once you've been here a few weeks, you'll barely notice its size."

On legs gone numb with awe, Cassandra started up the walkway, which was lined with ornate lampposts. At home, she had to be frugal with lantern fuel, lighting the lamp right before dark and turning it down whenever she could do without the light. Was Luke Taggart really so rich he could afford to have lamps burning in his yard at night?

The ornate wooden front door, she noticed as she stepped onto the porch, was another wonder. Carved in a busier pattern than a calico dress, it had a darling little peekaboo window at the top.

"Do you open that window and look out to see who's knocking?"

He laughed as he pushed the portal open. "Actually, the servants usually greet my callers. If it's someone I prefer not to see, they tell them I'm not receiving guests or that I'm out. The window is mostly for looks."

"They lie, you mean? Saying you're not here when you actually are?"

He furrowed his brow and appeared to mull that over. "It's a polite lie, one that's pretty much considered acceptable in more elevated social circles."

In Cassandra's books, a lie was a lie.

She stepped over the threshold into a huge foyer and found herself surrounded by panels of wood. Oak, she guessed, darkened to golden umber and polished to a high gloss. The floor was made of burgundy tiles with mosaic designs of gray stone that matched the mortar. To her left, a staircase climbed to the second floor, the newel intricately carved, the balustrade repeating the design until it disappeared from sight. Her gaze landed on a large, gold-framed mirror on the foyer wall that was flanked with smaller mirrors, greenery trailing from gold planters below them.

"Oh, my..."

"Like it?" His pride was unmistakable.

"Oh, yes." Cassandra tried to think of something to say, but she was so incredulous, her brain seemed frozen. "Oh, yes..."

He chuckled again, a deep, throaty rumble that she found utterly endearing. "I'm glad. For the next year, at least, this is going to be your home. If we get on well together and I renew your contract, you may stay longer. Who's to say?"

A man entered the huge hall. He appeared to be dressed for church in an odd, uncomfortable-looking black suit that had tails hanging down the backside. He strode briskly toward them, then came to an abrupt halt, clicking his heels and inclining his balding gray head. "Master Taggart, I do apologize. I had no idea you'd be returning home so early with a guest." With a military stiffness, he pivoted toward Cassandra, inclined his head again, then held out a hand. "Madam, may I take your wrap?"

Cassandra had never clapped eyes on anyone quite so solemn, except maybe old Mr. Faucett, the town's dour undertaker. Fighting a sudden dread, she slipped off her shawl and relinquished it. With a puckered expression of distaste, the man held the length of damp, cream-colored yarn aloft in one hand as if he weren't quite sure what to do with it. Cassandra nearly snatched her shawl back. It had once belonged to her mama, and even though it wasn't as fine as the wraps grand ladies wore, she was extremely proud that her papa had given it to her.

"Shall I tell Martha you'd like refreshment, sir?"

"No refreshment for me, Pipps. But I would like Martha to attend Miss Zerek. In addition to other things, I believe the young lady would like some tea served to her in her rooms. Would you summon Martha, please?"

The humorless, unfriendly gentleman turned on his heel, draped Cassandra's shawl over the arm of a coat tree, and then walked back the way he had come with heel-clicking precision, his back so stiff his coattails barely wiggled.

Cassandra leaned toward Luke and whispered, "Is he an eccentric relative?"

Luke stared down at her for a long moment, his expression curiously blank. "An eccentric what?"

"Relative. You know—an uncle or something?"

The corners of his firm mouth quirked. "He's a butler."

Cassandra had heard mention of a family of Butterworths in Black Jack, but to her recollection, she'd never encountered any Butlers. "From your mama's side?"

Luke bent his head closer to hers. "Why are we whispering?"

"So he won't hear. I wouldn't want to offend him. People can't help being strange, now, can they?" She patted Luke's arm. "You needn't feel funny about it. We've all got a strange relative or two, haven't we? My uncle Aristotle bats at cobwebs that don't exist, and my mama's sister Colleen frequently converses with leprechauns. Once she even caught one, but before he could reveal the whereabouts of his gold, he bit her finger and got away."

Luke blinked. Twice. Then he cleared his throat and straightened. "You don't say?"

"Not that we believe she *really* caught a leprechaun," Cassandra hastened to inform him.

He looked relieved to hear that.

"After all, everyone knows they're extremely difficult to catch, and Aunt Colleen isn't exactly quick on her feet. Arthritis in the toes, you know. It's so bad, she wears shoes two sizes too large, and they flop when she walks. Papa says she couldn't catch a cold, let alone one of the little people."

"Have you ever seen one?" he asked in an odd voice. "A little person, I mean?"

"Not yet," Cassandra admitted. "But then, I've lived my whole life in America, and not many little people immigrated here. A few, of course. The one at Aunt Colleen's was snooping

114

in her trunk, unbeknownst to her, and she accidentally locked him inside. When she arrived in New York and lifted the lid to unpack, he hopped out. He wasn't very happy about having been moved against his will to America, and he's been plaguing her ever since."

"I see."

He looked so appalled that Cassandra felt obliged to say, "You mustn't worry. She lives far away in Boston, and little people aren't fond of traveling. They have a tendency toward dyspepsia, you know. Because of the small size of their stomachs."

"You don't really believe in such things, do you?"

Cassandra gazed up at him, astounded that a worldly man like Luke Taggart possessed such an unfortunate gap in his education. "Of course. Don't you?"

Before he could reply, a door at the end of the hall swung open, and a woman in a serviceable black dress and spotless white apron appeared. Cassandra recognized her from church. "Mrs. Whitmire!" she cried, extremely pleased to encounter a familiar face. "How nice to see you."

The kindly widow smiled warmly. "Cassandra Zerek." She flashed a questioning glance at Luke. "What brings you here?"

In all the excitement of seeing the house, Cassandra had nearly forgotten about her papa and brother. Guilt washed over her in a crushing wave. "The way gossip travels, I'm sure you heard about the spot of trouble my papa and Ambrose got into last night."

Mrs. Whitmire's smile faded. "Yes, dear, I did. I'm so sorry."

"Well," Cassandra went on, "their being in jail put me and Khristos in an awful pickle, and Mr. Taggart has rescued us by offering me a job. His generosity will enable me to pay Papa's and Ambrose's fines, plus keep me and Khristos off the streets until they're released and can go back to work."

The older woman looked surprised for an instant before her gaze flickered toward her employer. "Well, we can certainly use another pair of hands. It's a large house. What position is she to fill, Master Taggart? We lost a kitchen girl last week, so we've a place for her there, and Deirdre is forever complaining she could use another girl upstairs."

Luke met Mrs. Whitmire's gaze evenly. "Miss Zerek has contracted to be my paid companion, Martha. I'd like you to show her upstairs, arrange for her to bathe and then get her settled in for an afternoon nap. I'll be requiring her company this evening, and I'd like her to be well rested. She'll be using the suite that adjoins mine. I trust it's prepared for occupancy as I requested?"

Mrs. Whitmire's warm smile seemed to freeze on her lips. She stared up at Luke for what seemed to Cassandra an endlessly long moment. "Miss Zerek is the young woman you've hired to be your...your paid companion, sir?"

"That is correct," he replied tersely, drawing his watch from his pocket. After flipping it open to check the time, he fixed Mrs. Whitmire with another cool stare. "While you're getting her comfortably settled into her suite, I'll write you up a list of instructions. You'll find it on my desk in the library. Please see to it that all is accomplished before my return, exactly as I've specified. I have some errands to run, and I'll be away for at least three hours, possibly longer."

"You won't forget to have someone go fetch Khristos?" Cassandra reminded him with a smile that wobbled only a little. "At the schoolhouse, at two o'clock. Remember?"

"I remember," Luke assured her, his gaze lingering on hers for so long that her cheeks grew warm and her heart danced a flutter step in her chest.

"Master Taggart," Martha whispered, her gaze sliding from his face to Cassandra's and back again, "this girl is barely out of the schoolroom. How can you possibly...your paid companion, sir? Surely not."

Luke's gaze turned frosty, and the room seemed to chill. Cassandra resisted the urge to hug herself. "Not another word, Martha, to me or to Miss Zerek," he said in a low, commanding tone. "You're overstepping your boundaries to presume it's any of your affair. The same applies to every other servant in this household, so pass the word. Do I make myself absolutely clear?"

The woman bowed her head. "Yes, sir. I apologize."

Luke turned to Cassandra, his dark face creasing in a smile that thawed the ice from his expression. Taking her hand, he bent toward her. "Look forward to the evening, Cassandra. Martha's staff sets a lovely table, and Cook prepares meals so succulent, they fairly melt in your mouth. After supper, we'll—" He broke off and held her gaze for a moment. "I'm sure it will be the first of many unforgettable nights. I'm looking forward to enjoying your...companionship with more anticipation and enthusiasm than I've felt in a good long while."

He seemed so confident she would prove to be good company that it made her a little anxious. "Shall I plan some activities? I don't want to bore you."

His amber gaze glinted like banked embers. "What sort of activities do you have in mind?" he asked huskily.

Cassandra's mind went totally blank. "I, um..." She shrugged. "Do you like to play games?"

"With such a beautiful lady? I would *love* to play some games."

"What kind?"

The creases at each corner of his mouth deepened in a slow grin. "Use your imagination, little one, and surprise me."

He bent his tawny head and touched warm, slightly moist lips to the back of her hand. The caress was like silk brushing against her skin. A tingle coursed up her arm, radiating out from her shoulder to ribbon down her spine. Cassandra still had goose bumps when he released her and disappeared through a doorway to her right.

Mrs. Whitmire had a stricken expression on

her face when Cassandra looked back at her. Summoning a cheerful smile, Cassandra said, "Please don't worry, Mrs. Whitmire. Just because there's a difference in our ages doesn't mean I won't make Mr. Taggart a good companion." She hesitated. "Exactly how old is he, anyway?"

"I don't know exactly, miss. Right around thirty, I would say, give or take a year."

Cassandra knew of women her age who were married to men far older than that. "There, you see? That's not so great a difference. I'm nearly nineteen."

The woman quickly averted her gaze. "Yes, well..." she said, gathering up her skirts. "If you'll just follow me, dear, I'll take you to your rooms."

Cassandra bent to pick up the satchel Luke had left on the floor and hurried on the heels of the older woman to go upstairs. At the landing, Mrs. Whitmire turned right. At the third door on the left, she stopped, sorted through the keys hanging from her waist, and inserted one into the lock. As the door swung open, she beckoned for Cassandra to follow her and disappeared inside.

Cassandra came to a dead stop at the threshold, scarcely able to credit her eyes. Never had she seen such a beautiful room. Decorated in brilliant red with gold accents, it was fit for a princess. The huge bed stood on a raised area that Mrs. Whitmire called a dais, and it had a coverlet of plushly quilted crimson silk. Sheer, shimmery gold curtains swept down from the ceiling in splendorous swags. They were affixed to the walls at either side of the white headboard with ornate gold brackets that contrasted richly with the red rugs and flocked red velvet wallpaper.

Oh, and the furniture...Cassandra had never seen its like. All of it was impossibly dainty, the stark white finish offset with delicate gilt on all the edges. Even the drawers had fancy handles, ornate little gold things that reminded her of miniature door knockers. As she moved into the room, she felt as though she were stepping into a dream.

"Oh, my..." she whispered.

"Gaudy, isn't it?" Mrs. Whitmire observed.

To Cassandra, it was gorgeous. Better, even, than patent leather slippers. Of course, she loved things that sparkled and shone, and in this room, things sparkled everywhere she looked. Even the ceiling. She dropped her head back and stared at her reflection. The entire ceiling was covered with mirrors. She'd never seen so many in one place. Never. Not even the time Papa had taken them to the carnival, and she'd gotten lost in the mirror maze.

"Oh, Mrs. Whitmire, I *love* it," she whispered, twirling around and staring upward at her reflection. "It's so bright and shiny and gay. Although I must say it may be hard to sleep in here. I'll feel as if someone's watching me."

"As might well be," Mrs. Whitmire sniffed. "This room wasn't designed with sleep in mind, missy."

Cassandra couldn't have agreed more. This

room had been designed to dazzle, and it was accomplishing that. She couldn't believe it was actually going to be hers. Dropping her satchel, she rushed to the ornate armoire and pulled open the doors. The clothing rod inside was four feet long if it was an inch, and it would be all hers. With only two dresses, she didn't need nearly so much space, of course, but maybe, after she paid Papa's and Ambrose's fines, she could buy herself a couple of gowns. Really pretty ones, befitting the occupant of such a beautiful room.

Cassandra saw several garments pushed to one end—odd-looking things, one of black lace, another with broad white ruffles. Forgotten by another guest, she supposed. Later, she would tell Luke they were there so he could return them to their rightful owner.

As she closed the armoire, she said, "Oh, Mrs. Whitmire, am I dreaming? Pinch me so I'll wake up!"

The woman sniffed again. "Let's leave the pinching to Master Taggart. He'd be the expert."

That suited Cassandra. If she was dreaming, she didn't want to be pinched any time soon. She gave the room another slow appraisal, then hugged her waist and shivered. "I can't believe I'm here. I just can't believe it."

Mrs. Whitmire's blue eyes took on an odd glint. "That's two of us," she said before stepping over to close the door that led to the hall. "Well, now, what's done is done, I suppose. We both have our orders." With a deep sigh, she turned back to face Cassandra.

"The bathing chamber is through that door behind you. Peel off those clothes, and I'll find you a sleeping gown to put on after you bathe."

"That won't be necessary. I've got my own in my satchel."

Mrs. Whitmire advanced on her. Bending to open the satchel, she plucked out Cassandra's nightgown and held it up for appraisal. "This won't do," she said haughtily. "It won't do at all." Her lips drew into a thin line as she put the gown back into the bag and straightened. "I'm sure there are one or two nightgowns in the bureau. Master Taggart's *guests* are forever leaving things behind."

Trying not to feel stung by Mrs. Whitmire's reaction to her nightgown, Cassandra began unfastening her bodice. "Does he have a lot of company?"

The older woman jerked a bureau drawer open. As she rifled through the contents, she said, "Yes, well, he's a bachelor, isn't he? That makes for loneliness."

"Not anymore," Cassandra replied, letting her dress fall to the floor. Tugging at the tapes of her dingy petticoat, she added, "Not for the next year, anyway. I'll be here to keep him from being lonely. Poor man. Can you imagine his feeling that he must pay someone to be his companion? He's so wonderful, I'd happily do it for free."

Mrs. Whitmire made an odd sound at the back of her throat. When Cassandra glanced up, the older woman looked as if she'd accidentally swallowed a fly. Cassandra smiled at her.

"I know he was terse with you downstairs a minute ago, Mrs. Whitmire, but I'm sure he didn't mean to be. It's probably an embarrassing situation for him, don't you think? Worrying what people will think when they find out about our little arrangement? I mean...well, it's just so awfully sad."

"Sad." Mrs. Whitmire's voice took on a strangled quality. Trying to hold back her tears, Cassandra suspected.

"Yes, sad." Cassandra sighed, her own eyes prickling. "Imagine, a fine, handsome man like that, feeling he has to pay someone to be with him. I think it's the most pathetic thing. For him to be that lonely. Why, it fair breaks my heart."

Mrs. Whitmire spun around and disappeared into the bathing chamber. A second later, Cassandra could have sworn she heard water running. After gathering up her clothing and laying it, neatly folded, on a chair, she followed the older woman to investigate.

"Oh, my lands!" Cassandra gaped at the claw-foot bathtub. Water streamed into it from a brass spout, and clouds of steam rose toward the ceiling. "Hot, running water? Where on earth does it come from?"

"There's a water vat in the attic, kept heated by a furnace," the woman said as she tested the water temperature against the back of her wrist. "Do you want bath salts?"

Cassandra giggled. "May I have pepper as well?"

Mrs. Whitmire lifted an eyebrow. "Bath salts are little crystals to make the water smell nice." She took a blue bottle from a small shelf above the tub. "Yea or nay?"

"Yes, please." Cassandra couldn't imagine water that ran hot with the turn of a knob, let alone salts to scent it. Hugging her naked breasts, she stared in fascination as Mrs. Whitmire sprinkled granules over the water.

"There you be," the woman said. "May as well climb in."

"Where might I find a towel?" Cassandra asked, not wanting to drip all over the beautiful red rug when she finished bathing.

"I'll have Deirdre send a girl up to assist you. She'll bring in towels and see to it you have everything else you need."

A little over an hour later, Cassandra lay on the deliciously soft bed, staring at herself in the looking glass directly above her. The ceiling seemed such an odd place to hang mirrors. She stuck one leg in the air to examine the bottom of her foot, which she'd never really gotten to study at length before. She had a fat big toe.

She sighed and let her leg flop. She missed her papa and Ambrose. Inside her chest, there was one little spot that ached, even when she wasn't thinking about them. Her papa and brother, locked up in a room without windows. It broke her heart to think of it, and tears welled in her eyes.

She quickly blinked them away. Papa would want her to make the best of this situation. He didn't cotton much to snivelers. *Put on a cheerful face,* he would say. Cassandra smiled at herself in the mirrors. She looked kind of like Lycodomes did when he snarled.

Taking a nap in the middle of the day seemed even odder than mirrors on the ceiling. She yawned and sighed again, not at all sure she could sleep. After a moment, she turned onto her side and punched the pillow. The silk pillowcase emitted the scent of lavender. She snuggled her cheek against it. As luxurious as it felt, she wasn't sure she liked it. Silk was slick, and the pillow kept getting away from her. She liked to roll hers into a ball and hook her chin over the lump.

The nightgown wasn't comfortable, either. Cassandra had never seen so many ribbons on one garment. Up each side, instead of a seam, there were ties to hold the cloth together, which left slits in between. More ribbons ran down the front. It made her feel like a gaily wrapped package under a Christmas tree. She would have changed into her own comfortable gown, but while she'd been in the tub, Mrs. Whitmire had taken all her clothes. Cassandra could only assume the housekeeper meant to wash them.

What Cassandra would wear until her clothing all dried, she had not a clue. The girl who'd helped with her bath had just shrugged and said, "Not to worry," every time Cassandra asked. Surely they weren't expecting her to wear any more left-behind clothing from other guests.

A sudden thought had her stifling a giggle. What would the good sisters say if she were to arrive tomorrow in time for daily Mass in a dress held together with ribbons? Oh, lands, it didn't bear thinking about.

Another yawn stretched her mouth wide. She blinked drowsily and then let her eyes fall closed. Maybe...just maybe...she could drift off, after all.

Her last thought before sleep claimed her was that she needed to ask Mrs. Whitmire if there was a checkerboard in the house. Cassandra hoped so, for, aside from games she'd made up to entertain Khristos, checkers was one of the few things she knew how to play.

She needed to plan lots of activities. Given the way she'd been raised, with only her immediate family, the nuns in various convents in the towns where they'd lived, and a long line of parish priests as her companions and teachers, Cassandra was aware that her knowledge of the world was limited. Her conversational skills were bound to seem lacking, if not downright dull, to her new employer. It wouldn't do to bore Luke Taggart to tears her first night on the job.

SEVEN

Luke braced a hand on the newel post's gleaming finial and stared upward, his jaw clenched. "Damn the woman," he muttered before spinning on his heel to resume his pacing. Back and forth he prowled, from one end of the foyer to the other, his heels clicking an impatient rhythm on the tiled floor.

Females and their primping. Since his

return to the house nearly two hours ago, he'd bathed and shaved, slipped into clean clothes *and* soothed his taut nerves with a large whiskey, all the while conscious of the silence abovestairs.

What the hell was keeping her?

Scowling, he directed an impatient glance toward the landing above, his mind filled with an image of Cassandra's lush curves filling out one of the gorgeous new gowns he'd bought her that afternoon.

His body stirred, and his scowl deepened. Five minutes more, he decided. After that, he would bloody well charge up those stairs to fetch her. And then what? Take her then and there, without the finesse she deserved?

Patience, man, he told himself with grim resolve. It didn't pay to appear too eager. He'd never met a female yet who hesitated to use her body as a bargaining chip.

Lord, but she was going to be beautiful in one of those gowns. Luke didn't give a shit which one she chose; they were all of fine silk or velvet and expressly designed to display a wealth of cleavage. He imagined feasting his eyes on creamy white skin and getting occasional glimpses of her nipples as the neckline of her dress dipped low. Ah, yes...

He missed a step as it occurred to him he had no idea what color her nipples were. Pert brown? Delicious pink? Lush rose? He was getting hard just thinking about it. A smile touched his mouth. First, they'd enjoy a leisurely supper by candlelight. He'd ordered something light, with delicate sauces to tease her palate while he engaged her in suggestive conversation. A little wine with the meal would help her to relax. Then, after a lush, sumptuous dessert, during which he would offer to feed her from his own plate, with his own fork, he'd take her to the drawing room.

Brandy for him, sherry for her. When the liquor had loosened her up and the moment seemed right, he'd coax one of her breasts from its nest of silk. Maybe he'd even moisten her nipple with brandy, then lick it clean, teasing and nibbling until the sensitive crest grew deliciously turgid. Ah, yes...then he'd nip her lightly with his teeth until she quivered and sobbed and begged him to take all of her into his mouth. He'd hold back, of course, denying her what she wanted. Make her squirm against him and plead with him to—

"Mr. Taggart?"

Luke jumped so violently, he nearly parted company with his boots. He whirled toward the landing. Cassandra stood above him, grasping the railing, her huge blue eyes filled with concern. Luke's gaze shot to her breasts, which were completely covered with—what the hell? The little minx was wearing one of his best shirts over her dress!

"Yes?" His voice sounded like an unoiled door hinge. He swallowed. "Cassandra, why on earth are you wearing my shirt?"

Her cheeks went scarlet. "I hope you don't mind my sneaking into your room for it."

Randy as a four-horned goat, Luke would have granted her nearly anything, just not his goddamned shirt. All that delectable cleavage, and it was hidden. He was so disappointed, he could have wept.

"Of course I don't mind." He clenched his teeth, flexing the muscle along his jaw. "Doesn't the gown fit you properly?"

"Well..." Her cheeks grew even pinker. "Sort of, and sort of not. I'm not sure how to explain."

Luke held out a hand, beckoning her to him. "Well, come down here, sweetheart, and try."

"But I'm not really dressed. I mean, not properly and all." She leaned out over the railing as if to check for interlopers in the foyer. "What if someone sees?" she whispered.

What if someone saw what? She was wrapped up like a package for long-distance mailing. Luke found it difficult to tear his gaze from her chest. Leaning out over the railing the way she was, with the wood pressing her breasts up—well, suffice it to say, his shirt was filled out in places it had never been before. *Jesus H. Christ.*

"No one will see, honey." His voice still had an unmistakable squeak. He sounded like an adolescent boy. He lifted his hand higher. "Please, come on down. We'll step into the drawing room for privacy, if that'll make you feel better."

Luke watched as she descended the staircase. The blue velvet dress she wore was exactly the right length. He'd taken her brown wool gown to the dressmaker, and the woman had gotten measurements off it to make some quick alterations on the ready-made garments Luke had selected. If the length had turned out this perfectly, how could any of the other measurements be that far off the mark?

"Is the waistline too snug?" he asked.

"No. The waist fits me well enough. In fact, it fits me pretty well everywhere."

"Then what's the problem?"

Her cheeks flamed again. When she reached the foyer, Luke took her hands in his. Making a great show of moving back to regard her at arm's length, he smiled and said, "I knew that color of blue would be beautiful on you. If you'd only take off that shirt, I bet you'd be a vision."

She licked her lips, which made his groin tighten, and then she glanced away, looking utterly miserable. "Oh, Mr. Taggart, I don't want to seem ungrateful."

"Luke," he corrected. How could he make love to the woman if she persisted in being so formal? "And what makes you think you may seem ungrateful?"

"Because I'm going to have to insist you return all the dresses. I can't possibly wear any of them."

"Why the hell not?"

The dresses had cost Luke a small fortune. Cassandra should be drooling over them. He'd gone the gamut: delicate underthings, lacy lingerie, expensive silk stockings, sexy red garters, and dainty black velvet slippers.

With extreme effort, Luke managed to modulate his voice before he spoke again. "I thought they were beautiful dresses, and I had the dressmaker alter them especially for you. How can I possibly take them back?"

"You mean you can't get your money back?"

"Not without going to a lot of trouble!"

Her gaze clung to his. Still smarting with disappointment, Luke returned her regard with unflinching resolve. If the gowns fit her, she could damned well wear them. He wasn't about to endure a bout of female histrionics every time something didn't suit her just so.

Even as he hauled in a deep breath to lay down the law to her, her beautiful eyes began to fill with tears. No wailing and sobbing, as he was accustomed to. *That* he could have handled. Oh, no. She just stood there looking crushed, with that incredibly sweet and luscious mouth atremble, and her small chin quivering.

An odd feeling swept through him, reminding him of the time he'd knocked over a vase in the brothel where his mother had once worked. With dreamlike slowness, he'd seen the vase falling, had known it was going to shatter if he didn't catch it. Heart in his throat and unable to breathe, he'd made a wild lunge, only to succeed in knocking over the table as well.

The infuriated madam had blistered his backside but good for his clumsiness while all the girls stood around and laughed at the sight of his bare ass. His mother had been part of the audience, of course. Betraying him, as always.

Heat climbed his neck even as he drew his brows together. Damn it all, Cassandra wasn't made of glass, and just because her chin quivered was no reason for him to feel panicked. He'd learned years ago never to let a

131

woman get under his skin. When they wept, it was usually to get their own way—a manipulative tactic, nothing more. And he refused to be manipulated.

Trying for a firm, no-nonsense tone, he said, "Cassandra, I have very little patience with weepy women."

A gigantic tear spilled over her lower lashes and trailed down her cheek. The awful, almost frantic feeling within him intensified.

"Honey, please, don't cry." He gripped her hands more tightly, not liking the desperate edge in his voice. So what if she cried? It wasn't as if the world would end. "It's not that important. If you don't like the dresses, you don't like the dresses. I'll buy you others."

"It's not that I don't like them," she said in a choked voice. "They're the most beautiful dresses I've ever seen!"

"Then why won't you wear them?"

She made one of the most god-awful faces he'd ever seen—a cringing, sour-lemon sort of look that wrinkled her forehead, squeezed her eyes closed and contorted the lush fullness of her mouth. "It's *embarrassing,*" she whispered. "I don't know how to even *say* it."

He drew her with him into the drawing room. "No one will hear you in here. Just tell me, flat out."

She scrunched her shoulders as if someone were dribbling ice water down her spine. "It's just—well..."

"Yes?" Luke urged.

"The dressmaker," she said in a hushed voice.

"She made some terrible miscalculations on some of the pattern cuts."

"Pattern cuts?" he echoed.

She went up on her tiptoes to whisper in his ear. "There is scarcely any *front* in any of those dresses. Practically all of my bubbies show."

"Your bubbies?" Luke had heard them called a lot of things, but never that.

"Sshh!"

"Your bubbies?" he repeated more softly. That was what all of this was about? He could scarcely believe his ears. How, precisely, did she hope to provide services to him as a paid companion *without* revealing her bubbies? "Cassandra..." Luke hesitated, choosing his words carefully. "You *are* my paid companion now, you know. Given the nature of our relationship—well, if the dresses are a little low-cut, I can understand your not wanting to wear them in public, but surely it's not a problem here in the house, where only I will see."

She drew back and splayed a hand over her chest. "Didn't you hear what I said? The dresses have no *front*!"

Of course they didn't. He rubbed his jaw, regarding her thoughtfully. In that moment, it began to dawn on him that she honestly didn't comprehend exactly what kind of duties he'd hired her to perform.

Those huge blue eyes, always so open and completely guileless. That absolutely angelic face. The sweet innocence in her smile. None of it was an act. The little featherbrain actually believed he had agreed to pay her five hundred dollars a month to keep him company.

"You're pulling my leg, right?" he asked with a halfhearted chuckle.

"No, I swear to heaven, the dresses have no fronts. At least not much. I couldn't possibly wear any of them without some other form of cover." She glanced anxiously toward the hall. "If I dared, certain parts of me would most assuredly fall out."

Luke could only hope. The corners of his mouth started to twitch. She looked as scandalized as if she'd just encountered a nude man on Main Street. He pitched his voice to an accommodating whisper. "Cassandra, surely you're exaggerating. All dresses have *some* front. Let me see."

She leaped back from his reaching hand. "I can't do *that*. You're going to have to take my word for it, that's all."

As jumpy as she was, Luke guessed she was right on that score. Much to his regret.

"I feel so bad," she told him. "To think that you spent so *much* money on so *little* material. That woman cheated you, and she's stark-raving mad, to boot. No lady in her right mind would wear this dress. And if you could see the nightgowns and underthings she sent? You'd simply faint!"

Luke had spent nearly an hour hand-selecting those nightgowns and underthings. "What, exactly, is wrong with those?"

"Holes."

"Holes?"

"In the lace," she expounded. "Very large holes. Or, if not that, barely any material, and that not sewn together, leaving slits everywhere."

"Surely not."

She nodded emphatically. Luke rubbed his jaw again and gave the plackets of his shirt a pointed glance. It wasn't lost on him that she'd selected one of the finest silk shirts in his wardrobe instead of a more serviceable cotton one, nor did he miss the way she frequently reached down to lightly run her fingertips over the soft velvet of her new dress. Like every other woman he'd ever known, this girl had a weakness for pretty things, no question about it.

"I'm so sorry," she said in a voice that quavered and yet managed to sound prim. "After all the trouble you went to, I hated to have to tell you. There's no way around it, though. You'll just have to return my old clothes to me and take all the new ones back."

That could prove difficult, given the fact that he'd had all her other clothing burned. "I see. Well…"

"Do you think you'll have any problem getting your money refunded?"

"I hope not." He assumed a pensive expression and told himself to ignore the hint of lavender wafting from her skin. "Odd, isn't it? I selected all those dresses from a display rack. On the hangers, they didn't look frontless. Maybe you should show me exactly what the problem is so I'll know what I'm talking about when I go into the shop for a refund."

Her eyes went round with what could only be described as horror. "Show you?"

"Just a quick peek," he assured her.

She pitched her voice to a whisper again. "But half my bubbies are bare."

A tight sensation grabbed Luke by the throat. He swallowed it down. "Cassandra, don't be silly. It can't be that bad," he chided gently. "All I want is a quick peek. I spent a lot of money. How will I ever get it back if I can't point out to the dressmaker what the problem is?"

She caught her lower lip between her teeth, biting down so hard the flesh whitened. "Well, I suppose...since you put it that way."

"It's necessary," he assured her. "And completely proper, under the circumstances."

"If you insist."

"I do."

With cheeks aflame and hands trembling, she shyly opened the shirt, holding the plackets apart only long enough to give him exactly what he'd requested, a very quick peek. Nevertheless, he glimpsed enough lovely breast and cleavage to drive a saint to rape.

As she rebuttoned the shirt, he wheeled toward the liquor cabinet. A stiff drink held sudden appeal. He sloshed brandy into a tumbler, recalling as he tossed down a hearty swallow how he'd fantasized about savoring the taste of it on her swollen nipples. Fat chance. She actually believed he wanted her to be his friend, for Christ's sake. How Milo Zerek had raised this girl in mining towns without her becoming corrupted, Luke didn't know. But somehow the sanctimonious little son of a bitch had managed.

Time, he assured himself. He only needed some time to seduce her. It was a goal he intended to achieve by evening's end. Innocent or no, she had the body of a temptress. And any woman who reached Cassandra's age with her virginity still intact had to be as randy as he was. Not to mention frustrated as hell. All he had to do was make her aware of the needs of her own body.

A virgin...an honest-to-God virgin. The word hung in Luke's head, and no matter how he circled it, he couldn't quite believe it.

Luke had sensed that Cassandra was different, of course, and he'd guessed that she'd led a more sheltered existence than most. But a virgin? To his way of thinking, there were laws of nature that always held true. Candles went out in a strong draft, sugar cubes melted in a downpour, and girls raised in mining districts got their bellies plowed at a very young age. Luke had never done the honors. Raised in a whorehouse and initiated into sexual relationships by an aging prostitute when he was twelve, he'd always preferred experienced bed partners.

What, exactly, was he supposed to do with a goddamned *virgin*? He wanted her in his bed, dammit. Tonight.

"Sherry?" he offered, glancing over his shoulder at her.

Still fastening the last button of his shirt—the one that joined the collar snugly beneath her chin—she looked up, her expression rather startled. "Sherry? Oh, heavens, no. I intend to join the convent, you know. I mentioned that to you this morning."

At the very thought, Luke bit down so hard on his back teeth that he nearly cracked a molar. "Ah, yes, I remember your saying something about that." He flashed what he hoped was a harmless-looking grin. "Surely sherry's allowed. It's wine, after all, and even nuns have a bit of that every day at Mass."

"I don't think it's quite the same thing. Do you?"

"A splitting of hairs."

His brandy snifter halfway to his lips, Luke studied her for a long moment, slowly absorbing the innocence in her gaze, the artless way she smiled. From the beginning, it had been those very things about her that had attracted him so strongly. Now they were becoming a very big pain in the goddamned ass. A man didn't lighten his pocket to the tune of five hundred a month only to look at a woman and not touch. She was his, bought and paid for, dammit. For a year, anyway.

He cleared his throat and schooled his features, glancing into his snifter before impaling her with his most wheedling smile. "Please, Cassandra, won't you join me?"

"If you wouldn't mind, I'd prefer tea."

Disgruntled, Luke reached for the bell to summon a servant. Before he could grasp the handle, she said, "Oh, please, may I go to the kitchen and ask for it myself?"

"Whatever for?"

"I'd like to check on Khristos. Mrs. Whitmire

said he was in the kitchen. I couldn't come downstairs earlier because I had nothing to wear, so I haven't had a chance to speak to him. I want to be sure he's settled in and that he isn't feeling afraid. He's only eight, you know, and with Papa in jail, he's already upset. Being brought here, being surrounded by strangers. I'm sure he doesn't understand what's going on. Do you mind if I go to see him for a bit?"

The last time Luke had checked, the kid had been sitting on a stool in the kitchen, devouring cookies faster than Cook could take them from the oven. Nevertheless, he could tell by the worried expression in Cassandra's eyes that nothing short of seeing Khristos for herself would ease her mind. "You won't stay long, I hope? I'd like to chat a bit before supper."

She gathered up her skirt. "I'll be back before you can blink." At the doorway, she spun around. "Oh, my...I nearly forgot. I can't go to the kitchen like this." She made a fist in the front of his borrowed shirt. "Would you mind terribly asking for my clothes to be brought back? It won't take me a minute to change."

Luke sighed and set down the brandy snifter. "Cassandra, I'm afraid I had your clothes burned."

"Burned?"

"They were little better than rags." He shrugged. "I had Martha dispose of the entire lot."

"Not my shawl," she whispered shakily. "You didn't burn my shawl?"

Judging by her stricken expression, Luke was relieved he hadn't. "No, I forgot about it. I think it's probably still on the coat tree."

She dashed out into the foyer. Stepping to the doorway, Luke watched her draw the shawl into her arms and hug it as if it were a long-lost friend. She glanced over her shoulder to smile at him. "It belonged to my mama," she explained. "I know it's old and ugly, but it's one of the few things I have left of her."

"You could wear it," he said, barely able to believe he was making the suggestion. Now she'd have another layer of clothing to hide behind. "That way, maybe no one will notice the shirt."

She did as he suggested, then graced him with a beatific smile. "You're right. It nearly covers it."

Leaning a shoulder against the door frame, Luke regarded her with an uplifted eyebrow. "I know it's probably a dumb question, but why are you so worried that someone may see you in my shirt?"

She did indeed look at him as if he were incredibly dense. "Only think how it would look!" She lowered her voice to just above a whisper. "Living here in your house, I'm going to have to be very careful. Otherwise, people may think...well, you know, that we're doing something *indecent.*"

EIGHT

&❧ Games...When Cassandra had made mention of such activities that afternoon, Luke had been hoping for games of a more seductive nature—when he finally joined her here in her bedchamber tonight. After devoting an entire evening to trying to seduce her, he was acutely conscious of the nearby bed, the flickering glow of the firelight, and the provocative decor that surrounded them. Cassandra seemed oblivious to all of it.

Crystal brandy snifter in hand, he leaned back against the chair cushions and regarded his brand-new paid companion across an ornate, custom-made chessboard. Seemingly unaware of his scrutiny, she sat in the gold-upholstered chair with her slender legs drawn up, one arm looped around her knees. Her glossy sable hair lay in a thick braid over one shoulder, the ends tied off with the same red ribbon he'd seen her wear twice before.

His gaze dropped to the thick velvet lapels of his black robe, which she had filched from his wardrobe to conceal the nightgown he'd bought her. Every once in a while, when she moved just right, the robe gapped open to reveal some of the scandalous lace she'd described earlier, but try as he might, he never got a glimpse of any holes.

More the pity...

Her brow furrowed in concentration, she studied the ebony and ivory chess pieces, contemplating her next move. A newcomer to the game, she was diligently following the rules he'd very patiently explained to her before they'd begun playing nearly two hours ago. All in all, he guessed she was doing well enough—for a rank beginner.

Even so, Luke had little hope she would ever truly challenge him, not even with years of practice. Chess was a complex game, one that required sophisticated tactics and a wealth of practical experience, not to mention a superior intellect. Which was why he wasn't putting much stock in Cassandra's skill as an opponent. Any girl who believed a man would pay her five hundred a month for the mere pleasure of her company wasn't exactly a genius, now was she?

Not that Luke faulted her for that. Hell, no, just the opposite. In his experience, the more featherbrained a woman was, the more uninhibited she proved to be in bed. And, to him, that was the bottom line.

"Check."

He abruptly stopped swirling his brandy. Some liquor slopped onto his lap. "Pardon?"

She beamed him a smile. "You heard me." She leaned slightly forward, revealing just a smidgen of lace beneath the robe. "Your king is trapped."

Tearing his gaze from the tantalizing display of creamy white skin, Luke focused on the chessboard.

She giggled. "Wiggle your way out of that one, Mr. Taggart!"

Luke studied his pieces. She had him cornered, nine ways to hell. "I'll be damned."

"Probably not. But you are soundly trounced!" she informed him cheerfully. "Unless, of course, you can think of some way out of it."

Luke knew his way around a board too well to believe there was any hope of that. He lifted his gaze to hers and looked deeply into those deceptively guileless eyes. Behind that veil of innocence, there was evidently a frighteningly sharp brain clicking away like a skillfully operated abacus. Either that, or he'd been so distracted by the occasional glimpse of lace, he'd opened himself up for attack.

"You're right," he said as he managed a smile. "I admit defeat. You win."

Her eyes sparkled like happy stars, and something moved inside him. Something dangerous and, therefore, best ignored. "Best out of three?" she challenged, her face alight.

He swallowed, his heart speeding. Perhaps she was more skilled at playing the part of a flirt than he'd first thought. "What are you willing to wager?"

She pursed her lips. "I could iron your shirts."

"I pay maids to do that."

"Bake bread?"

"Cook's job."

She took a deep breath and furrowed her brow. "I haven't any money."

Luke had plenty of money. What he sorely lacked was the warmth of her sweet body in his arms. He smiled slightly. "How about this? The loser has to be the winner's slave for a day, granting his every wish and desire, no limits."

"*His* every wish and desire?" Her eyes twinkled with laughter. "I don't think so."

"You're on," he said huskily.

Sitting rigidly erect, Luke concentrated his full attention on the second game, not allowing himself to so much as glance at the gaping lapels of his robe. His years of experience at chess stood him in good stead. Though she gave him a run for his money, he had her in checkmate by game's end. The fact that it had taken him another two hours hardly seemed important, considering the reward that awaited him if he could manage to win two games out of three.

Manage? As she set up the pieces for a third game, Luke sat back to study her. No featherbrain, this, but a very intelligent young woman. He'd made the mistake of underestimating her once; he wouldn't again. He had played chess against some of the best, yet this girl, who'd never clapped eyes on a chess piece before, had pushed him to the limit of his ability.

"Where did you attend school, Cassandra?"

"Here and there," she said distractedly, frowning as she tried to recall where the chess pieces went. "Papa always insisted that I be educated only by the nuns, so I never actually attended school like my brothers and other kids."

"How could he afford to give you a private education like that?"

"Oh, it didn't cost anything. I just went to the convent, and the sisters in the towns where we lived tutored me in their spare time. When they were too busy, I studied or read or helped out with chores to repay them for their kindness."

"And when you lived in towns where there were no nuns?"

She shrugged. "I didn't get any instruction then. I just tended to Khristos and read all that I could. Mostly from the Bible. Papa felt that was safe enough."

"Safe?"

She flashed him a grin. "He's always been very particular about what I am exposed to. He promised Mama he'd raise me to be a lady, and that isn't easy to do in mining towns."

Luke agreed. In fact, sitting across from him was the first genuine *lady* he'd ever spent time with. "And socially? Did you mingle only with—" He broke off, reluctant to credit the wealthier females in mining towns with being ladies. Most of them weren't. "How did a poor miner's daughter manage to mingle only with the upper class?"

She giggled. "I didn't. Mingle, I mean. Unless I'm over at the church or the convent, mostly I just stay home."

"So you have no friends your own age?"

"Not really."

"Don't you miss that and resent your father for depriving you of it?"

She looked at him as if the thought had never occurred to her. "You think I'm strange, don't you."

"Not strange. Remarkable, perhaps. Don't you want to have friends? And read books that don't have a religious theme? Poetry, maybe, or dime novels?"

Her eyes widened. "Papa says dime novels are scandalous tripe and would fill my head with foolish notions. Poetry is all right, but he likes to read it himself first to make sure it's suitable, and he doesn't have very much spare time for that." She hesitated, then leaned slightly forward. "I sneaked and read *Hamlet* once. I *loved* it."

"So, you like Shakespeare, do you?" Luke studied her over the rim of his glass. "But you feel guilty for having sneaked behind your papa's back to read some of Shakespeare's work?"

"Papa would be disappointed in me if he knew." She smiled slightly. "He only makes me abide by his rules to protect me. He loves me a lot. How can I resent that?"

"So you *choose* to remain ignorant to please him?"

Flags of pink dotted her cheeks as she returned her attention to the game board. "'Ignorant' isn't a very nice way to put it. I prefer to think of my choices as being selective. And, yes, I've chosen that. If we don't endeavor to please the people we love, then what is life all about?"

Luke had no idea. To him, life had become a boring chain of endless days, strung together by lonely, meaningless nights.

"It isn't as if Papa has neglected my education. I have a fair command of the English language, and he's taught me some Greek. I'm also very good with numbers, and I've gotten to study geography and a little bit of history. In my world, what more do I really need to know?"

Luke swirled his brandy. "There are other worlds, Cassandra. Even right here, in Black Jack."

"And this is one of them," she replied, dimpling a cheek. "Here I am, learning chess. Until tonight, I didn't even know such a game existed." Her eyes darkened as if a thought had just occurred to her. "I suppose I seem very dull to you, don't I? If that's the case, I'll understand if you want to get someone else to be your companion."

"And if I did, what would you and Khristos do?"

She gnawed her lower lip, her worried expression belying her bravely spoken. "We'll manage somehow. We Zereks always do."

Luke searched her gaze, the realization driven home to him once again that she was a rare gem in a town filled with unpolished pebbles. He finally allowed himself to smile. "As it happens, I've read all of Shakespeare's work and I've skimmed through enough dime novels to be in complete accord with your papa that they're tripe. In short, I don't find you at all 'dull,' Cassandra. 'Refreshing' is a better word."

"You needn't be kind to spare my feelings. I know I'm ignorant about a lot of things." She tipped her head and wrinkled her nose. "I guess the world is full of unopened doors, isn't it? And if we open them, we may find Pandora's box. Maybe I'm a bit of a coward, but when Papa tells me there are bad things behind a door, I steer clear of it. He's much wiser than me when it comes to things like that, and I trust his judgment."

Luke wished he hadn't chosen to use the word 'ignorant' to describe her. He'd hurt her feelings, and he really hadn't meant to. "How do you know the story of Pandora's box?"

"Papa told it to me. I assumed it was a Greek fable."

"The important thing is that the message in the story is true," he said softly. "You've been right to listen to your papa. There are a lot of evils in the world, and if you can avoid them, more power to you."

Only she hadn't, Luke thought, with an inexplicable regret. She'd walked right into the devil's den. Determined to shove that thought aside, he turned his gaze to the table. "Luckily, chess isn't one of those evils, and you seem to have a talent for it."

"I do, don't I?"

As the third game commenced, she began to banter with him. Tilting her head coquettishly, she said brightly, "I have this funny little tickle in my throat. When I win this round, I think the first thing I'll demand of my slave is a nice hot cup of tea."

Luke smiled as he made his move, then leaned back in his chair to rest a polished black boot on his knee. "The first thing *I'm* going to demand of *my* slave is that she remove that damned robe," he said softly. "I'm dying to see what's wrong with that nightgown you're wearing."

Her eyes widened. "Holes, I told you. And in very inconvenient places."

Luke knew that the bodice of the nightgown had been designed expressly for male pleasure, and if the holes were positioned where he thought they were, he'd happily show her their usefulness. "We'll see."

Clearly flustered by the prospect, she cast a vague glance at the board, then made her move. Luke's smile deepened. Not exactly a

148

fatal mistake, he mused, but if she continued in this vein, he'd have her trounced in another thirty minutes, possibly less.

His body stirred at the thought of all he intended to require of his lovely slave. It was wicked of him, he knew, and not fair play, but he couldn't resist rattling her concentration with yet another verbal thrust. Glancing toward the hearth, he said, "Holes or no, at least you won't get cold. That fire has the room nice and toasty." Leaning forward to make his play, he advanced with his rook, thus removing one of hers from the board. "Uh-oh. One of your best soldiers, dead on the field. Careful, Cassandra, or you may be parting company with that robe quicker than you think."

Startled, decidedly worried-looking blue eyes became fixed on his. "You wouldn't *really* make such a request. The bet is all in fun, right?"

"Absolutely. No limits, remember? What could be more fun than that?"

Her cheeks flushed a pretty pink. Returning her attention to the board, she said, "You are a caution. Judging by the way you go on, a body'd think you were a scoundrel of the worst sort. If I didn't know better, I'd be worried."

A few minutes later, when Luke once again had her in checkmate, he relaxed back in his chair, folded his hands behind his head, and flashed her a slow grin. "Well, well...it would appear our games for the evening are just beginning. Now we can play master and slave."

Fully expecting her to try and weasel her way out, Luke was more than a little surprised when she vacated the chair and dipped before him in a graceful curtsy, the neckline of the robe parting with the motion to reveal a tantalizing display of seductively exposed breast. "I am at your service, Your Royal Highness," she said, lifting the folds of the robe as though it were a skirt. "How may I please you?"

Enjoying the game, Luke cleared his throat, arranged his face into a stern mask and intoned solemnly, "I don't allow robes in my kingdom, my lady Cassandra. Please, take it off and remove it from my sight. I find it offensive in the extreme."

She dimpled a cheek at him as she straightened. "Seriously, what would you like? More brandy? A foot rub? Your wish is my command."

Unbidden, his gaze drifted upward. Directly behind her, the spacious, silk-draped bed awaited. And he was certainly ready. More than ready. But was she? Instincts he'd been honing since the age of twelve in the arms of countless prostitutes told him no. And taking a woman was always immensely more satisfying if she'd been properly aroused first.

Impatience roiled within him, but he relentlessly tamped it down, determined to do this right. He'd made numerous mistakes in his checkered past, but one thing he'd never done was go against his instincts. Especially not where it pertained to seduction. To Luke, sex was an art, and he prided himself on being a master.

Even so, he was sorely tempted to insist that she remove the damnable robe. Once it was off and the luscious holes in that lace were performing their purpose, she would no longer be able to pretend there was nothing going on between them. His body sprang taut as he envisioned her exposed nipples getting hard as cool air touched them. Then, of course, he would visually caress them until she was half mad with yearning.

Shifting his gaze to her blue eyes, he imagined the shattered trust he would see in them if he pressed the issue and forced her to expose herself. True, she'd made a wager with him, and she'd lost. According to the rules he lived by, winners took all, and losers wept. Their bet aside, to all intents and purposes, she actually *was* his slave, ensconced in this room expressly to please him. He was paying dearly for the right to enjoy her body in any fashion he chose, and if he did, she would have no legal recourse, for she'd contractually waived all her rights.

Only...the word hung in his mind, like the opening to a bottomless pit. He had an unbalanced feeling, as if he were teetering on a dangerous edge, and no matter which way he fell, he'd be lost. Cassandra. She stood before him, still grasping his robe in a half-curtsey, a ragtag princess with a bedraggled red ribbon in place of a tiara.

"Come here, honey," he heard himself tell her in an oddly husky voice.

Luke almost wished she'd hesitate, that he might see wariness in her eyes. Then, maybe, he wouldn't feel this unwarranted and totally absurd reluctance to betray her trust. But, of course, she didn't hesitate, and in her eyes he saw only openness and sweet honesty as she moved toward him.

"On your knees," he said in that same thick voice.

She bent her legs and knelt before him. Luke grasped her shoulders and turned her to sit on her heels between his spread thighs. The fact that she allowed him to move her about, exhibiting no trace of uneasiness, humbled him in a way he couldn't explain and had no wish to analyze. At the back of his mind, a niggling little question kept repeating itself. Who was in danger here, her or him?

Pressing his thumbs on either side of her spine, he began a firm rubbing motion.

"How about a back rub instead of tea?"

"I'm the one who lost," she reminded him. "You should be getting the back rub, not me."

"The bet was all just in fun, remember?" He found a tense muscle and worked it gently with his fingertips. "Besides, maybe this particular master enjoys giving back rubs better than he does receiving them."

"Hmm." She arched her slender back and made a little sound in her throat that reminded him of a cat purring. "Oh, that's nice." She leaned into the massage, letting the heels of his hands support her. With another little purring sound, she bent her head slightly forward to better accommodate him. "Oh, Luke, that feels—absolutely wonderful."

"It'd feel even better without this robe in the way." He smiled, admitting, if only to himself, that he'd never been a man to give up easily. Maybe it was that soft purring sound she kept making. It reminded him of the saying that there was more than one way to skin a cat. Or, in this case, to disrobe one. "Can I push it down just a hair?"

He felt her shiver slightly, and he doubted it was with cold. "Hmm," she murmured. "But only just a bit. The gown, remember."

How could he forget?

He ran his fingertips under the collar of the robe and drew the heavy velvet downward off her shoulders. She immediately caught the folds, clasping them modestly over her breasts. Luke grinned. For the moment, he was content to admire the loveliness of her bare shoulders. Her skin was so pale as to be nearly translucent and as soft as satin beneath his fingertips.

To give her a sense of space and a false sense of security, he relaxed back in the chair a bit, his gaze fixed on the ceiling. The mirrors provided him with an unimpeded frontal view of her. With skilled hands, he massaged the muscles in her shoulders until her body began to give with every pressure of his grip. Going nearly limp, she sighed and murmured something unintelligible. Her hold on the robe relaxed a little. He started massaging her shoulders, then her upper arms, inching the robe downward as he went. She'd evidently forgotten the reflective ceiling, for she made no attempt to stop him and never glanced up.

Luke supposed ceiling watching was an acquired habit.

At last, the velvet fell from her breasts, the heavy, thick folds catching at the bend of her arms. Creamy skin, ivory lace. Luke couldn't resist cupping his palms over her upper arms and sliding them up to caress the sweet roundness of her shoulders. God, she was lovely. Even beyond his expectations. A compact little goddess, every inch of her generously rounded and perfectly formed to please a man's eye. Ample breasts, a tiny waist, full hips. And, best of all, no bony sharpness anywhere. Just a delectable creation of feminine softness...

One look, that was all it took, and his gut was tied in knots. She hadn't lied. V-necked and extremely low-cut, the lacy nightgown had holes that displayed a wealth of flesh. Her breasts were like ripe melons, thrusting so taut and firm that her creamy skin had a satiny sheen. The crest of one nipple protruded through the ivory mesh. It was the exact same color as the wilted edges of a pink rose blossom, a delicate, dusky mauve.

A completely unexpected and inexplicable stab of guilt went through Luke. She'd been hugging that robe around herself for over four hours, and she clearly had no idea of what he was seeing now. Luke closed his eyes for a moment, wondering what the hell was the matter with him. A conscience? Just the thought made him want to laugh. Life had been a cruel teacher, and he'd learned long ago to look out for himself and no one else, to grab

154

his pleasures in any way he could and never berate himself. Ethics were for fools. The man who hesitated was the man who got ground under the heels of smarter men's boots.

Determined not to be plagued with stupid sentiments that might interfere with his gratification, he opened his eyes again. She was his, dammit. Bought and paid for, with her signature on the bottom line. If he wanted to look at her, he'd damned well do it.

The view made his heart start to pound. He wasn't sure he could trust himself not to catch her around the waist and bend her back over his arm. God help him, but he wanted her. If completing the act wasn't possible tonight, at least he needed to touch her, to hold her, to savor the taste of her.

Continuing to massage her spine with the pad of one thumb, he slipped his other hand to her neck on the pretext of rubbing it. There he began a campaign to assault her senses, pressing in deeply with his thumb and fingers one second, then lightly caressing the next. At the nape of her neck, silken tendrils of hair lay like down against her skin. He trailed his touch up the graceful slope of her neck, traced the shape of her ear, lightly smoothed her hair.

Her breathing became shallow and quick. He felt her shiver slightly and smiled to himself as she bent her head sideways to give him better access. Jesus, she was sweet. Wonderfully, incredibly, impossibly sweet. He no longer doubted he was the first to touch her like this. That was evident in everything she did, in every little huff of her breath. It wasn't a case of catching her with her defenses down, for she had none. Luke doubted she even realized he posed a threat.

Kneading her muscles, touching her in ways he knew would arouse her, he watched as the changes came over her. His pulse started to slam against his ribs when he saw her start to squirm, moving her sweetly rounded derriere on the heels of her feet, as if she suddenly couldn't get comfortable. The heavy robe, which was still caught at her elbows, lay rumpled about her breasts, the velvet grazing one exposed nipple. The peak, teased to erectness by the cloth, grew more distended and swollen with each pass.

"I feel funny," she whispered.

"You do?" Luke bent his head, pressing his lips ever so lightly against her hair. "Funny, good? Or funny, bad?" He moved his lips to her ear, letting his breath waft warmly against the lobe, knowing even as he did that most women were disarmed by the sensation. "Want me to stop?"

"No, it's just..."

"Just what?" he whispered against her temple.

"I don't think I'm supposed to feel this way," she said faintly, breathlessly.

"What way is that?"

"Shivery all over. I...I don't think nuns are supposed to."

Cautiously, Luke touched the tip of his tongue to the shell-like contours of her ear. "Is it a good shivery feeling?"

"Yes, but—"

"If it feels good," he whispered huskily, "then what's the worry? We're not doing anything wrong."

The soft huff of her breathing became more pronounced. The sound made Luke's blood rush, his pulse drumming in his temples. Jesus. He'd never gotten this hot just by kissing a woman's ear and touching her—

"Do I smell bad?"

Her voice was so faint that it took Luke a moment to register the question. He froze with his tongue thrust into her ear canal, tried to say "What?", which came out more a slurred grunt, and opened his eyes. He drew back and tried again. "What?"

She looked over her shoulder, fastening worried blue eyes on his. "You were sniffing." Drawing the robe higher on her arms, she said, "I used bath salts. Do I stink?"

"I wasn't sniffing."

Luke realized suddenly that he was still hearing the huffing sound as well—and that it wasn't Cassandra grabbing for breath with passion-starved lungs. She seemed to register the noise at the same moment he did and glanced around. "What is that?" she whispered.

Damned if Luke knew. Nudging her gently out of his way, he pushed to his feet, the hairs at the nape of his neck standing on end. When Cassandra started to speak again, he pressed a finger to his lips. Cocking his head, he turned in a slow circle, trying to pinpoint the noise. It was growing louder, almost a snorting now—a wet, muffled snorting. His gaze became fixed on the door that opened onto the outside hall. Cassandra followed his gaze, her face going pale.

"What is it?" she asked again in a barely audible voice, reaching out to grab Luke's trousers.

He jumped and immediately wanted to kick himself. What was he, some kind of Nancy-boy? It was one thing for Cassandra to be scared; the girl believed in leprechauns, for Christ's sake. But he was a grown man with both feet firmly rooted in stark reality.

After prying her hand off his trousers, he strode to the door, twisted the knob, and flung open the portal. Something large shot past him, a blur of white, yellow, and mud-brown.

"Lycodomes!" Cassandra cried with a relieved laugh. "I'd forgotten you were here, you silly dog!"

The silly dog, Luke noted, had been wallowing in mud. And he was extremely wet, to boot. In Luke's experience, wet dogs usually waited until they were near humans to rid themselves of the excess moist—

"No!" Luke shouted.

He was too late. Legs already spread for balance, Lycodomes gave himself a hard shake, showering Cassandra, Luke, and a good portion of the room with mud and murky rainwater. When Luke lowered his arm from shielding his eyes, he saw that Cassandra had acquired what appeared to be a bad case of freckles.

"Son of a—a—a *bitch*!" He advanced on the

dog, murder in his heart. "Come on, you mangy cur. The house is no place for you."

Cassandra was giggling, so she apparently didn't hear Luke's nearly snarled edict. Wrapping her arms around the dog's neck, she said, "Oh, Lye-Lye, you're a mess. What happened, sweetkins? Did you get locked out in the rain?"

At this point, Luke wished Lye-Lye would go drown himself in an inch of standing water. The animal was covered, absolutely *covered*, with mud. Luke's robe would never be the same. The rug probably never would be, either.

Luke grabbed the dog by its collar. "Come on, Lycodomes. There's only one place for you, and that's outside."

"Oh, but it's raining!" Cassandra cried.

"He can stay perfectly dry on the porch," Luke insisted, dragging the dog in his wake as he made for the door. "There's an overhang out there."

"Can't he visit, just for a minute?"

Luke shot her a look that should have spoken volumes. "Until he has a bath, this dog is *not* going to be in my house."

Once in the hall, Lycodomes began to snarl. Luke, in no mood to be intimidated, growled an obscenity under his breath. The two of them continued the exchange all the way down the stairs. By the time they reached the foyer, Luke was almost baring his teeth. "Go ahead. Bite me, you mangy, stinking bastard," he muttered under his breath. "Get your licks in while you have a chance, because I promise, your days are numbered."

Luke threw open the front door and shoved the dog out onto the porch. Lycodomes snarled one last time as the door swung closed.

Luke held up his hands. Mud and dog hair. And, oh, God, the *smell*! He started back up the stairs, so furious he wanted to gnash his teeth. He'd almost had her, dammit! A few more minutes, that was all he'd needed, and he would've had her in bed. Now, because of that goddamned, stinking dog, he would have to start all over again.

First, however, he had to wash up. He doubted Cassandra would find him very appealing with Lycodomes's stench all over him.

After rinsing her hands and wiping off her face, Cassandra played for a few minutes with the *twa-let* in the bathing chamber. Like everything else in her suite that wasn't red or white, the flush chain was gold. When she pulled it, water surged from a porcelain tank into the bowl, swirling round and round until it disappeared. She could only wonder where it went.

That thought made her stop tugging on the chain. If, as Ambrose had suggested, the water went to a sewage hole outside somewhere, she could cause a flood. Remembering how muddy and wet Lycodomes had been, an awful thought occurred to her. She sniffed at the sleeve of Luke's robe. *Nope.* Just plain old mud, thank heavens.

She wandered back into the bedchamber.

After standing before the fire for a moment, she grew restless and began to explore the room. On the dresser were a brush and comb set and a hand mirror laid out on a lacy scarf. She picked up a dainty-looking bottle with a funny little rubber ball on top. There was amber liquid inside, and the faint scent told her it was perfume. Only how did you get it out? She tugged on the ball. It didn't come off, so she pulled a bit harder. *Ssspphh*, went the bottle. From nowhere, it seemed, a cool spray hit her full in the face.

Gasping, she put the perfume back and waved a hand before her nose. *Lavender.* Evidently Luke frequently had a lady guest who liked that particular scent. His mother, maybe? Cassandra couldn't feature an older woman wearing a nightgown that was held together by ribbons. Unless she was eccentric, of course. Maybe it ran in the Butler family.

The left-behind perfume reminded Cassandra of the clothes she'd seen in the armoire. She really ought to mention them to Luke so he could return them to their owner. She stepped over to open the wardrobe doors as a reminder.

Buttoning the fresh shirt he'd just pulled on after a fast bath, Luke walked to the door that adjoined his suite of rooms to Cassandra's. When he stepped into her bedchamber, he froze. She stood before the armoire, holding a knee-length black lace pinafore up to herself. Luke's stomach dropped to somewhere around the region of his knees.

The costume was one of several he'd had made specially for female "guests" to wear for his private entertainment. Complete with black silk hosiery and black lace garters, the frontless pinafore was very fetching on a well-proportioned and otherwise nude female.

Shit! he thought as he bolted forward. Not entirely sure why, Luke snatched the black lace costume from Cassandra's grasp. He didn't want her to drape it against herself or, for that matter, so much as touch it.

"What are you doing?" he asked sharply.

"N-Nothing! I just saw some clothing in the armoire earlier, and I thought you might want to return it to the lady who owns it."

"What lady?" Luke reached past her to jerk all the other garments at the back of the wardrobe off the hangers. "Yes, of course...the owner. You're right. I should return all of this."

He bunched the milkmaid costume under the crook of his arm so Cassandra wouldn't see it. Next he grabbed the shepherdess outfit, rolling it into a wad as well. The shepherdess's staff, the handle of which had been hooked around the neck of the hanger, came loose and fell onto the floor. Cassandra gazed down at it in bewilderment.

"What's that?"

"Nothing." Luke bent to pick up the damned thing. As he straightened, he realized he was sweating. He shoved the armoire doors wide to make sure no other scanty garments lurked inside. Satisfied that he had everything, he said, "Excuse me for a minute, honey. I, um..." He

162

gestured with the staff. "I'll just put these in my suite so I remember to, um, return them."

Once back in the privacy of his own suite, Luke tossed the offending clothes onto a chair, then stood in the darkness, holding the staff in one hand, pinching the bridge of his nose with the other. What in God's name was wrong with him? What difference did it make if Cassandra saw these things? It wasn't as if she could stay innocent forever. In fact, if he had his way, the quicker she lost her innocence, the better. So why was he racing around like a madman, trying to hide things from her?

He was losing his mind, that was what. And getting a bitch of a headache while he was at it. He took a deep breath, then exhaled slowly, forcing the tenseness from his muscles. The oxygen cleared his head a bit, and he wiped his brow with the sleeve of his shirt, smiling slightly. A momentary lapse, he assured himself. Caused by that damned dog of hers. Someday soon, he might even have Cassandra model that black lace pinafore for him. In fact, he'd look forward to it.

He tossed the staff onto his bed and stepped back to the adjoining door, pausing to take another deep breath. "Well," he said as he reentered her rooms, "I've got that all taken care—" The breath he'd just inhaled rushed from his lungs as if a fist had impacted with his solar plexus. "Cassandra," he managed to croak, "what are you—"

"What's this?"

She turned from an open dresser drawer,

163

holding up an intricately carved wooden dildo. Fashioned in lifelike proportion, the thing looked wickedly huge, held aloft in her slender hand. Luke's heart gave a violent kick against his ribs.

"Good God Almighty," he cried. "Get out of that stuff and put that damned thing *down*!"

She leaped as though he'd struck her. The dildo flew from her hand, striking the floor head first, then bouncing across the rug. Barely aware he'd even moved, Luke took a giant leap and snatched the thing up before it stopped bouncing. Slipping it under his shirt, he turned back to Cassandra.

"You really shouldn't be looking in all the drawers," he said, descending on the dresser as he spoke. He cringed when he looked into the drawer she'd already opened. It was chock-full of salacious gadgets he'd forgotten were in this room.

"I thought this was my bedchamber."

"It *is* your bedchamber," Luke replied, trying to gentle his voice as he jerked the damned drawer off its runners. "It's just—" Objects clattered and clunked as he clutched the drawer to his chest. "Excuse me for a minute."

Back toward his suite he went. At the door, he hesitated to glance at her. "I won't be but a minute. Stay out of things while I'm gone. Okay?"

Once back in his own bedchamber, Luke set the drawer on his bed, then lit a lamp. After jerking a case off one of his pillows, he emptied the contents of the drawer into it, vowing that they would meet with the same fate Cassandra's clothing had earlier that day: incineration.

When he returned to Cassandra's room, she was standing with her back to the fire, looking downcast and chastened. He hadn't meant to snap at her. But, damn! Once he had put the emptied drawer back where it belonged, he systematically searched the others to make sure she wouldn't run across any more gadgets.

Finally satisfied that all things depraved or obscene had been removed from her proximity, Luke leaned a hip against the dresser and crossed his booted feet. He felt as if he'd just run a footrace through a shoulder-deep vat of congealed porridge.

Settling his gaze on Cassandra, who still stood by the fire, he couldn't help but notice how incredibly virginal and out of place she looked. This bedchamber was more suited to a prostitute with its bold red accents, gold bed-hangings, and gaudy Parisian furniture. A girl like her should be surrounded by soft pastels.

Luke made a mental note to have the room redone immediately. Tomorrow, in fact. What had seemed perfectly acceptable and even mood-enhancing to him yesterday now struck him as cheap and tawdry.

This girl was a precious find; she needed the proper setting. If he meant to keep her here for the next year as his live-in companion, which he most certainly did, then he had to make a few changes. After all, the entire appeal of hiring her had been to afford himself a sense of normality, to have a lady in his bed instead of a well-practiced whore. She wouldn't retain that innocent air for long if he bombarded her on all sides with the evidence of his own debauchery.

She suddenly clamped a hand over her mouth and stifled a huge yawn. Looking more closely, Luke saw that her long, lush eyelashes were beginning to droop. He stifled a groan, all hope of ending this evening by taking her to bed turning to dust. Hell, at this point, he wasn't even sure he had the necessary energy to accomplish the deed.

A snuffling sound drifted to him. Luke cast an incredulous glance at the door. Not the dog again. Biting back a curse, he strode angrily across the room and jerked the door open. Sure enough, there stood Lycodomes in all his muddy glory. The lower panels of the door, Luke noticed, were smeared with brown from the animal's filthy fur.

Great! Just bloody great!

NINE

As weary as Cassandra was, she couldn't sleep. The bed was too soft and the room was too quiet. So quiet she could hear the breath going in and out of her lungs. She missed the sound of Khristos's even breathing, Papa's rumbling snore, and the way Ambrose smacked his lips after he rolled over. She also missed Lycodomes, who always either slept with her on the cot or curled up nearby on the floor.

Across the room, the clock on the wall ticked off each slow, relentless second. Shifting light from the dying fire played over the walls, turning the mirrors above her to molten silver and making shadows that danced and swayed. She stared up at her reflection which, in the dimness, seemed blurred and indistinct. As blurred as the future that stretched in front of her.

Tucking her lower lip between her teeth, she tried to make sense of the jumble of thoughts and feelings that had been plaguing her since she'd bidden Luke good night. But the harder she tried to line things up in her mind, the more confused she became. After spending an evening in Luke Taggart's company, there was only one thing about herself that she knew with absolute certainty—her name.

For as long as she could remember, she'd yearned to be a nun. Now the yearning lay around her like shattered glass. She squeezed her eyes closed, so confused and filled with guilt she could barely stand it. But even so, she couldn't run from the truth. She was attracted to Luke Taggart. His smile, the lonely ache in his eyes, even the way he rubbed his nose when he was thinking gave her goose bumps. For the first time in her life, she'd begun to wonder if she had a true calling to the sisterhood.

But if she didn't take vows, what then was she to do? Even if Luke wasn't as strongly attracted to her as she was to him—even if nothing came of her feelings and they went away as suddenly as they'd come—she couldn't ignore the changes he'd provoked in her mind and body. Tonight had been a danger sign, a portent of doom for all her dreams. Nuns didn't feel shivery all over when they were near a man. A nun wouldn't have yearned to melt against Luke when his breath stirred her hair.

"I don't know what to do," she whispered, her voice breaking. She closed her eyes against a rush of tears. Even now, she felt all achy inside and tingly in places that had never tingled before. Ever since she'd told her papa of her intention to become a nun, he'd been warning her that this would happen, that someday she'd meet a man who'd make her heart go *pitter-pat* and her knees feel watery. She'd always laughed and said, "Not me, Papa. I'm not like other girls, getting all silly over boys."

And she never had. But then, Luke Taggart was far from being a boy.

Rolling onto her stomach, she angrily jerked the silk pillowcase off the pillow so she could wad up the down-filled ticking and hook her chin over the lump. Tears trailed in ticklish ribbons over her cheeks, and she prayed with an unprecedented fervency for God to take these feelings away.

She'd finished one prayer and started on another directed at the Holy Mother when a sudden thought brought her to a dead stop. What if Luke had somehow sensed her unusual...reaction to him?

The thought filled her with mortification. He needed a friend, not a twit who got all moon-eyed every time he entered the room. He was paying her a fortune to provide him with companionship, and it was her job to provide it. What would Luke think if he found out his nearness made her heart skitter? Her getting a silly fixation about him wasn't part of the bargain they'd struck.

In his mind, theirs was a business arrangement, from which he had clearly defined expectations that she was obligated to fulfill. Why, there'd even been one line in the contract to protect him in case they had an argument. She couldn't remember exactly how it was worded; something about any issue that might arise from their relationship, and her relinquishing all rights in that event. The poor man. What kind of life had he led that he trusted so little? If they had a quarrel and this arrangement failed to work, she'd never dream of holding him to their agreement and making him pay her a wage she wasn't earning.

They could have just shaken hands. According to her papa, shaking hands was as binding as any lawyer-written words. Yet Luke had felt it necessary to have every little thing spelled out, insisting she agree to it in writing.

A slight smile touched her mouth, and she nuzzled her face against the ticking to dry her tears. Little wonder he made her feel all funny inside. He was so tall and muscled all over, yet in many ways, he seemed vulnerable and uncertain. Sometimes, when she looked deeply into his eyes, the expressions she saw there made her ache, and she found herself having to resist the urge to give him a hug and try to reassure him. It broke her heart that he was so lost and lonely, and she could only guess how many times he must have been hurt. Otherwise, why would he be so hesitant to trust people?

In other ways, though, he reminded her a lot of her papa, always touching and patting, his gaze warm with affection. He was funny, too, especially when he tried to be stern and bossy. She could see right through those fierce scowls. Underneath it all, he was a big old softie. Even when Lycodomes had shaken mud all over the room, he'd dragged the dog from the chamber with an underlying gentleness. Cassandra had seen angry men grab dogs by their collars and jerk the poor animals clear off their feet. As furious as Luke had been, he'd been firm with Lycodomes, but not in any way abusive.

Maybe the way she felt about Luke was natural, a one in a million reaction to a man who was equally as rare. Maybe the funny feeling in her heart wasn't the *pitter-pat* Papa had warned her about, but a completely understandable response to the goodness she saw inside Luke. It wasn't often such a kind and benevolent person came along, after all.

She could like a man and still become a nun, she assured herself. She could like him a lot; there was no sin in that. And Luke Taggart was definitely a very likable sort. He also needed a friend, someone who'd be loyal to him no matter what.

A feeling of peace settled over Cassandra. Instead of getting all upset about the funny feelings she got when she was around Luke, maybe she should just wait and see what happened. Her papa was fond of saying that God could work in mighty strange ways, and he was right. Cassandra truly believed that God sometimes guided people in directions they never intended to go because that was where they were needed most. Maybe God felt it was more important that she be Luke Taggart's friend than that she become a nun. As a sister, she would have an opportunity to change a lot of people's lives, but maybe not to the same degree that she might be able to change Luke's.

She had to be open to God's will, she realized. In all things, He had a plan, and even when that plan wasn't clear, a person needed to be flexible. God called people to all kinds of vocations, sometimes to religious orders, sometimes not. It wasn't up to her to decide. If she kept her heart open by praying often, she'd know the right thing to do. She just had to be patient until the answer came to her.

Cassandra relaxed as the warmth of the down comforter seeped through her flesh and into her bones. Drowsiness settled over her like a heavy blanket, making her limbs feel languorous and her closed eyelids weighted. She stifled a yawn against the ticking, smiled sleepily, and let herself drift into the blackness.

In the adjoining room, Luke lay awake, staring at the ceiling. A dozen questions plagued him as he went over the evening he'd spent with Cassandra. How could she make him laugh with such complete abandon? Why had he felt so good in her company when she'd failed so completely to satisfy his expectations? And how, in God's name, had she wrangled him into playing chess their first night together, when he'd wanted to play lascivious games instead? Even more disturbing, why had he felt so disgusted and upset with himself when he'd found her examining the scanty lace pinafore? Or so ashamed and appalled when she'd opened that bureau drawer?

Finally the questions drove him from the bed. After throwing on his clothes, he went out into the hall and began to pace outside her bedchamber, tormented by images of her alone in that huge bed. By all rights, he should be beside her. Better yet, *inside* her. So what was he doing wearing a trail in the carpet runner? Why didn't he march right in there, lay down the law, and enjoy what he was paying for?

At the end of a year, he would have lightened his pockets to the tune of twenty-six *thousand* dollars, for Christ's sake. If he went dipping for honey a half dozen times a day, every day, for the entire year, he'd never get his money's worth. Quite simply, there wasn't a piece of ass on God's green earth that was worth twenty-six thousand dollars.

He was out of his mind, plain and simple. And going crazier by the goddamned minute.

An odd sound from downstairs brought Luke reeling to a halt. He stepped to the banister and looked down into the foyer. Bluish moonlight coming through the half-moon of glass over the entry door cast deep shadows that hindered his vision. He cocked his head to listen. After a moment, he heard the sound again—a muffled, eerie cry, sort of like a ghost wailing. Had some lunatic broken into the house?

Well, hell! What else was going to go wrong on this accursed night?

With a resigned sigh, he decided he'd better go downstairs to investigate. Except for Mrs. Whitmire and Pipps, who seldom stirred during the middle of the night, all the live-in servants slept in separate quarters above the carriage house out back. As a rule, none of them ventured into the house after once retiring to their beds.

Nothing seemed amiss as Luke moved silently from room to room on the first floor, and he heard no more unusual sounds. After touring the kitchen at the very rear of the house, he shrugged and nearly convinced himself his ears had been playing tricks on him.

As he was about to leave the kitchen, however, a low wailing drifted through the shadows again. It seemed to be coming from the storage room just off the kitchen. Luke stepped to the closed door, hesitated a moment to listen, then quickly shoved the portal open.

"What's going on in here?" he boomed.

The wailing ceased abruptly, a low growl taking up where the wailing left off. Luke peered through the gloom. Khristos, Cassandra's little

173

brother, sat huddled on a cot along one wall, Lycodomes curled on the floor beside him.

"What the hell are you doing in here?" Luke asked sharply.

"It's wh-where I'm s'posed to sleep," the child replied in a miserable little voice.

Luke swallowed the obscenity on the tip of his tongue. He'd told Mrs. Whitmire to get the boy settled in someplace, leaving the details up to her. He had assumed—wrongly, it seemed—that she would assign the child a downstairs bedroom and see to it that he was reasonably comfortable. Instead, she'd stuck him in a storage area. The enclosure was not only cramped; it was colder than a broom-riding witch's tit.

"Are you chilly?" Luke asked.

"N-No, sir." Piteously, the boy tugged the sleeves of his nightshirt down over his hands. "The lady gave me lots of quilts."

Luke sighed, making a mental note to speak with Mrs. Whitmire first thing in the morning. He knew she'd been shorthanded lately, but it was inexcusable to stick a child in here with the stores of food, as though he were no more important than a slab of meat. "Well...what's the problem, then?"

"Nothing, sir."

Something had to be wrong. The kid had been wailing. Luke cast a jaundiced glance at the dog. Now he knew how the mutt kept getting back inside. "Are you going to be all right in here, then?"

"Yessir."

Luke stood there for a moment, not liking

the idea of Khristos remaining in the storage room until morning. But...if he was warm, it probably wouldn't do him any actual harm, and it seemed silly to wake Mrs. Whitmire in the middle of the night without good reason. "Well, I'll be saying good night, then. If you need anything, Mrs. Whitmire is—"

"She done told me where she was," Khristos interrupted. "Her and the man with the tails—they sleep in them rooms off the kitchen, she said."

Luke smiled slightly at the boy's description of Pipps. "That's right. She's not far, if you should need her." He cast another glance at Lycodomes. "Don't be letting that dog wander through the house. I'll turn a blind eye to your bringing him in here tonight, but after this, he isn't allowed inside. Understood?"

"Yessir."

"I'll see you tomorrow, then."

Luke stepped out and drew the door firmly closed. He was about halfway across the kitchen when a muffled sob jerked him up short. He glanced back over his shoulder. The kid was crying again, dammit. If nothing was wrong, what the hell was he blubbering about?

Luke nearly kept walking. It was late. His patience was frayed. He was also exhausted. The last thing he wanted or needed was a bawling kid to deal with.

Cursing under his breath, he returned to the storage room and threw the door open again. "Khristos, what seems to be the

175

problem? Out with it, now. It's late, and I want to go back to bed."

"I'm scared," the boy replied in a muffled voice. "I ain't never slept all alone afore, and I keep hearin' noises, I do. I think you got haunts."

First leprechauns, now haunts. Luke hauled in a deep breath and let it out slowly between clenched teeth. "That's absurd. There's no such thing as ghosts, and you're far too old to be sleeping with someone. You have Lycodomes in here with you. Now I want you to be quiet. Do you understand? Pull the quilts over your head so you can't hear the house settling. But go to sleep."

Once again, Luke closed the door. This time he made it halfway through the dining room before Khristos's sobs jerked him to a halt. *Dammit!* Balling his hands into fists, Luke told himself he wasn't going in there a third time. But despite his avowals, he couldn't bring himself to keep walking.

Memories...unbidden, they flooded into his mind, hazy at first, but taking on clearer definition with each of Khristos's muffled cries. Luke saw himself at about Khristos's age, huddled in the dark hall outside his mother's bedchamber, trying to stifle his sobs so no one would hear and beat him for disturbing the customers. Hungry, cold, scared...and alone. In a house filled with people, there had been no one to comfort Luke.

"Son of a bitch."

Before he realized what he was about, Luke was retracing his steps to the storage room.

The boy's crying ceased the instant the door opened. Luke suspected Khristos was afraid of being punished and was holding his breath.

Ignoring Lycodomes's low growls, Luke stepped over to the cot, not entirely sure what he meant to do. It was with no small surprise, therefore, that he found himself scooping the boy into his arms. Luke had never been around children much since he'd been a child himself, and after his encounter with Khristos the night before, he wasn't sure he even liked the little buggers. Sticky, dirty hands and snotty noses weren't high on his list of favorite things.

Luke's first thought as he clasped Khristos to his chest was that the lad was far too thin. Bony arms and legs clamped around Luke's neck and waist. The child's ribs poked against him. Thinking of Tigger, the child he'd rescued a few days back, Luke realized it wasn't only homeless little guttersnipes who could be malnourished.

"You want some milk, kid?" he asked gruffly, amazed he was making the offer. "I can scrounge up some cheese and, um...do you like fried chicken? We had it for lunch yesterday, and there's probably some left in the icebox."

Khristos pressed his small face against the hollow of Luke's shoulder, nuzzling his shirt. Luke had a bad feeling the little rascal might be wiping his nose. "If you don't like chicken and cheese," he quickly amended, "I'll wager there are cookies in the cupboard."

"I like chicken and cheese," Khristos replied in a shaky voice.

Luke ran his fingertips up the little boy's spine. The vertebrae felt like small marbles, with scarcely any flesh as padding. "Well, then, we'll have all three."

Luke carried the boy to the kitchen where he placed him on a three-legged oak stool. "Sit still while I get a lamp going. I don't want you falling off in the dark and busting your ass, or Cassandra will have mine."

After rummaging in several drawers, Luke finally located the box of lucifers. He struck a match head on glasspaper and ignited a gas jet. With a sputter, the swing-bracket lamp flared to life, casting a golden glow over the room. "There we go," he said, rubbing his hands together as he stepped over to the icebox.

Khristos's eyes took on an eager glint when Luke returned to the work counter with a platter of chicken, a brick of cheese, and a bowl of leftover custard. "Better than cookies," Luke observed as he set the last on the butcher block. "You like custard?"

Khristos nodded enthusiastically, his pale cheeks still tracked with tears. As Luke set out dishes, silver, and drinking glasses, then sliced some cheese, he took a closer look at the child. He couldn't help but notice that Khristos's white flannel nightshirt was threadbare and yellow with age. Sable hair, cobalt eyes, pale skin: Milo Zerek's children all bore an unmistakable family resemblance. Luke wondered how it might feel to grow up belonging somewhere—to know your real last name, to have a father who loved you and a brother and sister who looked like you.

Luke's only known relative had been his mother, and she'd been a poor excuse for one, slapping him around, calling him filthy names, never even bothering to make sure he had food to eat. Born a bastard, Luke had learned to live up to the name at a very young age, stealing for his supper, lying to save his hide, doing unto others before they did it unto him. He hadn't taken the surname of Taggart until he'd turned thirteen and run away from home, a seedy brothel in Kansas City. He'd seen the name Taggart on an order board at a feed store, liked the sound of it and had been using it as his handle ever since.

As he straddled a stool, Luke tossed Khristos a hunk of cheese, then handed him a chicken leg. As the two of them began to eat, it occurred to Luke that he had a prime opportunity to learn more about his new paid companion. "So," he said, "tell me about your sister, Khristos."

The child fastened a bewildered blue gaze on Luke. "Ain't much to tell," he said around a mouthful of chicken. "Exceptin' that we always sleep right next to each other, with my papa and Ambrose on the other side of the room. That's how come I got scared, 'cause I ain't never slept alone. Not in my whole life."

Luke didn't miss the pleading look in the kid's eyes. Since the only bed partner he wanted for the night was Cassandra, which didn't seem likely given all that had happened, he ignored the hint. "You'll get used to sleeping alone. There's nothing to be afraid of. Besides, you've got Lycodomes." Having made mention of the dog, Luke glanced around to see where the mongrel was. Since there was no sign of him in the kitchen, Luke assumed Lycodomes was still lying beside Khristos's cot in the storage room. "It must've been hard on Cassandra, not having any privacy. As I understand it, most young ladies have their own sleeping area. If not a room, at least a privacy curtain."

Khristos looked surprised to hear that. "What for?"

His teeth buried in the meat of a chicken thigh, Luke eyed the boy for a long moment. Tearing meat away from the bone with his teeth, he pocketed it in his cheek. "To dress behind, for starters."

"What for?"

Luke drew his brows together in a frown. Looking into Khristos's innocent blue eyes was like looking into Cassandra's. Somehow, Milo Zerek had managed to raise at least two of his three children without their acquiring much carnal curiosity or knowledge. Luke didn't care to recall just how much sexual savvy he'd possessed at Khristos's age because it brought back bad memories. But he could say with absolute certainty that he'd been a storehouse of knowledge in comparison, and he'd definitely been curious about female anatomy. Of course, he'd been raised in whorehouses, where a woman's body was a much sought-after commodity, so maybe that explained it.

"Girls are put together differently than boys," he pointed out cautiously.

Khristos nodded sagely. "They can't whiz standin' up."

Luke circled that for a moment. "You mean take a piss?"

Khristos's eyes went as round as supper plates. "You better not say that in front of Cassie. She'll lye soap yer mouth, but good."

"Lye soap my what?"

"Yer mouth," Khristos repeated. "For sayin' bad words."

"You're telling me she puts soap in your *mouth*?" The very thought made Luke's chicken start to taste funny. "Jesus H. Christ!"

Khristos gave a startled laugh, choked on a swallow of milk, and sprayed the butcher block with white. He pressed the sleeve of his dingy nightshirt against his lips. "She's gonna get you good," he mumbled against the flannel, his eyes reflecting his mirth. "You'll be burpin' lather clear 'til next week!"

"She'll have to catch me first." Luke grabbed a towel off a rack behind him and swiped at the mess Khristos had made on the counter. "But I'll heed the warning, just the same." He smiled slightly. "Any other things I should know about her so I don't get in trouble?"

As he wolfed down his food, Khristos spouted information, all of which Luke filed away in his memory to be sorted out later. That their papa said Cassie was sharp as a tack in most ways, but not too smart in others, always trusting people she shouldn't, forever bringing home stray animals they couldn't feed, and always hankering for things they couldn't afford.

"I reckon we all do that, though," Khristos observed as he shoveled custard into his mouth. "Me, I hanker after a shotgun. And Ambrose, he wants a felt fedora hat."

Luke, who'd long since stopped eating, watched in stunned amazement as Khristos kept stuffing his mouth. "More milk?" he offered, as he served the boy more custard. Khristos nodded; Luke poured. "What kind of things does Cassandra hanker for?" he asked as he corked the jug.

"Mostly stupid stuff, like genuine patent leather slippers, like what's in the window over at the dress shop."

"Ah..." Luke recalled seeing those slippers as he'd passed the shop. As a general rule, he preferred to patronize Paulette's, on the other side of town, where more revealing clothing and seductive underthings were available.

"And she loves the sparklies."

"Sparklies?"

"You know, like that there brooch she wears."

"Jewelry," Luke clarified.

Khristos scraped his bowl clean and put a last spoonful of custard in his mouth. Luke was surprised the boy could consume so much without becoming sick.

"Well..." he said. "If you're finished eating, I guess we should go to bed."

Khristos's face fell. "Cassandra says I never even turn over once I go to sleep," he informed Luke.

"Oh, really." Luke pretended that the hint had gone straight over his head.

"And I ain't wet my covers since I can't remember when."

"That's nice."

Luke averted his gaze from the child's beseeching eyes and stacked the dirty dishes. Why he bothered, he didn't know. He paid servants a bloody fortune to clean up any messes he made. "Well, Khristos, it's really late, and I'm tired."

"Mr. Taggart?"

Luke felt the question coming and deliberately didn't glance Khristos's way. "What?"

"If I was to promise to be real still, and be real quiet, and not cry no more, would you let me sleep with you? Just for tonight, 'til I get used to it here and stuff?"

"Sorry, kid. I'm used to sleeping alone."

A frantic edge entered Khristos's voice. "You won't even know I'm there, I promise."

It was on the tip of Luke's tongue to say no, absolutely not. But then he made the mistake of meeting Khristos's gaze. There was something about great big blue eyes, he decided. One look into them, and all his convictions went flying out the window. "If you wet my bed, I'll have your—"

"I won't! I promise. Thank you, Mr. Taggart! You won't be sorry. Honest!"

There were, Luke mused an hour later, various measures of regret a man experienced when he'd made a bad mistake: sort of sorry, very sorry, damned sorry, and goddamned sorry. Luke was goddamned sorry. It was one thing to drift off to sleep with a skinny little runt of a kid lying next to you on a wide expanse of bed. It was quite another to be startled awake only minutes later by a hundred-plus pounds of damp, smelly dog landing smack dab in the middle of you.

"Son-of-a-bitching Christ!"

"Lycodomes! That's Mr. Taggart's side!" Khristos scolded. "Get back over here!"

Feeling as though his lungs had collapsed, Luke sat bolt upright, one arm clamped over his belly. "Get that damned dog out of my bed!"

Khristos hugged Lycodomes's neck, drawing the canine down beside him. Still bug-eyed from being so rudely awakened, Luke gaped at the interlopers in his bed, not quite able to believe what he was seeing. That stinking, wet, muddy, ill-mannered beast was lying on his imported white silk sheets? Even with nothing but moonlight to illuminate the room, Luke could see dirt smears.

Khristos, his small chin quivering, his eyes glistening with tears shot through by moonlight, stared back at Luke. "He'll be good."

Outraged, Luke jabbed a finger toward the hallway door. "Get...him...out!...of here!"

Khristos sailed off the bed as though he'd been catapulted, tugging the dog behind him. After Lycodomes exited the room into the hall, the child returned to Luke's bed, sniveling softly.

"Don't cry," Luke told him firmly. "It's nothing to cry about. I just don't like dogs. All right?"

"But Lycodomes always sleeps with me or Cassie," Khristos informed him tearfully. "He's lonesome."

Luke imagined the dog smearing mud all over the walls out in the hall and soiling the floors. But he'd be damned if he would get back up, get dressed, and go clear back downstairs again to put the beast outdoors. "He'll be fine, Khristos. Trust me. He'll sleep outside the door where he can smell you."

More sniveling.

Determined not to listen, or care, Luke closed his eyes and worked the muscle along his jaw. Finally, when he could stand it no longer, he said, "You promised not to keep me awake if I let you sleep with me, Khristos. Lycodomes is fine out in the hall, I tell you. So what's the problem?"

Gulp, shudder. "Maybe if you was to tell me a story I could go to sleep," Khristos finally suggested between loud sniffles. "Cassandra always tells me a bedtime story."

Luke searched his mind. The only stories he knew were the ones told by men in saloons and gambling houses. Besides, it was three o'clock in the goddamned morning. "I don't know any stories."

Gulp, sniff, shudder. Blessed silence. Then *gulp, sniff, shudder.* Luke opened his eyes and stared for a long while at the ceiling. He couldn't quite credit the fact that he was lying on sheets that now stank of dog, his bed partner a snot-nosed, blubbering little kid. And to think he was paying five hundred dollars a month, plus a twenty thousand year-end bonus, for the privilege. Something had gone seriously awry here. *Gulp, sniff, shudder.*

No more, Luke vowed. He'd reached his limit, by God. First thing in the morning, he would take Cassandra aside and lay down the law to her. By the time he finished with her, she'd understand *exactly* what her duties as his paid companion were, and she'd either start performing them, as of tomorrow night, or find herself tossed out into the street on her ear.

"I know lots of stories," Khristos said shakily. "Maybe I could tell you one."

So much for the kid being quiet, Luke thought sourly. At this point, though, he preferred almost anything to listening to him snivel. "Sure, kid. Tell away."

Khristos took a jerky breath, then wiped his nose on Luke's sheet. "Once upon a time..." he began, "a long, long time ago, there was a real ugly toad."

Luke shot him a look. "Don't you have a better story than that? I don't like toads."

"This is a special toad. He ain't really a toad at all, y'see. He's a prince."

"A what?"

"A prince," Khristos repeated. "It's a really good story, I promise. Cassandra tells it to me lots."

That caught Luke's attention. Maybe, by listening to the story, he could get some insight as to how the girl's head worked. "Okay, tell away, kid. I'm listening."

"Once upon a time," Khristos began again, then proceeded to spin a tale about a prince who'd been cursed by a wicked witch and turned into an ugly toad. Before Luke realized how it happened, he was hanging on the child's every word. When the story concluded with the toad's being kissed by a beautiful lady who magically restored the prince to human form, Luke was sorry to have it end.

"So...did they get married, or what?" he asked Khristos.

"Sure," Khristos said. "Cassie always ends her stories with 'happily ever after.'"

Luke snorted. "It's a pretty dumb story, if you think about it. What beautiful lady in her right mind would kiss an ugly toad?"

"Cassandra says the lady saw past the toad's ugliness," Khristos explained. "She knew there was a handsome prince hidden behind all the warts."

Luke snorted again. "Right. You don't really believe that stuff, do you?"

"Cassie says there's something wonderful and beautiful inside everyone," Khristos murmured drowsily, "if only people look deep enough to see it."

Luke, who lay with his arms pillowing his head, shifted his elbow to look at the child beside him. "You going to sleep?"

"No," Khristos said faintly.

Just seconds after he made the denial, the child began to breathe more deeply. Luke smiled to himself. Telling the story had done the trick; the boy was out like a candle in a strong draft.

Fastening his gaze on the ceiling again, Luke went back over the story Khristos had told him, particularly the ending. So Cassandra believed everyone had something good and beautiful inside them, did she? He smiled again, thinking that the girl had better be packing a shovel if she hoped to dig deep enough to find anything beautiful inside Luke Taggart.

She was obviously walking around with her head in the clouds, he decided, and it was high time she got her feet firmly rooted in reality.

Luke was nearly asleep when there came a soft scratching on the door. Determined to ignore it, he rolled over. But as the minutes passed, the scratching grew more persistent. Finally, Luke could stand it no longer. He shoved himself out of bed, strode angrily across the room, and jerked the door open, intending to scold the dog and put a stop to such behavior.

Big mistake. The second the door swung open, Lycodomes came barreling in and promptly jumped on the bed.

"Lycodomes," Khristos said drowsily and looped his arm around the dog's neck.

Luke heaved a resigned sigh and sat on the edge of the bed, thinking of the fleas that even now were probably breeding on his sheets. He couldn't quite believe he was actually considering letting the mongrel stay. But when he glanced back over his shoulder, he saw that Khristos still had one arm around the dog's thick ruff. Lycodomes, who had already settled in comfortably, licked the boy's face.

"Son of a bitch," Luke said.

With a groan, he lay back down. One good

thing about dog smell, he noted as he closed his eyes. After a few minutes, it lost its edge.

As that thought drifted through Luke's mind, something damp slapped him across the mouth. He sputtered and swatted it away, only to have it slap him in the face again. *Dog tail*, he realized. Too drowsy to fight the situation any longer, Luke anchored the wagging canine appendage under his arm. As he slipped into unconsciousness, he heard a low, threatening growl.

TEN

Luke rose from bed the next morning ready to lay down the law. The sooner Cassandra realized, in detail, exactly what was expected of her, the sooner Luke could stop wasting his energy on filthy dogs and homesick boys.

Already this morning, he'd had to drag himself out of bed twice—once to usher the mongrel outside before the damned thing clawed a hole in the expensive oak door, and once to show Khristos the way to the kitchen so the kid could get something to eat. By then, it had been well past time for Khristos to leave for school, of course, a situation Luke was determined would not repeat itself on the morrow. A good education would one day be of paramount importance to the boy if he ever hoped to make something of himself, and every day he missed school constituted lessons he might never again have an opportunity to learn.

Luke knew exactly how difficult it was to patch the holes in a ragged education—and how inadequate a man could feel when he was repeatedly reminded of his ignorance.

As though summoned by his black thoughts, a sour smell assaulted his nostrils and he scowled. *Christ on crutches*, he thought as he tugged on a clean shirt. Even now, his rooms reeked of wet dog. The first thing he intended to do this morning was speak to Mrs. Whitmire about having the whole damn suite disinfected. Well...maybe not the first thing. Before he issued mandates for the bedchamber to be cleaned, he was going to give the housekeeper a dressing down she wouldn't soon forget. Imagine the callous gall of the woman, sticking poor, scared Khristos in a storage room. Every time Luke remembered finding the child in there, his blood started to boil.

As he tucked in his shirt and buckled his belt with angry precision, his thoughts turned to Cassandra. For once, his mental picture of her sweet face did nothing to mellow his mood. Directly after breakfast, he was going to haul her into the study and put the fear of God into her. No preambling. No mincing of words. He'd just lay it on the line. There were plenty of women in Black Jack who'd give their eye teeth for this position. She could either earn her wage or pack her satchel, and at this point, he didn't particularly care which.

Or so he told himself.

When Luke finally found time to speak with Cassandra after he got downstairs, he quickly discovered that laying down the law to her was easier said than done. First, he had to get her attention, and short of snarling at her, which he was suddenly reluctant to do, he wasn't sure how to go about it. Every room in his house, not to mention the countless objects she encountered in them, seemed to fascinate her.

First she discovered the breakfast room, which, she hastened to inform him, was bigger than her whole house down in the mining district and, in her estimation, "totally extravagant." He already had a huge dining room that could easily seat forty people. How many eating rooms did one man need? Then she stumbled upon the octagonal solarium, where she stopped to examine and admire every plant, all the while marveling that she felt as if she were outside. By the time Luke finally got her headed toward his study, he was seething with impatience.

"Oh, my stars," she said in awed tones as he ushered her into the large room. "I've never seen so many books in someone's house in all my life!" Like metal shavings drawn to a magnet, she moved toward the bookshelves that lined one entire wall. "Oh, Luke, do you realize how very lucky you are? You could read for a year and never run out of material!"

As much as he enjoyed reading, Luke didn't think the books were the room's most interesting feature. For starters, a whole wall at one end was devoted to a fireplace made with gold-veined ore taken from one of his mines. Most people couldn't take their gazes off it and invariably asked if the gold was real.

In addition to the fireplace, he'd spent a fortune on the furnishings. A custom-designed leather sofa and two matching armchairs. A hand-carved oak desk. Imported crystal hurricane lamps. A gorgeous Persian rug. Everywhere Luke looked, he saw things that should have been capturing her attention. Instead, she seemed mesmerized by the titles she was reading aloud.

"If you enjoy reading that much, Cassandra, you're welcome to borrow a book any time you like," he offered when she paused for breath.

Once again wearing his white shirt over one of the dresses he'd bought her yesterday, she pressed a hand to the buttoned front placket and turned toward him, her eyes round with delight. "Oh, are you sure you won't mind? As I told you last night, I love to read, and I hardly ever get to."

He made an all-encompassing gesture toward the shelves. "Make free."

In his reading tastes, at least, Luke was fairly conservative and had nothing on the shelves that might pollute her mind. Unlike some men, he wasn't limited to seeking lascivious pleasures between the covers of a book, so he seldom chose that sort of reading material. To fill in the gaps in his education, which were gargantuan, he leaned more toward the informative or classic literature.

As she turned back to study more book titles, his gaze dropped to the shirt again. The tails fell well past her hips, revealing only the lower half of the dress. This one was crimson

192

silk, his favorite, the revealing style of which was totally camouflaged by the loose folds of white silk she wore over it. Luke counted himself lucky she hadn't joined him for breakfast this morning draped in that ugly old shawl of her mother's as well, undoubtedly because the combined layers of clothing were too stifling inside the warm house.

"Cassandra," he said in a firm voice, "I'd really like to talk to you. Do you think you could tear your eyes away from those books long enough to hear what I've got to say?"

She spun around again, her expression contrite. "I'm sorry. It's just...well, it's like being in a library. Papa took me to one once, you know. In Denver, when we were passing through. I could have stayed there for days."

Luke indicated that she should take a seat on the sofa. As she perched on the edge of a leather cushion, he leaned against his desk and crossed his feet.

"I've learned one of your secrets," she said suddenly.

Luke, who'd been contemplating the gleaming black toe of one boot while he tried to compose what he meant to say, glanced warily up at her. Her eyes were gleaming, and her lips curved in a particularly sweet way.

"What secret is that?" he asked in a cautious tone, his first thought being that he'd somehow missed a drawer when he cleaned out her room last night. Had she stumbled across some obscene little gadget or lewd garment?

She leaned slightly forward. "Your favorite color. It's red!" She indicated the pattern in the Persian rug. "In nearly every room I've seen, there are touches of it, just as bright as can be. When you did my rooms, it must have been your grand finale."

Luke's relief was as inexplicable as it was unprecedented. Suppressing the urge to reach out and smooth a tendril of dark hair from her cheek, he uncrossed his feet, crossed them again, and then began tapping the side of his thumb on the desk.

Wryly, he wondered why Cassandra Zerek brought out this odd streak of protectiveness in him. When he'd brought her here yesterday, he'd had every intention of introducing her to some of those gadgets eventually and insisting she wear scanty, seductive lingerie to please him, but that had been *before* she had turned his whole life upside down.

Maybe it was because she was so trusting, and so young and vulnerable, that she made him feel...what? Responsible for her? Or even a little guilty?

"Yes," he admitted, glancing at her skirt, "I guess you could say my favorite color is red."

At least, it had been until he'd seen her in that god-awful room last night and realized what a bawdy color it actually was. Recalling his decision to redecorate her bedchamber, Luke snapped his fingers.

"That reminds me." He turned to a pad of paper on his desk and jotted himself a note. "What's *your* favorite color, Cassandra?"

"Blue."

He made note of that as well, then tossed

down the pen. As he turned back to her, he sighed. "Cassandra..."

"Yes?"

"We have to reach a clear agreement. When I hired you to be my paid companion, I'm afraid you didn't understand the duties I expect you to perform."

"Oh...I'm sorry. I thought we had a lovely time last night. That is, I did. I guess—"

"I did, too," he hastened to assure her. "Truly. It's just—" Luke found himself at a loss for words. Speaking delicately was an art for which he lacked talent, and now that he was actually facing her, speaking bluntly didn't seem at all the thing. "I, um..."

Those eyes. Not even Luke, who'd always prided himself on being single-minded and prodigiously ruthless when he wanted something, could ignore their adoring glow.

"I'm paying you a very generous wage," he finally managed. "Can we agree on that much?"

She nodded, the loose curls caught up at her crown by the familiar red ribbon bobbing with each dip of her chin. "Absolutely."

He cleared his throat and told himself to ignore the singsong voice in the back of his mind that kept saying, *Bastard. You heartless bastard.*

If *this* was what it was like to have a conscience—a little voice resounding inside his head that called him insulting names—Luke decided he'd happily forego the experience.

"I don't think it's unreasonable of me to

expect you to perform the services I'm paying you for, Cassandra," he observed drily. "Do you?"

"Not at all." Her eyes grew dark, and her brows swooped together. "I guess I did fail to please you."

The last thing he wanted was to wound her. "I wouldn't put it exactly like that," he amended. "It's more appropriate to say that I'm afraid you don't understand the, ah, *specifics* of what I expect."

"Oh. Specifics. I see." She nibbled her bottom lip. "I'm sorry, Luke. Mrs. Whitmire assured me that you *love* to play chess."

"I do! It's just—" He threw up his hands. "Honey, it's just that talking and playing chess all evening weren't what I had in mind."

"I see."

Only, of course, she didn't. Gazing into her lovely eyes, Luke knew she didn't see at all. "Sweetheart," he said cautiously, "do you understand what wifely duties are?"

The smooth slope of her forehead pleated in another frown. After a moment, the bewilderment disappeared from her expression. "Wifely duties. Yes, of course."

"I'm not talking about your mending my shirts," he said bluntly. "I'm talking about other sorts of duties, the kind a wife generally performs late at night for her husband when everybody else is asleep and the house is quiet."

Cassandra got a knowing look in her eyes, which he took as a good sign. "Late at night duties," she repeated, nodding.

"It's *those* kinds of duties I've hired you to perform," he said softly.

She glanced nervously around his study. He suspected she was trying to avoid his gaze. After a moment, her expression went from concerned to downright alarmed. Before she could fly into a temper, he held up a hand.

"I'm a fair man. I realize you didn't enter into this agreement with a clear understanding of my expectations. And after getting to know you a bit better, I also realize you may not be—" He shrugged and sighed. "Well, suffice it to say, you may find such a position... demeaning. If you—"

"I'm not exactly in a position to be selective," she pointed out. "You've given me and Khristos a home. And Lye-Lye, of course. It's only right that I repay you in any way you think is fair."

Luke could scarcely believe how easily she'd acquiesced. Relieved, he flashed her a slow smile. "I'm pleased to hear that. And I must say, I admire your...well, shall we say, flexibility?"

Her smile was sunrise and sunset and a perfect day in between. "My papa taught us that, in order to survive, we have to be adaptable."

Luke nodded. "Your papa is a wise man." Bracing his hands at the edge of the desk, Luke shifted his position, inhaled a deep breath, then let it out with a chuckle of sheepish laughter. He settled a warm gaze on her. "To be honest, I was half expecting this discussion to get a little ugly. I'm glad you've decided to be

197

mature and not hold it against me. Being an unmarried man..." He let his voice trail away. "Well, I'm sure even you understand that a man has certain needs, and if you aren't willing to fulfill them, I'll have to hire someone else."

She looked so distressed he was tempted to reach for her. "Oh, please, don't consider hiring someone else. I *need* this position. Even though I know Khristos and I would manage somehow, we'd be in an awful fix if I lost it."

"As long as you fulfill your side of the bargain and your performance pleases me, I'll have no reason to hire someone else, will I?"

"I understand, Luke," she said earnestly. "And I promise not to shirk my responsibilities again. After all, it's not as if Mrs. Whitmire can take care of those sorts of things for you."

Luke barked with laughter. "Definitely not!" He searched her gaze for a moment, his chest going oddly tight.

"She's rather plump, isn't she?" She smiled again, conspiringly. "Don't tell her I said so, but I've noticed she gets breathless going up the stairs. I'm sure the duties she already has sometimes seem overwhelming to her."

Recalling the way she'd tucked Khristos away in the storage room to save herself trouble, Luke had to agree.

A tense silence fell between them. Luke finally broke it by saying, "I really did enjoy being with you last night, honey. Don't think I didn't."

A slight rosiness touched her cheeks. "I liked it a lot, too."

Their gazes remained locked for what seemed to Luke an interminably long while, but he couldn't look away. Not when her eyes were warming his face, and her smile was wrapping around him like a hug. "It's not that I don't want to spend evenings chatting and playing chess again. I do. It's just that I expect other things from you as well."

She nodded again. Strands of her sable hair caught the light, radiating gold. "No problem. I assure you, Luke, that I won't disappoint you again."

"You didn't disappoint me. Never that." He flashed her a meaningful grin, which she returned shyly. "I think *frustrated* would better describe how I felt."

She pushed to her feet and smoothed her skirts. "And that's perfectly understandable. If you hire someone to do a job and they don't—well, anyone would feel frustrated."

Luke straightened and shoved himself away from the desk. Closing the distance between them, he cupped her small chin in his hand and lifted her face. "I don't want you to feel nervous," he told her softly. "Promise me you won't. I know this is all new to you."

She laid her hand lightly over his wrist. "I'm a fast learner, Luke, and I know I can count on you to be patient. I may be a little...well, awkward at first. But with practice, I'll improve. The way I've lived, I haven't acquired a lot of experience, and certain aspects are likely to seem a little overwhelming to me."

"We'll take it slow," he promised. "Ease you into it. Where you lack experience, I have a wealth of it."

She drew back, still smiling. "I may draw from your expertise, then. When I take on a task, I like to do it right."

Luke liked the sound of that. Indeed, he had a feeling he was going to make a very enthusiastic teacher.

As Luke left the house a few minutes later, his mood was much improved. Despite the storm last night, the sun shone warmly on his shoulders as he stepped along the cobblestone sidewalks that bordered the well-kept yards of his neighbors, and the rain-washed air carried the acrid but oddly pleasant scent of smoke from backyard burning barrels. Plump housewives, dressed in serviceable basque day jackets and skirts protected by wrap-around overskirts, waved good morning to him from their porches, where they were either shaking rugs or sweeping steps. Dogs came running out to sniff at his tan woolen trousers, then wagged their tails in friendly recognition as they trotted off to mark their territory, christening bushes and white picket fence posts.

Luke couldn't suppress a sense of well-being, especially when he contemplated the coming night with Cassandra. No chess, no kid, no wet, stinking dog. Not tonight. For the first time in a very long while, he could scarcely wait for his day to be finished so he might hurry home.

As Luke angled across Gambler's Way to the

corner of Diamond, his gaze caught on the dry goods store. Jed Wilson, the proprietor, happened to be outside sweeping the front walk, his white apron flapping in the morning breeze. After checking both directions for approaching conveyances, Luke crossed the thoroughfare.

"Good morning to you, Jed!"

The plump store owner jumped with a start, then pushed up his spectacles to regard Luke's advance with myopic owlishness. Shifting the broom to one hand, he ran a palm over his shiny bald pate. "Ah, Mr. Taggart. How are you?"

"Doing well, doing well." Luke drew to a stop, hands thrust in his trouser pockets, his brown jacket swept back by his wrists to reveal his yellow silk vest. "Say, Wilson, do you happen to carry nightshirts, by any chance? Something to fit a small lad."

"Certainly." Stepping to the recessed doorway, Jed leaned his broom against the gray clapboard and waved for Luke to follow him. Once inside, he meandered down one aisle, then cut left up another, his hand trailing lightly over the bolts of cloth and sewing notions displayed on tables and racks.

"Ah, here we are," Wilson said as he drew to a stop. "What size are you wanting?"

Luke pursed his mouth. "Well..." He held out a hand to indicate Khristos's height. "About so tall, a skinny little mite. I need it for the Zerek boy, Khristos. Perhaps you know him?"

"Oh, yes! He's in Zachariah's class at

school." Jed shook his head. "I heard about his father and older brother getting tossed in the hoosegow. Crying shame, that. Milo Zerek always struck me as a decent sort, honest and forthright. I was mightily surprised to hear he'd taken to claim jumping, especially on one of yours. Never took the man for a fool."

"Yes, well, you can never tell about people, I guess."

Wilson shook his head. "I reckon not. Zerek never once tried to squeeze me for credit, like some folks do. In my books, that's usually a sign of good character." He pulled a blue flannel nightshirt from the center of a stack. "This one will fit." He rubbed the nap between his fingers. "Nice and warm it'll be, too."

Luke took the proffered garment and held it up for inspection. It looked awfully small to him. "You're sure it will fit?"

"If it doesn't, you can exchange it." Jed winked. "But I have an eye for sizes, you know. Especially as they pertain to boys that age, being's I have one of my own." Crossing his arms over his potbelly, Wilson rocked back on his heels. His brown eyes gleamed with curiosity behind his spectacles. "May I ask why you're buying the boy a nightshirt? Seems an odd thing to do, being's his pappy got caught red-handed stealing from you."

Luke laid the nightshirt over his arm. The speculative expression on Wilson's face set off warning bells in his mind. If he said the wrong thing, it would become fodder for the

202

gossips, and his pretty little mistress would be hurt. Normally, Luke didn't worry about what others might think. He did what he pleased, the devil take gainsayers. But that had been before he'd formed an alliance with an innocent young girl who wore her heart on her sleeve.

"Zerek's being arrested left his children on their own with no means of support," Luke said, striving for just the right note of offhandedness. "When no one else came forward to give them assistance, I offered to put them up at my place. Better that than see them tossed out in the streets. Not even I could sleep nights with that on my conscience."

"Ah..." Wilson's tone conveyed that he found the explanation highly suspect, which came as no surprise.

"What the child has by way of clothing— well, I can't very well let him run about in rags," Luke explained. "When I spotted you out on the sidewalk, it occurred to me you might carry at least a few of the things he needs."

"Mighty kind of you, if you don't mind my saying so, especially under the circumstances. Hell of a note when a man gets done dirty, then finds himself supporting the offender's children."

"Not really. My housekeeper, Mrs. Whitmire, can always use another pair of hands, and the girl is of an age to be helpful around the house. I figure she can more than earn their keep."

Luke wasn't sure where that had come from or even why he'd said it. In truth, it was silly to bother. Sooner or later, the townspeople would realize what was going on, and Cassandra's reputation would be in tatters. By evading the truth now, Luke was only delaying the inevitable.

"Ah, yes." Wilson smiled slightly. "As I understand, Cassandra's handy at domestic sorts of things. Cleans the Catholic church, you know, and I believe she helps out over at the convent on a regular basis as well. 'Little Miss Sunshine,' Father Tully calls her."

Luke smiled to himself, for the nickname fit her to a tee. When he was with her, he often felt as though the sun had just peeked out from behind a cloud. Some people claimed money couldn't buy happiness. Luke disagreed. He'd just purchased himself an abundant measure of it, all wrapped up with a tattered red bow in glossy sable curls.

Damn...instead of going to the office, he wanted to turn around and head directly home. To hell with waiting all day to have her in his bed. He wanted her now, with an urgency that made him ache. If there hadn't been business matters that required his immediate attention, he would have done exactly that.

ELEVEN

The smell of ammonia was strong enough to bring tears to her eyes, but Cassandra had long since stopped trying to wipe them away. Instead, she narrowed her gaze against the obnoxious fumes and concentrated on working faster.

Nevertheless, the job had turned out to be more difficult than she'd imagined. Luke's staircase was just about the biggest one she'd ever seen. Twenty-four steps in all. *Wide* steps. And every blasted one of them needing a good scrubbing, she thought as she rubbed industriously at the white film of softened wax on the tread above her. Though she was scarcely half finished, her back and knees were already killing her. Judging by the thickness of the wax deposit, Luke had delayed almost too long in hiring someone to take care of things like this. Cassandra was willing to bet these stairs hadn't had attention in two or three years, maybe even longer.

Whew! She tossed her rag back into the water where the scrub brush floated, handle side up, and swiped at the beads of moisture gathering on her brow. Ten steps finished, fourteen to go. Remaining on her knees, she wearily gathered the folds of her skirt in one hand and grabbed up the bucket with her other, preparing to move down another level.

As she was negotiating this rather tricky maneuver, a rapier voice cut through the silence. "What in the bloody *hell* do you think you're doing?"

Cassandra gave such a start, she slopped ammonia water all over herself and the stairs. Angling a glance over her shoulder, she saw Luke. He stood in the open doorway, one arm leaning against the door frame, his chocolate brown jacket hooked on a finger and tossed back over his shoulder. Behind him, the darkening sky looked almost as threatening as he did.

"Luke!" She scrambled to tug her skirt down and hide her ankles. "Oh, my! I, um, didn't expect you back quite so early."

Tawny brows drawing together in a fierce scowl, he pulled his watch from the pocket of his yellow silk vest and opened the engraved gold case with a flick of his thumb. "Early? It's nearly six."

"Is it that late? How time does fly when you're"—she wiped wax scum from her palm onto the apron she'd filched from the kitchen—"having fun. I, um…would have gotten started earlier, but Cook gave me a pie to take over to the jail this afternoon, so I walked to town to deliver it before I began."

Returning the watch to its pocket, he fixed her with a relentless stare, not so much as a hint of a smile touching his stern mouth. He had a dark, dangerous air she'd rarely noticed before, his amber eyes glittering like whiskey shot through with firelight. Cassandra gulped, intimidated in spite of herself.

"You didn't go in back to see your father and brother, did you?"

"No. The marshal wouldn't let me."

"Good. It's no place for a young woman."

"That's what the marshal said. But taking them the pie made me feel better. At least they know I'm thinking about them."

"I really don't like the idea of your going over there, Cassandra. Aside from the marshal and deputies, most of the men who have business at the jail are coarse individuals who wouldn't hesitate to take advantage of you."

Cassandra gulped, remembering all the times her papa had said the same thing. "But, Luke, I only took them a pie. I didn't stay more than a minute or two, at most."

"Nonetheless, after this I will escort you. It's no place for you to be going all alone. Do I make myself clear?"

He looked impossibly big standing there, broad across the shoulders and long of leg in the tan trousers. As much as Cassandra wanted to be allowed to take her papa and brother little treats to make their stay in jail less miserable, she found herself nodding. "Yes, very clear. I won't go again unless you take me."

He relaxed slightly. His white shirtsleeves, she noticed, were turned back to reveal darkly tanned, powerfully corded forearms. Even in a relaxed stance, he projected an aura of raw power.

He looked past her at the stairs again. "You never did answer my question," he said in that same dangerously silken voice. "What do you think you're doing?" His gleaming gaze dropped to her person. "And where, may I ask, did you get that horrible rag of a dress?"

"Oh!..." She plucked nervously at the gray wool. "I, um...borrowed it from one of the maids. I didn't want to ruin one of the new dresses you bought. One little stain, and you wouldn't be able to get a refund."

A muscle along his jaw started to tic. His

gaze seemed to burn into hers for an endlessly long moment. "Cassandra, I thought we had reached a clear understanding when I left this morning, and now I come home to find you—" His gaze shifted to the stairs. "What, *exactly*, are you doing?"

"Stripping off the wax." Wiping her other hand reasonably clean on the apron, she pushed to her feet. "I, um…made out a list. You know, of all the things around here that need to be done. Stripping off floor wax is one of them. I, um…thought if I took the house in sections, I might get the first floor done this week, then start on…" She let her voice trail away and swallowed. "Were you hoping I'd start something else first?" She glanced around the foyer. "The lamp globes, maybe? I know the soot buildup on them is frightful, but all things considered, I thought cleaning them was of secondary importance."

"The lamp globes?" he repeated in an oddly strained voice, his gaze moving slowly over her face.

"Is something wrong?" she questioned, her heart giving an anxious flutter.

"Apparently." His scowl deepened. "Perhaps you will recall that I told you, very clearly and precisely, what I expected of you tonight?"

She nodded, still mystified but determined to do whatever was needed to please him.

"In my recollection, I said *nothing* about floor wax or lamp globes."

A burning sensation washed over Cassandra's eyes, and she had an awful feeling it wasn't from ammonia fumes. She'd wanted so badly to please him, and she'd worked so hard and fast to get a lot accomplished before he got home. "I'm sorry, Luke. I guess I should have asked you to draw up the list."

"What list?"

"The list of—" She licked her lips and swallowed again. "You know, the list of wifely duties you'd like me to perform."

"We need a list?"

"Yes, well...I like to be organized and plan ahead. Otherwise, things have a way of not getting done. Like these stairs, for instance. I'll bet it's been ages. The wax buildup is so thick, it's going to take me twice as long as I thought. Several more hours, probably. That's why I started before everyone went to bed. I had to wait until the maids had completely finished upstairs, of course. But then, I started straightaway. It was either that or do the job a few steps at a time."

"Hours?"

He pushed away from the door frame and moved into the foyer, a forbidding figure with the stealthy surefootedness of a large, predatory cat.

Even looking down at him, she thought he seemed taller than ever before, lean yet well-muscled. His thick tawny hair lay in loose, glossy waves over his forehead, one slightly curly hank teasing the prominent bridge of his nose. His expression stamped with forbidding sternness, a tendon along his jaw rippling with agitation, he came to a stop just before the stairs and gazed up at her with derisive golden eyes that seemed to miss nothing.

"I'm sorry, Luke," she whispered tremulously. "You've only to tell me what you *would* like me to do, and I'll have it done before you can blink."

The rigid set of his mouth softened slightly at the corners, and she thought some of the anger ebbed from his eyes. "Cassandra, what am I going to do with you?"

"Give me clearer instructions?" she suggested hopefully.

He extended a hand toward her, his lips quirking with a smile he seemed determined to squelch. "Come down here, sweetheart. I'll have Mrs. Whitmire assign some of the staff to finish this."

"But you can't do that! You're paying me a great deal of money. I can't leave jobs half finished for others to do. How would that be fair?"

For the life of him, Luke couldn't think of a good answer. Not that it should have surprised him. With Cassandra, he seemed unable to get a point across with any clarity. So much for speaking delicately. Judging by the reception he'd gotten this evening, he may as well have delivered an oratory to the girl in Greek. Scotch that. She undoubtedly *understood* Greek, what with her father having been born in Greece. It was English she seemed not to grasp.

He curled a hand around the ornate finial atop the newel post, a part of him wishing it were her lovely little neck. He cast a glance at the unfinished stairs, which were now filmed with white from soaking in ammonia water. "But, honey, this could take you hours. What about supper?" *And my making love to you until dawn,* he silently added. "I've been looking forward all day to spending time with you."

She cast a worried look at the softened wax all over the stairs. "I, um...maybe you could bring in a chair and visit with me while I work. After you've had supper, of course. I think I'll just skip eating tonight."

"Don't be silly. I won't have you going without supper." Not able to believe he was getting suckered into this, Luke tossed his jacket over the bannister and began rolling his shirtsleeves higher. This was going to be the first time in a very long while that he had broken a sweat outside the bedchamber. "We'll get it done faster if I help," he told her with a wry smile. "Then we'll sneak into the kitchen for a snack. How's that sound?"

She gave an airy little laugh. "And you call me silly? It isn't as if I might waste away if I miss supper. Please, Luke...just leave me to finish this and go eat."

He gave her figure a quick appraisal. "You say that as if you think you're fat."

She bent to retrieve the scrub brush from the bucket. "'Stout' probably better describes me."

"You are *not* stout." Luke allowed his gaze to trail over her once more. He supposed that, strictly speaking, taking her measure with a purely impartial eye, she might be a little too curvaceous for her height. But how could a man notice when he got so deliciously preoccupied while admiring the curves? "You have a lovely shape."

She bent to scrub the next riser, her posterior, which he counted as one of her finer features, raised for his perusal. "Ample, anyway," she replied in a voice gone breathless with exertion. "Ambrose says I'm built like a—" She broke off. "Well, suffice it to say, his nickname for me isn't very complimentary."

Luke, who now stood only two steps below her, yearned to grasp her by the waist and draw that wonderfully well-rounded fanny snugly against his hips. In fact, if she were to get on her knees and he were to kneel behind her, it would be an ideal position for—

"Hi, Luke! Thanks a heap for the clothes you got for me!"

Luke gave a guilty start as Khristos came to a skidding stop next to the banister, Lycodomes coming to a halt perilously close behind him. The kid was grinning from ear to ear, and the dog was wearing a self-satisfied look Luke didn't much like at all. He felt his temper fraying.

"I thought I gave strict orders for that dog to be kept outside."

Cassandra poked her head between the banister rails to gaze down at her brother. "Oh, my, don't you look handsome!"

Khristos grinned and turned in a slow circle to show off his new red shirt and blue jeans. When he came back about, he thrust out a foot. "New boots, too, Cassie. Ain't they grand?"

Cassandra fixed shimmering blue eyes on Luke and smiled with such melting warmth he forgot all about the damned dog's being in the house. "Oh, Luke, you shouldn't have. How will I ever repay you?"

Right off the top of his head, he could think of a dozen delightful ways. If this was the sort of reaction he got for buying the kid clothes, next time he'd take him to a tailor. "I don't expect repayment. I wanted to get them for him."

Luke felt his newly acquired conscience give him a hard kick. Ignoring it wasn't as easy as it had been this morning. *What the hell?* he asked himself. Sucking up a little gratitude he didn't really deserve wasn't the worst thing he'd ever done. Not by a long shot.

"And this ain't all!" Khristos informed his sister proudly. "Two new nightshirts! And rubber boots. I got more shirts and trousers, too. And socks, lots and lots of socks! Mr. Wilson had them delivered right to the back door, like I was rich or somethin'!"

Cassandra assumed a stern expression that Luke found adorable. "Well, see that you show Luke your appreciation by taking good care of them. No throwing clothes on the floor. Or ripping your pants climbing over fences."

"I'll wear my old clothes to play in," Khristos assured her.

Luke was about to protest that he didn't want the boy to wear those rags again, period, not for play or anything else, but Cassandra cut him off. "Good idea, Khristos. That way, you'll always have nice things for school and church. Speaking of which, I want you up bright and early for school in the morning. Did you tell Mrs. Whitmire to wake you, like I asked you to?"

"Yep. She says she'll set her alarm clock and tell Cook to fix me breakfast."

Cassandra bent back to her work. "Mrs. Whitmire is a very kind lady. We can't have you missing any more school. Your marks will start failing."

Khristos wrinkled his nose at Luke, clearly not enamored of the thought of returning to the classroom. Luke was chuckling as he nudged Cassandra aside and commandeered the scrub brush.

"What are you doing?" she cried. "Offering a bit of help is one thing, but taking over is quite another. It's my job, and you're paying me most generously to do it."

Luke made a broad sweep over the wax-filmed oak with the brush bristles. "I'm not going to stand around being useless while you do all the work." He glanced upward. "Does that other bucket have rinse water in it?"

"Yes, but—"

"Cassandra," he warned in a firm voice, "no more arguing. I *want* to help. All right?"

"I'll help, too!" Khristos cried. Looping an arm around the newel post, he swung onto the bottom step. "What part can I do?"

"I suppose you could fetch clean rinse water," Cassandra said, handing him the other bucket. "Mind you don't slosh, though. We can't have water spilled on the floors."

Khristos had no sooner returned with a refilled bucket than Luke felt water splash all over his left trouser leg. He turned a narrowed eye on Cassandra. She grinned impishly and flicked the moisture on her fingertips directly into his face.

For an instant, Luke could only stare at her in stunned amazement. "You really shouldn't have done that," he said softly.

She pressed closer until they were nearly nose to nose. "Oh, my, I am *so* terrified. What are you going to do? Drown me?"

Luke laughed in spite of himself. "You, young lady, haven't the common sense God gave a gnat! Do you have any idea who you're dealing with? I'm a feared man in this town."

She wrinkled her nose. "You're a big faker, is what you are!"

She flicked water in his face again. Luke blinked, then wiped the wetness from his eyes. She was still grinning, clearly challenging him to retaliate. Then she delivered the final insult by tucking her hands in her armpits and flapping her elbows while she squawked like a chicken. Khristos, who looked on from the bottom step, started to guffaw, apparently delighted by her antics.

"Git him, Cassie! Git him good!"

Luke couldn't remember the last time he'd played. But suddenly he wanted to. With a sharp, almost hungry yearning. "Do you know what I do to people who flick water in my face?" he asked in an ominously low voice.

"No, what?"

Luke made a lunge for her. She shrieked and tried to evade his grasp, which set her off balance. Afraid she might take a tumble down the stairs, he grabbed for her in earnest, hooking an arm around her slender waist. Lycodomes, excited by all the commotion, began to bark.

"Git her, Luke!" Khristos cried. "Yes! Git her good!"

With a twist of his upper body, Luke pinned her beneath him on the stairs, taking care not to crush her with his weight. Giggling and shrieking, she flailed her arms and kicked futilely with her feet. Then, to his amazement, she grabbed hold of his nose. "Unhand me, sir! Or wind up with a Greek snout as big as mine!"

Chuckling at her audacity, Luke made fast work of capturing both her wrists, then forced her arms above her head. "Hmm...it seems I have a tasty little morsel to devour. Where shall I begin?" He growled and bent to nibble the sweet slope of her neck. She shrieked again, which only made Lycodomes bark all the more loudly and actually dare to nip the calf of Luke's leg. The filthy, stinking canine's days in the Taggart household were definitely numbered, Luke thought as he trailed gentle nips along Cassandra's throat up to her ear. "Ah...you are delicious."

"Forgive me for interrupting, Master Taggart, but is there a...problem?"

Luke jerked his head up to see Pipps peering at him through the banister rails, his austere expression compromised only by the startled look in his eyes. "Nothing I can't handle, Pipps," Luke told the butler. "Go on about your business and leave me to mine."

Clearly rattled by the dog's loud barking and Khristos's shrill giggles, the butler executed a smart pivot on one heel, raised his chin in the air, and marched back the way he had come. Returning his gaze to Cassandra, Luke leered down at her. "You see, my lovely little morsel, I have absolute power here. No one will come to your aid."

"Tickle her ribs!" Khristos encouraged. "She hates it."

"Shut up, Khristos!" Cassandra cried.

Locking both her wrists in the grip of one hand, Luke settled a palm at her waist. "Ticklish, are you?"

Breathless with laughter, she gazed up at him without a trace of apprehension in her lovely eyes, a fact that touched Luke as nothing else might have. Didn't she realize that this kind of play was not only inappropriate, but could easily escalate into a situation beyond her control? Luke hadn't lied. He did have absolute power in this house. If he chose, he could toss her over his shoulder, carry her upstairs, and have his way with her. No one would help her. No one would dare.

Luke settled for tickling her instead—mercilessly—until her lushly curved body went limp with exhaustion beneath him and her cheeks had gone rosy from laughter. Lycodomes, the only one who seemed to recognize a toad when he saw one, grabbed hold of Luke's boot several times and gave it

217

a violent shake. Luke was having too much fun to care.

"Have you learned your lesson?" he finally asked Cassandra.

"Yes," she said weakly.

Slowly, Luke released her, then levered himself up so she might move. It was one of the hardest things he'd ever done, for God only knew when he'd have her beneath him again. While tickling her, he'd been granted the opportunity to explore the curve of her waist, the delicate framework of her ribs, the plump underside of her breast. The contact may have seemed innocent to her, but it had been a purely carnal pastime for him, one that he longed to continue behind locked doors. Only good old Lycodomes, damn his ugly hide, seemed to have sensed the danger.

As Cassandra scrambled out from under Luke and twisted onto her knees, he regarded her well-turned backside with a lascivious gleam in his eye. With his thoughts otherwise occupied, he was, therefore, caught by surprise when something cold and dripping wet slapped him full in the face. He jerked, then just sat there for a moment, blinded by the cloth that clung tight to his features like a second skin.

"Ooooh," Khristos said with a horrified laugh. "He's really gonna git you now, Cassie. You better run!"

Luke peeled the wet rag away from one eye and peered at his recalcitrant little mistress-who-wasn't through a waxy, ammoniacal haze. She feinted, as though to make a frantic dive down the stairs, then changed directions to scramble upward. Tossing away the rag, Luke grabbed her by an ankle to halt her flight, then set himself to the business of wetting his hand and rubbing her face. While he was thus engaged, she groped blindly for the bucket, cupped her hand full of water, and flung it at his head.

From that moment forward, war was declared and the water fight was on, with Khristos and Lycodomes diving in and out of the fray, becoming as wet as the combatants, and Luke getting sharply pinched by damnable canine teeth more than once. Water on the stairs. Water on the walls. Water on the foyer floor. By the time exhaustion claimed its ultimate victory over both Luke and Cassandra, the entrance to Luke's home looked as if a gigantic rain cloud had rolled in and dumped its contents.

Weak from laughing so hard. Luke collapsed against the stairs to get his breath, Cassandra a damp little lump beside him, Khristos and Lycodomes several steps below them.

Pipps chose that moment to wade back into the foyer. He paused at the banister. "Master Taggart, sir. Are you sure there isn't a problem?"

Luke pushed up to look around. Cassandra was damp from head to toe, her sable hair hanging in wet tendrils around her flushed face. Water dripped off the oak panels above her. Glancing down at himself, Luke saw that he wasn't in much better condition.

"Does it look as if there's a problem, Pipps?"

The butler arched an eyebrow. "Not at all, sir."

"We've just been playing," Luke explained.

"Playing. Yes, sir."

"Have you an objection?"

"Not at all, sir. It's simply not your usual habit, Master Taggart, and we in the kitchen became concerned. There was a great deal of barking and screaming going on out here."

"Well, *un*concern yourselves," Luke said crisply. "Habits can change, and as you can see, I've decided to change mine. We've just been having a bit of fun."

"Fun." Pipps repeated the word as though he'd never heard it before and glanced around at the puddles of water. "I see. I apologize for the intrusion."

Luke leaned closer to the banister, lifted a drippy hand, and flicked water in the humorless butler's face. The man jerked but otherwise maintained the same expressionless countenance. "Relax a little, Pipps. If you continue to scowl like that all the time, your face will freeze that way."

The butler pivoted on his heel again and marched rigidly away. Luke gazed after him, wondering why he'd ever hired the man. No wonder he used to dread coming home. Under Pipps's rigid rule, no one in this house ever dared to smile, let alone laugh.

TWELVE

Lamplight played over the kitchen, bathing the brick walls and highly varnished oak cupboards with flickering, muted gold. Sitting astraddle a three-legged stool, Luke tried to ignore the stink of ammonia clinging to his shirt as he applied himself to his meal of ham, mashed potatoes, snap beans, and butter-rich yeast rolls. Somehow Cook had managed to keep the food warm and reasonably moist while Luke and Cassandra finished stripping wax.

Cook had looked appalled when she realized her master intended to eat his supper in the kitchen to protect the upholstery on the chairs in the other rooms. At the time, it had seemed like a good idea to Luke, but now, seated between Cassandra and Khristos at the simple oak worktable, he was having second thoughts. Cook and her fellow servants, Pipps and Mrs. Whitmire, didn't know how to react to Cassandra, who seemed to have no notion of class distinction.

"Please, Cook, won't you sit back down?" she pleaded for the second time in less than as many minutes. "I won't be able to eat a bite if you persist in standing. Come finish your tea."

Cook was a rotund, gray-haired woman with three impressive rolls of flesh at both chin and waistline. Shy and retiring, she seemed more at ease with her pots and pans than she was with people. But while she'd been in Luke's employ, he'd learned the woman had a heart as big as she was and expressed her fondness for people with the food she prepared, ever eager to please, one ear always cocked for clues as to their favorite dishes. Since Khristos's arrival, Cook had baked cookies every single day, an attempt, Luke knew, to make the boy feel welcome. Just this evening, she'd prepared pies to be taken over to the jail.

Rubbing her hands clean on her apron, the hefty woman cast Luke a nervous sideways glance, clearly uncertain of the reception she might get if she did indeed sit across from him at the worktable. Her behavior made him feel vaguely guilty. Was he such an ogre that his help felt intimidated? In truth, Luke had never given his servants' feelings about him much thought. Until Cassandra's entrance into his life, he hadn't spent much time at home. He'd found all the big, empty rooms lonely. His household staff had been peripheral to his life, people he paid well and tended to ignore unless they fell down in their duties.

"Please, Cook," Luke said, "sit down and finish your tea."

The massive servant waddled over to the stool she had vacated earlier. With a surprisingly agile twist, she planted one half of her broad backside on the seat. The stool groaned and creaked under her considerable weight. Luke sneaked a glance at Khristos, on his left. The boy was eyeing Cook with the same fascinated horror he might afford a boulder balanced atop a hill, poised to come crashing down on his head.

"There now," Cassandra said cheerfully, "isn't that better?" She glanced up at Pipps, who stood at rigid attention across the room, then at Mrs. Whitmire, who seemed to have taken root near the stove. "There's plenty of room for you two to join us as well."

"Thank you, but no, miss," Pipps replied, looking down the bridge of his nose at Cook's back with almost palpable disapproval.

"Oh, please." Popping a piece of ham into her mouth, Cassandra leaned across the butcher block and patted a spot beside Cook. "All three of you were sitting down when we came in. I feel as though we've run you off!"

Luke made a mental note to take steps in future toward being on more friendly terms with his servants. For the moment, however, he could do little but shoot the butler an eloquent glare. "Pipps?"

His usually pallid cheeks flagged with pink, Pipps stepped off the distance to the worktable and maneuvered himself onto a stool without seeming to bend at the middle. Hands folded on the butcher block before him, gaze fixed to a spot on the wall behind Luke, the man sat in rigidly silent disapproval.

"Mrs. Whitmire?" Luke glanced around Cassandra at the housekeeper. "Please, won't you join us?"

Mrs. Whitmire lowered herself onto the stool next to Pipps, her expression equally humorless. Regarding the pair as he chewed

223

a mouthful of succulent ham, Luke decided they reminded him of two mismatched bookends. It was almost as if they were afraid to let on that they were human and not automatons, the blame for which Luke laid directly on his own doorstep. The potatoes in his mouth suddenly tasted like paste, and he had difficulty swallowing. It wasn't as if he were royalty, for God's sake, yet he'd taken their deference for granted. They weren't convenient fixtures, he realized now, but individuals with thoughts and feelings.

"Now, isn't this far more pleasant?" Cassandra suddenly bounced off her stool and stepped over to the stove to fetch the teapot from the warmer. After returning to the table, she refilled Cook's teacup, a kindness that made the hefty woman look as if she'd accidentally swallowed a very large bug and was even now feeling the wiggle in her throat. "Where is your cup, Pipps?" Cassandra asked.

The butler shot Luke an imploring glance, which he ignored. "On the counter next to the sink, miss," Pipps grated in stiff tones.

Cassandra stepped over to get the cup, which she placed, filled to the brim, before Pipps's folded hands. "And yours, Mrs. Whitmire?"

"I don't take tea in the evenings," Mrs. Whitmire replied. "It makes me restless."

"Some milk, then?" Cassandra offered.

"No, thank you, miss," the housekeeper declined regally.

Cassandra put the teapot back on the warmer and returned to her seat. "It's so nice, isn't it? Getting an opportunity to chat like this, I mean."

As far as Luke could discern, no one but Cassandra seemed to be talking. He smiled slightly to himself as he cut another bite of ham, marveling that someone so artless and naive had so very much to teach him. Not about the world as he knew it, but as she saw it—a rosy, happy place where people were inherently good, and one had only to dream to make wishes come true. If given a choice, Luke decided, he'd take Cassandra's version of reality any day and cast his own to the wind.

Glancing at her sweet profile, Luke felt as if a hand was squeezing his heart. Sometimes he felt as if he were drowning in blackness, and she was a bright little candle flame that might be snuffed out at any moment. The thought made him feel vaguely frantic.

"So, Pipps," she said. "In what way, exactly, are you related to Mr. Taggart?"

"Pardon me, miss?"

Cassandra munched on a mouthful of green beans and swallowed politely before she spoke again. "Are you an uncle, a cousin?"

Pipps put up his chin. "I am a butler, miss."

"Yes, I know." Cassandra glanced inquiringly at Luke, her blue eyes warm and sparkling. "Are the Butlers on your mother's side?"

Pipps sniffed. "I am in charge of the household staff. The *butler*, miss. An employee of Mr. Taggart's. We are *not* related."

An odd expression crossed Cassandra's features. "Do you mean to say that Mr. Taggart *pays* you to stand in the foyer?"

Luke gulped back a startled laugh as he swallowed a mouthful of ham. Pipps, however, didn't seem to see the humor. "I don't just *stand* in the foyer," he corrected. "I manage the household." With that haughty proclamation, Pipps listed some of his duties.

"Imagine that, Khristos," Cassandra said with a wide-eyed glance at her brother. "Mr. Pipps does *all* of that and still manages to stand in the foyer all day to open and close the door." Cassandra smiled very sweetly. "That's amazing, Pipps. It's rather like managing to be two people at once."

For the first time in Luke's recollection, the butler looked totally nonplussed. "I don't stand in the foyer all day, miss. It only seems that way because it is my responsibility to be on hand should Mr. Taggart need me."

"In the foyer?"

Pipps cleared his throat. "Well, yes, miss. For instance, if he should require the carriage to be brought around, or need his coat, or happen to bring in guests. It is *my* job to see that all is taken care of by the staff as expeditiously and efficiently as possible."

"Hmm. So it's your job to see that everyone else does theirs?"

"Yes, miss."

"Well, little wonder you always seem to be glowering," Cassandra observed sympathetically. "It's not easy to be well-liked when it's your primary function to boss everyone else around." She reached out to pat the butler's hand. "If you should ever feel lonely, Pipps, I always enjoy a good chat."

"Thank you, miss. I shall bear that in mind."

Luke thought he glimpsed a fleeting smile on Pipps's mouth, but before he could tell for sure, the butler raised his teacup to his lips. After buttering a roll and reaching around Luke to place it on Khristos's plate, Cassandra turned her attention to Cook. "And what about you? Have you any duties here besides cooking?"

"No, miss. I supervise the kitchen help, of course, but only as it pertains to meal preparation. Mrs. Whitmire plans the meals and does the grocery orders."

Mrs. Whitmire added, "I also oversee the running of the household. Even Deirdre, who manages the upstairs maids, takes her direction from me."

"I see." Cassandra dimpled a cheek. "My goodness, I never realized how very *complicated* it all was. Which explains why it's such a pleasant place to be."

"You've enjoyed your stay thus far, then?" Cook asked.

"Oh, yes!" Cassandra replied, her face fairly beaming. She turned an adoring gaze on Luke. "Mr. Taggart has been so *wonderful* to me and my family. If not for his offering me this position, I don't know what might have become of me and Khristos." She glanced down at the dog, who napped before the stove. "Or Lycodomes, either, for that matter. We'll be forever in his debt."

Trying to conceal the disapproving twist of his mouth behind his teacup, Pipps raised one eyebrow and glanced uneasily at Luke. "Without doubt."

"Now," Cassandra said cheerfully, "if I can only just get the *specifics* of my job mastered."

The butler choked. Tea came up his nostrils and, judging by his strangled cough, went down his windpipe as well. Cassandra leaped off her stool and raced around the table to whack him on the back. "Oh, dear, are you all right?"

Tears streaming, his face tomato-red, Pipps nodded and fought for breath. "Yes, miss," he finally wheezed. "Right as rain. A bit of tea just went down the wrong way."

"Either that, or it had a bone in it," she said gaily, still patting him on the back. "Better?"

"Yes, miss, much better."

Luke hid a smile as Cassandra, who evidently had no clue that *she* had caused the poor man to strangle, came back around to her seat. "Now, then, where were we?"

Mrs. Whitmire shot Luke a glare. "I believe you were saying something about the specifics of your job."

"Oh, yes." Finished with her meal, Cassandra pushed her plate aside and cradled her teacup in her hands, both elbows propped on the butcher block. "I'm having a smidgen of difficulty understanding exactly what sorts of things Mr. Taggart wants me to do. But, otherwise, our arrangement is working out very well so far. We had a great deal of fun playing games in my bedchamber last night, at any rate, and—"

Pipps choked again. This time, Luke feared

the poor man was going to fall clear off his stool before the thumps Mrs. Whitmire dealt to his back helped him to catch his breath.

"Oh, my...I do hope you're not coming down with something," Cassandra said.

"I'm fine, miss. Really."

"I hope so, not just for your sake, but for the sake of the children at the orphanage. I have to be very cautious about colds and things like that, you know, visiting there as frequently as I do. If one child gets the sniffles, they all do, and it's incredibly hard on the good sisters trying to get them all well again."

"I didn't know you went often to the orphanage," Cook said.

"Well, I haven't been since coming here," Cassandra replied. "But if Luke continues not to require my services during the day, I'll probably start going again."

Luke felt three disapproving gazes shift his way. Cassandra seemed oblivious.

"What do you do at the orphanage?" Cook asked her.

"Anything that needs doing. I especially enjoy telling the children stories, but mostly I just work. Cleaning, usually. Or helping with the laundry. With so many children, there's a virtual mountain of it to do on any given day." Cassandra shrugged. "It's good practice for me. When Khristos turns twelve, I hope to become a nun, you see."

This revelation earned Luke startled looks from his servants, which quickly turned accusing. Luke could only marvel at how quickly Cassandra had managed to win over his servants, particularly Pipps. To his knowledge, the butler had never bent an inch or exhibited affection of any kind for anyone. Now, the man had a look on his face that put Luke very much in mind of an outraged father's.

Turning his gaze to Cassandra, Luke decided that perhaps it wasn't such a marvel, after all. She still sat there, chattering away, completely unaware of the undercurrents of tension around her, the shimmer of innocence in her eyes so obvious that only a blind man could fail to see it.

Before she caused a mutiny amongst his household staff, Luke opted to retreat. Remarking upon the hour, which was growing late, he directed Mrs. Whitmire to please see that Khristos got settled into a bedchamber on the first floor. Then he requested that a maid be sent to Cassandra's room to attend her while she bathed.

Cassandra was still chattering to Pipps as Luke ushered her from the kitchen. "What a very *nice* man he is, once you get to know him," she observed as Luke led her through the foyer. "One would never guess it, the way he scowls all the time. In fact, he reminds me a little of you."

That brought Luke's head around. "Of me? I don't scowl all the time."

"No," she agreed, "but you do sometimes, and when you do, you look ever so fierce."

"I do?"

"Very." She lifted her gaze to his, the azure depths shimmering with warmth. "I'm not afraid, though."

"Maybe you should be," he told her in a voice that had gone oddly husky. "There are a lot of people in this town who would tell you I'm not a very nice man. They might even describe me as ruthless."

As the words left his mouth, Luke wondered what had possessed him to say such a thing. Being candid about his faults had never been one of his trademarks, particularly not when being honest might weaken his hand. Cassandra, however, seemed not in the least unsettled by the revelation. Indeed, she apparently thought more highly of him for having confessed such a thing, if her radiant expression was any indication.

"Well, they're wrong," she said softly. "I know firsthand what kind of man you are, Luke Taggart, and there's only one word to describe you."

Luke was almost afraid to ask what that one word was. Her mouth curved in a particularly sweet way as she moved up the stairs with him.

"Wonderful," she whispered. "Absolutely wonderful."

This was becoming a habit, Luke thought later that night as he stalked along the hallway outside his and Cassandra's bedchambers, silently counting his strides. What was worse, the thoughts going through his head had started to remind him of a phonograph when a cylinder got stuck. *Tomorrow morning, I'll lay down the law.* Why did that have a familiar ring? *I have rights, dammit, for which I'm paying dearly, and I'm going to exercise them.* Now *there* was an original plan.

Raindrops struck the octagonal gable window at the end of the hall, lacerating his nerves like needles. He was furious with himself for being such a weakling, frustrated with Cassandra for confounding him so, and tired of wrestling with his conscience, which was quickly becoming a royal pain in the ass.

So what if the girl believed he was wonderful? If he had any brains, he'd use her naivete to his advantage. He *did* have rights, goddammit. Twenty-six thousand dollars' worth, to be exact. So what the hell was he doing, wandering up and down the hall outside her rooms like a moonstruck lad? Was he out of his mind?

Yes. A raving lunatic, that was him. Any minute now, he was going to explode. The girl had him waffling as he never had before, decisive one moment, hesitant the next, until he wasn't sure which way was up. He'd seen the maid leave Cassandra's rooms well over an hour ago, and yet here he was, pacing up and down the hall.

In all his life, Luke had never wanted anything more than he'd wanted to join Cassandra in her bathing chamber. But instead of going in, he'd hovered outside her rooms, aching with frustration, yet hesitant to destroy her high opinion of him, until he'd missed his chance. Now she was undoubtedly asleep. *Asleep,* for Christ's sake.

A picture filled his mind: pale, satiny skin flushed to a rosy glow by the steamy hot water. Soap bubbles flirting with pink nipples that were swollen with warmth and glistening with wetness. Sable hair gathered atop her head in loose curls, revealing the sensitive nape of her neck and the graceful slope of her gently rounded shoulders. A goddess in her bath, just waiting for him to claim what was his by right.

Even now, she lay in there, like a flawless pearl on a cushion of silk. Priceless and breathtakingly beautiful. Her skin, still moist from soaking in a hot tub and lightly scented with lavender, would be warm satin beneath his lips, a heady delight for him to kiss and taste and caress. He imagined pressing his body to hers, his throbbing hardness sinking slowly into a moist velvet sheath, passion-slick limbs entangled, breath coming quick and hard, hearts pounding with arousal.

Fed up, Luke strode decisively to her door and grasped the brass handle. He was going in, dammit. The devil take her luminous blue eyes. He just wouldn't look into them. Women's bodies had been his playground for nearly eighteen years. He knew where to touch Cassandra, how to use his hands and mouth to inflame her senses. He could have her trembling with need and begging him for it in ten minutes, maybe less. Afterward, he'd be happy, and she'd be—shattered.

He stood there with his hand clenched over the brass, his body straining, his mind clamoring with arguments, none of which seemed to make sense anymore. *Cassandra.* She'd turned out to be everything she'd promised to be when he first saw her, magical and warm and infectiously funny. He wanted her more now than he had in the beginning. Needed her more. Yet he knew if he satisfied that need, she'd never be quite the same again.

If he went into that room, she'd be a little fallen angel who'd lost her wings and halo by the time he finished with her. Never again would she look at him as though he'd single-handedly hung the moon. With one hard thrust of his body, he would bring her face to face with *his* world, where ugly toads out-numbered princes, and innocent young girls were fair game to lecherous, conscienceless men.

Luke relaxed his hold on the door handle and closed his eyes. *Wonderful, absolutely wonderful.*

With a low groan, he turned and planted his back against the door. Nobody had ever believed in him the way she did. Nobody. For as long as he could remember, he'd always been a lesser being, a whore's bastard as a child, a ruthless bastard as an adult. Years ago, he'd ceased to care and had begun watching out for himself. Luke Taggart, always number one, and to hell with every-body else. He'd chased a dream of striking it rich; then the dream had come true. The whore's bastard had suddenly had the world at his feet, and he'd been kicking it in the proverbial teeth ever since.

He curled his hands into throbbing fists, a vision of Cassandra's face drifting through his mind. *Those eyes.* Damn those beautiful eyes of hers. So blue. So luminous and expressive.

When she looked at him, she made him feel fine and brave and noble and kind. Not a whore's bastard, but a hero. And he liked the feeling. He liked it a lot. Which was the whole goddamned problem.

The image she had of him was like candy being dangled before a baby. He wanted to reach out and grab it and never let go. To feed off of it like a starving man. Only her vision of him was a lie, dammit—a lie that existed only inside her head. A huge, goddamned lie that not even he, the master of deceit, would be able to pull off. Sooner or later, she was going to see him for what he actually was. If he didn't do something himself to destroy the image she had of him, which would be a miracle, then her father would enlighten her the moment he got out of jail.

Hauling in a deep breath, then slowly exhaling, Luke stared into the shadows that clung to the vaulted ceiling above the foyer. *That* was his reality—shadows that always hovered, waiting to envelop him. A darkness in his soul that had been growing like a cancer all his life and had reached gargantuan proportions these last few months. When he'd seen Cassandra, she'd seemed like a beam of sunlight to him.

She'd brought the sunshine into his home, into his life. And now that he'd gotten a taste of having her with him, now that he knew how it felt to see her smile light up the gloom, he couldn't bear the thought of losing her.

That left him with few options. Knowing that it was only a matter of time until she discovered what a rotten, ruthless bastard he actually was, he had to bind her to him somehow, and the only way he knew to do that was the same way he'd originally planned—by holding her to the letter of their contract.

It was late tonight, and he knew she was exhausted after working so hard to strip the wax from the stairs. But come tomorrow night, no more waffling. She *would* share his bed. With a little luck, their coupling might even result in her getting pregnant, which would give him even more leverage over her. The long and short of it was, he couldn't let her go, not now.

Holding a shattered, fallen angel in his arms was better than no angel at all.

THIRTEEN

At precisely eight-fifteen the next morning, Luke descended the long flight of freshly waxed stairs to the first floor. Sunlight filled the downstairs with a lemony cheer. Blending with the not-unpleasant odor of wax was the tempting aroma of freshly brewed coffee and a variety of breakfast foods, the most tantalizing of which were eggs, fried bacon, and bread still hot from the oven.

Nevertheless, Luke felt sure he also smelled wet dog, even though he'd taken a bath after rising and donned fresh clothing. The foul smell seemed to have permeated everything in his bedchamber, including the clothes in his wardrobe.

And little wonder...he'd no sooner drifted to sleep last night than Khristos and Lycodomes had once again invaded his bed. The boy had been frightened, he'd told Luke, of all the things in the huge house that went *bump* and *creak* in the dark. When Luke had inquired as to why the child chose *him* as his protector instead of Cassandra, Khristos had haltingly explained that Cassandra was a puny girl, not much bigger than Khristos himself, while Luke was big enough and strong enough to keep away the haunts. Since Luke hadn't been able to think of a logical argument for that, he'd resigned himself to spending another night abed with his eight-year-old houseguest and the stinking mongrel.

To Luke's dismay, Khristos had repaid his generosity by regaling him with yet another of Cassandra's fanciful bedtime stories, once again about a charming young man who rescued a lovely damsel, then carried her off into the sunset to live with him in marital bliss, happily ever after. Luke knew better. Bliss was just another word for sex, a hard truth Luke intended to set before Cassandra posthaste. In about ten minutes, to be precise.

As Luke crossed the foyer, he found himself following a trail of muddy paw prints that led over the burgundy tile to the kitchen door at the rear of the house. Along one wall, there was a smear of mud where the huge beast had evidently lain down after coming in wet and muddy from outdoors. Damn, but his house was beginning to look like a dog kennel. Worse, it was starting to smell like one.

Today, Luke vowed. This very morning he would speak to his man of affairs. The instant he got to his office. By sundown Lycodomes would be out of his house for good. Gone, and good riddance. Because Cassandra loved the mongrel so much, Luke would order his man to find the dog a good home—somewhere far away from Black Jack, preferably—but there his magnanimity ended.

Cassandra would be distressed for a few days, of course, but she'd get over it. Perhaps, Luke mused, he would buy her a kitten to replace the mongrel. Or possibly even a very *small* dog. Something she could lavish her affection on, that wouldn't completely destroy his home.

When Luke reached the open doorway of the breakfast room, he paused on the threshold to admire the lovely sight that greeted him. Cassandra sat alone at the table. To his amusement, she seemed to be fascinated by his rose-patterned, gilt-edged china and was holding a delicately made teacup up to the light, turning it slowly to admire the intricately painted flowers. Luke supposed that everything in his house seemed impossibly luxurious to her.

Everything but the wildly expensive wardrobe he'd purchased for her, that is. This morning, beneath his blasted and ever-present shirt, she wore a lovely yellow day dress, the color of which rivaled the sunlight pouring in through the white lace curtains. Indeed, she resembled a creation made of sunlight, with the beams glistening in the artless sable curls piled atop her head and the pale yellow walls around her reflecting the warm glow.

Leaning a shoulder against the door frame, he took a moment to study her. Soon, he promised himself, he would have to relent and take her to the dressmaker, whose orders to create a custom-made wardrobe for her were temporarily on hold. Cassandra obviously wasn't going to wear any of the revealing gowns he'd bought her without a shirt over them, and he was becoming heartily sick of being denied the pleasure of admiring her lovely shape. Even in a modestly designed dress, he'd be able to see the swell of her breasts, the indentation of her waist, and the tempting flare of her hips.

A sardonic smile curved his firm mouth. A nun? Every time he pictured this girl swathed from head to toe in black wool with rosary beads dangling from her waist, he wanted to laugh. She was absolutely unsuited for the role, far too enamored with material things, for one, and too exquisitely lovely, for another. She'd been made for a male's carnal enjoyment, every curve of her body begging to be possessed. She'd see a narrow, hard cot in a nun's cell over his dead body.

"Good morning," he said softly.

She gave a startled jump and turned slightly on the chair to fasten surprised blue eyes on him. A radiant smile curved her temptingly full mouth as she carefully returned the cup to its saucer. "Oh, Luke! Good morning! I've been waiting for you."

He strode slowly into the room. The sideboard

to his right was laden with food, which made him wonder why she hadn't helped herself. "You should have gone ahead without me. Sometimes of a morning, I take coffee in my suite and enjoy my solitude while I read the paper."

She lifted a shoulder, which looked amazingly small within the generous folds of his silk shirt. "With all those little candles burning under the serving dishes, nothing is likely to get cold."

Luke reached her chair and bent to press a kiss on her forehead. "Those are called 'warmers,'" he explained. Reaching to the opposite end of the table, he grabbed his plate. "I don't know about you, but I'm starving. Let's dish up. Then we'll visit over breakfast."

She got her plate and followed him to the sideboard, velvet and silk whispering around her like a sensual promise. "Have you ever wondered why we pronounce it '*break*fast'?" she asked. "The word was derived way back in the olden days, you know, because people considered the stretch of time between evening and morning meals a fast, and when they finally ate, they were breaking it."

A self-educated man, Luke had had enough trouble learning to spell without investigating word origins. "Really?" He considered for a moment. "It makes sense, I guess. Let's break our fast then, why don't we?"

He piled creamy scrambled eggs, crisp bacon, and fried diced potatoes onto his plate while Cassandra took samples of the less traditional fare: eggs slathered in a French cheese sauce, stuffed mushrooms, fruit custard, and buttery croissants. She glanced at his plate, then plopped a spoonful of mushrooms beside his potatoes.

"Don't be boring."

Boring? Luke prided himself on trying everything at least once, sometimes twice, perverted sexual exploits notwithstanding. Yet he laughed in spite of himself. If there was one thing he could count on from Cassandra, it was that she never seemed intimidated by him. "I've never managed to acquire a rich man's palate. Cook keeps trying to tempt me, but—" He shrugged. "When I grew up, if I was lucky enough to eat, I had plain food, and I still lean heavily toward the ordinary at mealtime."

Shadows crept into her lovely eyes. "You went hungry? When you were a boy, I mean?"

Luke hadn't intended to divulge that morsel of information. He felt heat creeping up his neck. "I told you I once lived in the mining district, and to me, the shack I rented there was a pretty fancy place. Before living in the mining district, I guess you might say I saw some very lean times."

"You did go hungry," she summarized.

"Sometimes." Uncomfortable with the pity that shone in her gaze, Luke grabbed a piece of toast and returned to the table, where he busied himself pouring them each a cup of coffee. "Don't feel sorry for me, Cassandra. As you can see, I survived quite nicely."

She took her place opposite him, her luminous

241

eyes still aching with sympathy. "It can't have been easy. When I imagine Khristos going hungry—well, it nearly breaks my heart."

Still intensely uneasy, Luke swallowed a mouthful of egg. He resembled her little brother about as much as a stone resembled a pussy-willow catkin. He snorted at the very idea.

"Do I look like I went hungry?" he challenged, narrowing his gaze.

A twinkle of laughter crept into her eyes. "I suppose not. You're rather large, and—" Her gaze dropped to his shoulders, then to his chest, and a becoming flush colored her cheeks. "Well, there is quite a *lot* of you, here and there."

Here and there, there was quite a lot of her as well. Luke studiously avoided looking at the twin mounds of luscious female flesh that filled out the front of his shirt. It was enough to know she wasn't physically unaffected by him, that the sizzling attraction he felt for her with his every waking breath and sometimes in his sleep was reciprocated. "Cassandra, we have to have another talk. About your duties here."

Her face fell and she fixed her gaze on a mushroom, which she chased around her plate with the wrong fork. Luke felt the corners of his mouth trying to curve upward and relentlessly tamped down the smile. "Cassandra, the smaller fork placed to the outside is for salad and stuff. You use the larger one for your main course."

A little frown drew her delicately arched

eyebrows together. "Really?" She glanced at the sideboard. "There isn't any salad."

"Yes, well...the staff puts out a full place setting, regardless. Sometimes, there's an even littler fork, for hors d'oeuvres."

"For *or what*??"

"Hors d'oeuvres," he repeated with a chuckle. "It's a French word, I believe, meaning little appetizers served before your meal. Shelled crustaceans in sauces...tasty little things, usually, served in a small dish. You'll get it all down eventually. Watch other people; then follow their example." He inclined his head at her napkin, which still lay in an undisturbed, decorative fold beside her plate. "You should also spread that over your lap."

"My lap? Whatever for? I thought it was to wipe with."

"It is. But it's also to catch any drips from your eating utensils, and proper etiquette demands you unfold it and spread it over your knees before you start to eat."

"My *knees*?" She rolled her eyes. "Rich people must be very sloppy eaters."

Luke laughed again, realizing that he'd gotten completely sidetracked, which happened a lot when he was with her. He observed her as she dutifully placed her napkin over her lap, a movement that drew back her shoulders momentarily and thrust her breasts forward. The silk front of his shirt clung to the upper swells of bared flesh underneath, tying his gut into aching knots.

Luke cleared his throat. "As I was saying...about your duties?"

She lifted a hand. "Tonight, Luke, I promise not to disappoint you. I was thinking of starting on the lamps, if that will be all right."

He shook his head. "I didn't bring you here to clean for me or to play chess with me, Cassandra."

Her eyes filled with bewilderment. "Then what am I supposed to do? So far, I've done nothing to earn my wages, save for stripping the wax, and correct me if I'm wrong, but I don't think you wanted that done."

"Do you remember my telling you last night that some people say I'm a very ruthless man?"

She nodded.

Luke hauled in a deep breath. "Well, in all honesty, I'm that and more. I brought you here for purely nefarious reasons, Cassandra. Do you understand what 'nefarious' means?"

Again, she nodded. "Wicked," she said faintly.

"That's right, wicked." He stabbed his fork into his eggs, the tines clinking against the china. When he swung his gaze back up to hers, he looked deeply into her eyes, hardening himself to the vulnerability he saw there. "I want to be intimate with you—in every way. I'm not paying you this astronomical wage so we can have a casual friendship. I want an *intimate* relationship, the kind that will raise the eyebrows of decent folks. In the contract you signed, you agreed to be intimate with me in that way. Legally, you're committed, and I intend to hold you to that. Do you understand?"

The color had washed from her face. "I believe so, yes."

Luke could tell by the appalled look in her eyes that he had indeed finally gotten through to her. "Tonight I have a meeting, and I'll miss supper. When I do get home, I expect you to be waiting for me in your bedchamber. You will be appropriately attired and prepared to be intimate with me. Is that absolutely clear? You will not wear my robe over your nightgown. I would like you to arrange for the maids to bring up wine and candlesticks, so we can create the right mood. No more chess. Any games we play will be of an extremely *intimate* nature. If the thought of that embarrasses you, I'm sorry. But that's what I'm paying for, and that's what I will have. Any questions?"

When she shook her head, Luke leaned back in his chair and tossed down his fork. He couldn't quite bring himself to meet her gaze again, fearful of what he would surely see there. The girl who believed in magic and fairy tales had just had a headlong collision with reality.

"I can't say I'm sorry for wanting you the way I do," he finally managed to say in a voice that had gone oddly gravelly. "In many ways, you weren't wrong in your assessment of me. I'm a very lonely man, and I need someone like you in my life. It's as simple as that."

Luke threw his napkin on his plate and abruptly shoved back his chair. "As I said, I have a busy day planned, so expect me to come in late tonight. Be waiting for me, as

245

instructed." At the door, he hesitated, still keeping his gaze averted from hers. "No nonsense, Cassandra. From this point on, consider yourself on the same plane as Pipps and Mrs. Whitmire, with specific duties to perform. I'll be patient with you while you grow accustomed to your new role, but only to a point."

With that, he exited the breakfast room, so anxious to escape her presence that he all but bolted.

For a long while, Cassandra simply sat there, staring at her untouched breakfast, Luke's words circling endlessly in her mind. When she could bear the sordid implications no longer, she closed her eyes, but even that didn't shut out the whispers. *Intimate with me.* She knew what that meant—vaguely, anyway. Her papa being the sort of parent he was, she'd not been directly exposed to what he called the "seedy aspects of life," but neither was she completely ignorant. She knew that married couples shared a special kind of love that produced babies, and that that special kind of love was frequently referred to as "marital intimacy."

Only she and Luke weren't married. They weren't even engaged! And he'd understood from the first that she hoped to one day become a nun. That being the case, how could he possibly expect her to be that kind of "intimate" with him? Did he plan to marry her? Was that it? Or did he want to exercise those sorts of privileges without marrying her?

The very idea appalled her. She was a good Catholic girl, and once every two weeks, she went to confession. How would she explain such behavior to Father Tully? Even worse, how would she ever get into a convent if she engaged in such activities? Not that she was entirely sure that becoming a nun was even what she wanted anymore. Since meeting Luke, she wasn't sure about much of anything.

Just as Luke had done earlier, Cassandra left her meal untouched and fled upstairs to her rooms. Once inside, she leaned against the door with her eyes closed, trying desperately to sort out all that he had said. The Luke Taggart she knew and the one she'd just seen downstairs were entirely different men, one kind and gentle, the other relentless and...and frightening.

Panic was beginning to well in Cassandra's chest when she took a firm grip on her thoughts and began to scoff at herself for even entertaining the notion that Luke would demand such things from her. He'd been kindness itself ever since she'd come here. She was doing him an injustice and a great disservice by even thinking this way.

She had misunderstood him, that was all. The word "intimate" had several different meanings. She would think the best and not let this shake her faith in him until he proved her wrong. That was how her papa had raised her—to believe in people and always give them the benefit of the doubt.

Yes, that's exactly what she would do, she told herself, squaring her shoulders. After all,

Luke was her protector. And Khristos's too. He had to be. Until her papa and Ambrose got out of jail, there was no one else.

"I want that damned dog out of my house," Luke said succinctly. "Take him a goodly distance away—preferably to another town—and find a good home for him."

Donald Brummel, who'd been taking notes on Luke's instructions for the day, laid down his pen and sat back in his chair. "Luke, have you considered just disposing of the beast? Finding a home for a child is one thing, but for that *dog*? I can't work miracles, you know."

Distracted, his thoughts darting back and forth, then doing circles, Luke shoved a hand through his hair. "I take it you found a place for Tigger?"

"Don't I always?" Donald sighed. "I contacted Father Tully and, through him, located a childless couple who live at the edge of town, have a little farm. As I understand it, they're interested in adopting Tigger's little brother and sister as well."

"That's great," Luke said, but without much enthusiasm, although he truly was glad. "I can always count on you." He leveled a meaningful look at his man of affairs. "I'm sure, if you work at it, you can find a solution to my dog dilemma as well."

"Yes, well, as I was saying, the animal's not exactly a prime specimen with all that hair missing on one side. And that's not to mention the rest of him is shaggy, dirty, and beyond ugly. How in the world can you expect me to find a decent home for him, Luke? Who in his right mind will want him?"

Luke kicked back in his leather office chair and planted his crossed feet on the polished surface of his mahogany desk. He settled his gaze on Brummel. "Use your imagination. Pay someone handsomely to take him in, if you must. All I care about is getting rid of the damned mongrel. He's a nuisance." Eyeing a mark on the side of his boot left by one of Lycodomes's teeth the previous night, Luke scratched behind his ear, then began to wonder if he had fleas crawling on him. The thought made him shudder. "He's single-handedly destroying my house. Mud everywhere, not to mention the stink. Damn animal's as big as a horse."

Brummel picked up his pen. "Have I carte blanche? I don't want you blistering my ears for paying too much to get the animal settled somewhere."

Luke raised an eyebrow. "I don't care what it costs; just get him out of town. And, for God's sake, whatever you do, don't let Cassandra or her little brother see you taking him."

"It would be far simpler just to shoot him."

Luke had considered that, and the embarrassing truth was, he couldn't bring himself to issue the order. Though he detested the flea-bitten mongrel, he knew Cassandra and Khristos loved him. For that reason, and that reason alone, Luke knew he wouldn't be able to look himself in his shaving mirror every morning if he did the animal any harm. Just removing the dog from the area was going to plague his conscience badly enough.

Conscience...Luke fixed his gaze on the white plaster wall opposite him. Lately, that word had begun to slip into his thoughts with alarming frequency. He shifted his gaze to an oil painting at the center of the wall, which happened to be one of his favorites, a restful depiction of a wildflower-strewn field with an aspen-lined brook meandering through the grass. Sometimes, when the tension of cutthroat business negotiations got to him, he could gaze at that painting and separate himself from reality for a moment, which was usually enough to calm him. This morning it didn't work.

Suddenly the door to his office crashed open. Reflexes sharpened by years on the streets brought Luke shooting to his feet, fists knotted, body braced to spring. He felt a little silly when he saw that the intruder was Cassandra, whose height barely cleared the strike plate of the door lock by two feet.

Before he could gather his composure, she gave a shrill cry and came flying across the room. Luke spread his arms in the nick of time, catching her against his chest as she launched herself at him. He fell back a step under the impact of her slight weight, then tightened his arms around her, vaguely aware that she'd traded his shirt for a waist-length burgundy cloak he'd bought for her.

"Luke! Oh, Luke!" She let loose with a string of sobs that nearly broke his heart. "Th-they sent me a-a-way! Th-they said I'm n-not fit c-company f-for the ch-children!"

Surprise mushroomed to full-blown rage

within Luke so suddenly that it took him off guard. "Who said that to you?" He tightened his embrace, wanting to throttle the sons of bitches. "Who, sweetheart?"

"The s-sister-rrs! They don't w-want me th-there anymore!"

The nuns...Luke closed his eyes as understanding dawned. He'd known the rumors would come home to roost eventually, of course, and that the self-righteous citizens of Black Jack would begin to snub her. But he'd never expected the *nuns* to turn on her. What about Christian forgiveness and all that other bullshit they were constantly preaching?

Cassandra leaned against him, her sobs so deep and tearing, he was afraid she might hurt herself. *Christ.* He'd never dreamed she would get this upset. The women he'd kept company with in the past had taken the low opinion of others in stride.

"Oh, sweetheart..."

"They say it's be-because I'm y-your paid com-companion. Even th-though they love me and und-understand I h-had no choice but to take c-care of myself and Khristos in any w-way I could, they c-can't allow me to be around the innocent ch-children anymore. Wh-why, Luke? Why would they say that? I'm no dif-different now than I w-was. Just living in a dif-different h-house."

"No," he agreed softly, beginning to sway with her in a rocking motion. "Of course, you're no different, honey. Not a bit. It's all right, sweet. Shhh...it's all right. I'm here."

Going up on her tiptoes, she wrapped both

arms around his neck and clung to him as though he were the only solid fixture in her world. Luke shifted his arms to lift her against him, trying to absorb the body-shaking force of her sobs.

As he rocked her, he noticed Brummel studying her backside with a lustful gleam in his eye. Even with the waist-length cloak to conceal its suggestive lines, the gown she wore was revealing from there down, the clingy material lacking the usual flounces and layers of petticoats to camouflage her shape. Luke shot a glare at his employee. The man leaped up from his chair and made a hasty retreat, mumbling something about paperwork.

Watching the door close behind him, Luke decided that Cassandra had been right; he had to get her another wardrobe, and quickly. He didn't want other men ogling her.

As for Cassandra's not being able to work at the orphanage, Luke had very little to say. "Honey, sometimes people say hurtful things they don't mean. They're just narrow-minded, that's all, and cruel. Anyone who says you're not the same sweet girl you always were is mis-informed. We'll get this straightened out, I promise you. The sisters will let you work at the orphanage."

They would allow it, Luke vowed, because even nuns could be bought if the offer was right. If he laid enough money on the table, they'd let every whore at the Golden Slipper visit the orphans, and smile while they were at it. The hypocritical bitches.

Luke pressed his cheek to her hair and breathed in the heady scent of lavender, which called to mind visions of Gloria in a black pinafore. He made up his mind to get Cassandra her own bath salts and perfume, something with a light rose scent to better suit her innocence. When he held her close like this, he wanted no memories of his sordid past intruding.

A wave of regret such as he'd never experienced washed over him. God help him, he'd never meant for her to be hurt like this, never dreamed the pain would cut her this deep. He was so accustomed to people looking down their noses at him, even while showing him obsequious respect, that he scarcely noticed anymore. At some point in his life, he had cared, and cared deeply, but somewhere along the line, he'd developed a skin so thick it no longer hurt.

A sudden memory slammed into him. At about seven years of age, he'd decided one Sunday morning that he wanted to attend Sunday school like the other children did. Shortly after his arrival at the church, he'd been tossed out on his ear by an irate minister who'd called him "the spawn of Satan." Luke could still remember the hurt and shame of that, which had quickly turned to scorn for Christianity. It was a scorn he harbored to this day.

Oh, yes...he understood the pain Cassandra was feeling, and he was as outraged in her defense as he'd once been for himself. Heads were going to roll, wimples or no.

Even as the thought ricocheted through his head, Luke knew he wasn't being entirely fair. The nuns had a reputation to uphold, and fallen women frequenting the orphanage threatened that. Ultimately, the head that should roll was his own, for he'd caused this. In his single-minded lust for this girl, he'd destroyed her good name.

What was done was done. Luke knew there was very little he could do now to fix things. Her reputation was in tatters, and it would remain in tatters. His only option was to take her mind off what the nuns had said to her.

For several minutes he simply stood there, holding her until her weeping had turned to occasional sniffles. Then he said, "You know what I think we ought to do?"

"No, what?" she asked thinly.

"I think we should go shopping and buy you some new dresses. Would you like that?"

In a muffled voice totally lacking enthusiasm, she said, "I guess."

Luke worked a hand between their bodies to grasp her chin. When he turned her face up, her large blue eyes reminded him of drenched velvet. "Sweetheart, please, don't let those silly old women make you sad."

The corners of her mouth turned down and her chin quivered. "It's just—" She hauled in a shaky breath and gulped. "They used to be my friends. And now they're not. All because I'm living at your house. They think I'm wicked now, don't they?"

Luke couldn't bring himself to answer

that. "You don't have a wicked bone in your entire body."

"Then why did they send me away?"

Luke wanted to say he had no idea, but since meeting this girl, lies didn't spring to his tongue quite as easily as they once had. He fell back on evasion. "I really think we should go shopping and forget what they said. Things always look better once you've stepped back from them a bit and given yourself time to calm down. I understand from Khristos that you've had your eye on those patent leather slippers in Miss Dryden's dress shop window. What say we go buy them?"

She wrinkled her nose. "I guess."

Luke felt out of his depth. He'd never met a woman yet who didn't brighten at the thought of going shopping. "Just think, sweet. Anything you want. The sky's the limit. I'll buy you a dozen of the prettiest, most costly dresses in town." Her glum expression didn't change. "And all the accessories. Shoes, hats." She still looked sad. "And how about some jewelry? Every lovely woman should have diamonds. Have you ever owned a real diamond?"

"No."

"Then let's go shopping!"

"Oh, but Luke, you've already spent a small fortune on me, and you never returned any of those things. I can't let you buy more."

He narrowed an eye at her and assumed a teasing scowl. "Pardon me, but you and whose army intend to stop me? You can't go around in dresses without fronts."

255

She glanced worriedly over her shoulder. "Shhh. Someone will hear."

He lowered his voice. "Give me any argument, and I'll shout it to the rooftops."

She sniffed again and worked one hand from around his neck to dry her cheeks. "What I really want most, I'm afraid you can't buy, Luke." Fresh tears filled her eyes. "The sisters were my friends. And now I've lost them."

"Nonsense. I'll iron that out, you'll see. Soon you'll be back with the children, telling them stories. Now stop this crying. You're going to make your pretty eyes all red."

She sniffed and swiped, then fluttered her lashes. "I'm sorry. I don't mean to be a bawling baby. It just hurt my feelings, that's all."

Despite her attempts to brighten, there were still shadows of sadness in her eyes when she looked back up at him. He drew his handkerchief from his pocket and dabbed at her face. Her eyelashes clung together in long, black spikes, making it appear as if someone had drawn stars around her eyes.

"Better?" she asked as he returned the handkerchief to his pocket.

"Perfect," he whispered, and meant it, though he was setting himself to the task of straightening her hair even as he spoke.

When all the necessary repairs to her appearance had been done, Luke tucked her hand over the crook of his arm and led her from his office. Brummel glanced up from his desk to nod farewell, careful this time to keep his eyes where they belonged.

As they exited the brick office building onto the cobblestone sidewalk, Luke heard a familiar bark and glanced up to see Lycodomes at the opposite side of the busy street. At the sight of Cassandra, the huge dog gave a joyful *woof!* and bounded forward.

He was heading directly into the path of an oncoming wagon.

FOURTEEN

For an instant that seemed years long, Luke couldn't react while details were imprinted on his brain like hot iron on leather. Lycodomes, legs churning, tongue lolling, his soulful brown eyes fixed on his mistress as he bounded happily toward her. Horses' hooves flashing. A heart-stopping blur of gold and white fur, tumbling and going down under those dangerous, thrashing feet. The wagon wheel spokes spiraling in a dizzying circle. Cassandra screaming. Then an awful, bone-shattering crunch and the dull *whump* of flesh being sandwiched between iron wheels and stone.

Luke found his legs then and broke into a run, hearing Cassandra's heartbroken shrieks behind him and the dog's pathetic cries ahead of him as he shoved through the crowd of people that had already started to form. Shopkeepers in white aprons, women out to do their marketing in walking suits and flowery little hats with veils, children too young to attend school. The colors of their garments swam together in a blur that made

Luke feel as if he were plunging through a garishly bright rainbow.

The horses, panicked by all the noise, began to rear, whinnying and striking the air with their hooves. At the edges of his benumbed mind, Luke knew it would be only a matter of seconds before the animals bolted if the driver couldn't get them under control.

When Luke finally reached the wagon, he found Lycodomes lying crumpled behind one of the wheels, his right back leg badly mangled. Blood seemed to be everywhere. Knowing that the driver of the wagon would not be able to hold his team much longer, Luke grabbed the dog by its front shoulders and dragged him away from the treacherous wheels, knowing even as he did that it was a wasted effort.

"Lye-Lye!" Cassandra cried. "Oh, Lye-Lye!"

Luke caught Cassandra just as she would have dropped to her knees beside her pet. Clamping a hand over the back of her head, he spun her toward him and pressed her face against his chest. Struggling for calm, which had always come easily to him in a crisis, he glanced around, feeling, for the first time in his life, like a panicked fox searching for a bolt-hole. He didn't want to deal with this. *Jesus.* Why did it have to be Cassandra's dog? Why not some homeless mongrel nobody cared about?

A man in the crowd said, "You'll have to put him down, Taggart. With the leg busted up like that, there's nothing else to do."

Luke felt the jolt that ran through Cassandra. "Easy, honey," he soothed, tightening his arms around her trembling body. Holding her fast, he gazed over the top of her dark head at Lycodomes, his emotions in a tangle and his gut knotted. The way he saw it, he had two choices. He could do the dirty work himself, or he could take the coward's way out and let someone else take care of it.

"A gun," Luke said softly when he met the gaze of a nearby shopkeeper. "Get me a gun, please, so I can put him out of his misery."

"No!" Cassandra struggled against his embrace and finally wrested her face free. "No! You can't! Please, Luke, no!"

"I've got a revolver right here," said a brawny miner with saddened blue eyes and a beard the color of cinnamon, as he stepped forward out of the crowd. "The chambers are all full." He glanced down at the dog, who was whining pathetically with pain. "Want me to do it, Mr. Taggart, sir? It might come easier for me, not knowin' the dog and all."

Luke handed Cassandra into the keeping of Mr. Wilson, owner of the dry goods store, who had just shouldered his way through the throng. Then he turned to the miner and held out a hand for the weapon. "No, I'll do it. He deserves that much, having a friend do it."

A friend? Luke's stomach lurched. Some friend he'd been, plotting the dog's disappearance. Maybe there was a God, after all...a cruel trickster who manipulated events to teach people a lesson. *Be careful what you*

259

wish for. You just might get it. How many times had he heard that saying? And ignored it.

What a fool he'd been. He'd wanted Lycodomes out of his house...and he was getting his wish.

The portly driver of the wagon had finally managed to calm the frantic team, which was now standing nervously in the traces. Tying off the reins and setting the brake, the teamster jumped down from the wagon and turned to Luke. "Damn, I'm sorry about this. He ran right out in front of me. I tried to stop, but there wasn't time."

"These things happen," someone said. "I saw it. There was no way you could have stopped, man, so don't be blaming yourself."

These things happen. The words hung in Luke's brain. As he closed his hand around the cold butt of the revolver, Cassandra broke away from Mr. Wilson and dropped to her knees beside her dog. With a sob, she lifted Lycodomes's head onto her lap. Knowing what he had to do, Luke stood over her, his jaw clenched. He gave her a moment to say her good-byes before he finally spoke.

"Cassandra," he said gently. "Sweetheart, he's in pain. The sooner we end it, the better for him."

She lifted tear-filled eyes to his, and guilt sliced through him.

"Please, Luke, please," she said, each word shuddering from her slender throat on the crest of a sob. "We have to try to save him. We can't just shoot him without even trying."

"Sweetheart, he's hurting bad, real bad. It wouldn't be a kindness to wait any longer to put him out of his misery."

The miner who'd lent Luke the gun stepped forward and grasped Cassandra gently by the shoulders. "Come, lass. You come along with old Mike, eh?"

As the miner drew Cassandra to her feet, she kept her gaze fixed on Luke. The pain in her eyes made him feel physically sick. This wasn't the kind of hurt that would pass in an hour or so. She *loved* that stinking dog. Not lightly. Not offhandedly. But with all her heart.

Love was a word Luke had grown to despise, for with its utterance had come the most nightmarish experience of his life, an experience he had shelved in the darkest recesses of his mind, the memories of which he couldn't face, not even in the stark light of day.

And yet...looking at Cassandra's stricken face, he could no longer deny that love did exist. At least for some.

With remarkable gentleness for so large a man, the miner led Cassandra away so she wouldn't witness what was about to happen. Luke gazed after her a moment to be sure she wasn't going to twist free again and run back. Then, feeling defeated, he returned his attention to Lycodomes.

His hand tightening around the butt of the pistol, he knelt beside the dog and pressed the barrel against the animal's temple. Almost as if he understood Luke's intent, Lycodomes whined and nudged Luke's knee, his liquid brown eyes filled with silent pleading.

Luke tightened his finger over the trigger. This had to be done. All he had to do was pull the goddamned trigger.

His arm began to tremble; then his hand started to shake. He strained to draw back on the firing mechanism, but for the life of him, he couldn't do it. Not with those soulful brown eyes staring up at him.

"Dammit, Lycodomes," he whispered. "Don't look at me like that."

The dog continued to implore him. It was absurd, of course, but Luke could almost believe the animal was trying to communicate with him. *Don't shoot me. Please, don't shoot me.*

"Quick and clean," Mr. Wilson urged from somewhere behind Luke. "I know it's hard, but you've got to do it. The poor thing's suffering."

Luke swallowed and tightened his finger on the trigger again. *We have to try to save him. We can't just shoot him without even trying.*

"You want me to do it?" Wilson asked.

Luke relaxed his hold on the gun, knowing even as he did that every man in the crowd was going to think him a spineless coward. He didn't care. Chances were, the dog couldn't be saved, and Luke had never been a man to play against bad odds. But this wasn't a goddamned poker game where the only thing at stake was a pile of money, either.

The revolver dangling in his lax hold, Luke assessed Lycodomes's injuries more closely. He knew next to nothing about dogs, but he'd seen plenty of men get hurt when he'd been working in the mining tunnels. Small cave-ins. Toppling ore carts. Wet nitro on men's boots, detonated by sparks from pickaxes glancing off stone. More times than he could count, Luke had helped carry another miner from a tunnel, convinced with every step that the man's injuries were so severe, he couldn't possibly survive, only to see the fellow return to work a few weeks later. Sometimes injuries looked worse than they actually were.

He pushed decisively to his feet and handed the revolver to Wilson. "I need someone to help me carry him," he said as he peeled off his jacket.

"Carry him?" Wilson repeated. "If you don't have the heart to do it, Mr. Taggart, step aside and I'll finish him for you."

Luke shot the shopkeeper a searing glare as he spread his jacket on the ground beside Lycodomes. "I need a volunteer. He's busted up too bad for me to carry him myself."

The miner who had led Cassandra away shouldered a path back through the crowd. "I'll help you."

"It's cruel, if you ask me," some woman said. "Better to put the poor thing out of its misery."

Luke saw Cassandra pushing through the crowd behind the miner. When her gaze found Luke's, adoration blazed in her eyes, making his heart catch. In that moment, Luke knew he'd made the right decision. If there was no hope for the dog, so be it. But before he made that call, he had to know for sure.

Shaking his head, Mr. Wilson handed the

miner's gun back to him. "If you ask me, you're just prolonging the inevitable, Taggart. Nothing short of a miracle will save that dog, and you know it."

"I'm not asking," Luke bit out. "Just move back out of our way, please. We need some room here."

After shoving the revolver into its holster, the stocky miner crouched down beside the dog. "He's liable to bite when we try to lift him, Mr. Taggart."

Luke hunkered near Lycodomes's head. "I'll take the biting end, just in case. It's going to hurt like hell when you touch his hindquarters. Be as careful as you can."

The miner nodded. "Once we get him onto the jacket, I think we can lift him without jostling him too much."

Luke slipped one arm under Lycodomes's shoulders, using his other hand to support the dog's head. The position brought Luke's face within easy snapping distance of the animal's teeth. He envisioned himself with half a nose or a badly scarred cheek, then shoved the thought away. Lycodomes wouldn't bite him. Why Luke believed that, he wasn't sure, but he would have bet his last dollar on it.

Lycodomes whined pitifully as Luke and the miner lifted him between them. "I'm sorry, boy," Luke whispered. "Hold tight."

Relief washed over Luke when the dog was finally positioned on the coat. At least that much was over. Cassandra dropped to her knees beside Luke. With a trembling hand, she lightly stroked her dog's muzzle.

"I'm here, Lye-Lye. It's going to be all right. You'll see."

Looking down at her, Luke realized she truly believed he was going to work some kind of miracle and save her dog. What was worse, Luke wished with all his heart he could. He couldn't bear to see her cry.

There was no veterinarian in Black Jack, so Luke directed the miner to head for the doctor's office up the street. The sidewalk was narrow, so Cassandra walked in the gutter along the curb to stay abreast of them, her skirt gathered in her hands to keep the hem from trailing in the water. Her worried gaze seldom strayed from Lycodomes, which resulted in her stumbling more than once, when she encountered drainage grates.

"I really don't think it's a good idea for you to be wading through that muck," Luke told her once. "Why don't you just walk behind us?"

"I'm fine, Luke. Honestly."

Luke could tell by her pallor that she was too upset to be thinking clearly, but he refrained from arguing with her. Carrying the dog between them, it was slow going for the two men. They had to walk sideways, and with every step, it became more difficult to keep a good grip on the jacket.

"He's a heavy one," the miner said with a grunt as they crossed an alleyway and stepped up onto the next curb. "A hundred and twenty pounds, if he weighs an ounce, I'll wager."

Luke had to agree. His jacket was barely large enough to serve as a litter. To Lycodomes's credit, he didn't so much as snarl, even though the jostling had to be causing him a great deal of pain.

Doctor Mosley's practice was located a block north. By the time they reached the brown clapboard building, Luke's arms were beginning to cramp, and he noticed that the miner wasn't faring much better. The man's face had turned florid, and he was heaving for breath. Cassandra ran ahead of them to open the door, a bell overhead jangling loudly to herald their arrival. The smell of disinfectant and ether assailed Luke's nostrils as he and the other man maneuvered the huge dog through the doorway.

Luke scanned the dim interior of the waiting area with one sweeping glance. Three metal-framed chairs with sagging leather cushions took up one wall; a battered bookcase stood opposite them, with a collection of paintings—all garish and poorly done—arranged haphazardly around it. Luke nodded toward a door adjacent to the bookcase.

"Through there, I think."

Cassandra scurried around them to open the door. Just as she reached for the knob, the portal swung open and Doctor Mosley stepped out. A plump, bald little man with a shining pate, spectacles that flashed like mirrors, and a tidily trimmed gray beard, he looked like a fat penguin in the black trousers and vest he wore over a crisply starched white shirt.

Upon spying the bleeding, badly injured dog, the doctor hooked his thumbs in his belt loops and rocked back on his heels, peering up at Luke as if he were a lunatic. "You can turn right around and go back out the way you came in, Taggart. I don't treat animals."

Luke glanced at Cassandra. "Honey, you wait out here for a minute. All right?"

At her nod of agreement, Luke shouldered his way past the pompous little doctor, and the miner executed a clumsy sidestep to keep pace. The room they entered was dim, the only illumination being a few feeble rays of sunlight that came through a high, two-foot-square window. Shelves filled with bottles of every conceivable color and size lined the walls. An examining table occupied center stage, its worn leather upholstery permanently depressed where countless patients had lain.

"Don't you dare put that filthy dog on my table!" Mosley cried.

The doctor's tone made Luke's temper rise. Working in tandem with the miner, he gently laid his whining, bloody burden on the well-padded table, then turned to retrace his steps. After motioning the miner back out into the waiting room with Cassandra, he softly closed the door so she wouldn't overhear what was said, then pivoted toward the doctor.

"Back off, Mosley."

"Now wait just a minute—"

"Since we don't have a vet in these parts yet, I'll make it worth your trouble. Just name your price."

Raising his eyebrows high above the rims of his spectacles, Mosley puckered his lips, which, surrounded by gray beard, reminded Luke of the south end of a northbound jackass. "I don't treat dogs, Taggart."

"You do now."

Mosley sighed and shook his head. "You don't understand. I know next to nothing about dogs. If I try to treat the poor thing, I may make matters worse instead of better."

"He's going to die if you don't, dammit! Can't you at least look at him? How does a thousand dollars strike you?"

Mosley's eyes bugged behind the polished lenses of his spectacles. "A thousand dollars? Are you out of your ever-loving mind, Taggart? No dog is worth that."

Luke didn't need Mosley to tell him that, but the animal's worth wasn't the issue. "It's my money," he said softly.

The doctor sighed and rubbed his bearded chin, his gaze fixed on Lycodomes. "That girl out there must mean a lot to you, that's all I can say. A thousand dollars?"

"That's right. You save that dog, and it's yours."

"It's your money," Mosley said as he reluctantly approached the table.

After lighting the gas lamp suspended from the ceiling, he examined Lycodomes at length. When he finally looked at Luke again, the expression on his plump, bewhiskered face was solemn.

"Is the hip broken?" Luke asked.

"Not that I can tell. But there may be internal injuries. I've no way of knowing for sure."

Luke swallowed. "Bleeding inside, you mean?"

The doctor nodded. "If so, he's a goner. There's nothing I can do."

"How about the leg? How bad is it?"

"Bad," Mosley replied. "That's the least of my worries, though. I think I can set it. I cannot, however, promise that the dog won't be lame. If he lives, and I stress the 'if.'" He hesitated a moment, as if to let that sink in. "I'm sorry, Mr. Taggart, but it's my recommendation that we put the animal down. I can do it painlessly. A bit too much ether, for a prolonged period of time. He'll just go to sleep and never wake up."

Luke stared down at Lycodomes's chest, noting the dog's rapid breathing, a sure sign of pain. Less than an hour ago, Luke had been making arrangements to get rid of the dog. Now, he would have given almost anything to save him. He closed his eyes for a moment, imagining the shattered look on Cassandra's face when he told her the news.

"I've seen lots of lame dogs," Luke said gruffly. "Most of them seem to get around all right. Even three-legged ones."

"True enough. It's your call. Just understand that if he's bleeding internally, there's not a damned thing I can do."

Luke opened the surgery door and stepped through. Cassandra had leaped up from the chair when she heard the creak of the hinges. Surprised to see that the miner had already left, Luke motioned her into the surgery. The instant she entered the room, she ran directly to the table to hug her pet.

As gently as possible, Luke laid out the facts to her. "It's up to you, honey. I'll leave the decision to you."

Cassandra straightened and pressed a hand over her mouth, her aching gaze fixed on Lycodomes, who lay there panting and whining, clearly asking her, in the only way he could, to do something to help him. Finally, she looked up at Luke again. Two gigantic tears hovered on her lower lashes, then spilled onto her cheeks, trailing like liquid diamonds to her quivering chin.

"You decide, Luke. I'm afraid I'll make a selfish choice." Her mouth twisted in a tremulous spasm.

"Sweetheart, I can't make this decision for you."

"Please? You'll do what's best for Lycodomes, and I'm afraid I won't. I love him so much."

Luke felt as if he'd just been sucker punched. She stood there, looking at him with her heart in her eyes. She actually meant it. If he voted to destroy the dog, she would abide by his decision, no questions asked.

He turned his attention back to Lycodomes, not entirely sure he wanted this kind of responsibility. He didn't deserve her trust, dammit. He was a rotten, lying, conniving bastard. Everyone else in town realized that, so why didn't she? Only she didn't...and he was beginning to feel like a spider trapped in its own web.

Looking at the doctor, Luke asked, "Can you ease his pain?"

Mosley ran a hand over his bald pate. "I can

try. Just as long as you bear in mind that I'm shooting in the dark. Even too much of the right thing could kill him."

Luke heaved a sigh. Finally, he said, "Then I think we should do what we can for him." He met Cassandra's gaze. "As you said, we can't just give up without a fight. This way, at least he's got a chance."

"How much will it cost?" she asked, turning to the doctor. "Will it be frightfully expensive? I have wages coming at the end of the month, but right now, I haven't much money. Do you mind waiting for payment?"

Luke didn't want her to know that her entire first month's wages wouldn't cover what he'd offered the doctor. "Money isn't the issue." He turned to Mosley. "Go to work," he said softly. "If you can save him, the price we agreed on is yours. If he dies, I'll pay your regular fee and not a cent more."

The insult, though not spoken in so many words, was blatant. Mosley's mouth hardened. "You can't blackmail me, Taggart. If I take on a patient, human or canine, I put forth my best effort, whether there's payment involved or not. Take your money and get out of here."

For an awful moment, Luke thought the doctor meant he should take the dog away as well. But then the older man stepped to the surgery table, his expression intent. "Go on," he said vaguely, his complete attention already focused on Lycodomes. "Wait outside. I don't work well with people standing over me, gawking."

• • •

Waiting...pacing...waiting. From the chairs to the bookcase, Luke wore a path in the waiting-room floor, hands clasped behind his back. Every minute seemed to last an hour, each hour a lifetime. Luke's thoughts were never far from the dog, the only exception being when he contemplated the girl who sat huddled on the chair, head bent, shoulders sagging. If Lycodomes died, Luke knew a part of Cassandra would die with him. A precious part of her...and Luke was going to mourn the loss.

Doctor Mosley had been closeted in the surgery with Lycodomes for approximately two hours when a tap on the waiting-room window brought Luke reeling to a stop. He glanced through the dusty blind to see Donald Brummel standing outside on the sidewalk, a newspaper held in one hand to shield his head from the afternoon rain, which came almost daily in the Rockies. With his free hand, Brummel motioned for Luke to step outside.

"I heard about the dog getting run over," he said when Luke joined him on the sidewalk.

Raindrops pelted Luke's face. The pinpricks of cold wetness on his skin felt good, and he hauled in a deep breath of the fresh air, flexing the stiffness from his shoulders. "We're still not sure if the doctor can save him."

Donald smiled slightly. "I thought you wanted to get rid of him."

"Keep your voice down, goddammit. She may hear you through the glass."

Donald lowered the newspaper, tapping its damp folds lightly against his tweed trouser leg. Within seconds, his honey-brown hair glistened with raindrops. "Shall I take this to mean I should forget your orders to make arrangements for the dog's disappearance?" he asked with a quizzical gleam in his eye.

There was no mistaking the man's amusement, and Luke had an unholy urge to plant a fist squarely in his mouth. "I underestimated Cassandra's affection for the animal," he said softly. "She's devastated. If the dog lives, and I hope to God he does, he will remain in Black Jack."

"So, it's finally happened."

Luke lifted an eyebrow. "What's finally happened?"

"The indomitable Luke Taggart, brought to his knees by a pretty little swatch of calico. I never thought I'd live to see it."

"I hardly think my concern for the girl's feelings equates to being brought to my knees," Luke ground out.

"Not an easy thing to admit, is it?" He shook his head. "I still deny it after fifteen years of marriage." He shrugged. "No need to look so stricken, Luke. It happens to the best of us, and in the long run, it really doesn't change anything. I still rule my household with an iron hand." His mouth quirked at the edges. "And I have my wife's permission to say so."

He turned and walked away. Luke fixed a glare on the man's back. Brought to his *knees*? Not likely.

Still disgruntled, Luke reentered the doctor's office to find Cassandra gazing morosely at the floor, her small face pale, the skin drawn tightly over her cheekbones. Luke sighed and sat down beside her to take her hand. "Sweetheart, he's going to be okay," he said with far more confidence than he felt.

She forced a smile—a ghost of a smile, compared to the radiant ones she usually bestowed on him. Luke missed the shimmer that was often in her eyes, the glow that always seemed to emanate from her.

"Even when he was just a pup, Lye-Lye always protected me," she said, barely above a whisper. "And all the people I love as well. Every day, he walked Khristos to school, and sometimes he'd lie outside in the rain and snow, waiting to walk him home. I never worried, not for a second, that any harm might befall my brother, not when Lycodomes was with him."

Luke recalled the first time he'd encountered Lycodomes, how the dog had sensed a threat and snarled a warning.

"He always protected me. Oh God, Luke, why couldn't I protect him?"

"Oh, honey." Luke hooked a hand around her nape and drew her face to his shoulder. "Don't," he said softly. "It was an accident. Lycodomes knows that."

She made tight fists on the front of his expensive silk shirt—a shirt that was smeared with blood and covered with dog hair. Strangely, Luke didn't care. All he could think about was her pain and how helpless he was to ease it.

The door to the surgery opened, and Doctor Mosley stepped out. His eyes twinkled with a smile that didn't quite reach his mouth. "I don't believe he has any internal bleeding," he said briskly. "That's a good sign."

Luke sprang to his feet, his heart kicking against his ribs. "And the leg?"

Cassandra remained seated, her arms hugging her waist. "Could you fix it?" she asked in a thin voice.

"It was broken in three places," Mosley replied. "But I set the fractures and splinted the limb. The rest is up to God and Mother Nature. It'll either knit nicely, or it won't." He held up his hands. "All you can do now is take him home and wait. If he makes it through the next twenty-four hours, he should live. We'll be able to rule out internal injuries, at any rate. Whether or not he'll be lame is a question we can't answer until the splint comes off in approximately six weeks."

"So he still isn't out of the woods?" Luke pressed.

"Not by a long shot. He's lost a lot of blood, and infection could set in. Any number of things could go wrong." Doctor Mosley looked at Cassandra. "I did my best. I'm not a veterinarian, you understand. A dog's leg is made differently than a human's. There are bone angles and tendons I'm not familiar with. All I could do was make my best guess and try to put him back together."

"Thank you, Doctor Mosley," Cassandra said. "Even if he dies, I'll never forget your having tried to save him."

Luke rubbed a hand over his face, exhausted now that some of the danger had passed. "You wait here," he told Cassandra. "I'll go to the house and get the carriage. The less we jostle him around getting him home, the better."

At the door, Luke stopped and spun back. "Your money," he said to the doctor. "I haven't paid you."

Mosley smiled. "Keep the money." He winked at Cassandra. "Consider it my gift to the young lady."

Back braced against the wall, one leg extended, Luke sat on the kitchen floor with one arm curled loosely around Cassandra, his other arm resting on his upraised knee. Limp with weariness and fast asleep, she lay against his chest, her head cradled on his shoulder, her face tipped up so her every breath caressed the underside of his jaw. The single lamp burning on the wall above them cast a nimbus of light all around them, a soft, hazy orb of amber.

Though it was well after two in the morning and everyone else, including Khristos, had long since gone to bed, Luke didn't feel the least bit sleepy. After sitting in the same position for nearly three hours, his body was starting to cramp, but he wouldn't have moved for anything. He was afraid he might wake Cassandra, and he wanted to continue holding her.

Feeling her slightness within the circle of his arm, her softness pressed so innocently against him, having the scent of her all around him—it was as close to heaven as he ever hoped to get.

Heaven...three days ago, Luke would have scoffed at the very notion that such a place existed. Now, resting his gaze on Lycodomes, who lay on a pallet of blankets near the stove, he could almost believe. The dog had skated very close to death this afternoon and was still on thin ice. Yet Luke was beginning to hope he had a chance. A good chance. The dog's chest no longer rose and fell quite so rapidly, and he seemed to be resting peacefully. That had to be a good sign.

It was almost as if some invisible power had worked a miracle, Luke thought as he regarded the dog. To that end, Cassandra had certainly said enough Hail Marys—so many, in fact, that Luke nearly had the prayer memorized himself. A slight smile touched his mouth. Maybe he wasn't the only one who couldn't bear to see Cassandra cry.

A funny, shivery sensation crawled over Luke's skin, and he drew his gaze from the dog to glance uneasily about the room. Could it be that there really were divine forces at work all around them? Luke had lived his whole life convinced otherwise. If some divine being had been following him all these years, looking over his shoulder and keeping a tally of all his bad deeds, he was in deep shit.

He shook the thought away. If there were a God, then where the hell had He been when Luke was a kid?

Luke pressed his lips against Cassandra's

dark, silken hair and hauled in a deep breath. Pale lavender blossoms, sunlight filtering through green leaves, birds trilling—those were the things that came to his mind. Clean, sweet things. He could never settle for black lace again, not after having her in his arms.

She stirred slightly. Luke dipped his chin, watching her dark lashes flutter against her ivory cheeks. "How is he?" she asked groggily.

Luke glanced at Lycodomes. "I think he's better," he told her softly. "Maybe your prayers helped, hmm?"

The husky tenderness in Luke's voice made Cassandra's heart catch. Tipping her head back, she gazed up at his burnished features. His whiskey-colored hair lay in loose waves over his high forehead, lending him a tousled, little-boy appeal. As she met his gaze, she remembered how she'd once compared his golden-brown eyes to those of a tiger. The thought amused her now, for tigers were fierce, dangerous creatures, and Luke was one of the most gentle men she'd ever met.

Oh, he had hard edges. She didn't fool herself about that. She had seen that side of him more than once when he dealt with other people, and that very morning he'd even been gruff with her. She had no doubt he could be dangerous. When he got angry, a harsh, brutal set came over his features, and a merciless glint entered his eyes. Yet with her, he had been patience itself, his hands always lightly caressing her arm or her hair, his eyes cloudy with tenderness. He hadn't hesitated to try and save Lycodomes, either, and she knew he'd done it only for her. She wasn't blind to the looks he sometimes gave the dog, as if he'd like to strangle him.

Cassandra couldn't understand the feelings she was developing for this man. Sometimes she wanted to draw his head to her shoulder and stroke his hair, to tell him everything would be all right. It was a silly urge, given that he always seemed so strong and in command with everyone else. It was only when he looked at her that he got that uncertain, yearning look—like a lost little boy who was searching for home and had no idea where to turn.

Unable to resist the urge, Cassandra reached up and pressed her palm lightly against his cheek. The whiskery nubs along his darkly tanned jaw pricked her skin. Smiling, she rasped her thumb over the roughness. Not a little boy, she reminded herself, but a very large man whose body was roped with steely muscle. Yet the look in his eyes reminded her of Khristos when he woke from a bad dream.

Turning his head slightly, Luke caught her thumb between his teeth. The wet, silken heat of his mouth made her tummy flutter. It was a startling sensation, yet she liked it very much.

An awful, uncertain feeling went through her. She didn't know who she was anymore. Being with Luke so much these last few days had changed everything, making her question herself at every turn.

He smiled slightly when she drew her hand back, his eyes gleaming as if her startled reaction amused him. Then, almost imperceptibly, he bent his head. Cassandra's breath snagged in her throat, for she knew he meant to kiss her. The fluttery feeling in her stomach turned hot and storm tingly, excitement ribboning from its center to make her breasts swell and a shiver run up her spine. She *wanted* him to kiss her, she realized. She wanted it more than she'd ever wanted anything.

Lycodomes whined suddenly. Luke jerked his head up, and Cassandra sprang away as if his broad chest had suddenly become a bed of hot coals. Twisting onto her knees, she bent over her dog.

"Lye-Lye?" The dog fastened worshipful brown eyes on her. Blinking away tears, Cassandra smoothed a hand over his head, then toyed gently with his curly ears. "Oh, Luke, I think you're right. He seems better."

His pulse slamming and his breath coming quick, Luke pushed to his feet, trying without much success not to resent the dog for choosing that particular moment to wake up. Two more seconds, that was all he'd needed, and he would have been kissing her. Luke straightened his shirt, tucking in the tails with jabbing fingers.

"Do you think maybe he's hungry?" he asked when the dog continued to whine.

Cassandra bit her full bottom lip—a lip Luke would have given his right arm to be nibbling on himself. "I wonder if it would hurt him to have some milk."

Milk...Luke glanced blankly around the kitchen, trying to orient himself. As he moved across the room to the icebox, he silently lectured himself on appropriate timing. What had he hoped to do, take her on the kitchen floor? *Jesus.* He had to maintain some control. He drew the jug of milk off the shelf and slammed the icebox door closed.

"One bowl of milk, coming up," he said with a lightheartedness he was far from feeling. To his surprise, Lycodomes eagerly lapped up the bowl of milk when he set it on the floor in front of him. "Well, I'll be damned," Luke said with a laugh.

"He *is* better! Oh, Luke, he truly is!"

The light was back in her eyes, Luke thought as he met her gaze. Seeing that was better than getting a kiss, any day. "I'm totally ignorant about dogs," he told her as he knelt next to the empty bowl, "but I'd say it's unlikely he has internal injuries. I don't think he'd drink anything if that were the case."

Cassandra gave a glad little cry and bent to hug her dog's neck. Luke felt warm wetness on the back of his hand where it rested on his knee. He glanced down to see that Lycodomes was licking him. When Luke failed to respond, the huge dog nudged his fingers with his wet nose.

"Do you think he's asking for more milk?" Luke asked Cassandra when she straightened.

"No, I think he wants you to pet him."

"Why would he want that? He doesn't even like me."

She watched the dog nudge Luke's hand. "Maybe he's changed his mind. He's a very good judge of character, my Lycodomes."

A good judge of character? The words hung between them for a long moment. Then, with a hesitancy he didn't bother trying to hide, Luke relented and moved his palm to the dog's massive head. Lycodomes made a soft whining sound as Luke began to stroke his fur. Then the animal relaxed and rested his nose on his paws, closing his eyes.

In that moment, Luke felt something hard and cold inside him begin to thaw. He was very much afraid it might be the thick crust of ice he'd formed years ago around his heart.

FIFTEEN

By mid-morning, Lycodomes was showing marked signs of improvement. Not only did he consume another bowl of milk and some meat Luke gave him, but with Luke's help, he even managed to walk outside.

"I can't believe I'm doing this," Luke grumbled as he supported most of Lycodomes's weight and helped him to hike his leg. "Helping a goddamned dog piss on my shrubs!" Lycodomes lifted a liquid brown gaze, his canine face looking concerned. "Why it surprises me, I don't know," Luke added. "I can't believe a lot of the things I've been doing and saying the last few days."

With a low whine, Lycodomes licked Luke's face, a gesture that earned the dog little popularity with the recipient of his affections.

"Do you know how much just one of these shrubs cost me?" Luke asked as he dodged wet kisses. "A bloody fortune, you mangy mongrel. More than you're worth, by far."

By the time Luke got to his office shortly before noon, his mood had gone from sour to downright foul. After nearly snapping Donald Brummel's head off for committing the unforgivable offense of bidding him good morning, Luke locked his office door and sat down at his desk, where he accomplished next to nothing. The long and short of it was, he couldn't concentrate on any of the paperwork he tried to tackle.

Finally admitting defeat, he planted his elbows on his desk and rested his aching head in his hands. He felt like a sock Cassandra was wringing out, the emotions roiling within him as confusing as they were painful.

The bald truth was, he no longer liked himself very well. His life up to now had counted for absolutely nothing. Milo Zerek was a poor man who had raised his family in leaking hovels, but compared to Luke, he had the whole damn world in his pocket. No matter how much rain poured through the leaky roof over their heads, or how threadbare their clothes might become, Milo's kids still felt safe and, damn it, loved.

Luke couldn't think of a single person in his life who'd even been fond of him. Except, of course, for Cassandra and Khristos, who'd swallowed all his lies—hook, line, and sinker. Oh, yes, he was a real hero, all right. A goddamned public benefactor. Saint Luke, who had so magnanimously taken them into his home and so generously seen to it that their dear papa and brother served light sentences. Luke Taggart, who'd offered Cassandra more money for her friendship than most people saw in a lifetime. Luke Taggart, the liar, who had manipulated them from the first, using trickery to lure them into his clutches.

As he had done so often of late, Luke couldn't help but remember the story Khristos had told him that first night about the frog who was actually a handsome prince.

Just the reverse was true of Luke, a man pretending to be a prince when he was actually a toad, enticing a gentle, innocent girl into his snare so he could possess her. Little had he known that his sweet little princess would become his captor instead. And like all captives, he now felt frantic. The feeling kept coming over him in waves, a suffocating, tight-chested sensation.

In desperation, Luke finally fled his office and went to the dressmaker's to purchase Cassandra another ready-made wardrobe. If he saw her wearing one of his shirts over a beautiful new gown one more time, he was going to wring her pretty little neck.

After making arrangements for the wardrobe to be delivered to his home, Luke headed directly for the Golden Slipper, his former home-away-from-home. Taking a corner table situated in the shadows, he ordered a jug of Mon'gahela whiskey and one glass.

Halfway into the bottle, he joined a poker game, began placing crazy bets—which was totally uncharacteristic of him—and started losing money, hand over fist. He didn't care.

It felt good to be back in his own world, damned good. At least here everyone was exactly what they appeared to be—crass and shallow.

After drinking and gambling his fill, Luke followed a redhead named Estelle upstairs. She'd entertained him in her private suite many times before, and he looked forward to having sex with her. Raw, lewd sex. No innocent blue eyes. No shy blushes. No feeling guilty every time he had a lustful thought. Just flesh, bought and paid for, from a woman who had no illusions about him.

Luke, the toad, frolicking in the slimy pond of vice.

In addition to her other talents, Estelle's specialty was oral sex. When Luke kissed her, he smelled the fishy odor of man on her, and it instantly repulsed him. Shaken, he set her away from him and met her gaze. What he saw there made him feel as if the floor had suddenly vanished from under his feet. Behind the hard glitter of her eyes were myriad emotions, none of them pretty: boredom, distaste, desperation, all confusingly stirred together with an underlying hatred.

Maybe it was the liquor he'd drunk, but suddenly Luke didn't see her as an object he could rent for a few hours. She was a young woman who had thoughts and feelings, just as he did. He had no idea what had led her to this pass; he only knew she wasn't in this room servicing men because she wanted to be.

The revelation stunned Luke so badly that

he couldn't think his way past it. She leaned into him again, rubbing her bosom against his chest, an enticement he might have interpreted as desire months ago, but now recognized as a well-practiced and completely fake ploy. This was a job to her, nothing more—a way to feed herself and keep a roof over her head, two feats that weren't easily accomplished by a young woman on her own. Luke, and dozens of other men just like him, took advantage of her circumstances, tossing coins to her as they might to a street organist's monkey for a performance well rendered.

Shaken, he turned away from her to look out the window.

"What's the matter, big boy?" She came up behind him, running her arms around his waist, her hands fumbling with his belt buckle. With a throaty laugh, she murmured, "I'll bet I know what you want."

Keeping his gaze fixed on the window, Luke felt the fly of his trousers fall open. Estelle ran groping fingers over his crotch, nuzzling his back as she tried to arouse him. In the darkness beyond the window glass, Luke imagined he could see Cassandra, her sweet face uplifted, her eyes filled with admiration and trust. He tried desperately to drive the image away, but he couldn't.

What would she think of him now? he wondered. Luke, her prince in shining armor.

Estelle knelt beside him. Closing his eyes to block out Cassandra's image, Luke willed himself to stand fast, to let himself respond.

But he couldn't. Everything about Estelle seemed suddenly pitiable to him.

Restraining himself so he wouldn't roughly shove her, Luke set her away from him and hastily refastened his pants. "I think maybe I've had a little too much to drink," he said with a weak laugh.

It sounded lame, even to him. Thrusting a hand into his pocket, Luke drew out a wad of money and tossed it on the bed as he went to collect his jacket. At the door, he paused. "I'll come back some other night. All right, beautiful?"

"Sure, Luke."

Estelle pushed to her feet. In the candlelight, she was indeed beautiful, every man's dream come true, a tall, lushly curved redhead with rouged lips, impudent nipples displayed to best advantage, and legs created to ride a man's hips. There was nothing wrong with her, not even in Luke's critical estimation. He just didn't want her. And, if the truth were to be known, she didn't want him, either.

Luke's hand slipped away from the brass knob, and he turned to press his back against a wood door gone slick with the oil from hundreds of men's hands. He gazed across the room at the young woman he'd almost bought and used.

He felt ashamed. In all these years, he'd never looked deeper than the surface when he'd been with a woman, never cared enough to bother.

"What?" she asked with a faint smile that didn't reach her eyes.

Luke resisted the urge to fish more money out of his pocket. No matter how low she'd sunk to stay alive, she still had some pride. He wouldn't have liked it if someone had humiliated him by offering him charity, and he doubted she would, either.

"Have you ever considered another kind of work?" he asked.

She laughed softly. "Like what? Being a laundress and selling my favors to unwashed miners to help pay the rent? No, thanks."

"I have some connections," Luke told her, his mind working in fast circles. "In Denver and San Francisco and Sacramento. You're too intelligent a woman to waste your life in a place like this." He drew one of his calling cards from his breast pocket and tossed it onto the bed near the money. "If you're interested, go see my man of affairs at my offices."

A gleam of interest had slipped into her eyes, but there was wariness there as well. "What kind of work? I don't know how to do anything else. And I don't have enough money to reach Denver, let alone Frisco."

Luke smiled. "You can get training, Estelle. Nowadays, women even go to college back east."

"Sure. And pigs can fly, too."

"Do you think you're too stupid?" he asked, with just a hint of challenge.

"I think I'm too poor," she shot back.

"I'll give you a loan. Fair interest, low payments, which you can start making after you get another kind of job." He trailed his gaze over her, bringing it to rest on her slender,

288

long-fingered hands. "There are all kinds of things you could do, Estelle. Typesetting, secretarial, or clerical. You don't have to stay here." He turned back to open the door. Stepping out into the hall, he said, "Take your time and think it over. If you want to get out of here, I'll help you go."

As he descended the stairs and exited the saloon, Luke nearly convinced himself he *had* had too much to drink. That had to be what was wrong with him. He'd not only just passed up an opportunity to bed a beautiful woman, but he'd offered her a way out of her chosen profession, which meant he might never get another crack at her. If that wasn't crazy, he didn't know what was.

Striking off toward home, he hauled in several bracing breaths of the crisp night air, trying not to remember all the times he'd consumed far more whiskey and still managed to perform quite adequately in bed. To analyze his behavior and his failure to perform, he would have to ask himself questions he was neither ready nor sober enough to answer.

The house was dark when Luke let himself in. He crept quietly up the stairs, relieved to find his bed empty when he entered his suite. Khristos was evidently growing accustomed to all the strange noises the house made as it settled at night.

Stepping into his bathing chamber, Luke ran water into the sink and scrubbed his face, brushed his teeth, and gargled with one of Cook's homemade mouth rinses, a concoction of rose extract and tincture of myrrh. When all trace of Estelle's kisses were washed away, he pressed a towel to his face, breathing deeply of its clean smell.

Christ. Luke couldn't remember the last time he'd felt so drained. Loosening his tie, he returned to the bedchamber. As he came to a stop beside his bed, he noticed a thin crack of light coming from under the door between his bedchamber and Cassandra's. Surprised, he couldn't resist opening the door to see if she were still awake.

The sight that greeted him made him freeze. Candlelight. Everywhere Luke looked, a candle flickered, the overall effect one of liquid amber dancing over the room. Atop the bureau sat a silver tray bearing a wine jug, with two goblets beside it.

Leaning a shoulder against the door frame, Luke settled his gaze on Cassandra. She sat in one of the armchairs by the small table where they'd played chess that first night, her knees drawn to her chest, one arm dangling over the armrest, head bent, dark hair cascading in tousled waves over her flannel-covered breasts. She'd obviously sat up waiting for him and fallen asleep.

Seconds before, Luke hadn't believed anything could make him smile. He should have known better. What a little corker she was. Until now, he'd completely forgotten the talk he'd had with her two mornings previously. Glancing once more around the room before swinging his gaze back to her, he realized she had followed his orders to the letter, right down to the flannel nightgown she wore, a god-awful rag she must have borrowed from one of the maids. He shook his head and grinned. The damned thing covered her from chin to toe.

Drawn to her like a moth to a flame, Luke tried to tiptoe across the room, *tried* being the operative word. With three-quarters of a jug of whiskey sloshing in his gut, "Grace" wasn't exactly his middle name.

Cassandra blinked awake, then stifled a yawn with dainty little fingers. When she spied Luke, her bleary blue eyes widened and a glowing smile curved her sweet mouth. "Luke," she said sleepily. "You finally came home. I've been waiting forever."

Luke hunkered beside her chair, leaning a little heavily on the arm for balance. Reaching up to smooth her hair back from her face, he couldn't resist trailing a fingertip along her sculpted cheek. "How's Lycodomes?"

If possible, her smile grew even more illuminating. "Oh, Luke, he's *wonderful*! He ate a huge dinner."

"He did?"

"Yes! And Pipps helped me take him outside several times today—although, I have to say, I'm not sure Lycodomes needed the help. He's swinging that splint out from his body and hobbling around as if he's worn it forever."

Luke forced himself to draw his hand away from her silken cheek. "I'm glad, sweetheart. I guess all your prayers worked."

Her eyes warmed with that worshipful look Luke had come to crave. "I think you're the one who has answered all my prayers. No offense to God or anything, for I'm sure He's been up there orchestrating things and that if it weren't for Him, I never would have met you."

"You think so?" Luke rocked back on his heels, nearly toppling over in the process. He grabbed for the chair to catch himself. "Somehow, I doubt that."

If God did exist, Luke doubted He was in the habit of leading virginal young girls into the arms of lascivious males.

"Well, I don't doubt it. Not for a second," she said decisively. "You truly are a godsend, not just to me, but to my whole family. Do you know what Cook did today? She fixed enough extra supper for Papa and Ambrose, then sent the gardener over to the jail with it posthaste so they could eat it hot. Pie and fresh bread. And little chunks of beef simmered in gravy. They haven't eaten so well in a long time."

"You didn't go to the jail, did you?"

Her face fell. "No. I promised you I wouldn't unless you went with me. But I sorely wanted to."

Luke relaxed slightly. "It was thoughtful of Cook to send them supper. I'll have to thank her."

"I only wish I could think of some way I might thank *you*."

Cassandra, draped head to toe in a dingy flannel gown, was the most tempting creature he had ever clapped eyes on. He smiled when he noticed that she was also wearing someone's oversized gray wool socks on her small feet, which made them appear disproportionately large. Sexy? Yes. Desirable? Absolutely.

"I, um…" He coughed and glanced around the room. "It looks as if you had plans for us tonight. I hope my being late didn't ruin them."

She rubbed under one eye. "I'm starting to wake up now, but you look dead on your feet."

Drunk, more like it, Luke thought with a wry smile. "I'm not that tired." He looked around at all the candles again. The scene had been set for seduction, but he knew better than to get his hopes up. "What did you have in mind?"

"You said you wanted to be intimate."

His heart lurched. "Yes, I did say that."

Her dimple flashed in an impish grin. "Well, I got everything prepared, just like you wanted. Are you ready to start?"

Luke locked gazes with her. "With what?" he asked cautiously.

"With getting intimate." She lowered her feet to the floor, the overly long toes of the gray socks flopping. Wrinkling her nose, she said, "I thought we might play a game." Apparently Luke's disappointment registered on his face, for she rushed to add, "An *intimate* game, of course."

Somehow he doubted her idea of intimate bore any similarity to his.

Well aware that he was drunk, Luke knew he should probably go straight back to his own bedchamber. With Estelle still so fresh on his mind, though, Cassandra seemed so innocent and refreshingly sweet that he didn't want to leave her. She was everything Luke had never had, everything he had ever wanted without realizing he wanted it. And she was there, as tempting as a gaily wrapped box of chocolates.

An intoxicated man falls prey to temptation so easily.

Swaying to his feet, Luke stepped to the bureau. "It would be a shame to let the wine go to waste. Will you join me?"

Her light laugh reminded him of a crystal bell tinkling. "I've never had wine before."

"Never?"

"Well…only a smidgen at Holy Communion or when my papa poured me a tiny bit to celebrate a special occasion. Papa says a lady should never touch spirits unless she is in the company of a male relative, for doing so may get her into a pickle."

Luke smiled to himself. "Your papa is a very smart man."

"I suppose it's all right tonight, though," she added, "because I'm with you."

Luke could have done without the vote of confidence. It was exceedingly difficult to be a bastard when she had such utter faith in him. He stood there, the wine bottle poised over her goblet, his lust at war with his conscience. In the end, he decided that exceedingly difficult did not equate with impossible. He poured her a full glass of wine, set it on the table beside her chair, and took a seat across from her, the wine jug dangling from one hand.

As she lifted her glass, she swirled the burgundy, gazing thoughtfully into the crimson depths. "I can trust you to take good care of me if I get tipsy, can't I?"

Luke lifted his goblet to her in a mock toast. "You have my solemn word on it. I *always* take very good care of tipsy ladies."

He watched without comment while she upended the glass and downed the wine as though she were drinking fruit juice. When her glass was empty, he leaned across the table to refill it, his gut knotting at the way she licked the corners of her mouth.

"It's sort of nasty," she said with a delicate shudder.

"The second glass will taste a lot better," he told her in a voice gone husky.

He felt no guilt for urging her to drink more. He wanted this girl, needed her in a way he couldn't and didn't wish to define. He wasn't going to play the fool and vacillate about how he got her into bed. He quickly emptied his own glass and refilled it as well. The effect of the wine, on top of the liquor he had consumed earlier, filled him with warmth. *Cassandra.* He watched her with heavy-lidded eyes, yearning to have her in his arms so fiercely that it bordered on pain.

Glancing at her attire, which was about as seductive as that damn nun's habit she professed to want, he comforted himself with the thought that at least the setting was right. And hell, drunk or not, he could dispense with the infernal nightgown and socks quickly enough, after all.

"Well," she said gaily as she polished off half of her second glass of burgundy, "shall we begin?"

Luke was more than ready. "By all means."

She bent to pick something up from the floor beside her chair. He saw that she held some slips of paper and two pencils in her hand. As she slid some paper and one of the writing tools to him, she said, "It's a game I made up, so you have to promise not to laugh."

Cry, maybe. Laugh, never. Luke took up the pencil, thinking to himself that he had another, far more appropriate tool for the occasion— one that was equally long and rigid, which he could put to far better use. "What is the object of this game?"

"To become intimate, of course."

That suited him. "And the rules?"

"It's called 'Secrets,'" she explained. "Khristos and I have played it on rainy days. It's sort of fun."

Just what he wanted, to play a game she'd played with her brother. "I'm all ears."

Her eyes lighted with a mischievous twinkle. "What you do is write one of your most closely guarded secrets on your piece of paper. I'll do the same on mine. Then we turn the papers facedown and try to guess what the other person has written. We can give little hints, of course. By the time we're done, we'll know all kinds of things about each other and be well on our way to a much more intimate friendship."

Luke set the wine jug and his goblet aside, then smoothed his slip of paper on the table.

He quickly jotted down his most closely guarded secret and turned it face-down. When he looked up, he saw that Cassandra was still holding her pencil poised over the paper, her forehead creased in a frown. She was obviously taking this all very seriously.

Luke smiled to himself, trying to imagine what sort of thing she might reveal to him. Knowing Cassandra, it wasn't likely to be anything earthshaking.

She finally wrote something and turned her paper over. "Okay, you start."

Luke studied her for a long moment. "Aren't you going to give me a hint?"

She nibbled on her bottom lip. "Well...it's something that's really, really bothering me. A lot. And it has to do with the way I've been feeling lately."

"Lately," he repeated. "Meaning six months, a few weeks, a few days?"

"A few days." Her blue eyes darkened like the sky on a stormy day.

Luke had always thought her eyes revealed her every thought and emotion, but never more so than now. One look into those gigantic spheres of blue, and he knew exactly what her secret was. "Cassandra, do these feelings have anything to do with me?"

She averted her face for a moment. When she finally looked back at him, her expression was apologetic. "I'm sorry. I guess this was a dumb idea. I should have written something else down. This particular secret has me really upset."

Luke tossed his pencil onto the table.

"Let's forget the game, then, honey, and talk about it. What's bothering you?"

She gazed at him for an interminably long while. Finally she said, "Ever since I was a little girl, I've wanted to be a nun."

"I know. But what has that to do with me?"

She shrugged. "Now I'm not sure I should become one."

Luke's pulse quickened. "Why, sweetheart?"

Crimson flooded to her cheeks. "Because of the way you make me feel. When I'm with you, I feel like I swallowed butterflies—a funny, fluttery feeling in my stomach—and shivery all over."

Luke's first reaction was to feel elated, but there was no ignoring that bruised, worried look in her eyes.

"All my life," she whispered raggedly, "I've wanted to devote my life to the church. Now I'm beginning to feel as if all my plans are falling apart. I like you far too much, and the more I'm around you, the more deeply I'm coming to care about you."

Even as intoxicated as he was, Luke could see how very confused she felt. He also realized she'd deliberately chosen to play this game so she might tell him of her feelings, that she was hoping he would say something wonderfully wise that would put everything into its proper perspective.

Which meant they were both in deep shit here, because—damn it all—he was as confused as she was, and sinking fast. Over the last few years, women had fawned over him, showered him with compliments, and shamelessly tried to entice him with their bodies, all of which had left him emotionally unaffected. Yet Cassandra's admission that she was beginning to worry about "liking him" in a way she shouldn't left him shaken.

He knew she had no idea how vulnerable she was making herself to him. She had already consumed one glass of wine and was well on her way toward finishing the second, her cheeks prettily flushed from the alcohol.

"Sweetheart," he said very gently, "has it ever occurred to you that you may not have a true calling to the sisterhood, that maybe God has other plans for you?"

"Like what?"

Luke took a slow sip of wine, studying her over the rim of his goblet. "Like being a wife and mother, for instance. That's a very important calling as well."

The startled expression in her eyes soon turned to a liquid-looking dreaminess, and the smile she bestowed on him was beatific. "Do you think the way I'm feeling means I'm falling in love with you?"

A suffocating sensation crept up Luke's throat. There was that word again, *love*. "I think it may mean you're coming to care very deeply."

"How do people know for sure?"

A master at seduction, Luke knew every erogenous zone on the female body and how to titillate it. "There's one surefire way for you to learn if you're truly developing an affection for me." He patted his knee. "Come here, sweetheart."

SIXTEEN

&❧Her eyes wide and wary, she set down her wine-glass and rose to her feet. He smiled slightly. The girl was innocent, yes, but far from stupid. She seemed to realize she might be taking an irrevocable step.

Luke held out a hand to her. "Don't you trust me, honey?"

His heart squeezed when she pressed a shaky hand to her waist and moved toward him. "Yes, I trust you, Luke," she murmured. Instead of pleasing him, her words made him feel like a contemptible manipulator. A very intoxicated contemptible manipulator who wanted her so badly, he didn't give a shit.

When she finally placed slender fingers across his outstretched palm, Luke took a firm grip, afraid she would to try to bolt. Even if she tried, she wouldn't get more than a step or two before he hauled her back. Now that he had her where he wanted her, at long last, he damned sure wasn't about to let her get away.

"Here, honey, sit on my knee a minute. Just for a minute."

Though she slanted him a shyly worried look, she did as he asked. Unfortunately, because of the liquor they'd both consumed, his leg was weaving, and her aim wasn't all it should have been. He nearly dumped her on the floor.

"Son of a bitch!"

He made a wild grab. A full breast pressed against one of his palms, and he had a handful of deliciously soft fanny in the other. He managed to maneuver her onto his spread thighs. She slumped against his chest and giggled. Luke saw that her nightgown had hiked up, revealing one slender leg. Flawless ivory skin shimmering like silk in the candlelight caught his undivided attention. He curled a hand over her delicately made knee, his fingertips lightly tracing the sensitive skin at the back. She went instantly still, and he heard her breath quicken, then come to a shuddering halt.

He met her gaze. Big, startled blue eyes looked back at him. Eyes that searched and probed and...tugged on his black soul. In some distant part of his benumbed brain, Luke realized she wasn't the only one who'd stopped breathing. His body felt electrified, every pulse-beat seeming to explode through him. The press of her bottom had turned his cock so hard, it ached. He swallowed, hoping she couldn't feel his arousal.

It was a futile hope, he realized as her eyes widened. With a soft exclamation of alarm, she tried to slip away from the hard bulge pressing against her softness.

"It's all right, honey. Don't be afraid." His voice, gravelly with desire, cracked on the last inflection. "I won't hurt you."

"I know," she whispered.

Luke hauled in a deep, shaky breath and exhaled through clenched teeth. She placed a hand on his chest. Until he felt her fingers splay lightly over his bare skin, he'd forgotten that his shirt hung open. He knew she must feel his heart slamming against his ribs like a sledge.

Dainty little fingertips moved lightly over the contours of his chest, testing the hardness of muscle, the texture of skin, the coarseness of his body hair. His gaze still locked with hers, Luke realized she was exploring him and that the fear he'd seen in her eyes moments before had turned to wonder.

"You feel so different. Than I do, I mean."

Luke swallowed, hard. He would have liked very much to draw his own comparison. "Do I?"

She trailed a light, inquisitive touch down the pectoral cleavage at the center of his chest to the inverted triangle of dark blond hair below, her crescent-shaped nails tracing each rung of muscle on his belly. "Are you this hard all over?"

Christ, yes. Like a rock. He bit down hard on his back teeth and nodded, feeling sweat pop out on his forehead. She lowered her gaze to follow the path of her fingertips. "Oh, Luke, you're beautiful."

He'd been called a number of things, but never "beautiful."

She found the ridge of a scar that curled from his back around his side, and her touch hovered there. "What happened to you here?"

The lash of a leather belt had cut him when he was a boy, but Luke saw no point in telling her that. He doubted Milo Zerek had ever so much as lifted a hand to any of his children, let alone beaten them, and the longer Cassandra remained ignorant of that kind of ugliness, the better. One of the things Luke treasured most about her was her naivete, and he didn't want to taint that with his own jaded outlook. Not now, not ever. The longer she continued to live in her little fairy-tale world, the longer he could escape into that world with her.

The thought made Luke stumble mentally, and he backed up like a man who'd just stubbed his toe, to see what the hell had tripped him. It was true, he realized. Cassandra did live in another world, a very sweet, pure little world of her own creation—or maybe of Milo's—where the harsh facts of life not only never intruded but didn't exist. In that world, she saw everything through rose-colored glasses, and when he was close to her, he could share in the magic. No ugliness, no deception, nothing to fear. In that world, even Luke Taggart, the whore's bastard, was somebody wonderful.

Someone beautiful.

A stinging sensation washed over Luke's eyes, and an awful choking grabbed hold of his throat. The need inside him was a sharp hunger that went far beyond the physical. This girl had become as necessary to him as the air he breathed.

"Luke?"

He jerked and refocused his gaze on hers. "What, sweetheart?"

"You didn't answer me. How did you get this scar?"

"I don't remember." The truth was, he didn't want to remember, and for the first time in his life, he'd met someone who helped him to forget. "It happened a long, long time ago."

"It must have hurt dreadfully," she whispered, her fingertips tracing the still sensitive ridge of scar tissue. "How could you forget something like that?"

Because to remember nearly drove him mad. "I just have, that's all."

Tracing the delicate features of her face with a lingering gaze, Luke shoved away the memories that always hovered at the back of his mind, concentrating instead on the feel of her pressed against him. Holding her like this, he decided, was like stirring a generous dollop of honey into strong black coffee. Somehow, she took the edge off, making his life bittersweet instead of completely unpalatable.

His face hovered only scant inches from hers, and he closed the distance, settling his mouth lightly over her lips. She gave a startled gasp, her breath sweet with the taste of wine when she finally exhaled. Luke clamped a hand over the back of her head to hold her fast, then sent his tongue on a cautious foray for a more thorough taste of her. It was her turn to jerk, a violent little arch of her body that brought her breasts fully against his chest. He slipped an arm around her waist to anchor her there.

Careful, the voice of his newly discovered conscience whispered at the edges of his mind. Cassandra was no Gloria or Estelle. Contracts, legal jargon, proprietary rights—none of those things concerned him right now. Now his only thoughts were for Cassandra and the feelings he was arousing in her.

No matter how patient he had to be, or how long he suffered, he was determined to give her pleasure instead of pain. Satisfaction instead of fear. Later, when they were lying sated and entwined, he didn't want her to feel humiliated or used. Or bought.

A man who'd engaged in nearly every sexual deviance that existed, Luke wasn't sure he even knew how to be a gentleman in bed. Somehow, the sexual act and good manners had never struck him as behavior that went hand in hand. Even so, he sensed that he needed to move slowly. He couldn't just dive in like a starving man devouring a plate of food.

To his surprise, her lush lips opened for him like delicate flower petals to sunlight. At first, she kept her tongue withdrawn from his, shying away from the contact he craved. Luke allowed her that, using his hands to arouse her senses instead, lightly caressing her back and feathering his fingertips over her nape. Then he pulled his mouth from hers to trail kisses over her face, kissing her eyes closed, tracing the shape of her ear, whispering to her. He hadn't memorized a repertoire of sweet nothings; in his social circles, they'd never been necessary. So he fell back on honesty, asking her to trust him, telling her how lovely she was, how much he wanted her, that she shouldn't be frightened. Eventually he began to realize it wasn't so much what he said but how he said it that mattered. She responded to the gentleness in his voice, the tension flowing from her, bit by bit, until she relaxed against him.

When he kissed her again, she parted her lips and, with a shy hesitancy that made his breath catch, touched the tip of her tongue to his. He moaned into her mouth and felt her gulp, taking his breath into herself. Dear God...he wanted to thrust more than just his breath into her.

Warning bells went off inside his head again. She'd never done this before, and he had to ease the way, yet backing off was difficult. He wanted to devour her...now, this minute. Taste all of her. Lose himself in her. Possess her so completely that his touch would be indelibly branded on her skin. His. He had to make her his, not just for tonight, but for all time. Because to face life without her now would be unbearable.

Gently and cautiously, Luke twined his tongue with hers. She stiffened slightly, but after a moment, she relaxed again, letting him taste her. He coaxed and teased until she finally slipped her tongue fully into his mouth. He met the shy invasion with light nips of his teeth. She shuddered and pressed closer, at the same time offering up her mouth more completely by parting her lips wider and letting him suckle her tongue.

Heaven...hell. Luke felt caught somewhere in between, her surrender to him so sweet he gloried in it, yet his need to take more so brutal his body quaked. Hands buried in her luxurious tresses, he ended the kiss with teasing nibbles, tormenting her already swollen lips in ways he knew would make her nerve endings scream. Her breath had started to come in jagged little pants when he finally lifted his head, and her eyes had a dazed look. He could feel every beat of her heart thrum through her body where it rested against him. No bones poked him anywhere, not even the point of an elbow. She was like holding a down-filled pillow, light and incredibly soft, every contour shaped to fulfill a man's fantasies.

Moving his hands up to cup her face, Luke dragged a thumb lightly over her mouth. It wasn't as difficult to go slowly with her as he had anticipated, for he wanted to savor everything about her, committing it to memory. Her breath puffed against his hand, hot and moist and quick. She was aroused, he knew, her sense of preservation numbed by the wine she'd drunk. He lowered a hand to the prim collar of her nightgown and flicked a button from its hole with practiced fingers.

Her eyes went wide, and she caught his wrist in halfhearted protest. "Luke? What are you doing?"

He nearly smiled at the question. His intent had to be fairly obvious, even to her. "I want to look at you, sweetheart. Please, won't you let me?"

For a long moment, she gazed up at him, her face mirroring her hesitancy. Then she let go of his wrist, giving silent permission for him to continue. As she released her hold, Luke realized what a precious gift she was offering him with such sweet generosity.

He started to unfasten another button, acutely aware that his hands had started to shake. He, Luke Taggart, who'd taken women with casual disregard all his adult life. Sex had always been a game to him. Now it suddenly seemed sacred—a melding of himself with something so pure and good, the thought terrified him. Cassandra wasn't the only one who was about to take an irrevocable step. He had a feeling that once he took her, he'd never be the same again.

The button refused to part company with the buttonhole, an unprecedented development. Normally Luke could have divested a woman of her clothing with both eyes closed and one hand tied behind his back.

"Do you n-need help?" she asked in a tremulous voice.

She reached up to assist him, her slender fingers claiming victory where his own had suffered defeat. Her cheeks pinkened as the fastener fell away, telling Luke that the thought of a man seeing her naked was not easy for her to contemplate. Yet her small hands descended to the next button, her fingertips slipping the iridescent disk from its hole. Her gaze clung to his, as if by looking at him, she drew courage. That humbled him even more.

With each downward progression of her slender fingers, his heart slammed more violently. When at last she'd undone every button, she let her hands fall to her lap and lowered her gaze, her dark lashes forming thick, silky crescents against her flushed cheeks. Not a blush of pleasure, he realized, but one of shame.

Luke's heart twisted. This girl had dreamed her whole life of becoming a nun, and now she was about to commit an act of fornication. The magnitude of that wasn't lost on him, not now that he'd gotten to know her. She was sacrificing everything she'd dreamed she might one day be, everything she'd yearned to be.

He caught her chin in his hand and forced her to look up at him. "Sweetheart, don't feel ashamed. It breaks my heart."

It was a sappy thing to say. He didn't *have* a heart, for Christ's sake.

And yet...

Luke swallowed, unable to escape the appeal in those melting blue eyes. His hand shook as he smoothed a rebellious tendril of curly dark hair from her cheek. "Have you any idea how lovely you are?" he asked her softly. "Or how much I need you?"

"Oh, Luke..." She placed her small hands on his shoulders and leaned forward to rub the tip of her nose against his. "Do you truly need me?"

Luke had never rubbed noses with anyone in his life. It didn't surprise him that he was being introduced to the activity by Cassandra or that he actually found it enjoyable. Her nose, like everything else about her, was soft, the bridge so pliable it gave way against his. When she drew back, he couldn't help but smile.

"I definitely need you," he said huskily. Right then, his body was screaming with need. Setting her slightly away from him again, he reached up to smooth back the front plackets of her gown. "And I want to look at you more than I've ever wanted anything."

The flush on her cheeks darkened. "I want you to," she admitted. "I know it's wrong, but—"

"No, dammit. It isn't wrong. It's absolutely right."

As he parted the flannel to bare her breasts, he feared he might die of anticipation. Days, he'd waited...endless days, longing to rest his gaze on those delicious swells of ivory flesh.

She whimpered low in her throat, and her body convulsed as the cloth dragged across her nipple. Luke trailed his palm in the wake of the material, letting the heel of his hand brush over the erect nubbin, slowly and lightly. She jerked again and arched her spine, pressing closer for his touch.

"Luke?"

"It's all right, sweetheart." Was that his voice, so gruff and shaky? Grasping her by the waist to hold her erect, he leaned back in the chair to feast his gaze on her. God, she was lovely. Her breasts were as round as plump melons, the skin flawless ivory, the nipples a tempting strawberry-and-cream that instantly made him salivate for a taste. "Oh, Cassie, you're beautiful."

She made another whimpering sound, a feminine noise deep in her throat that aroused his every male instinct. Her hands had locked over his wrists again where he grasped her waist, her knuckles white with the force of her grip. He let his palms move over her hips, pressing in above her pelvis with his thumbs and massaging deep. She sucked in her breath and held it, which thrust out her breasts.

Keeping a firm hold on her hips, he leaned forward to touch the tip of his tongue to a nipple. He could feel every thrum of her heart in that turgid peak of flesh, which pebbled and begged for suckling at the first instant of contact. She moaned and released her hold on his wrists to make tight little fists in his hair—whether to shove him away or urge him closer, he wasn't sure. She didn't leave him to wonder long. She drew him closer with an unmistakable urgency that nearly undid him. Her lashes drooped low over her lovely eyes, and her breathing came even more quickly.

"Luke," she whispered raggedly, "this must be wrong—terribly wrong."

"No," he cried hoarsely against her silken skin, "nothing that happens between us can ever be wrong, sweetheart. Never. It's wonderfully right."

Nothing could have made him stop. He latched onto her breast, drawing sharply. She cried out and arched against his mouth, offering herself to him without reservation. He caught the tip of her nipple between his teeth and began to roll the sensitive flesh, sending jolt after jolt through her slender body until she was sobbing with need, shaking with it.

Luke ran a hand under the hem of her nightgown. Silken thighs parted beneath the pressure of his hand. His fingertips homed in

311

on the nest of curls at their apex and invaded the shy folds of femininity to find a hot wetness that surprised even him. She jumped when he laid claim to the button of flesh he sought. He felt her stiffen. But he continued to suckle and tease her breast, dragging her back down into the vortex of passion with him until she once again relaxed her legs.

After teasing her there for a few minutes, frustration drove Luke to clasp her in his arms and shove to his feet. With four long strides, he reached the bed, where he laid her on the mattress. He positioned her lush bottom at the mattress's edge and knelt on the floor, parting her knees with the breadth of his chest.

She shrieked when he settled his mouth where his hand had played only moments before, the sound ripping up from her with a shrillness he feared might wake the whole house. She pushed at his shoulders, half-heartedly trying to dislodge him, but he'd firmly staked claim with his mouth and wasn't to be so easily dispatched.

Such earthy intimacy was bound to embarrass her initially. But it was also the one surefire way he knew to bring her mindless pleasure. Acting quickly, he began to suckle on that throbbing flange of sweetness, the pull of his mouth drawing the flesh there into a taut peak he could flick and tease with the tip of his tongue.

She cried out again, the sound strangled and muffled, her slender body jerking under his ministrations like a puppet manipulated by invisible strings.

"Luke! Oh, Luke, please!" She bucked and twisted, groping blindly for him, telling him in a language as old as womankind that her maidenly shyness was quickly being overcome by need. "Oh, Luke!"

He felt the flesh he tormented start to swell, then grow hard. With a growl, he caught it gently in his teeth, tugging and massaging until she dug the heels of her feet into his back, lifted her hips to him, and made fists in his hair to hold him closer.

When she finally climaxed, her body went into paroxysmal spasms. Luke stayed with her, gentling his ministrations but not desisting, barely allowing her first orgasm to subside before he pushed her to have another, then another. Later, when she remembered this, he wanted the ecstasy to be foremost in her mind, so overwhelming that the crudity of it dwindled in importance. Only when she lay limp and quivering, so exhausted that a fine sheen of moisture covered her skin, did he finally draw back.

Crawling up onto the bed, he settled beside her and trailed kisses over her face. She ran her arms around his neck and drew him down to her, pressing eagerly against him.

Luke clasped her in his embrace. She was magic and miracles, fairy tales and impossible dreams.

"Oh, Luke, I love you! I love you so much. I truly do. I love you. I love you."

"Oh, Cassie, I—"

Luke felt as if someone had just slapped him stone-cold sober. *Love.* To him, the word bordered on vile, and he bit it back. Then, grabbing frantically for control, he jerked away from her. He'd nearly said he loved her, and what was worse, he'd nearly said it with absolute conviction.

He swung off the bed and stumbled across the room to the door of his own bedchamber. He burst into the other room, locked the adjoining door and leaned against it, so weak at the knees that he couldn't stand without the extra support.

Stunned by Luke's abrupt departure, Cassandra lay in the flickering candlelight, tears of shame and humiliation welling in her eyes until the illumination seemed to swim. She'd heard the key turn in Luke's door and knew he'd not only left her, but locked her out of his rooms as well.

Oh, God. She rolled over and buried her face in her pillow, wanting to die. After giving herself to him that way, after allowing him— no, begging him—to do all those things to her, he'd turned away from her. He didn't want her love. He didn't even want her body.

A sob welled in her chest as she recalled the look on his face as he'd drawn away. As the picture gained clarity in her mind, the need to weep dissipated, and sheer puzzlement took its place. She pressed her closed eyes against the cool silk, remembering every detail of his features. Unless she was very, very wrong, the expression that had been stamped upon them hadn't been disgust.

It had been heartache—the kind that ran so deep, it couldn't be put into words.

Cassandra sat up with a suddenness that made her dizzy. Holding her breath to listen, she stared at the door that led to Luke's bedchamber. From the other side, she heard the shuddering intake of his breath. Her heart caught at the sound. She couldn't exactly say he was sobbing—not as she did when she cried, at any rate. But maybe men didn't make the same kinds of noises.

All her life, Cassandra had been more sensitive than most to other people's feelings. Her papa said it was because she wore her own feelings on her sleeve, which gave her special insight. Whether that was true or not, she did believe she had seen straight into Luke's heart a few seconds ago.

Such pain.

She wasn't sure what troubled him. She only knew he needed her. It didn't matter that he'd conveyed otherwise by locking the door between them. He needed her. She sensed it, clear to the marrow of her bones. Indeed, she could almost feel the waves of desperation emanating from him, even through the walls.

Remembering the door that opened from the hall into his bedchamber, she scrambled off the bed. She no sooner gained her feet than she hesitated, held fast by a sudden shyness and indecision. He hadn't said he loved her. He'd just done those embarrassing things to her person, then left her without a word. Somehow, it didn't seem very dignified to go after him. Or even very right. If he wanted to be with her, why had he left?

Then her gaze fell on the folded scrap of

paper he'd left lying on the table. She stepped over to pick it up. When she read the secret he'd written down, fresh tears came to her eyes. *I'm a toad pretending to be a prince.*

Cassandra knew by heart the story he referred to. As a small child, she'd heard it from her mother, and when she'd grown older, she'd embellished the tale for Khristos's entertainment. Apparently Khristos had told the story to Luke. And Luke had given it his own interpretation. Luke, handsome on the outside but ugly within.

Nothing could have been farther from the truth. Nothing. She didn't know why he would think such a thing, but he obviously did. *Some people might even tell you I'm ruthless,* he'd once told her. *I'm not a very nice man.*

She made a tight fist over the piece of paper, as if by sheer force of grip she could obliterate the thought from his mind. He wasn't ugly inside. He *wasn't*! And she couldn't let him go on believing he was.

Luke couldn't stop shaking. The worst of it was, he knew he was shaking with fear. He leaned more heavily against the door, closing his eyes. Afraid of a sweet, completely harmless girl half his size? It was absurd.

Oh, God, he'd nearly told her he loved her. He squeezed his eyes more tightly shut, trying to block out the thought, refusing to acknowledge even so much as the possibility. He couldn't love her, wouldn't love her. It was madness.

Yet Luke couldn't deny the feelings, the

tenderness and protectiveness that had taken root deep within him—feelings that transcended the physical, that had nothing to do with sex and everything to do with his heart.

Feeling as though he'd been physically battered, he staggered to the bed and collapsed across it, his face buried in the silk comforter. Memories assailed him as he recalled another time he'd lain with his face buried against a mattress, only that bedspread had been made of faded chenille and had reeked of the semen that permeated the nap, the leavings of his mother's countless customers.

There's a good boy. Let old Hank love you, son. Don't you want me to love you?

Luke wasn't sure how old he'd been on that long-ago night. He guessed he must have been about Khristos's age, still naive enough to trust a kindly man with a gentle voice and strong hands. Still naive enough to believe in his mother when she told him to let Hank "love" him and not be afraid. At that age, Luke had wanted to be loved more than anything else in the world, even if it was by a total stranger with whiskey on his breath.

Only there was no love to be had for him that night, just betrayal that had cut so deep, the wound still festered within him. He could remember his mother, shoving one of her stockings into his mouth to muffle his shrill screams of pain...slapping him afterward for crying and disturbing the other customers.

Luke angled an arm over the back of his head in a futile attempt to ward off the memories. On the back of his tongue, he could almost taste his mother's soiled stocking, the nasty stench of her dirty feet nearly strangling him. He felt as if he were going to vomit, an overpowering urge that had him gritting his teeth.

Please. The word became a litany inside his head, a silent plea to an unmerciful God to stop the remembering, to numb the pain. Only, of course, he expected no answer. If there had ever been anything he could count on, it was God's turning a deaf ear. No miracles, not for Luke Taggart. No angels appearing from out of nowhere, working their celestial magic.

Then, suddenly, in the darkness, Luke *did* feel an angel beside him. Cassandra, her small hand brushing lightly along his arm, then drifting to his hair. Her voice, soothing him, saying nonsensical things, warming him deep inside where he had always felt cold.

"Cassie?" Luke couldn't believe she'd come to him. After what he'd done to her, he just couldn't believe it. Christ, he treated his whores with more consideration, at least making a polite excuse before he walked out on them.

"Oh, Luke," she whispered. "Of course it's me."

Luke stiffened, absorbing her presence through the pores of his skin, so glad she was there that it was all he could do not to drag her into his arms and hold on for dear life.

She pressed against him much as she had earlier, only this time he was the unlearned child, she the wise one. As light as gossamer, she trailed her fingertips over his hair again, then brushed her knuckles along his temple. Luke couldn't stop himself. He turned his face toward her hand, craving her touch. Her small thumb caught one of the tears on his cheek, and he heard her breath catch.

"Oh, Luke..." she whispered in a tortured voice. "What's wrong? Tell me what's wrong."

It was the one thing Luke could never do. What had happened to him was too terrible, too ugly, to share with her. He didn't want her to know there were men in the world so vile they would do such things to a little boy, or that there were women so cruel and heartless. His mother had rented him out to good old Hank for fifty dollars. How could he tell Cassandra that? If he did, she would be forever changed by the knowledge. He didn't want her to change, dammit. He needed her to be just what she was, an angel with stars in her eyes.

He rolled onto his side and caught her to him. Almost afraid he might hurt her, he squeezed so hard, yet was unable to gentle his hold. "Don't leave me." The words erupted from him raggedly, a muffled testimony to his weakness, which at any other time would have humiliated him beyond bearing. He pressed his face against her wonderful hair. "Promise me, Cassandra. Promise you'll never leave me."

"Oh, Luke. Shhh. Shhh." She wrapped her arms around his neck, one hand splayed over the back of his head. "I'm here. I'll always be here. Shhh."

Cassandra. In her touch and in her soft,

whispering voice, Luke finally found the tenderness that had eluded him. She pressed against him, her arms a precious haven; the kisses she trailed over his jaw, light caresses that he treasured the way some men did jewels. She made no request for money. There was no bargaining before she offered herself to him. In short, she had no ulterior motive. She was just a simple, uncomplicated girl making a gift of herself to him in a simple, uncomplicated way.

Luke cupped a shaking hand over the silken nape of her neck, drawing her face closer to his so he might taste her mouth again. Not a carnal kiss this time, but a hesitant searching, hers born of innocence, his of wonder. The taste of her mouth washed away the bitterness at the back of his throat and eased the pain of his memories.

When he drew back, she whispered, "I love you, Luke."

He closed his eyes, wishing with all his heart he could tell her the same. Instead, all he could say was, "Tell me again. I want to hear you say it again."

She caught his face between her hands, smiling radiantly as she kissed the tip of his nose, then his lips, then his chin. "I love you. Silly me, thinking I wanted to be a nun. Papa warned me, but I wouldn't listen. I *love* you, Luke Taggart. I love you with all my heart."

Luke drew her into the circle of his arms again. She was so precious, this girl. A stolen bit of sweetness. He had no right to her, yet he couldn't hold himself away from her.

Luke drew the coverlet over them, a deep, abiding peace settling over him as lightly and warmly as the down. He gently settled Cassandra's head against his shoulder, then smoothed her silken hair over his chest like a soft blanket. Sighing contentedly, she snuggled close, hooking one leg over his hips and clinging to him like a baby opossum. That suited him just fine.

Long after Cassandra's breathing changed, he lay awake, staring at the ceiling. Moonlight filtered through the lace sheers between the drapes at the windows and cast designs across the plaster. He counted spots until his eyelids finally grew heavy.

His last thought as he slipped into slumber was: *She loves me. She really does love me.*

SEVENTEEN

It seemed to Luke he'd just closed his eyes when the mattress sagged at the other side of the bed. The ensuing jiggle brought him groggily awake.

"What the hell?" he whispered.

He blinked to clear his vision, sitting up and staring at the blurred outline of a child kneeling on his bed. The white nightshirt and tousled dark hair finally registered on his befuddled brain.

"Khristos?" he whispered, still keeping his voice down so as not to awaken Cassandra. "What the hell are you doing in here?"

"Don't be mad, Luke. I had a bad dream, is all."

321

"I'm not mad, kid. Just...surprised."

Cringing because the boy had caught him in bed with his sister, Luke raked a hand through his hair. *Christ.* How was he going to explain this one?

"Did you have one, too?" Khristos asked.

"One what?" Luke asked stupidly.

"A bad dream." The child glanced at his sister, who still slept peacefully, her dark hair a fan across Luke's pillow, her hand curled loosely beside her head. "Did Cassie come in to tell you stories and chase the scaries away?"

"You might say that." Relieved, Luke smiled in spite of himself. Reaching over to jerk the covers back on the other side of the mattress, he patted a spot for Khristos to lie down. "Now that you're here," he whispered, "you may as well stay."

Khristos didn't need a second invite. He dove for the pillow like a contestant in a greased pig contest, looping his thin arms around the silk-covered down and burying his face in it. "Thank you, Luke," he said in a faint voice.

"You're welcome," Luke whispered back.

He was about to lie back down when he heard an odd thumping sound. Leaning sideways on an elbow, he searched the darkness beside the bed. Slowly, a very large dog began to take shape in the shadows.

"He wouldn't stay downstairs," Khristos explained, "so I kind of helped him get up here."

"Kind of?"

Cassandra came awake, rubbing her eyes and yawning. "What's going on?"

Luke couldn't believe the poor, busted-up dog had come all the way up those stairs. Given the fact that he had, however, Luke didn't have the heart to carry him back down them.

"We have some company," he finally told Cassandra.

"Company?"

As Luke slipped from the bed, she pushed up on an elbow. "Lye-Lye? Khristos? What are you two doing up here?"

Khristos explained his and the dog's intrusion a second time. "I only had to pull a little to help Lycodomes climb the stairs," he elaborated. "He misses sleeping with you really bad, I guess."

Luke had a hunch Lycodomes wasn't the only one who missed sleeping with Cassandra. Taking care where he placed his arms, Luke lifted the dog and deposited him gently at the foot of the bed on Khristos's side. The child was small. His lack of leg length would give the animal plenty of room to lie down. Like a wolf circling an area to check for snakes, Lycodomes turned around and around on the coverlet until he found a good spot.

When all four of them had finally gotten situated and reasonably comfortable in the bed together, Luke turned onto his back and drew Cassandra's head to his shoulder again, one arm looped loosely around her. On her other side, Khristos snuggled as close as he could get.

"Isn't this fun?" she asked. "We're having a sleep party."

Luke couldn't help but chuckle. Only Cassandra could find a bright side to this. Personally, he felt like a sardine stuffed into a can.

Something thumped Luke sharply across the shin. Lycodomes's splint, he realized. Cassandra and Khristos were both so short, the dog had evidently decided to claim the entire lower fourth of the bed as his area.

"Oh, look!" Cassandra said suddenly. "There's George Washington."

Luke wasn't surprised. Everyone else had barged in on him; why not a dead president?

"Where?" Khristos asked.

She pointed at a shadow on the ceiling, cast there by moonlight coming through lace. In spite of himself, Luke studied the design. For the life of him, he couldn't see how it resembled good old George.

"Oh, and look there! It's a teapot!"

"I see it!" Khristos cried.

And so it went, for at least twenty minutes. Finally Cassandra yawned and drifted off to sleep, her withdrawal from the game forcing Khristos to grow quiet as well. Or so Luke thought. After a long while, the boy asked in a hoarse whisper, "Did it work, Luke?"

He glanced over Cassandra's shoulder at the child's shadowy face. "Did what work?"

"The story Cassandra told you. Did it chase your scaries away?"

When Luke finally answered, his voice was gruff. "Yeah, I guess it did."

"Good. I'm glad. What story did she tell?"

Luke thought a moment. "The one about the ugly toad that got magically transformed into a prince by the love of a beautiful lady."

"Good. I like that one." Khristos snuffled and thrashed with his skinny legs to get comfortable. Luke gazed at the ceiling, searching for George.

The following day, a deep, bone-chilling fear settled over Luke and stayed with him even when he finally escaped the house and went to the office.

As a kid far younger than Khristos, he'd learned to lie with the best of 'em. *No, I didn't touch the bread on the tray. No, I never took your money, Ma.* In the early years, lying had been his only means of getting what he needed. Only later did he learn to lie to get what he *wanted*. Necessary lies, glib lies, cruel lies, manipulative lies. He'd never felt a twinge of guilt. Now, however, the lies he'd told to possess Cassandra—the tricks he'd played to place her in an untenable position—had gotten him into a hell of a fix.

If she ever learned the truth, she would despise him. And she would discover it the instant she got an opportunity to speak with her father. Milo Zerek was poor, not stupid. Luke had seen the expression in the man's eyes the night of his arrest. Milo knew exactly how Luke had engineered the trap to ensnare him. At the first opportunity, he would tell his daughter.

Scowling at his desk blotter, Luke considered confessing everything to Cassandra—

and rejected the idea almost instantly. To do that, he would have to count on her to forgive him, and that was asking a hell of a lot. Yet, at the same time, he knew if he kept going as he was, he would only dig himself into a deeper mess.

One thing was for sure; keeping the Zerek men locked up in small jail cells for three months, as he'd originally planned, no longer seemed a good idea. Later, when Cassandra learned the truth, he didn't want her looking back and feeling bitter because her father and brother had been made to suffer unnecessarily.

Head cradled on his hands, Luke tried to think of some way he could keep the two men away from Cassandra, yet still see to their comfort and well-being.

Time...the word became a litany in Luke's head as he sat there with the heels of his hands pressed against his aching eyes. He needed more time. He couldn't let her learn the truth until he had an unbreakable hold on her heart.

Exhausted, Luke finally pushed up from his desk, hooked his jacket from the back of his chair, and grabbed his hat. A plan was taking shape in his mind—a very good plan, if he did say so himself. Now all he need do was visit his attorney and implement it.

Ten minutes later, Luke pounded his fist against Daniel Beauregard's paneled front door with such urgency that the carved oak trembled. From inside the two-story brick house, he heard running footsteps as someone raced to answer his knock. An instant later, the door swung open.

In his rush to see his attorney, Luke shoved past the solemn-faced butler, nearly knocking the skinny old man off balance. Grabbing the servant's arm to steady him, Luke said, "Hello, Stevens. Is Daniel home?"

"Mr. Taggart!" the butler sputtered, his bald pate shining in the light from the chandelier. "Good day to you, sir."

Luke swept his gaze over the entry hall. The seasoned oak doors, which contrasted starkly with the unadorned white walls, were all closed, giving no clue to where the master of the house might be. "Daniel is here, I hope? I've important business to discuss with him."

Straightening his black frock coat, the servant said, "I do beg your pardon, Mr. Taggart, but Mr. Beauregard is presently indisposed."

Luke drew his watch from his vest and flipped it open to check the time. "It's well after noon. Would you please tell him I'm here?"

The butler looked flustered. "Actually, sir, he's got a bit of a headache and gave me strict orders that he isn't to be disturbed."

A hangover, more than likely, Luke thought impatiently. Daniel made a habit of staying out late and tipping the bottle a bit too often. Nonetheless, he was a shrewd attorney, and Luke could always count on him. "I'm sure he'll make an exception for me," Luke told the butler firmly. "Where is he, Stevens? I'll take responsibility for disturbing him."

With a long-suffering sigh, Stevens finally

gestured with a pale, blue-veined hand at the set of double doors at the far end of the entry hall. "In there, sir. He and a houseguest are at breakfast."

Breakfast? Luke shook his head. One major difference between himself and his attorney was that Daniel often stayed abed late, then piddled away half the day once he arose. Luke had always been more regimented in his work habits.

His boots tapping a sharp tattoo on the gleaming hardwood floors, Luke traversed the long hallway. At the double doors, he twisted the ornate brass handle, pushing a shoulder against the panel. As he entered the room, he reeled to a stop. Daniel was at breakfast, all right, the main course a voluptuous brunette whose bodice gaped open, her pale, thrusting breasts smeared generously at the tips with strawberry jam. One hand braced on the table, her other on the back of Daniel's chair, the woman was bent forward and moaning delightedly as Daniel loudly suckled the preserves from her distended nipples.

"Oh!" she cried when she spotted Luke.

"Goddammit!" Daniel said with a snarl. "Doors were made to knock on, Taggart! Where were you raised, in a barn?"

Luke softly closed the door behind him and crossed his arms. His attorney, who still grasped his ladylove by the waist, had a smear of jam on his chin. The brunette, eyes glazed with ebbing passion, was about to impale her lover's ear with the tip of one strawberry-smeared breast.

"Actually, nothing so fine as a barn," Luke said with a grin. "Good afternoon, Daniel." He glanced at the woman, whom he recognized as the wife of an affluent city councilman. Under other circumstances, Luke might have beat a fast retreat. As it happened, he admired the councilman very much and couldn't help but feel angry on the poor fellow's behalf. "Hello, Mrs. Jackson. Good to"—he cast a pointed look at her exposed bosom—"see you."

A flush that rivaled the red smears on her breasts shot to her cheeks. With a choked murmur, she straightened and began jerking at her bodice to cover herself, cringing when the fine lawn of her chemise connected with the preserves and stuck to her skin. The moment all the buttons were fastened, she dashed from the room, slamming the door so hard behind her that the sound echoed off the dining room walls.

Luke turned a chair and straddled it, folding his arms across its back as he sat down. "Really, Daniel. Is there anyplace you draw the line? Rutherford Jackson is a nice man. That woman's got two little children and goes to church every Sunday."

Daniel grabbed up a napkin from beside his plate and scrubbed angrily at his jaw. Gazing at him, Luke had to admit the attorney was handsome, with refined features, dancing blue eyes, and wavy dark hair. More dangerous than his good looks, though, was his silver-tongued charm, which served him well in both the courtroom and the boudoir. Perhaps a little too

329

well, if Lindy Jackson's behavior this morning was any indication.

"*You're* lecturing *me*?" Daniel asked in amazement.

"I'm just pointing out that women like Lindy Jackson aren't exactly fair game."

"Since when? What did you do, get religion since I saw you last?" After straightening his amber silk robe and tightening the sash, Daniel reached for the china coffeepot at the center of the table. "Care for some? I can ring for another cup."

"No, thanks." Luke helped himself to a slice of toast, took a bite, then tossed the uneaten remains back onto the plate. "And, no, I haven't gotten religion. I just hate to see a perfectly good marriage ruined because you couldn't resist preying on a bored young wife. There are plenty of unattached females in town."

"You should know, Taggart." Daniel took a sip of coffee, eyeing Luke over the rim of his cup. "What brings you here this morning?"

"It's afternoon, and I came on business. I do have you on retainer, if you'll recall."

"Prior notification that you'd like to see me would be nice."

Luke chuckled and shook his head. "You have jam on the end of your nose."

Daniel swiped with the napkin again, a flush spreading across his high cheekbones. "Please, don't hesitate to enjoy yourself at my expense."

"I won't," Luke assured him. "Now that I'm thinking about becoming a married man myself, I find adulterous liaisons rather distasteful."

Daniel, in the middle of taking another sip of coffee, strangled on the liquid. He grabbed wildly for the napkin again. When the choking spasm finally passed, he fixed watery blue eyes on his employer. "What did you say?" he croaked.

"I said I'm thinking about becoming a married man."

"The Zerek twit?"

Luke narrowed an eye. "Cassandra is not a twit." He raked a hand through his hair and glanced around the room. "What are the legal ramifications?"

"Of what?"

"Marriage," Luke said impatiently. "If I marry her, will it weaken my hold on her? Nullify the contract we drew up?"

Daniel cleared his throat and dabbed at his eyes. "Well, it would certainly make the contract unnecessary. Your main goal was to bind her to you legally for a year. Marriage will accomplish the same thing, except for a lifetime."

Luke smiled at the note of warning in his attorney's voice. "I'm well aware of the usual duration of marriage, Daniel." He paused a moment. "What about any issue that should arise from our relationship? If we have a child, I have legal claim as things stand. If I marry her and we have a child, can she leave me and take it with her?"

Daniel sat back in his chair, his initial surprise ebbing, his gaze growing thoughtful. "In the event of a divorce, which is rather rare, the courts usually grant the father custodial rights to the children." He shrugged. "Occasionally, a man will specifically request otherwise, for whatever reason, but normally he gets custody and most of the assets as well. For one, the man is usually better able to support the children, and for another, a woman seeking divorce is generally looked upon with disfavor by a judge. Not a fair situation, to be sure, but that's the way it stands presently. Why?"

Luke sighed. "Before I do anything, I just want to be sure of my position. In essence, then, what you're saying is that a wife has very few rights in the event of a divorce."

A frown pleated Daniel's forehead. "Practically none."

"So, if I marry Cassandra, my legal hold on her will be as strong as it is now?"

"Stronger."

"Great!" Luke flashed his attorney a grin. "Just what I was hoping to hear."

"No, it's not great," Daniel came back. "It's an injustice, is what it is. No matter how miserable a situation may be for a woman, it's damned hard on her if she decides to sever the matrimonial tie. Someday, I hope to see that change."

Luke spared him another brief grin. "Don't get on your high horse. I didn't mean it's good that women have few rights in a court of law. I simply meant it makes it possible for me to marry Cassandra."

"Why marry her? By contract, you already

have all the rights of a husband for the next twelve months. I saw to that in the wording."

"But at the end of the twelve months?" Luke shook his head. "I've decided I want to keep her with me longer than that. Marriage, as you pointed out, will bind her to me for a lifetime."

"Unless she divorces you," Daniel reminded him, "which she'll very probably do the minute she talks to her father. You can't keep the man in jail forever, Luke. She's bound to find out what you've done, sooner or later."

Luke saluted the man's savvy with a curt nod. "That's exactly why I've been concocting another plan, which I want you to handle."

"Lord, help me."

"I pay you well, Daniel. Occasionally, you have to earn your money. I need you to buy me some time. A few months will probably suffice. Once Cassandra is with child, she won't consider divorcing me. Not if it means leaving her child behind."

"And if she isn't pregnant by the time her father is released? What then?"

Luke leaned forward over the chair. "Trust me, Daniel. I plan to work very hard to see that she is *very* pregnant before she ever sees her father or older brother again."

The attorney snorted. "And be bound to a woman who despises you for the rest of your life? Champion plan, Luke. I don't know why I didn't think of it."

"Have you got a better idea?" Luke challenged. "I can't lose her, Daniel. And I will if I don't lock her into this."

"No," the other man admitted with a sigh. "I don't have a better plan. I wish to God I did because this one has holes in it large enough to accommodate a horse." He shook his head. "Are you sure this isn't a passing fancy? There are a lot of women out there."

"I don't want any other woman; I want *her*."

"And her father and brother? What're you going to do, keep them in jail until they have prison pallor?"

"I've decided to have them released from jail and transported over the mountains to my silver mine."

Daniel raised his eyebrows. "To keep them prisoner there, you mean? Luke, stop and think."

"I have," Luke said firmly. "Look at things as they stand. The poor fellows are locked up. They'll be much better off over at the silver mine. Able to work, for one thing."

"Which equates to kidnapping and slave labor."

"I intend to pay them twice what they earned here—more than any other man in the mine—to compensate for the fact that they're more or less being sent there against their wills."

"Big of you."

Luke sighed. "Come on, Daniel. What else can I do? I care about this girl. I want to keep her with me. If I keep her father and brother in jail for three months, she'll never forgive me. This idea is much more"—Luke broke off, searching for the right word—"humane."

Daniel rubbed his jaw. "How the hell do you intend to keep them at the silver mine? The first opportunity they get, they'll hightail it back here."

"Not if they're kept under armed guard, they won't."

"Dear God, you really *have* gone over the edge. What if they try to run? Are you going to order that they be shot?"

"Of course, not. But they don't have to know that."

"Pardon me for saying it, but this is not a very good way to get off on the right foot with your in-laws."

"I'm not concerned about what my in-laws think of me," Luke retorted. "There's only one person whose opinions matter a damn." More than a damn, he realized with a mental shiver. "This plan will work, Daniel. I'm counting on you to see to the details."

EIGHTEEN

A twelve-branched candelabra at the center of the dining-room table cast a flickering amber glow over the pristine white tablecloth; long-stemmed goblets filled with darkest burgundy caught the light like prisms. Luke toyed absently with the base of his goblet, giving it a half turn, then twisting it back to its original position, his gaze fixed on the twinkling beveled edge of the glass. He had no appetite for the tender morsels of beef swimming in mushroom sauce on his plate, or for the baby potatoes and onions simmered in butter. In his recollection, he'd never been so nervous in his entire life.

How, exactly, did a man broach the subject of marriage? Luke couldn't imagine himself on bended knee. Yet, at this point, he would be willing to do even that if it would assure him a positive response.

Seated to his right, Cassandra glowed as richly as the goblets, her new, wine-colored silk dress, recently delivered from Miss Dryden's shop, shimmering in the candlelight, the ecru lace of the prim collar and cuffs complementing the flawless ivory of her skin. In the soft illumination, her sable hair, caught up at the crown in the usual loose array of curls, gleamed with highlights.

Gazing over at her, Luke felt his gut twist in an aching knot. What if she refused his proposal? All aspects of his plan except getting her to agree to marry him had already been executed. That afternoon, her father and brother had been removed from the jail and transported out of town to Luke's silver mine, the marshal having been generously bribed to ensure his complete cooperation. Milo and Ambrose Zerek were now under armed guard—a different form of incarceration, to be sure, but one that, in Luke's estimation, would be far more forgivable when Cassandra eventually learned the truth. Though still enduring imprisonment, both men would be well-treated and given far more comfortable living accommodations than they'd ever enjoyed before—not to mention much better wages—until such time as Luke elected to have them released.

Essentially, life for the two men wouldn't be much different than when they'd worked for Luke in Black Jack. Better, actually. Warm, dry shelter; good food, and plenty of it; plus great pay. The only major difference was that neither man would be allowed to see Cassandra or Khristos until Luke gave the word. It really wasn't an evil thing he was doing, Luke assured himself. More like "unusual." And it was necessary.

"Cassandra," he said in a strained voice that sounded nothing like his own, "there are some things I need to talk to you about."

She fixed that liquid, drowning gaze on him, her lush lashes so long and thick they swept up to her brows. "What kind of things?"

Luke toyed with his goblet, working his jaw. "First of all, about your papa and brother."

The blush along her cheekbones drained away. "Are they all right?"

"Yes, they're fine," he hastened to assure her. "Better than fine, actually." He managed to flash her a smile. "I've been feeling so guilty about their being kept in that jail. After the things you've told me, I know it's been sheer torture for your papa, being locked up like that. So...I, um...took the liberty of pulling a fast one."

Her color restored now that she knew her loved ones were all right, she frowned slightly. "A fast one?"

"You remember my explaining to you that I couldn't let them off scot-free, for fear that other men might begin jumping my claims?" At her nod, Luke continued. "Well, that is still a concern. So today, I had your papa and brother transported from the jail under armed guard to one of my silver mines. I've put out the word that they're being sent there to do hard labor to reimburse me for damages. But the truth is, they'll be doing the same sort of work they did for me here, only for much higher wages, and I've arranged for them to have nicer housing for the duration of their stay and a lot better food than they'd have gotten at the jail."

She laid her hand over his wrist, her already-shimmering gaze turning even more luminous. "Oh, Luke...you never cease to amaze me. How *sweet* of you to do that for them."

He shrugged a shoulder, eager to get past the dirty business of lying to her again. After a lifetime of lies, telling one more should have been as natural as breathing. It unsettled him to find that it was just the opposite.

"I figured they'd be a lot happier this way, and they're bound to feel better about things, now that they'll be drawing good wages for the duration of their sentence. It's a more palatable situation, all the way around." He swallowed. "I won't pretend I did it for unselfish reasons." He met her gaze. "I've come to care very much about you, you know. I can't bear the thought of your harboring bitter feelings toward me because of what's happening to your papa and brother. This way, my conscience is clear."

Luke only wished it truly was. Instead, guilt gnawed at him.

"Bitter feelings? Oh, Luke, you're such a silly man. You've been nothing but kind to all of us. How could you think I would harbor bitter feelings toward you, for anything? Just the opposite. I owe you a debt I can never repay."

"I don't want you to feel indebted to me. It's extremely important to me that you don't feel that way, in fact." He took a sip of wine to moisten his suddenly dry throat. "I have a question I want to ask you, and if you say yes, I don't want it to be because you feel obligated to."

"What question is that?"

Luke tightened his fingers around the stem of the goblet. "I, um...I've been thinking—about you and me. Having you here has made me very happy."

Her eyes brightened with sudden tears. "Oh, Luke, have I made you happy? Sometimes I've wondered. The specifics of my duties have been a little difficult for me to grasp, and lots of times you've seemed so frustrated with me that—"

"Forget the damned job, Cassandra, and your...duties." He hauled in a strangled breath. "I want you to marry me."

Sudden silence. Luke sat there, his temples thrumming with every beat of his heart. When she didn't say anything, he rushed to add, "Please, Cassandra, don't say no without thinking it through. I have a lot to offer you, if you'll only just—"

She interrupted him with an airy laugh. "'Don't say no?' I thought we'd already settled this last night."

Mouth lax and feeling as if he were standing at the edge of a hole, swinging his arms to keep from falling in, Luke gaped at her. "Pardon?"

She shrugged her slender shoulders, the expression in her eyes quizzical. "Well, didn't we? Settle it, I mean? That I wasn't going to be a nun because my true calling was to be your wife and the mother of your children? I thought it was all understood."

Scenes from the previous night flashed through Luke's mind: himself playing the role of intoxicated, conscienceless seducer. He'd gotten her tipsy, then nearly taken her virginity. As he recalled, he'd never said a damned word to her about any permanent arrangement, much less about marriage.

At his continued blank expression, Cassandra suddenly smiled and touched his cheek, her slender fingers feathering lightly along his bunched jaw. "You're so funny sometimes, Luke. As if either of us would even consider doing such...um...what we did if we didn't intend to get married."

He caught her hand to hold it against the side of his face, craving her touch in a way he couldn't define. "Then your answer is yes?"

She rolled her eyes and leaned toward him. "Of course it's yes. I would never have...well...engaged in such activities if I hadn't already decided to marry you. As it was, we did a terribly wrong thing, jumping the gun as we did. We really should have waited until Father Tully blessed our union."

She withdrew her hand and reapplied herself to her meal, taking dainty little bites of the succulent beef and chewing industriously. Luke stared at her, dumbfounded. Once again, it was driven home to him like a sledge hammering a nail that the two of them had come from entirely different worlds.

What struck him most strongly, however, was her complete confidence that it had been his intention to get married. Hell, if she'd been any other woman, he would have walked out and never looked back, not once considering himself obligated in any way. After all, he hadn't actually coupled with her. Yet in Cassandra's mind, they'd taken an irrevocable step.

He smiled, relieved beyond description on the one hand and amused to his jaded soul on the other. To think that he'd sat here at this table through half the meal, sweating and agonizing and unable to eat, scared to death that she might say no, and all the while, she'd been convinced that marrying him was the only option. *She* had decided, had she?

He smiled as he took another sip of wine, the choking sensation in his throat miraculously gone. She was his, as simply as that. No arguments, no getting down on his knees, not even a prettily worded proposal. The little minx *expected* him to marry her because, quite simply, it was the right thing to do. He kept forgetting he was supposed to be a prince, God help him.

"May I ask when you plan for this wedding to take place?" he asked, laughter lacing each word.

"Well, as soon as Papa and Ambrose get back, I would think." Her lovely brow pleated with a sudden frown. Leaning toward him again, she added in a low voice, "Unless, of course, my curse doesn't come."

"Your what?"

Her cheeks turned a pretty pink. "You know, my...um...curse. If it doesn't come, we can't possibly wait until Papa can be here to give me away."

It suddenly hit Luke what she meant by "curse," and it was on the tip of his tongue to disabuse her of the notion that she was in any danger of being pregnant. Then it occurred to him that she'd just supplied him with the perfect excuse to rush things.

"Sweetheart, it's for that very reason we don't dare wait until your papa gets back. If you're...well, in the family way...how would it look if the babe came nearly three months early? People would know that we...um...jumped the gun, and the shame of it would stay with our child forever."

Her eyes darkened with concern. "Oh, my..." She refocused, meeting his gaze with a question in her own. "Is it likely, do you think? That I'm...well...you know."

Luke had already told so many lies that one more hardly seemed an issue. Or so he assured himself. "It only takes once."

"Oh, my..." She sank back against her chair, letting her fork fall with a clatter onto her plate and putting a hand over her waist. "Oh, Luke, when I get married, I want my papa there to walk me down the aisle!"

Luke saw tears welling. That always made

him feel slightly panicky. His feelings about this girl defied explanation or reason.

"Honey, how about this? Let's be married quietly, with just Khristos in attendance, and two witnesses. I'm sure Pipps and Mrs. Whitmire would happily volunteer. Then, when your papa returns, we'll have a second ceremony—a grand wedding, with all the trimmings. You can wear a beautiful white dress, and he can walk you down the aisle. Ambrose can be my best man."

She immediately brightened at the suggestion. "Can we do that? Get married twice?"

"Of course, we can. What do you say? Isn't that a grand idea?"

"Oh, yes! It's perfect! And that way," she pitched her voice low, "it won't raise anyone's eyebrows if I'm...well...you know."

Luke never missed a beat. "Just in case, I think we should see Father Tully, posthaste. I'll convince him to waive the posting of banns and marry us immediately."

Given Cassandra's destroyed reputation, Father Tully was more than eager to see Luke make an honest woman of her. To that end, he not only waived their having to post banns, but he postponed a baptism the following afternoon to perform the quick ceremony. So eager was the priest to get them married, in fact, that Luke had the distinct impression the old man was half afraid Luke might change his mind and skip town.

Not a chance. Luke was getting exactly

343

what he wanted: a lifelong contract that gave him legally sanctioned rights to the girl who stood beside him before the altar, her face aglow as she vowed before almighty God to love, honor, and obey her husband until death did them part. Luke, determined never to utter the word *love*, subsituted the word "cherish" in his vows to her as he slipped a two-carat diamond wedding ring onto her slender finger.

Slightly off to the right, Pipps, Mrs. Whitmire, and Khristos stood witness to the ceremony. Pipps and the boy beamed with approval, but the housekeeper kept sending dagger looks at Luke to convey her displeasure. Luke wasn't sure why the older woman disapproved of his marrying Cassandra, and for the moment, he was too happy to care.

When at last Father Tully made a sign of the cross over Luke's and Cassandra's bowed heads, Luke was able to breathe a sigh of relief. It was done. She belonged to him, the union blessed by a priest, and no man—not even her beloved papa—could put it asunder. Catching Cassandra by the chin, Luke settled his mouth over hers, the kiss sealing her promises to him and binding her to him for a lifetime.

"Congratulations," Pipps said when the matrimonial kiss ended, stepping forward in a stiff, pompous manner to shake Luke's hand. In a voice pitched for Luke alone to hear, he said, "I wish you all happiness, sir. It's pleased I am that you changed your mind and decided to marry the young lady instead of—" Pipps grew flushed and cleared his throat. "Well, enough said. Congratulations."

In that instant, Luke knew that his servants had somehow determined the truth, that Cassandra was still as sweetly virginal as she'd been the day he brought her to the house. The upstairs maids had probably been watching for telltale signs of blood on the sheets or, God forbid, eavesdropping at the doors. That was the way of it when a man lived in a large house with bored hirelings lurking around every corner.

For a heartbeat, Luke felt slightly embarrassed. He'd made no secret of his intentions when he'd hired Cassandra, and it stung his male ego to think his household staff might be snickering at him behind his back for having failed to carry through. On the other hand, Cassandra wasn't just any woman, but his lady-wife, and he was glad that at least his servants realized she hadn't come to his bed before their marriage.

"Yes, well, Pipps, it was the specifics that proved to be my stumbling block," Luke said softly. "I had a devil of a time explaining them to her, and finally I just gave up."

The butler released a loud and very undignified snort, his face turning beet red. "The specifics. Ahem! Of course. They can trip a fellow up, to be sure."

As the butler turned toward Cassandra, his flush receded and the usual rigidity in his expression softened, his stern mouth turning up slightly at the corners. To Luke's surprise, instead of bowing low over his mistress's hand, the older man made a rumbling sound low in his throat and gathered Cassandra in his arms. "God bless you, miss. I mean, madam. I wish you a lifetime of only good things."

Cassandra went up on her tiptoes and hugged the butler's neck. "Oh, Pipps, thank you!"

Glowing with happiness, Cassandra drew away from the butler to embrace Mrs. Whitmire. Then she bent to enfold her little brother in her arms. "Ah, Khristos! What have you to say, hmm? Your sister's an old married lady now!"

"I'm just glad you married Luke!" Khristos shot his newly acquired brother-in-law a grin. "Fancy that. My sister married to the richest bloke in town."

"Khristos!" Cassandra exclaimed.

"Well, he is. Ain't nobody in town richer."

Luke winked at Father Tully, whose round face was creased in a grin, his kindly blue eyes twinkling. As he shook hands with Luke, the old priest said, "Treat her well, Luke. She's a rare gem."

Luke was well aware of the treasure he had, and he could scarcely wait to get her home to the privacy of his bedchamber to consummate their marriage. A slight snag, that. How Cassandra might react had him slightly worried. When he made love to her, she was bound to be surprised, after all, believing as she did that they'd already engaged in sexual intimacy to its fullest extent.

Luke brushed the concern aside, assuring

346

himself that he would barrel across that bridge when he came to it. Besides, by the time he actually did take her virginity, she'd be so mindless with passion, she'd scarcely notice.

His mind filled with visions of lovemaking, Luke signed the marriage documents and made his way from the church rather blindly, genuflecting on the wrong knee when Cassandra tugged on his sleeve, then dipping the fingertips of the wrong hand into the holy water before crossing himself. A Catholic, he wasn't. But to please her, he would happily go through the motions. Might as well get into practice. To marry her, he'd had to sign papers to the effect that he'd raise their children in the church and see to it that they received Catholic religious education. A small price to pay, Luke assured himself.

During the walk home, Luke kept one arm around his wife's slender shoulders, his senses attuned to her every movement as he took in the loveliness of the evening. Darkness was about to fall, and the crisp chill of winter hung in the air, making their breath crystalize into little clouds that dissipated around their warm faces. Chimney smoke trailed from the houses along the streets, the smell of burning wood mixing with the pungent scent of autumn leaves left in decomposing piles in the gutters. It was, Luke thought, a beautiful night. A night he wanted never to forget. His wedding night.

The insane urge to jump up and click his heels came over him. He wanted to run and shout his good fortune to the world. Instead, he tightened his arm around Cassandra's shoulders and fixed his gaze on her lovely profile. Whenever he looked at her, something inside him went all soft and warm. She wasn't precisely beautiful, at least not as the word was usually defined. Her nose, a miniature of her Greek papa's, was the most prominent feature of her face, jutting from between her brows. If not for the impressive thrust of her ample bosom, it would have preceded her everywhere she went. But to Luke, that nose was perfect. He wanted to kiss it, nibble its tip, feel its softness rubbing against his. And, God, that mouth. In profile, the bow of her top lip curved sweetly upward at the cleft, inviting a man's kiss.

He wanted to take her home and unwrap her as he might a gaily decorated Christmas package, to gaze at her to his heart's content, to examine every little detail of her face and body. Before this evening ended, he promised himself, he would memorize every inch of her, know the taste of her, the texture of her. She was his, absolutely, without limitation. He could linger over her tonight like a man over a succulent feast. Anticipation had his blood surging and his groin turning hot and hard.

Once at the house, Luke found himself swept away on a tide of celebratory jubilation amongst his staff. Cook had baked a cake and made ice cream, which she served in the kitchen to her master and new mistress, the other servants, Khristos, and the dog, with no pretense, formality, or folderol. There were toasts, good wishes, and much laughter all around before Luke finally felt he could whisk his wife upstairs without raising any eyebrows. But when he turned to claim his bride, he discovered that Mrs. Whitmire had beaten him to the draw and spirited the girl away for a woman-to-woman chat in the storage room.

When the two finally emerged, Mrs. Whitmire looked solemn and Cassandra, a little pale. Luke attributed her pallor to weariness. His bride had had a long, exciting day, with scarcely a moment to herself since she'd risen from bed early that morning. All the more reason for him to call an end to the festivities and take her upstairs as swiftly as possible. Leaving strict orders with Mrs. Whitmire that Khristos and Lycodomes were *not* to join him and Cassandra in his bedchamber that night—under any circumstances—Luke grasped his wife's elbow and ushered her from the kitchen.

When they were finally closeted alone together in Luke's bedchamber, Cassandra turned suddenly shy, asking if he would mind allowing her a few moments of privacy in her room to prepare for bed. Since she asked so sweetly, Luke had little choice but to grant her wish, but he felt a niggling alarm as he watched her leave. Had that been fear he'd seen in her eyes when she looked up at him?

Given the sweet passion with which she'd responded to him two nights ago, Luke shoved the thought away, scoffing. Why would she suddenly feel frightened? More than likely, she was only a bit shy.

Glancing around his bedchamber, he

decided a sudden case of shyness on her part was understandable. His suite had been prepared for seduction, per his orders, with candles lighted in strategic spots to cast a romantic glow over his room. A low fire burned in the grate, its cheerful crackling a perfect touch on a chilly evening. Wine awaited them on the small table near the hearth. Cassandra would have had to be blind and slightly dumb not to realize what he planned for the evening. Given the intimacy they'd already shared, maybe she was just feeling a little embarrassed at the prospect of doing those things with him again.

Pacing the floor, Luke rubbed his hands together, whether to ward off the evening nippiness or with anticipation, he wasn't sure. Then, growing impatient, he jerked at his tie and unfastened the three top buttons of his shirt. Back and forth he paced, one ear cocked toward the adjoining door between his bedchamber and Cassandra's, alert to the slightest noise that might herald her entrance. What the hell could be taking her so long? He checked his watch and saw that she'd been out of his sight only ten minutes. Not all that long, he assured himself.

Returning the timepiece to his pocket, he peeled off his vest and tossed it in the general direction of his dresser, where it hit and slid off to land in a puddle of gray, the watch going *kerthunk* as it struck the hardwood floor.

Christ. Luke stopped pacing and pinched the bridge of his nose. He needed to calm down, he lectured himself. Take it slow. Think about something else. Otherwise, he'd leap on the poor girl the moment she entered his bedroom. He didn't want to turn her from the intimacies of marriage with a crass display of unbridled passion, grabbing and groping and generally making an ass of himself.

"Luke?"

At the sound of her voice he nearly parted company with his skin. She stood in the open doorway, a vision in white. Like a goddamned fool, Luke just stared at her. Gone was the dingy flannel nightgown she'd borrowed from one of the maids, and she wasn't wearing one of the seductive gowns he'd purchased for her, either. This sleeveless creation was...Luke swallowed, hard. A flowing cloud of virginal white, it floated over the voluptuous curves of her body like moonspun magic, the low-cut bodice made of the same peekaboo eyelet lace as the overskirt, which lay in gathers over sheerest lawn to fall in graceful folds around her slender feet.

Her hair, brushed to a sheen, lay in a rippling dark curtain around her shoulders, one long tendril forming a loose curl over her breast. The bodice displayed enough ivory cleavage to drive a man mad, yet was still modest enough to befit an angel. Except, of course, for the fact that the eyelet was transparent enough for the outline of her nipples to show through.

"D-Do you like it?" she asked, pressing a trembling hand to her midriff.

Did he like it? Luke couldn't feel his feet.

He'd seen females in every stage of undress imaginable, had had them parade before him nude, striking suggestive poses and performing lewd acts to whet his desire. Yet Luke could not recall ever having felt so thunderstruck.

"I...um...asked Miss Dryden to help me choose it," she whispered. "I...it...if you don't like it, I'll go change."

Luke nearly tripped over his own feet walking toward her. "Don't you dare," he said with a choked laugh. He took both her hands in his and swirled her farther into the room, keeping her at arm's length so he could examine her from head to toe. At perusal's end, he hadn't changed his mind. She was still the most gorgeous thing he'd ever clapped eyes on.

"Oh, sweetheart," he said huskily. "You are...indescribably beautiful."

She wrested a hand free to splay it over her bare chest. A hand that was shaking in a way he didn't like at all.

"In truth, I feel a little...naked. This...nightgown hasn't much of a front, but Miss Dryden insisted it was just the thing. I...um...didn't have any money of my own, so I put it on your account. I hope that's all right?"

Luke nodded. Words were suddenly beyond him. Gazing into her luminous blue eyes, he realized she was frightened, that he hadn't imagined it earlier.

"Luke?"

The way she whispered his name jerked him back to his senses, and he realized he was making her horribly self-conscious, staring at her as he was. Hands shaking like an adolescent boy's, he stepped closer and cupped her face between his hands.

"I'm sorry, sweet. It's just that you're so lovely, I can't stop looking."

"I'm not...that is, you don't have to...sweet-talk me." She took a breath and focused wide eyes directly on his chin. "I know I'm short and stout, and I have a big nose."

Luke raised an eyebrow. "You're middling tall and generously rounded. And your nose is adorable."

She crossed her eyes to look along the bridge of the feature in question. "I have freckles."

"Adorable freckles, and you have to look close even to see them."

Her lips trembled in a brave attempt at a smile, but her small hands were clasped together so tightly her knuckles poked whitely against the skin. He wanted to kick himself for failing to take control and put her at ease.

"Honey, are you afraid I'll hurt you?" he asked, acutely conscious of how badly she'd begun to shake.

"I...um...yes...no...not exactly. It's just—" She gnawed on her lower lip for a moment, her gaze clinging to his. "Mrs. Whitmire gave me a motherly talk in the storage room, that's all. To prepare me for tonight. And from what she said, I gathered that...um...well, that maybe we didn't—" She broke off, looking hesitant. "Oh, Luke, please don't get angry with me for saying this, but I fear we may not have done things exactly right the other night."

Luke was beginning to get a very bad feeling about this. "What did she say?"

Her cheeks turned a bright pink. "I'd rather not go into detail." Her mouth quivered at the corners. "I'm just...well, a bit worried."

Luke could have cheerfully strangled Mrs. Whitmire. God save the world from well-meaning biddies. "Sweetheart, you shouldn't listen to Mrs. Whitmire, especially not when she's advising you about this sort of thing."

Before she could guess what he meant to do, Luke caught her around the waist and, with three long strides, pressed her back against the wall. She gave a squeak of startlement, making fists on his shirt. "What are you— Luke?"

He bracketed her shoulders with braced arms, his booted feet spread, one on either side of hers. His face hovering only inches above hers, he said, "Forget everything that frigid old woman told you. Marital intimacy isn't a chore, Cassie, and it's perfectly natural, and there's *nothing*, absolutely nothing, for you to be worried about."

The dubious expression in her blue eyes made Luke smile.

"Cassandra, do you trust me?"

"Yes, with all my heart."

Which was far more than he deserved. His smile broadened. "Then believe me when I say this isn't going to be some trial to endure. All right? Didn't it feel nice the other night?"

"Yes, but—"

"No buts. It will feel even nicer tonight. As nice as I can possibly make it for you. No bearing up. No wifely duty. Just sweet pleasure. I promise."

Luke's heart caught at the expression that came into her eyes as she raised her slender arms to encircle his neck. *Love.* She didn't need to say the word. The emotion poured from her, the warmth of it surrounding him.

"If you promise, then I believe you," she whispered. "You've never lied to me. If you say it will be wonderful, then I know it will be."

Luke had lied to this girl more times than he could count. He didn't deserve her trust. Yet he was going to take it, just as he'd taken everything else she had to give.

NINETEEN

ঙ Pressed against the wall and imprisoned there by Luke's muscular arms and firmly planted feet, Cassandra could sense his desire for her in the bunched hardness of his body, could hear it in the altered cadence of his breathing and the thunderous pounding of his heart. His dark face above hers had drawn taut, his features cast into harsh shadow by the flickering candle and firelight, his eyes agleam with an urgency she didn't understand.

Though she'd vowed to trust him, to believe in him and his promise not to hurt her, Cassandra couldn't seem to push Mrs. Whitmire's dire

355

warnings out of her head. Nor could she forget the shiver of doom that had shrouded the housekeeper's voice as she'd pronounced the fateful words "conjugal rights" as though they were worse than any disease.

When Luke suddenly moved away from her to lock both doors, she threw a dread-filled glance at the bed. The key rasped in its lock, the sound making her leap. She clamped a hand to her waist in a vain attempt to stop the lurching of her stomach. *Nothing to be afraid of, nothing to be afraid of.* The words skittered through her mind, but no matter how many times she thought them, they didn't calm her jangled nerves.

"You know, Luke, maybe we should have a little wine and…um…talk for a while," she suggested with shrill eagerness. "Wouldn't that be nice?"

In the flickering shadows, he looked tall and suddenly sinister as he turned from locking the door. His tawny hair gleamed like a lion's mane, his whiskey-colored eyes alert to her every expression and slightest movement. "Sweetheart, are you still frightened?"

Cassandra gulped and closed her eyes. *No matter how bady it hurts, you musn't struggle or cry out,* Mrs. Whitmire had warned direly. *Just bear up, lass. If he's the sort of man to have a care, it'll be over with quickly enough. And if he's not—well, even then, nothing lasts forever. If the bleeding doesn't stop soon after, cold cloths can help stanch the flow. If that doesn't work, the tearing may be uncommonly bad and you might have to send for a physician.*

"Cassandra?"

She fastened a startled gaze on his when he curled a finger under her chin. "Don't sneak up on me like that. You nearly made my heart stop."

He chuckled, a low, warm sound. "Cassie, for God's sake, what did that old biddy say to you? You look scared half to death."

"I'd just like some wine, that's all. Bridal jitters, I guess."

"Bridal jitters?"

She nodded. "That's what Mrs. Whitmire said I'd feel at this...moment."

He firmed his grasp on her chin, lifting her face slightly. "I see. And what else, besides bridal jitters, did she enlighten you about?"

Cassandra averted her gaze. Suddenly, the air in the room seemed terribly thin, as if the candles were burning away all the oxygen. "Luke, will you promise me one thing?"

"Anything within reason," he said, his voice thick with what sounded like suppressed laughter.

"If...um...it should prove necessary, you won't hesitate to go get Doctor Mosley, will you?"

He leaned around to see her face, his gaze giving hers no quarter. "Mosley? Why the hell would we need him?"

"If cold towels don't stop the bleeding."

"Jesus Christ." His hand on her chin tightened until the grip of his fingers was almost bruising. He forced her head around. "Cassandra, look at me."

She did as he instructed, wishing with

357

every breath she drew that she didn't have to. After a long moment, he gentled his hold on her chin, but his gaze remained relentless. In a measured voice, he said, "Mrs. Whitmire should be horsewhipped. Why she took it upon herself to have a 'motherly chat' with you, I haven't a clue. But the world could do without her brand of mothering. You aren't going to bleed enough to need cold towels, let alone a doctor. Virginal bleeding is a smear, at most—such a minute amount that we may need a magnifying glass to find it on the sheets afterward."

"Truly?"

He sighed and leaned down to press his forehead against hers. "Truly."

Gathering her courage, Cassandra blurted out the rest. "She said it was going to feel as if you were tearing me apart inside."

He moved his hands to her shoulders. His fingers curled warmly over her bare upper arms, their grip gentle, yet hinting at leashed strength. "Let's make a bargain, all right?"

Cassandra figured beggars couldn't be choosers. "All right."

"If it begins to feel as if I'm tearing you apart, all you need do is tell me, and I swear I'll stop."

"Y-You will?" Mrs. Whitmire had cautioned her against asking him to stop. Indeed, she'd said it was "absolutely unacceptable," and that Luke would grow angry if she made such a request, which would result in the ordeal being far worse for her in the end. "Do you promise not to get mad at me?"

He bent slightly to kiss the bridge of her nose.

"Remind me to let Mrs. Whitmire go first thing in the morning," he whispered huskily. "The old witch. I can't believe she's done this to you."

"Oh, you can't let her go! She was just trying to...well, prepare me. What with my mother being dead, and all. I g-guess she thought I needed to know what to expect."

He cupped a hand over the back of her head and pressed her face to his shoulder, muffling whatever else she meant to say. "Don't start worrying about Mrs. Whitmire," he whispered fiercely. "I won't really let her go." His fingers tightened convulsively over her scalp, conveying a depth of emotion she felt vibrating through his muscular body. "God, Cassandra...how could you think, even for a moment, that I would hurt you that badly and not stop?" he asked in a throbbing voice. "I'd rather cut off my arm, sweetheart. Anything but hurt you."

By the very shakiness of his whisper, she knew he meant it, and shame flooded over her for feeling afraid. Wresting her face to one side, she said, "Oh, Luke, I'm sorry. Of course you wouldn't. Not intentionally, anyway."

His chest shook slightly with a low chuckle. "Not intentionally, nor otherwise." He moved back a bit to capture her face between his hands again. "Ah, Cassie, girl. I want you so...."

Cassandra wished he would tell her he loved her, but for reasons she couldn't understand, *love* was a word Luke seemed reluctant to say. He had, however, told her that he cared about her. Looking up into his golden brown eyes, she decided that his actually saying the words wasn't necessary. The message was there, in his gaze, in the warmth and depth of feeling that could only be love, whether he expressed it aloud or not.

Very carefully, he pressed her back against the wall again, keeping enough distance between their bodies so he had room to unfasten the little ribbons of her bodice. Two nights ago, he'd seen her naked bosom, but to Cassandra that seemed a lifetime ago. Making fists at her sides, she fought against the urge to capture his hands. Slowly, bow by bow, her bodice parted, baring her breasts.

She hauled in a burning breath when he sent the nightgown sliding off her shoulders. Like a whisper, the eyelet and lawn fell to the floor, puddling about her bare feet. He moved back slightly and lowered his gaze. When she started to cross her arms, he caught her wrists.

"Oh, no..." he said huskily. "Let me look at you."

Cassandra yearned to close her eyes. She felt like a bug pinned to velvet, a specimen he meant to study. And study her, he did. Suddenly and horribly conscious of every flaw of her body, she died a little with each passing second, convinced he'd cease to want her when he saw how ugly she was: the round swell of her belly, the plumpness of her hips, her short legs, her big breasts. She recalled those few times she'd glimpsed herself nude in a full-length mirror—the last time, that very afternoon at Miss Dryden's dress shop. In

Cassandra's estimation, she looked like blobs of bread dough someone had lumped together. It was humiliating to think Luke might be making the same comparison. He'd seen parts of her the other night, but not the whole of her, all at once.

"My God, you're glorious," he whispered raggedly.

Cassandra blinked. "I am?"

"You are," he assured her.

There was such awe in his voice. Cassandra's superstitious Irish nature got the best of her, and she absolutely had to look down, just to make sure the little people hadn't been up to some mischief, a part of her almost hoping they had. She would have welcomed a bit of leprechaun magic right now, to smooth out her lumps and skinny up her fat spots. But, no, it was the same short, stout body down there that she'd always had.

"I have a fat bum," she blurted out.

Luke arched a tawny eyebrow. "Do you now?" Still imprisoning her wrists in his firm grip, he leaned around to look at the body part in question. Cassandra flattened herself against the wall in an attempt to foil him. "It looks like a pleasingly plump bum to me," he said warmly.

"That's what Papa says, that I'm 'pleasingly plump.'"

"What's wrong with his saying that?"

"I *hate* it. What he really means is that I'm fat, but he thinks I'm cute in spite of it."

Luke threw back his head and laughed. The sound so startled her that she was taken completely off guard when he suddenly drew her away from the wall and released his hold on her wrists to step slowly around her, his gaze glinting as he surveyed her, front and back, head to toe. She crossed her arms and cupped her palms in an attempt to conceal her breasts, which another girl had once told her were so big they looked like cow udders.

"Your papa is absolutely right," Luke finally said. "You are 'pleasingly plump.' And you know what?"

"No, what?"

"*Pleasingly* is a word kind of like *breakfast*, I'll bet, one that came to be over hundreds of years." As he finished circling her and came to a stop at center front, he flashed a slow smile. "A word people invented, I'm sure, to describe things that pleased them or gave them pleasure. And you know what, Cassie, girl? You please me."

"Do I?" It was difficult to squeeze enough air out of her lungs to form words.

"Know what else?"

She shook her head. He reached out suddenly and touched the tip of one nipple with a fingertip, making her jump.

"You missed a spot," he informed her.

Cassandra moved her hands to correct that. He merely smiled and touched his fingertip to another spot she'd inadvertently exposed in the attempt.

"I think your biggest problem is that your hands are too small," he whispered huskily as he stepped toward her, grasping her wrists as he advanced. "Too small to cover everything

362

you seem determined to hide, at any rate." He drew her arms down to her sides. "I think you need a larger pair of hands to do the job. Don't you?"

He settled his palms over the places her own had just vacated. Cassandra dragged in a breath and held it as a liquid warmth rippled from the tips of her breasts and began to roll through her. He bent his head, his lips hovering inches from hers, his gaze delving deeply into her eyes.

"You're beautiful, sweetheart. Absolutely beautiful. Do you know what I like the very best about you?"

"No, what?" she managed to croak.

"That you don't realize how very lovely you are." His lips moved marginally closer, every moist huff of his breath caressing her mouth like spring mist, making her senses thrill, yet sending shivers over her skin. "Every other beautiful woman I've ever known has been vain. It's delightful to finally meet one who isn't, to be able to tell you you're lovely and have you look so surprised to hear it. My God, Cassandra, how can you not know? Haven't you ever looked in a mirror?"

"Of course. That's one of the reasons I decided to become a nun."

"Over my dead body. You're mine—every sweet inch of you—and don't you ever forget it."

The throbbing intensity in his voice quickened her pulse. A rushing sound began in her ears, slight at first, like the distant sound of a rising wind that gained force and definition within her as he lightly touched his lips to hers.

Luke. Everywhere he touched her, she felt a melting, liquid heat, her skin so sensitized, even the downy hair on her arms began to tingle. He ran his hands from her breasts to her shoulders, then down to her elbows, his fingertips touching her so lightly, she felt as if she were standing nude in the rain. Each trailing touch of his fingertips was like a raindrop sluicing over her skin, the rivulets imbued with electricity from bolts of lightning that hadn't yet struck.

Luke was the lightning, she thought nonsensically. A sizzling electrical feeling seemed to emanate from him. As he touched her, he lingered here and there, tracing every curve, every crease, as though to commit everything about her to memory. Stirring shivers radiated outward from every place he settled his hands.

Then, hard and searing, he settled his mouth more firmly over hers, the contact so compelling and urgent it made her heart skitter. Wet silk. That was how his mouth felt, like wet, lush silk.

With no warning, he suddenly lifted her into his arms and carried her to the bed. After depositing her gently on the satin coverlet, he stood over her, his gaze molten amber as he surveyed her. Fire and candlelight created a shining nimbus around him, casting his broad shoulders and tawny hair in flickering gold, throwing parts of his face into shadow. He finished unbuttoning his shirt, the burnished planes of his well-padded chest revealed as the white silk fell open to his waist. An instant later, the shirt whispered to the floor.

Cassandra gazed up at him, mesmerized. *He* was the beautiful one, she thought, not her. With each move he made, the bulges in his shoulders and upper arms rippled and bunched, his dark skin gleaming as though rubbed with oil. He knelt beside her on the mattress, the bare breadth of his chest bathed in firelight, which somehow seemed to meld with him, making it difficult to tell where the tawniness of his hair and skin ended and the flickering amber began.

With a reverence that nearly brought tears to her eyes, he moved his hands to lightly trace the upper swells of her breasts. Her breath caught as the callused heels of his hands skimmed the tips of her nipples. He smiled at her shuddering reaction, then leaned forward slightly, his chest a canopy of bronze above her.

Cassandra forgot to feel afraid. Instead, she reached up to touch a fingertip to his collarbone, tracing its planes. From there, she trailed her hand down to explore his flat nipple, which gleamed like a coppery nugget in a light furring of golden hair. His breath caught, and she could almost feel the tension in him mounting. He was magic. He was firelight. He was a molten heat that washed over her and into her.

Her breasts burned and ached, craving more of his touch. He slipped an arm under her, catching her at the small of her back and splaying a hand beneath her spine. With seemingly little effort, he lifted her so she lay arched over his forearm, her head back. With silken lips, he tasted the hollow beneath her ear, his tongue resting there a moment to measure the erratic fluttering of her pulse. Then, as if sampling a rare delicacy, he nibbled at her throat, his hot, open mouth settling above the V of her collarbone to once again measure her heartbeat, which was quickening with every breath she drew.

When his free hand settled low on her belly, Cassandra felt as if she were immersed in white-hot fire. He ran his palm slowly toward the apex of her thighs and the nest of dark curls there.

"Luke?" she managed to whisper.

"Trust me, Cassie," he urged in a throbbing whisper. "Please, don't be afraid of me. It tears me apart."

Those last words called to her mind Mrs. Whitmire's dire warnings. Cassandra made a feeble grab for his wrist just as he found the moist center of her femininity and slipped a fingertip inside her. Surprise jolted through her at the sensation. Her breath snagged in her throat, and for the space of a heartbeat, she was terrified that pain would surely follow. But just as she tried to voice a protest at the invasion, he pushed deep, his clever touch making her feel like a mirror that was shattering. Oh, yes...Blinding sparkles floated up from the center of her. She moaned and pushed hard against his hand, wanting, yet uncertain what it was she wanted.

His hot mouth settled over one of her nipples, the drawing heat igniting, and every brush of his tongue fanning the flames. Cassandra made fists in his hair. Mrs. Whitmire had been right; he was making her come apart. Only it was wonderful. Absolutely wonderful. The most glorious feeling she'd ever experienced.

Luke felt the glow of Cassandra all around him, a sweet, bone-melting radiance that made it difficult for him to retain control. He wanted to make this perfect for her, but that didn't seem to be in the cards. He had trouble kicking off his boots. The fastenings on his pants defied his clumsy fingers. With years of practice, he'd long since honed his sexual skills to a fine art, enabling him to divest a woman and himself of clothing with seductive ease. How, then, had he gotten his trousers tied into goddamned knots around his ankles?

Somehow, he finally worked one foot free, infuriated with himself for having to twist and jerk and shake his leg to accomplish the feat. Christ. Every time the mattress bounced, Cassandra blinked to focus. He didn't want her to focus, dammit. He wanted her mindless. With one final shake of his leg, he divested himself of his pants, then bent to kiss her again, his heart pounding so hard he could scarcely think.

It didn't seem to matter....She opened her mouth to him, and he forgot nearly everything. She tasted like mulled wine spiced with cinnamon, warm, full-bodied, and intoxicating. God, she was sweet. So impossibly, incredibly sweet. If he hurt her in doing this, he'd never forgive himself.

The thought came over him like a dash of icy water. She was a virgin, and the first time was bound to be painful. He'd promised her only a slight bit of discomfort and a trace of blood. But what if Mrs. Whitmire was right, and it turned out to be an ordeal?

The truth was, Luke didn't know for sure; he'd never been with a virgin. He had lied to this girl so many times he'd long since lost count. Please, God. He didn't want her to look back and believe he'd lied to her about this as well.

His breath coming in ragged bursts, Luke braced himself above her. Her eyes half closed, her rosy mouth slightly swollen from his kisses, she restlessly moved her legs, her expression conveying that he'd filled her with urgent yearnings she didn't quite understand.

Luke knelt between her silken thighs, his throbbing manhood poised at her entrance. He looked down at the glistening folds of her femininity, moist and ready. One thrust. All he had to do was drive forward, and it would be over. Just one forward motion of his hips.

He jerked his gaze back to her face. Her dark lashes fluttered upward, and those blue eyes looked into his. There was no fear reflected in them, just an utter trust he would *never* deserve.

Every muscle in Luke's body tightened and began to shake. From somewhere at the edges of his mind, a little voice said, *Go for it, man. Don't be a fool. So what if it hurts like hell this one time? She'll live through it, and you'll have what you want.*

But wasn't that just the problem? That

he'd always taken exactly what he wanted, to hell with her and everyone else?

"Luke?"

That was his name. At the moment, that was about the only thing Luke was absolutely certain of. He rolled away from her, landing on his back beside her, his masculine pride as limp as an overcooked noodle against his thigh. He angled an arm over his eyes, sick with shame. He felt like an idiot and could only imagine how she must be feeling. *Great job, Taggart.* He'd probably turned the poor girl away from sex forever, if his clumsy groping and failure to complete the act could even be called "sex."

"I'm sorry," he managed to grate out between clenched teeth.

He felt her move. The next second, her trembling body pressed full-length against his side, her slender arm draped over his chest. "Oh, Luke, what is it?"

Smart girl. Even she realized he hadn't performed up to snuff. "I'm sorry," he rasped again.

How could he tell her he was a liar and a trickster who wasn't fit to kiss her feet, let alone take her virginity? How could he explain that just once, just one goddamned time in his whole miserable life, he wanted to be something better than what he actually was?

It was laughable. He was a pathetic piece of slime who had grabbed onto her sweetness and tried to escape the gutter his life had become. He'd been crazy to think he could make this work. Out of his mind. He'd schemed to have her, concocted lie after lie without a qualm. Eventually all those lies would catch up with him. When they did, they'd suck him under like quicksand. Daniel Beauregard was right; this whole plan was utter madness. Contracts, then marriage and shipping her male relatives off to the silver mine under armed guard. He was digging himself into such a deep hole, he'd never be able to climb out. He ought to just tell her the truth. All of it. And be done with it. To beg her forgiveness and pray to God she would grant it to him.

She ran a hand lightly over his chest. Her touch made his muscles jerk, an instinctive withdrawal he couldn't control. With a fierce little cry, she ran her arm up to hug his neck and pressed her face against the hollow of his shoulder.

"Luke, what is it? Please, tell me what's wrong."

He squeezed his eyes closed, hands clenched to keep from reaching for her. Even now, his body screamed with wanting her, and he didn't trust himself not to grab and take her. God help him, taking was all he knew.

"Don't," he bit out. "Don't touch me, please."

She went still and silent for a moment. Then she whispered, "Why? I love you, Luke. I want to touch you."

A harsh laugh tore up from his chest, chafing his throat with burning, bitter heat. "You don't love me, Cassandra. You don't even know me."

"Oh, yes, I do. I know everything I need to

know, at any rate. You're a wonderful man, Luke. Why can't you believe that?"

The hardened tips of her breasts branded his skin like burning embers, her silken softness beckoning him. Unable to bear it, Luke grasped her shoulders and lifted her away, his gaze locked with hers. "Let me tell you about Luke Taggart, the man you *think* you know so well. I'm a liar and a thief. I've lied to—"

She pressed a hand over his mouth, her blue eyes swimming with tears. "Stop it! Just stop it! I won't let you say things like that about yourself! I won't!"

He wrenched his face to one side. "You're not listening to me. I'm telling you, I'm a liar. I've even lied to you. And I've done some terrible things, Cassandra. Things you may never—"

"It doesn't matter."

"It *does* matter. When you learn what I've—"

She clamped a hand over his mouth again, her eyes blazing with love for him. "Don't!" she whispered fiercely. "It doesn't matter, Luke. Nothing matters. Don't you see? I don't care. All that matters to me, and all that should matter to you, is right now, and how we're going to go forward from here."

God, how Luke wished he could believe that.

"Are you going to lie to me again?" she asked softly.

Looking deeply into her blue eyes, Luke knew with a certainty that was foreign to him that he never would. That he couldn't. Grasping her slender wrist, he moved her fingers from over his mouth.

"No," he rasped, "I'll never lie to you again. Never. But I—"

"Well, then?" She bent her head to trail feather-light kisses along his temple and jaw. "Don't be this way. Please? This is our wedding night, the first night of the rest of our lives. We should be looking forward, not back. Who cares what went before? It's *now* that counts. Only that."

Luke couldn't stop himself. He caught her close, his arms trembling with quiet desperation. An armful of heaven. That was how she felt, so soft and warm, her body melding with his. God, how he wanted the absolution she offered. *The first night of the rest of our lives...* The words rang in his mind, a promise he was afraid to believe in, yet one he wanted to grab onto with both hands.

"Make me your wife," she whispered. "You didn't finish. Mrs. Whitmire said that you'd put yourself inside me. Why did you stop, Luke? Don't you want me that way?"

He gave a strangled laugh that was almost a sob and cupped a hand over the back of her head, his fingers tightening like a vise. "God, yes. I want you more than I've ever wanted anything."

"Then why did you quit?" she asked in a muffled voice. "Until we do it, we're not really married."

"I don't want to hurt you."

"But you said—"

"That's one of the things I lied to you about," he admitted raggedly. "I don't know for sure how bad it'll hurt, or how much you may bleed. I've never—" He broke off and swallowed. "I've never been with a virgin, Cassandra. I said all that to put your mind at ease, but the truth is, I don't know for sure. I don't think it's all that bad. But, hell, what do *I* know about it?"

He felt her stiffen slightly. Then she levered up on an elbow, resisting the pressure of his hand at the back of her head. In the firelight, her blue eyes shimmered like sun-washed sapphires. Her gaze clung to his for several seemingly endless seconds. "Then I guess we'll have to find out what it's like together." Her slender throat worked as she swallowed what he suspected was a lump of fear. "If it hurts too much, I'll tell you, and you can stop, just like you promised."

That she trusted him to do so meant more to Luke than he could say. For years, he'd believed that the fortune he'd managed to amass in gold could buy him anything, that he truly had it all. Now he realized he'd had nothing. This girl was the treasure he'd always sought—better than gold, better than power, better than anything.

Luke groaned and rolled with her, keeping one arm firmly locked around her slender waist to keep her body pressed to his, wedging his hips between her thighs as he came out on top. He was only human, and life hadn't taught him much self-restraint. How could he resist her? The plain and simple fact was, he couldn't. Not when she pleaded so prettily with him to take her.

Bracing himself on an elbow, he levered himself

above her, their gazes still locked. "Do you promise to stop me?"

She caught her lower lip between small white teeth. After a moment, she nodded. Luke could feel the tension in her, and he regretted that as he'd regretted nothing else in his life. Sometimes, he realized, lying to people made things easier for them, little white lies to allay a virgin's fears. Only where did he draw the line? Where did the white lies become slightly gray, or the gray, black? He knew firsthand that the delineation grew blurred after a while, that lying became a treacherous habit, something one did almost instinctively. No more...if he meant to build a life with this girl, he had to change, and that meant never telling her another falsehood, no matter how well justified.

Once again, in what felt like a miracle, his manhood throbbed with readiness, jutting against her hip. He knew she felt the rigidity and, thanks to Mrs. Whitmire, realized what it portended. He also sensed that her building anxiety would make it nigh unto impossible for him to arouse her again. If he tried, he'd only prolong the torture.

Shifting his body slightly, Luke positioned himself for entry. His gut clenched when the sensitive head of his shaft nudged against hot wetness and vulnerable, satiny folds of flesh. He just thanked God she was still ready for him.

"Put your arms around my neck, Cassie girl," he whispered tautly.

She did as he asked, her gaze conveying the

dread she felt, the tight clutch of her fingers at his nape echoing it. "Luke? Hold me tight while you do it. Hold me tight, please, so I won't feel scared."

His heart twisted at the fear in her voice.

He drew her close and pressed his face against the hollow of her neck. She clung to him, so tense he was afraid to enter her—afraid to even try. Her thighs were clamped against his in a futile effort to close her legs. Her breath came in jagged bursts.

"Sweetheart, you have to relax," he whispered. "Otherwise, it'll hurt for sure."

She released a tremulous breath, and he felt her body loosen slightly. Slightly wasn't enough. Tensed as she was, her inner muscles would resist his entry, making the pain a lot worse.

"Do it," she urged in a thin voice. "Hurry, Luke, and just—"

He eased his hips forward, his movement cutting her off. Liquid heat. Velvet softness. He clenched his teeth, felt sweat pop out on his face. Her spine arched, and where his palm was clamped to the slope of her back, he felt her muscles knotting. He pressed in another minuscule bit, encountering her maidenhead. The walls of her channel spasmed around him, and she sucked in a breath, her fingers at his nape tightening, her nails digging at his skin.

He knew he was hurting her. He could feel a difference in the tautness of her body now, the muscles rigidly contorted against the pain. *Damn it.* Poised above her, he began to

375

shake nearly as badly as she was. His manhood was about to burst with the pleasure of being partially inside her, his heart breaking a little because what felt so damned good to him was excruciating for her.

"I can't," he ground out. "Goddammit, Cassie, I can't do it if it's going to hurt you like this."

He no sooner spoke than she tucked her legs over the backs of his and bucked sharply upward with her hips, impaling herself with a jolting impact. Her thrust was slightly off-center, ramming the hard length of him against sensitive inner flesh as he ripped through her maidenhead. The low cry that tore from her throat made Luke recoil, but she held tight with her legs, riding him upward, her body convulsing as waves of pain coursed through her.

"Oh...God!" She sobbed and arched her head back. "Oh, God!..."

Luke grasped her hips and shifted his own to correctly align their bodies. He cursed foully under his breath when he saw crimson on her pale thigh. "Dammit, Cassandra! Why did you—"

He bit back the rest and gathered her close to rain kisses over her face. Her body was quivering, her chest rising and falling. With one final shudder, she managed to drag in a deep breath. He felt some of the tension ebb from her. Then her dark lashes lifted, and she dipped her chin to fasten luminous blue eyes on him.

"There." The note of triumph in her quavery

voice produced a burning sensation in his eyes. "It's d-done."

"Not quite," he said through clenched teeth, his groin pulsing with urgency.

Her eyes filled with confusion. "Y-You mean there's more?" she asked, horrified.

Luke wasn't sure this was a good time for honesty. So he evaded the question. "Has it stopped hurting yet?" he managed to ask.

"Why?" she squeaked. "Wh-what're you going to do?"

Luke gave an agonized laugh and withdrew a bit from her. She jerked and clutched at his shoulders, clearly startled by the sensation. He nudged forward again, making her gasp. "Sweetheart, does it hurt?"

"Y-yes. D-don't—" she broke off as he withdrew again, then dug at his shoulders with her nails as he thrust cautiously forward. "Oh, my..."

"Does it hurt?"

"Oh, dear..."

Luke was quickly losing control. "Cassie? Dammit, answer me. If it hurts too bad, I'll stop."

She answered him with an inexpert bump of her pelvis against his. "Oh, Luke!"

He tightened his hold on her hips again. "Let me do this, all right?" A deafening roar filled his ears as she wiggled her derriere on the coverlet, trying to arch against him. Every flex of her muscles, every slight movement of silken heat over his shaft, nearly made him lose it. "Be still, dammit. You've got rotten aim."

She bumped against him again and moaned.

"Oh, Luke! Let go of me. It feels so—" She caught her breath and held it. On the exhale, she cried, "Ohhh...yes!"

Yes. It was the sweetest word Luke had ever heard. He relaxed his hold on her and surged forward, burying himself to the hilt. She cried out and undulated her hips, instinctively striking a rhythm as old as man and womankind. Luke retightened his hold on her to control her off-center movements, afraid of hurting her again. With his hands to guide her, she bucked upward to meet his thrusts.

Through a red haze of passion, Luke gazed down at her face and the rapturous expression that was tightening her small features. He wanted to take it slow, make it perfect for her. But then her hot, wet passage tightened around him and went into spasmodic orgasm. The pleasure was so intense, crashing over him in such mind-dazzling waves with each contraction of her body, that he couldn't hold back. Male instinct took over, his muscles knotting, his hips hammering against her. Then...ecstasy. He went rock-still in the throes of it, not breathing, his heart thundering, his release a white-hot eruption. Cassandra cried out and arched up. With his last bit of strength, he accommodated her, resuming the driving rhythm until she tensed and quivered, then fell limp.

Luke collapsed on top of her, trying with very little success to support most of his weight on arms that suddenly felt like pudding. She flung an arm around his neck, her hand dangling limply over his shoulder, her chest heaving, the rapid fluttering of her pulse out of harmony with the wild slamming of his own.

"My God..." The words rushed from Luke on the crest of a groan. Never in all his life had he experienced anything like this. And now, to be heart-to-heart with her, her body pressed full-length against his...he felt complete in a way he couldn't explain, as if he'd finally found the other half of himself. "Oh, Cassie girl..."

She lifted a hand to his hair, her fingers trailing lightly over the tousled waves. "Oh, Luke, I love you so."

His throat tightened. He wanted so badly to say the words back to her, sensing that she needed to hear them and knowing she deserved to. But he couldn't force them out.

Tell Hank you love him, you little bastard. He's paid good money, damn you!

His mother's voice slipped out from the darkest corners of his mind, hammering at him, filling him with bitterness he couldn't get past, not even for Cassandra. He had finally obeyed his mother that long-ago night and sobbed out the words. Over and over, like a litany, he'd said them, his body raging with pain, his dirty little hands knotted on the coverlet, until the words gave way to screams. Afterward, when he'd huddled, torn and bleeding, in a dark corner of the cold hallway, he'd vowed never to say those words again, not for anyone.

It was the one promise in his entire, misbegotten life that he'd ever kept.

TWENTY

As Cassandra opened her eyes the next morning, sunlight dappled the bedchamber with bright splashes of cheery yellow, and birds sang a serenade just outside the windows.

Feeling lazy and wonderfully relaxed, she stretched, yawned, then blinked sleepily, not at all sure where she was. When she felt the heat of Luke's body beside hers, she smiled and ran her thumb over the wedding ring that encircled her finger. *Mrs. Luke Taggart.* A delicious happiness flooded through her as she tried out the name in her mind. She was married, really and truly married. The only thing that came close to marring her happiness was that Papa and Ambrose hadn't been present at her wedding. But even that couldn't dampen her glow for long. Luke had promised her a formal wedding later, and she'd have her papa walk her down the aisle then, just as a father should.

She rolled onto her side to study her new husband, whose dark face rested only inches from her own on the same pillow. He lay with one arm encircling her, his big hand splayed loosely over her ribs, one thumb snug beneath her breast. She trailed her gaze over his powerfully muscled shoulder, then down the length of his arm, loving him with her eyes. His skin was so dark compared to her own, his chest so powerfully muscled. She touched a fingertip to the mat of golden hair that ran in a furry wedge toward his waist, fascinated by its crispness.

The touch startled him, and his eyes snapped open. For a moment, he lay tense and wary, as if he didn't recognize her. Then a slow grin spread across his firm mouth. "Good morning, Mrs. Taggart," he said in a voice gone rough with sleep.

"Mmm, say it again. I love the sound of it."

His grin broadened. "Mrs. Taggart, and don't you forget it."

After all the liberties he'd taken with her body last night, making love to her again and again until nearly dawn, Cassandra doubted there was much chance she'd forget she was his wife. A blush warmed her cheeks, and as if he guessed why, he chuckled, low and deep.

"Feeling shy?"

She hugged the sheet a little more snugly around her. "Not really."

"Then come here," he said huskily.

The way Cassandra saw it, she was already nearly on top of him, but apparently she wasn't close enough to suit him. "Luke, it's morning."

He glanced around. "So it is." His hand tightened over her ribs, drawing her inexorably toward him. "I waited all night, and now it's finally daylight."

"Broad daylight."

"The better to see you by."

She resisted the pull of his hand. "I should

probably get dressed and go see if Khristos made it off to school."

"You should probably obey your husband," he said with a mischievous glint in his amber eyes. "I'd hate to start off our very first day of married life by having to paddle your backside."

"You wouldn't."

He raised up on an elbow. "Wouldn't I?" He slid his hand from her ribs down to her rump, his long fingers kneading the softness as he leaned closer. "How do you know I'm not a woman-beater? You never asked me."

"I just know." Cassandra felt a familiar heat pooling low in her belly. She shot an anxious glance at the window. "Luke?"

"Hmm?" He bent his head to nibble at her ear.

"I'd…um…really rather wait until it's dark again."

"And I'd really rather we not. Want to cut the deck for it?"

"You'd win. You're an expert at cards."

"That's the whole idea," he said with a throaty laugh.

Her pulse began to quicken as he nibbled his way from her earlobe down her neck. "Luke, it's so light in here."

"Keeping secrets, Cassie girl?"

"No, I just—" She tugged a little frantically to hold the soft ivory sheet over her breasts, a nearly impossible feat when he was under it with her. "Luke?"

"Hmm?"

"I guess I *am* feeling a little shy at that." Her

pansy-bright eyes pleaded with him to understand. And he did. His tigress turned timid
when she wasn't cosseted by the dark.

"Give me five minutes," he whispered,
trailing searing kisses along her collarbone.
"Will you do that, Cassie, sweet? Just five minutes?"

"Only five?"

His kisses moved marginally lower. "That's
the deal. After five minutes, if you still want
to wait until dark, we'll wait."

"Three minutes," she bargained.

"Deal," he whispered, then promptly jerked
the sheet down.

With a startled squeak, she cried, "Luke?"

He rose to meet her gaze, his eyes a molten,
brilliant gold in the shaft of sunlight that
spilled over his face. "Who else?"

"What?" She blinked, having difficulty following his meaning.

He bent his head to drag the tip of his
tongue over her nipple. "Has someone else done
that?" he asked, looking back up.

"No."

He moved to the other breast. "Or this?"

"No," she replied a little breathlessly.

He slid a hand between her thighs. "How
about this?"

"No," she said, the word more a moan.

He trailed warm, teasing kisses over her ribs,
tracing each from her side to her sternum, his
tongue lapping lightly at her skin. When he'd
finished there, he moved lower to explore
her navel. "Are the three minutes up yet?"

She arched toward him, gasping when the

heat of his mouth closed over the most sensitive part of her. "Not yet," she managed to say as his tongue dragged over electrified nerve endings.

"How much longer?" he murmured against her, the vibration of his voice sending jolts of sensation through her.

"Th-thirty sec-seconds, give or t-take."

"You counting?"

She made tight fists in his tawny hair, trying to draw him closer, her body already hopelessly addicted to the mindless pleasure she knew his mouth could give her. "No."

He raised himself suddenly. "You know, now that I think about it, it *is* awfully bright in here."

Her hands still fisted in his hair, Cassandra stared up into his twinkling eyes.

"Since we've got less than thirty seconds left..." He let his voice trail off and shrugged a muscled shoulder. "I s'pose I may as well stop."

It took Cassandra a few seconds to gather her senses, not to mention a few threads of her composure. When at last she had the presence of mind to speak, she said, "Don't you think it's terribly sad when handsome young men go prematurely bald?"

A puzzled expression swept across his dark, rugged features. "I guess. What does that have to do with now?"

She smiled very sweetly. "Because, dear husband, if you stop what you're doing, you're about to go."

"Where?"

She tightened her hold on his hair. "Bald."

Despite her having what she clearly believed to be a very firm hold on his hair, Luke threw back his head and laughed so hard he damn near choked.

Downstairs in the kitchen, the servants paused in their morning duties as the sound of deep, masculine laughter drifted through the house to them. Pipps smiled slightly and lifted his coffee mug to Cook in a mock toast. "I would say the young mistress is going to make Master Taggart a very happy man," he observed.

Cook dusted flour from her hands, picked up her coffee mug, and clicked its edge against the butler's. "I do believe you're right, Pipps, and the way I see it, he's overdue. A fine man, our Master Taggart. Many's the time I've wiped a tear from my eye, watching him ramble about, always so alone in this big old house."

With a loud *harrumph*, Mrs. Whitmire, who sat at the work table, lifted her gaze from the menu she was compiling for the upcoming week and frowned at both of them. "Let's just hope he isn't laughing at her expense," she said with a sniff. "You go ahead and waste your tears on the master," she told Cook sourly. "I'll save mine for that poor wee lass. Break her heart, he will, a thousand times if he does it once. Sow's ears don't become silk purses, no matter who they marry. A year from now, we'll be watching her scurry to do his bidding, leaping at her own shadow, all the sparkle gone from her pretty smile. Mark my words, it'll come to pass."

Pipps drew his bushy gray eyebrows together. "I do say, Mrs. Whitmire, I don't believe you have a very high opinion of marriage."

"Or of men," she said succinctly. "In my estimation, the entire lot of you isn't worth the powder it would take to blast you to kingdom come." She laid down her pencil, then picked it back up, clearly distracted and more than a little distraught. "I'm only surprised he married her. We all know he had less than honorable intentions when he brought her here. God only knows what made him change his mind. I can only say, with all confidence, that it had nothing to do with his moral bent or his having her best interests in mind."

Pipps assumed the austere expression that had always served him so well in dealing with subordinates. "The voice of experience?"

"Twenty years of marriage to a heavy-fisted skirt chaser who placed more importance on having his corn whiskey than supporting his wife and children," she replied grimly and bent back over her menu. "The day I buried Harold Whitmire was the happiest day of my life."

"Master Taggart's no drunkard," Cook pointed out, "nor heavy-fisted, either. I'm pleased as can be that he's found a measure of happiness."

"It's a free country. Think however you like," Mrs. Whitmire retorted. "Just don't expect me to celebrate with you. I'm surprised we didn't hear a ruckus last night, him being the kind of man he is, and her so young and unsuspecting. I did my best to prepare her, but even at that, he probably gave her a rough time of it."

Pipps shot the housekeeper a startled look. "You did your best to prepare her? For what?"

She narrowed an eye at him over her wire-rimmed spectacles. "For the pain and misery she was about to face. There's nothing worse than to walk into it blind, a starry-eyed bride trusting a man to be gentle. Nothing worse, I tell you."

Pipps settled a concerned gaze on her. "My dear Mrs. Whitmire, not all new husbands are unkind toward their brides. If you believe that, you've been ill advised."

She gave a disgusted snort. "There's a wise old saying, crass but true: 'A stiff prick has no conscience.'"

"Well, I never!" Cook turned back to her dough, kneading it with a vengeance. "I'm shocked to hear you talk so plain, Mrs. Whitmire. Shocked, I tell you." She punched the dough with a plump fist, the impact making her broad posterior shake under her skirts. "And in mixed company, no less!"

Pipps, who was still standing near the counter, set down his coffee mug. As he crossed the kitchen on his way to the foyer, he settled a saddened gaze on Martha Whitmire's bent head. Despite her age, she was still a fine figure of a woman. In the years since they'd begun working together for Master Taggart, Pipps had oft wondered why she seldom smiled and always seemed reluctant to look him directly in the eye. Now the mystery was solved.

As he moved past her, Pipps slowed his stride and reached out to rest a hand on her shoulder—just a light touch, nothing more. She leaped as though he'd pinched her fanny, color flooding her face. At precisely that moment, laughter rang through the house again, a clear, lilting laughter that was unmistakably feminine. Martha Whitmire cocked her head, her eyes reflecting her disbelief.

Pipps raised an eyebrow. Then the strangest thing happened. The butler's face began to crinkle, deep creases appearing on either side of his mouth, tinier ones fanning from the corners of his eyes. The next instant, his stern mouth curved sharply upward in a smile.

"Ah, yes," he said softly, for Martha's ears alone. "The poor little miss. It's a rough time he's giving her, make no mistake. I think we should hang him by his balls from the highest yardarm."

Happiness...it was a new experience for Luke. Oh, he'd felt occasional moments of elation, especially since striking it rich in the goldfields. But fleeting jubilation and an enduring sense of joy were two different things. Over the next few days, he got a taste of the latter.

Cassandra. Part angel, part imp. Except for the occasional long faces she pulled because she missed her papa and Ambrose, she filled up his life with sweetness and laughter, mischief and chaos. Luke never knew what to expect from one moment to the next.

Though he was reluctant to leave her, he did still have business matters to attend to at the office, and one afternoon when he came home, he found Pipps, Cook, Cassandra, and Khristos all out in the yard, trying to give Lycodomes a bath. Because they didn't want to get the dog's injured leg wet, they had him on a tether and were chasing him about with pots of water. Luke had never seen such a drippy, bedraggled foursome, and within the space of ten minutes, he was just as drenched as they were.

"How did I get roped into this?" he asked, shaking a pant leg that Khristos had just doused. "Blast it, Khristos, you got it in my boot."

"I'm sorry, Luke."

Luke relieved Pipps of the tether, taking a firm grip on both the dog and the situation. "All right, Lycodomes, enough of this non-sense. You're going to stand still while we rinse you. Understand?"

With a wide swing of his splinted leg, the dog plopped down on his soapy side and fixed Luke with a baleful gaze. Luke hunkered down to lift the animal back onto his feet. Major problem. Lycodomes was as slick as snot. Luke couldn't get a good enough hold on him to lift his considerable weight.

Someone snickered. He glanced up, trying to locate the culprit. Four sober faces peered back at him. "This is *not* funny. Whose brilliant idea was it to give him a bath in the first place?"

"Yours, sir," Pipps reminded him.

"Yes, well." Luke managed to slip an arm under the dog again. "That was before he got run over. I never would have suggested you try to give him a whore's"—he broke off, glancing at Khristos and Cassandra—"I mean, a spot bath. Without being able to confine him to the tub, how did you hope to get him rinsed?"

"By dipping water over the soapy parts," Cook inserted, her huge bosom heaving from the unaccustomed activity. "It seemed a sound idea…at the time, anyway."

Luke strained to lift the dog. "All right, Lycodomes, up you go! Enough of this nonsense!"

At precisely the moment Luke put all his strength into trying to lift Lycodomes, the dog suddenly decided to push to his feet. Caught off guard, Luke's upward momentum carried him over backward, and he landed on his ass in the flower bed. A very muddy flower bed. He lifted a hand covered with well-fertilized, wet soil.

"Son of a—a—a bitch!"

Snicker, snicker. He glanced up and saw that Cassandra had a hand clamped over her mouth, her eyes large and round, her cheeks going red.

"Are you *laughing*?" Luke demanded, scarcely able to believe she'd dare. His trousers were ruined. His jacket was saved only because he'd had the good sense to remove it. "Just what, exactly, strikes you as being so funny?"

She shook her head and pointed at him. A

second later, Cook chuckled. Pipps snorted. Even Khristos finally joined in. Luke drew up his legs to rest his arms on his raised knees, filthy hands dangling. "You're all crazy," he observed drily. But even as he spoke, he felt a smile breaking out. "Stark-raving mad, every last one of you. A dog bath in September?" He held up a muddy finger to test the wind. "It's colder than a well digger's ass out here."

An hour later, after Lycodomes was rinsed and patted reasonably dry with towels, Luke learned there were definite advantages to giving a dog a bath in September, or at any other time of the year. Afterward, everyone involved required a bath as well, and he was more than pleased to dismiss the maid and play attendant while his lovely young wife took hers.

Happiness...one moment blended into the next, mornings into afternoons, afternoons into ecstasy-filled nights, when he made love to his wife. For the first time in his memory, Luke felt content.

The rest of our lives. Cassandra's words on their wedding night kept floating through his mind like a promise. It was a promise he was starting to believe in. She was right: what had gone before, didn't matter. He'd done some bad things, yes. But he was doing his damnedest to make up for them now. Her father would be pissed at him for a while, and so would her brother. But after a time, they'd surely see he hadn't treated them all that badly.

Everything would come right in the end, Luke assured himself. It simply had to. He couldn't lose Cassandra. Life wouldn't be worth living without her.

TWENTY-ONE

Luke jerked awake and searched the gloom-filled room. For a moment, he didn't know what had jarred him from sleep, only that he thought he'd heard something. Judging by the weak light coming through the lace curtains, dawn was barely breaking. He sat up in bed, glancing down at the shadowy outline of Cassandra, who still slept peacefully beside him, one knee drawn up to nudge his hip.

After listening a moment and hearing nothing out of the ordinary, Luke nearly lay back down. But just as he started to ease back against the pillows, there came a wall-shaking racket that had him bolting upright again. It sounded as if someone were pounding the hell out of the front door downstairs. As Luke slipped from the bed, Cassandra stirred and yawned, rubbing her eyes.

"Luke, what is it?"

"Someone at the door, I think. I'll take care of it, sweet. You go back to sleep."

"Will you come back to bed?" she asked drowsily.

Luke smiled as he jerked on his trousers. His sweet little wife had taken to marital intimacy like a chocolate lover to bonbons. As a rule, he made love to her at least twice each night, then again the next morning before they rose to face the day. Though still in the clutches of slumber, she obviously didn't want to miss out on their usual morning activities.

"I'll be back," he assured her, bending to kiss her cheek. "Nothing could keep me away."

She murmured something and burrowed more deeply into the cocoon of silk. As Luke bent to find his boots, another flurry of angry thuds resounded through the house.

Jesus, what the hell was going on? Had there been a cave-in at one of his mines? Or a fire? His heart started to pound. As fanatical as he was about safety, there was always the danger of an accident. The thought made his blood run cold.

Grabbing his shirt and shoving his arms down the sleeves as he exited the bedchamber, Luke cursed beneath his breath. If this wasn't an emergency, he'd have someone's head.

At the landing, Luke heard Pipps coming from the back of the house at a run. Luke was halfway down the stairs when the butler entered the foyer, his long white nightshirt billowing around him, his slippers flapping sharply against the tiles. The mirrors and planters on the walls shook as another knock at the doors rattled the large house.

"I'll get it, Pipps," Luke called as he descended the remaining steps in a flying leap. The bastard on the other side of the door had better have a damned good reason for being there.

As Luke pulled the door open, his heart kicked violently against his ribs. Milo and Ambrose Zerek stood on his porch. Even in the gloom, Luke could see that they were filthy and disheveled. "Angry" didn't begin to describe the expression on their flushed faces. Milo stood with his feet spread, his large laborer's hands knotted into fists at his sides. Upon seeing Luke, he made a visible effort to refrain from physically attacking him.

"I've come for my son and daughter!" the older man grated out, every inflection of his voice throbbing with rage. "And so help me God, Taggart, if you try to keep them from me, I'll kill you with my bare hands."

Luke's heart, which had given such a violent start when he first saw the two men, felt as if it were dropping to his knees. He didn't know how the Zereks had managed to slip away from the silver mine, but they obviously had. The minute they saw Cassandra, the truth would come out. Whether or not Luke liked it. Whether or not he was ready. If Cassandra wasn't awake by now, she would be soon, what with Milo's voice pitched at such a volume.

Milo's threat of physical violence didn't intimidate Luke; neither did Ambrose's menacing stance. Luke had kicked and clawed and pummeled his way to adulthood. If pushed, he could teach both the Zerek men a thing or two about fighting—not that he discounted either of them as an unworthy opponent.

Luke opened the door wider and gestured the men inside. "I have no intention of keeping your son or daughter away from you, Milo."

"Intention, be damned. I want what's mine." Milo burst over the threshold, fists still knotted at his hips. "Where are they, you bastard?"

"Asleep. Or they were before you tried to kick down my front door." Struggling for calm, Luke glanced at the butler. "Pipps, I realize it's an ungodly hour, but would you brew us some coffee?"

"Immediately, sir."

"Forget the coffee! Get my boy and girl out here!" Milo yelled after the servant.

The butler paused to give Luke a quizzical look. Luke nodded his assent. There was little point in trying to keep Cassandra upstairs, not with this ruckus going on. "Wake Khristos first," Luke said, hoping against hope that he might get Milo calmed down before his wife spoke to him.

As Pipps headed for Khristos's room, Luke turned back to his "guests." Raking a hand through his hair, he sighed, then motioned toward the study. "We'll talk in there."

When Milo opened his mouth to protest, Luke added a terse "Please" that seemed to mollify the two big men somewhat. He needed time, he thought as he followed the Zereks over the threshold. Time to explain, to plead his case. Time he was desperately afraid he wouldn't get.

Once inside the book-lined room, Milo began to pace over the Persian rug like a caged bear, his muddy boots leaving a trail behind him. "I want my children!" he hollered. "And I want them now!"

Luke closed the door in hope that Milo's voice wouldn't carry through the whole house. Ambrose stood just inside the room, his stocky body braced to fight. He didn't give an inch when Luke stepped past him to approach his desk and light a lamp. As the wick flared, Luke turned back to meet his father-in-law's glittering gaze.

"I will happily turn over Khristos and Lycodomes to you, Milo," Luke said in a carefully measured voice. "And you're certainly welcome to see your daughter and stay here to visit with her as long as you wish. However, before we continue this talk, I should apprise you of the fact that since your departure from Black Jack, I've made her my wife."

Milo's craggy face went scarlet, his features contorting. After sputtering and working his mouth, he finally managed to rasp, "You *what*?"

"Cassandra and I were married three weeks ago," Luke said softly. "All right and proper, the union blessed by God in the Catholic church."

Milo's anger became so intense he began to shake. His gaze burned into Luke's. "You miserable, rotten, pitiful excuse for a man! How dare you stand there and speak of God! If you have a soul, it's as black as Satan's own!"

"No doubt," Luke admitted ruefully. "Nonetheless, Cassandra and I are legally married." He lifted his hands, searched in vain for words, then pinched the bridge of his nose and heaved a weary sigh. What could he say to this man? That he was sorry? "If it's any consolation to you, Milo, I regret the things I've done, and I'm making an honest attempt to reform."

Ambrose moved forward. "You married Cassie? You made my little sister marry you?"

Luke dropped his hand and blinked to clear his fuzzy vision. Ambrose, like his father, looked as if he'd crawled half the distance to Black Jack on his belly. Mud smeared his ragged clothing, dirt streaked his face, and there were bits of debris clinging to his dark hair. The two men had clearly risked life and limb to get here.

"Cassandra hasn't yet reached her majority," Milo cried. "The marriage isn't legal! I didn't give my consent!"

Luke shrugged. "What will you do, Milo? Contest its validity? Have it annulled? Trust me when I say the marriage has been well consummated. If you take Cassandra away, her reputation will be destroyed."

"Better that than the rest of her life! She'd be happier in a convent than married to a scurvy bastard like you!"

"She could very well be pregnant," Luke informed him coolly. "Do they take babes at convents?"

"If there's a babe, I'll help her raise it." Milo leveled a finger at Luke. "I'll have the marriage annulled, mark my words! No daughter of mine will live under the thumb of a monster like you. I wouldn't leave my dog in your care."

"Let's think about this, Milo." Luke leaned his hips against the desk, struggling against rising panic. Without Daniel Beauregard to advise him, he wasn't sure if Milo could have the marriage annulled or not. "Cassandra is eighteen, well past a marriageable age. Do you really believe a judge, especially one any-where in Colorado, will annul a consum-mated marriage into which she entered of her own free will? Especially a marriage to me?" For a long moment, Luke held the older man's gaze. "I'm not proud of what I've done, and if there were any way on God's earth I could undo it, I would. But that doesn't mean I'm willing to let my wife walk out of here without putting up a fight. I think you've learned, firsthand, of the power I wield in this town."

"We'll get a lawyer and fight you. If all else fails, she'll get a divorce."

Though uncommon, divorces were some-times granted to women if they had grounds to file for one. In his mind, Luke pictured Cas-sandra, large with child. Then images of her and his babe, living in penury, flashed through his head. Luke couldn't bear to let that happen, not even if it meant adding to his already-considerable transgressions against this family. He would use every bit of leverage at his disposal to hold her father at bay.

Giving both the Zerek men a wide berth— not because he felt intimidated, but because he didn't want to compound his trespasses even more by pummeling his wife's father and brother to a bloody pulp—Luke stepped to the wall safe. After withdrawing the contract Cassandra had signed, he returned to the desk and tossed the document onto the blotter.

"Read it," Luke bit out. "And don't bother ripping it up. I had Cassandra sign three copies, one of which is in my attorney's safe-keeping. You will note, as you read, that Cassandra will be legally bound to me even in the event of a divorce."

Milo snatched up the papers. His gaze darted back and forth as he skimmed the words. The flush of rage on his face drained away, leaving him milk-white. "Dear God…" He fixed a condemning gaze on Luke. "The girl couldn't have understood what she was signing," he said raggedly. "But you didn't care, did you?"

"Papa?" Ambrose stepped forward. "What is it?"

"A contract," Milo said, his voice a throbbing whisper. "A contract your sister signed, committing her to service this…man." Milo closed his eyes and let his arm drop, the documents rustling against his mud-smeared trousers. "Dear God, Taggart. What kind of scum are you?"

The question cut deeper than Luke let on—so deep he felt as if he were bleeding way down inside. *Scum* was too bland a word for the kind of man he was. In retrospect, he couldn't believe he'd taken such merciless advantage of a young girl's trust. But he had. And in the event of a successfully contested marriage, the contract would stand up in court. Daniel Beauregard had composed it with his usual shrewdness. Luke felt absolutely confident there were no loopholes.

"She isn't legally of age," Milo said wearily. "I can fight this and win. To use one of your favorite phrases, her signature isn't worth the paper it's written on."

Luke raised an eyebrow. "Assuming, of course, that you can find a judge anywhere in Colorado who will rule against me."

The cold hatred in Milo's gaze chilled Luke's skin. "Oh, yes. The high-and-mighty Luke Taggart. I nearly forgot you own the whole town and have business interests across the state. You don't have to abide by the law like the rest of us poor bastards."

Luke knew he was fighting dirty, and that Milo's disgust of him was well deserved. Nonetheless, his possibly pregnant wife wasn't going to endure a harsh Colorado winter without proper shelter and nourishment—not if he could prevent it.

Ambrose snatched the document from his father's lax hand. After skimming a few lines, he raised a cobalt gaze that was very like Cassandra's to glare at Luke. "How could you do this, Taggart? You made a whore of my little sister." He slapped the paper with the back of his hand. "How could you do it?"

Luke knew that any explanations he tried to make would fall on deaf ears. How could he explain that he'd had a change of heart after bringing Cassandra into his home, that once he'd come to know her, he couldn't carry through with his original plans?

"Cassandra came into the marriage a virgin," Luke said evenly. "As for an annulment or divorce, if you try to convince her to get either, that contract is still in effect."

"And you'll use your wealth and political clout to hold her to it?"

Remembering the newspaper-covered cracks in the walls and the water that had streamed through the ceiling of the Zerek shack, Luke said, "Without a qualm."

Milo gave a harsh laugh. "Over my cold corpse."

Luke was tempted to tell the man he needn't resort to murder, that, in case Milo had forgotten, Luke could still have his ass tossed back in jail. But there lay the path to only more regret.

At just that moment, the study door opened, and Cassandra poked her tousled dark head into the room. Her face went radiant with delight when she saw her father and brother, and with a cry of joy, she launched herself across the room and into Milo's arms, her nightgown and wrapper drifting around her curvaceous form in folds of white.

"Papa! It *was* your voice I heard! Oh, Papa! I thought not to see you for almost two more months!" After hugging Milo with all her might, she broke away to embrace her brother. Ambrose caught her close with one sturdy arm, still holding the contract in his other hand. "Ambrose, it's so good to see you. So good."

Brother and sister just stood there for a moment, swaying with the intensity of their emotion. Watching them, Luke knew how formidable the obstacles he faced might prove to be. He'd never loved or been loved like this. The blood ties in this family were unbreakable, forged to steel by the kind of loyalty and caring Luke had only just recently begun to understand.

Quite unexpectedly, Cassandra drew away from her brother and turned to throw her arms around Luke's neck. "You knew they were coming, didn't you? It was a surprise! Oh, Luke, how did you manage it? How long can they stay?" She leaned back to look up at him with tears in her eyes. "You never cease to amaze me. I tried never to complain of how much I missed them, but you knew, didn't you?"

Luke wished with all his heart he could say yes, that he could claim responsibility for their arrival. "Actually, sweet, I'm as surprised to see them as you are. Maybe more so."

"Get away from him, Cassandra," Milo said in a steely voice.

Cassandra threw her father a startled look. "Papa?"

"I said, get away from him. He's slime from the sewer, and I won't have his hands on you."

Luke felt Cassandra's body go tense. She flashed a bewildered look up at him, then directed it back at her father. "Papa, don't talk that way. Luke is my—"

Milo reached out and grabbed his daughter's arm, nearly jerking her off her feet to separate her from Luke. The horrified expression on Cassandra's suddenly pale face told Luke it was probably the first time in her life that her father had touched her in anger. Luke's gaze shot to where the other man's fingers bit into his wife's arm.

"Milo, gentle your hold. You're hurting the girl," Luke said with a note of warning.

Milo instantly released her. Cassandra rubbed her bruised elbow, her bewildered gaze trailing over the faces of the three men who stood around her. "What is this about, Luke? Haven't you explained that we're married?" She splayed a hand over the front plackets of her wrapper. "That's it, isn't it?" A shaky little laugh trailed from her as she glanced down at herself. "Papa, it isn't how it looks. Luke and I are married."

"No, you're not!" Milo retorted. "I never gave my consent."

Cassandra stretched out a hand toward her father. "But, Papa, we're going to have a formal wedding as well. You can still give me away, just like you used to talk about doing."

"To another man, maybe. Never to the likes of him."

Cassandra caught her bottom lip between her teeth and threw an agonized look at Luke. He could see how torn she felt, uncertain whether to go to her father or return to her husband. No more than a second passed, but to Luke it seemed an eternity. Then, visibly trembling, Cassandra turned her back on her father and stepped over to Luke. He caught her close, an anguish he never thought to feel coursing through him. She had chosen him over the father she adored.

Dear God…

Never had he hoped she might come to love him so much that she would forsake her family for him. The fact that she had, and that she'd done so with no encouragement from him, nearly broke his heart. He didn't deserve this kind of devotion from her, and any minute now, she'd begin to realize it.

"Cassandra, don't shame yourself any more than you already have," Milo said hoarsely. As he spoke, he snatched the contract from Ambrose's hand and shoved it at her face. "Read it, girl! He set us up. Don't you see? That fellow, Peter Hirsch? He was hired by Taggart to trick us, so we could be thrown in jail for claim jumping. He wanted you helpless, without the protection of your father and brother! So you'd be without any money, defenseless and at his mercy. It was all a vile trick so he could make you his whore!"

"His what?" she whispered.

"His *whore*!" Milo repeated harshly. "His *boughten* woman," he expounded when she still didn't seem to understand. "Like Mary Magdalene, lass. Remember in the Scripture? The story of the sinful woman who repented, and Jesus forgave? Until that time, she was a whore, Cassie girl. A woman who fornicated with men."

With a bewildered look, Cassandra drew back slightly from Luke, her gaze fixed on the contract. Finally she took it from her father and moved away from Luke to reread the cleverly worded lines. Milo hovered at her shoulder.

404

"You see? His 'paid companion,' it says, which is polite wording for 'whore!'" Milo jabbed at the center of the page. "Read it, child, this time with your eyes open. You agreed that he could take any liberties with your person he wished! And you gave up all legal rights to any issue! That means a baby, love. You gave up your rights as a mother. Good God, Cassandra, where was your head when you signed this?"

In the clouds, Luke thought sadly. That was where her head had been, and he'd taken ruthless advantage of it. Judging by her expression, she was crashing back to earth now. She turned disbelieving eyes on him. "Luke? Tell Papa it isn't true, that you never meant me to be your—" She broke off, and her huge eyes filled with anguish. "Tell him, please."

Luke wished with all his heart that he could. But he'd sworn never to lie to this girl again, and that was a promise he would not break.

"Tell him!" she cried.

Luke couldn't bear to see the pain in her gaze, yet he couldn't take the easy way out and look away. He'd done this to her. He could place the blame on no one else.

She began to tremble. Luke didn't think she could possibly grow more pale, but she did, the blood draining from her face until she looked chalky. "It's true?" she asked softly.

It wasn't really a question. She pressed a hand over her mouth, then crumpled the contract in rigid, white-knuckled fingers to hold her other hand fisted against her waist. Eyes closed, face contorted, she just stood there, shaking violently. "You *arranged* to have my papa and brother thrown in jail?"

Ironically, yet so characteristically, she seemed more appalled by the injustices he'd inflicted on her loved ones than by those he'd heaped on her. "How could you do that to my papa and brother?" she asked in a thin voice. "And then pretend you were being generous and fair?"

Luke didn't know what to say. As crazy as it seemed, even to him, he was a different man now than he'd been then. "Sweetheart, I am so sorry," Luke whispered. "I'd undo it if I could. I am so sorry."

The words rang out in the room, pitifully inadequate in compensating for the transgressions and, at the same time, condemning him. A man didn't apologize for something he hadn't done. The starch went out of her spine, and before his very eyes, she seemed to diminish in size, as if half the life had been drained from her. For endless seconds, she continued to stand there, eyes closed, face drawn. Luke thought she might burst into tears or fly into a rage. But, oh, no...not his Cassie. She finally hauled in a shaky breath, lifted her chin, and squared her shoulders.

When she opened her eyes and turned her gaze on him again, Luke nearly dropped to his knees. From the first instant he'd seen her, one of the things that had most enchanted him about her was the glowing innocence in her eyes. It was gone now. Shattered.

Stepping to the desk, she smoothed the contract upon its gleaming surface to go over the wording again, as if she had to look at it once more to convince herself of his treachery. Milo, still hovering at her shoulder, bitterly explained some of the legal jargon to her.

"He bought you, lass, as if you were no better than a piece of livestock. A grand price, I'll admit, but a purchase, all the same."

"But he married me," she whispered shakily.

Milo's mouth twisted. "To some men, marriage doesn't mean squat and divorce even less. Mark my words, he would have sent you packing the moment you ceased to entertain him."

"That's a goddamned lie!" Luke cried.

"And you, sir, are a goddamned liar!" Milo shot back. Then, with a look of chagrin at his daughter, he whispered, "I'm sorry, lass. I didn't mean to swear."

Yet another count against him, Luke thought a little frantically—that he cursed like a sailor.

Cassandra stood with her hands planted on Luke's desk, her shoulders bent, her head hanging, her tousled hair a dark curtain around her face. Milo gave Luke one last scathing look before continuing to point out all the clauses in the contract that were particularly condemning. When Cassandra finally straightened and directed her gaze at Luke again, her lovely blue eyes had gone suspiciously bright.

"Luke?" she whispered tremulously. "Say something. Anything at all. But, please, say something."

Her heart was in her eyes, Luke thought. And with every second that passed, he could see it breaking a little more. "Sweetheart, I tried to tell you. On our wedding night."

"You must not have tried very hard!" Milo put in.

Luke flinched, the words slicing at him like a knife. "I tried," he repeated, his gaze still delving deeply into Cassandra's. "I realized, even then, how wrong I'd been, and I wanted to set things right between us. Remember? You said—"

"'Set things right'?" Milo cut in. "While her papa and brother were being held prisoner at your silver mine? And before that, in jail at your behest? 'Set things right'? Don't listen to him, lass. He's lying even now." Milo slammed his hand down on the desk. "This contract tells the truth—that you thought of her as a plaything you could buy and then toss aside. Deny it, if you will! Go on. Look her in the eye and tell her that was never your plan!"

Luke couldn't do that. But, God help him, he wanted to. Oh, how he wanted to. Not just to save his own ass, but because the truth was destroying her. He stood there, helpless to stop it from happening, as much a victim of his own deceit as she was.

"You said it didn't matter," he whispered. "That we could start afresh. Please, Cassandra, can't we do that now? I care deeply about you. Surely you realize that. Knowing you, being with you…it's changed me. I'm not the same man who had that contract drawn up. Please...give me a chance to prove it to you."

Milo snorted. "Excuse my language, lass, but this is such horseshit, a man with no nose would puke at the stench! He's fond of bedding you, nothing more."

Cassandra jerked at the words. Luke clenched his hands, wanting to strangle Milo Zerek so bad he ached with it. "Cassandra, please, come upstairs with me for five minutes so we can talk privately," Luke entreated. "We can't get anything settled with your father bellowing at me every time I speak."

"You'll be alone with her again over my dead body!"

Luke was beginning to relish the thought. "That can be arranged," he ground out.

"I'm surprised you haven't already arranged it!" Milo accused. "It seems you stopped at nothing else! Tossed in jail, we were, for something we never did. You did it all to make us look guilty. Then hauled us off to your silver mine, to work us like slaves."

"I sent you to the silver mine to improve your circumstances. I felt guilty as hell! Dammit, I'd told so many lies, I couldn't see any way out. So I tried my best to fix things." Luke drilled Milo with a glare. "Tell her, damn you! Did you, or did you not, have good accommodations at the silver mine? Nice shelter, fine food, incredibly good wages! Tell her!"

Milo sneered. "Oh, yes. The finest of food, great pay. All the while with a shotgun pointed at our backs while we worked and slept. Even when we took a leak! Fine treatment we had!"

"I had to keep you away," Luke said hopelessly. "I needed more time before you told her what I'd done."

"Time for what?" Milo shot back. "To dip for a bit more honey?"

"Surely you must know that I regret what I've done and that I—" He broke off, the words he yearned to say burning in his throat like acid. "I obviously hold your daughter in very high regard, or I wouldn't have married her, for God's sake! Say what you like, but a divorce isn't all that easy to obtain. What legal grounds would I have for divorce with someone like her?" He shot Cassandra a pleading look. "She's damned near perfect."

"Perfect? High regard?" Flags of humiliation dotted Milo's cheeks. "Your esteemed whore?"

Luke knew how bad this looked. Dear God, in the beginning, he had even thought of her that way, as a plaything he'd purchased and brought home to enjoy. At the time, he hadn't cared a whit about her reputation or her plans for her future. Or her feelings.

He couldn't recall exactly when his sentiments had changed because it had happened gradually. He only knew he *had* changed, that he'd rather rip out his own heart than watch hers being broken this way.

"How you must have laughed at me," she whispered shakily. "Stripping the wax off your floors when what you wanted all along was my services in your bed. You *bought* me? Like a prize pig at the fair?"

"Cassandra, no. You can't believe that, sweetheart. Think about—"

She cut him off by turning her back on him. "I pray to God and all that's holy that I don't carry your child." Clutching her father's arm as if she no longer had the strength to stand by herself, she cried, "Get me out of here, Papa. Please, take me far away."

Luke took one step after her, then forced himself to stop. "Cassandra, please, don't leave. You have to know how much I care about you. I did a terrible thing; I know that now. And I'll spend the rest of my life trying to make it up to you. But, please, don't leave!"

In that moment, Luke realized just how much he actually had changed. Less than five minutes ago, he'd sworn to Milo Zerek that he wouldn't hesitate to call all his trumps into play to force her to remain with him. But now that the time had come, he could no more do that to Cassandra than any of the other rotten things he'd once planned. She wasn't just a plaything to him, as her father believed, but a sweet, precious woman who had come to mean more to him than drawing breath.

"Please, Cassandra," he said again. "Whatever you want. Anything. I'll do anything. Buy you anything. Take you anywhere, show you wonders you've never imagined. Just please don't leave."

Luke stood there, watching her move woodenly beside her father toward the door. A dozen wild thoughts went through his head. That he could have Milo and Ambrose thrown back in jail. That he could wrest her from her father's grasp, carry her upstairs, and force her to listen to him. He was Luke Taggart, goddammit. He had money, connections, political clout. Nobody bucked him. Nobody.

"You can't go out dressed like that," he heard himself protest. "At least go upstairs and get your clothes, sweetheart. It's cold outside, and raining."

She leaned her head against Milo's arm. "He bought the clothes, too, Papa," she said hollowly.

Glancing back over his shoulder, Milo impaled Luke with a burning gaze. "Then you'll not be wearing them, lass. The Zereks will take nothing from Luke Taggart."

Luke imagined her stepping out into the weather in nothing but her nightgown and wrapper. Her feet were bare, for Christ's sake. "Milo, don't be a fool. Do you want her to catch her death?" No answer. "At least let me give you some money. I owe both you and Ambrose three weeks' wages."

Luke hurried to his desk, yanking open drawers to locate his bank drafts. He doubted either of the Zerek men had a penny on them. The thought of their taking Cassandra away— the possibility that she might get wet and cold, that she might go hungry. God, he couldn't bear it.

"We'll not be taking your money, either," Milo Zerek said proudly, "so don't bother with a bank draft. You can owe us. God strike me dead if it's ever the other way around."

Luke lost it then. He brought his fist down hard on the desk. "Damn you, Milo, get your head out of your ass! Will you sacrifice that girl for your pride? How will you clothe and feed her? And what about Khristos? You don't even have a shack to go to. All your things are in storage. Have you even a miserable blanket to offer her?"

Milo opened the study door. Khristos and Lycodomes stood outside in the foyer. The boy's small face was pallid, his eyes huge splashes of blue against his colorless skin. Luke knew by the child's expression that he'd been listening at the other side of the door and, to some degree at least, understood how grave a situation this was.

Placing a hand on his small son's head, Milo stopped at the threshold to gaze back at Luke over his shoulder, his features stony.

"Milo Zerek takes care of his own."

Seconds later, Luke heard the front door open and close. He stood motionless, the pain in his chest so acute, he could scarcely breathe. His sweet Cassie was gone.

TWENTY-TWO

ʖ❧ Shame clung to Cassandra like a sodden cloak as she walked along the sidewalk within the safe circle of her papa's arm. With every step, she put more and more distance between herself and Luke's big house, where she'd left all her dreams—and very likely her heart.

It was a beastly morning, cold and wet, with an ugly wind blowing the raindrops side-ways. As soon as they'd left Luke's house, Papa

413

had thrown his coat over her shoulders, which left him exposed to the elements. Ordinarily, Cassandra would have been worried sick, afraid he might catch cold. But even though worry hovered someplace at the edges of her mind, she couldn't quite grab hold of it.

Nothing seemed to matter. Raindrops, hitting her face like pinpricks. A cold that seeped through the bare soles of her feet to make her shins ache in a strange, distant way. Boots impacting with the cobblestone, Khristos's smaller feet tapping a rapid tattoo that was completely out of rhythm with the slower, heavier tread of the men. Wood smoke that trailed from chimneys to flavor the icy air. Cassandra heard, felt, saw, tasted, and smelled, but nothing seemed real. Nothing but the awful, choking lump in the center of her chest that wasn't exactly a pain, yet not exactly an emptiness.

"Papa, where're we gonna go?" Khristos asked in a frightened little voice. "Lycodomes's leg is gettin' wet. It ain't s'posed to get wet, you know."

"First we'll go to the church," Milo said kindly. "Not to worry, Khristos. God has always taken care of us before, hasn't He?"

"Yes."

"Well, He will again," he assured the child. "We have to get your sister some clothes and a few things to set up housekeeping. Father Tully has that room at the back of the rectory. Remember? Filled with stuff that rich folks have donated for those less fortunate. Today, we're the 'less fortunate.' Down on our luck, we are. Father Tully will give us everything we need, that he will. And Lycodomes will be dry soon. So stop your worrying, lad. We'll be all right."

"But where will we set up housekeeping?" Khristos asked in that same shaky voice. "We ain't got a house, Papa. And me and Cassandra ain't even had breakfast yet."

In a voice that rang with false cheer, Ambrose inserted, "We're gonna go to our digs, Khristos! Won't that be fun, living in a cave? Papa and I have it all figured out. We'll be like the very first settlers."

"What did the first settlers eat?" Khristos asked.

"Whatever Father Tully has on hand to spare," Milo put in. "We'll keep our bellies full, Khristos. Haven't we always? It'll be all right, son. Trust your old papa, hmm?"

"I trust you, Papa," Khristos replied. "More'n anybody in the whole world."

Milo chuckled, but the sound lacked its usual warmth. "I know you do. And because you do, I won't ever let you down, son. Not you nor your brother or sister. This morning, after we get us a house fixed up in the cave, Ambrose and I are going to find work of some kind here in town. We'll make enough coin to buy food, mark my words. And soon we'll have enough to leave Black Jack. I've had a hankering to leave here for quite some time, truth be known. Been hearing lots of stories about rich veins being struck. We'll follow the gold, eh?"

"And strike it rich?" Khristos asked excitedly.

"Rich beyond our wildest dreams."

"Will you buy me a shotgun then?"

Milo tightened his arm around Cassandra, his big hand squeezing her arm in a comforting fashion. "I'll buy you whatever your heart desires, lad. Anything you want. Just as soon as I find that gold."

Cassandra stubbed her toe on an upraised cobblestone. Only her papa's quick reaction prevented her from taking a headlong spill. Ambrose said something under his breath, the ring of it reminding her of Luke when he swore and didn't want her to hear.

Luke. At the thought of him, agony hit her. It rolled through her in waves, welling up from inside her and erupting with such force, it cut off her breath. Huge, flattening waves of pain that made everything else seem far away, separated from her by a cottony haze.

"Papa, she's hurt her foot."

"Holy Mother, what else?"

"Cassie, does it hurt? Thunderation! It's bleeding."

Detached, Cassandra glanced down. Way, way down. At a foot that seemed to belong to someone else. And Ambrose was right, the foot was bleeding. Funny, that. It didn't hurt, that poor, torn toe. It felt a million miles away from her.

Suddenly the world seemed to turn sideways. She gulped back a wave of nausea and blinked. Ambrose had scooped her up and was carrying her, she realized. With a grunt, he jostled her, trying to reposition his arms to support her head, which thumped sharply against his sturdy shoulder. Even that discomfort seemed far away, as if she were watching someone else.

She gazed up at the rooftops that bounced and undulated in her vision. Green tiles, red tiles, plain brown shingles. Wasn't it strange how a person seldom looked up and noticed things like roofs? They were really quite pretty, all wet and shiny from the rain.

"Papa, I don't think she's even with us."

Of course, she was with them. Hearing the concern in Ambrose's voice, Cassandra blinked again and tried to focus on things that were up close. The worn, tweed-covered button of her older brother's jacket swam into her vision. Slowly, it took on clarity. She hauled in a deep breath, and some of the fogginess in her brain moved away.

"I'm all right," she managed to say. "Put me down, Ambrose."

"Don't be silly."

Cassandra dragged in another deep breath to clear her head. "You'll hurt your back."

"Packing a wee little thing like you? Don't insult me!"

In Cassandra's recollection, Ambrose had never referred to any part of her as little. That he did so now told her how worried he really was about her. She stirred and lifted her head. When she thought of Luke, pain threatened to flatten her, yes. And the shame she felt was so thick she could barely breathe. But that didn't mean she had to make her family suffer. They'd already endured enough, thanks to Luke, and would endure still more before this was over.

"Put me down, I said. I want to walk on my own two feet, Ambrose."

"One of them is bleeding."

"A scratch, nothing more." She grabbed her older brother by his ear, striving to put a note of playful bossiness in her voice. "Now, Ambrose. Enough mollycoddling."

Ambrose drew to a stop, his arms tightening for a moment as his blue eyes searched hers. "I love you, Cassie," he whispered. "You know that, don't you?"

Tears filled her eyes, and she hugged her brother's strong neck with all her might. He said the words so easily. *I love you, Cassie.* And the sincerity with which he said them shone in his expression. This was how it should be between people who cared about each other, she thought. More the fool she, for not realizing that before now. She'd kept making excuses for Luke, assuring herself that he loved her but simply couldn't say so. *Pig slop.* The man had no difficulty articulating when it came to any other subject.

No, she was the one at fault, dreaming her foolish dreams about a magic prince. Believing in the fairy tales she told Khristos. Oh, yes, she'd fooled herself, all right, and in the process, she'd made a fool *of* herself. She couldn't blame Luke. Or anyone else. *So you've chosen to remain ignorant to please your papa?* Luke had once asked her. She had replied that she preferred to think of it as being selective. Now she realized she'd been stone blind instead, refusing to see the bad in someone even when it was right in front of her nose. Selective? "Stupid" was more like it.

Cassandra Zerek was responsible for the shambles her life had become, and it was up to her to put everything right again.

As Ambrose set her on her feet, Cassandra took her crumpled pride and emotions firmly in hand. She was young and strong. Shattered though she felt, she still had all of herself here somewhere. She had only to fit the pieces back together.

Her gaze landed on Khristos, who stood with one small hand on Lycodomes's broad head. Her little brother's eyes looked nearly as big as flapjacks. Cassandra felt a different kind of shame crash over her now. How could she be so self-centered? Her family needed her—Khristos, especially. She was the only mother the little fellow had.

Remembering her own mother, whom she'd always tried to emulate in her dealings with Khristos, Cassandra shook the last vestiges of fuzziness from her mind. Time enough later to feel sorry for herself.

"Khristos, just look at you! Hat in your pocket, your coat hanging open. I swear, I have to watch you every second." She drew the red knit cap Luke had purchased down over Khristos's head, tugging so the ribbing would cover his ears. Then she quickly buttoned his new warm jacket with fingers gone oddly numb. "It's wintertime, in case you haven't noticed. Soon snow will be flying."

On shaky legs, she bent to hug her younger brother. When he hugged her back, she felt him shaking as well. This was a frightening situation, to be sure, having no home, no food, no money. Even Khristos understood that they were in a world of trouble, and that only charity from the church would save them.

"Let's play 'Thank Goodness'!" she suggested, inserting as much enthusiasm into her voice as she could.

It was a familiar game to everyone in the Zerek family, one that they played to cheer themselves up when times got bad. Ambrose immediately said, "Thank goodness we don't have bunches of curtains!" When everyone looked at him quizzically, he grinned and expounded. "Living in a cave, we'll have no windows!"

Milo chuckled as he bent to help Cassandra stand up again. Falling into a walk, he tugged her along, motioning for Khristos and Lycodomes to follow. "Thank goodness I haven't got heaps of money! When I got tossed in jail, they took my wallet!"

"Thank goodness we don't got a horse!" Khristos cried, skipping to catch up. "We ain't got no hay to feed it!"

"Thank goodness I'm not carrying a saddle! It would be too wasteful to throw it away, and without a horse to wear it, it'd be mighty heavy!" Cassandra put in.

"Thank goodness we don't still have all our furniture," Ambrose said. "It'd look silly in a cave."

"Thank goodness we have no furniture, for if we did, I'd have no reason to build new!" Milo added.

And so it went, all the way to the church.

As her papa helped her to climb the steps to St. Mary's double front doors, Cassandra thought, *Thank goodness I feel separated from everything right now, for if I didn't, I think I'd be dying.*

"Nothin' like a wee bit of good Irish whiskey to cure what ails ye," Father Tully exclaimed a few minutes later as he held Cassandra's foot suspended above a white-enameled washtub and sloshed alcohol over her injury. "We'll have ye fixed up in no time. Yer papa will find some clothes and shoes to fit ye, I'm sure. I've got boxes stacked taller than I am back there in that storage room."

Gripping the edges of the chair on which she sat in the cheerful rectory kitchen, Cassandra said, "We're grateful for the help, Father. Thank you for being so kind."

"Think nothin' of it. I'll be glad to get rid of some of that stuff." He flashed her a smile. "To make room fer more. People are always droppin' things by."

Vaguely aware of her papa's and brothers' voices somewhere at the back of the house, Cassandra fixed her gaze on a wooden cross hanging on the white wall behind the priest. "Lucky for us they do, I guess."

"Yes, well...Milo will get back on his feet soon." The priest sloshed more whiskey over her toe. "I'm sorry, lass. 'Tis bound to sting like the very devil."

Cassandra glanced down, wondering why she felt no pain. Her toe was badly stubbed, and the priest was pouring alcohol directly over the wound. "It's not bad, Father. Truly, it isn't."

The plump, gray-haired priest propped her heel on his black-clad knee and reached up to smooth her hair back from her cheek. His touch, as always, reminded her of Papa's, warm and gentle and full of love. "I've a feelin' ye're hurtin' so bad in other places, that toe seems like a small thing."

Cassandra closed her mind to the pictures of Luke that tried to creep in. "It's been a rough morning, to be sure," she said hollowly.

"And Luke? What has he to say about all this?"

Thanks to her papa's ranting and raving after they'd entered the church, Father Tully knew everything, including the fact that the wealthy, arrogant Luke Taggart had tricked Cassandra into signing a contract to make her his whore.

Shame. It crawled over Cassandra's skin, a cold, slimy feeling that she could scarcely bear—a feeling that seeped to the marrow of her bones when she allowed herself to think about it. "He didn't say much of anything, Father."

"Come, lass. He must have said somethin'."

Cassandra bit her lip and averted her gaze. "Papa was yelling so loud, Luke kind of got drowned out, I guess. He...um...said he was—" She broke off, gulping back the hurt that threatened to suffocate her. "He said he was sorry." She lifted her gaze to the ceiling, staring and swallowing again, this time almost frantically, in an attempt not to cry. "I, um…guess that means it was his intention. To make me his—his whore, I mean. Papa says he undoubtedly planned to divorce me once he got bored with me, that divorce to a man like him would mean nothing."

Father Tully sighed, drawing her gaze back to him. There was an oddly preoccupied look on his face. "Yes, well. It sounds to me as if ye might be wise to go back and speak with Luke when yer papa isn't around to drown him out."

Cassandra closed her eyes. "I can't. I just can't, Father. I'm too ashamed. It's hard enough just to meet Papa's gaze, or yours. I feel so—so dirty. And everyone knows. Luke and Papa and Ambrose and Khristos. Even you."

Father Tully set the whiskey aside and lowered her foot to the floor, then stood to drag another chair from its place at the table. After planting his backside on the seat, he leaned toward her with his elbows on his knees. His gaze caught hers and gave no quarter, searching relentlessly. "What, exactly, are ye ashamed of, Cassandra?"

"You heard my confession before the wedding. You know what I mean."

"Refresh me memory a wee bit. I hear lots of confessions."

"Before we got married, I let him do things I shouldn't have, the kinds of things husbands do to their—" she broke off, unable to continue. "I *trusted* him. I thought he loved me, and I loved him. Now I realize I did all those—those things with him, and all the while, I was nothing but a plaything to him. Papa accused him of exactly that, straight out, and even then Luke didn't deny it or say he loved me. Just that he was sorry, and that he'd make it up to me if he could. That must mean it's all true!"

"So ye feel ashamed?"

She cupped a hand over her eyes. "Wouldn't you? I soiled myself. Made a laughingstock of myself. He didn't just *try* to make me his whore, as Papa keeps saying. He succeeded!"

"I can remember a time in the no' so distant past when ye did no' know the meanin' of that word, lass."

Cassandra lowered her fingers slightly to look at him. "'Whore,' you mean?"

Father nodded. "'Tis a filthy word. I guess I hate it most because 'tis used to describe a human being, one of God's children. The world is full of people, all of 'em walkin' different paths. I believe God loves us all. What, exactly, is a whore? A bad woman? Or is she only someone whose life has led her to walk a path different from our own? Does God love her less for that? Or does He love her more? Maybe He looks down on her and sees, not a sinner, but only someone who's lost her way."

"Someone like me."

"Aren't ye bein' a little hard on yerself, lass? How could ye be on guard against somethin' ye did no' know existed? Until meetin' Luke Taggart, did ye even realize some women sold their bodies?"

"No. But I knew there were certain intimacies that were forbidden, and that if I let anyone touch me like that, it was a sin." She forced herself to meet the priest's gaze. "Luke said it wasn't, that nothing we did was wrong, but I knew better, and I let him. Even worse, I *wanted* him to. I sinned with him, Father. Make no mistake!"

Father fell silent for a good long while, then finally nodded. "Ye're right. 'Twas a terrible, terrible thin' you did."

"The worst part is, everyone knows!" she said thinly. "When Papa and Ambrose look at me, I can see it in their eyes—that they're ashamed for me. I think that's what hurts most of all—that they'll never think of me quite the same again. It's done, and I can't ever undo it. The taint will stay with me the rest of my life."

He nodded again. "Trustin' the man, givin' yerself to him, lettin' him touch ye before marriage, lovin' him, believin' in his lies." He heaved a weary sigh. "Ye've dug yerself into a black hole, that's fer sure."

"To be toyed with like that. Thinking I was something special to him and letting him—letting him *use* me. I wish I could die," she said with a sob.

"I do no' blame ye."

"I can't face Luke again. Never. Not after all we did, and him not loving me the tiniest bit! If he so much as looks at me, I'll crawl under a mopboard!"

"The scoundrel. He should be horse-whipped."

"And me along with him!"

Father shook his head, his expression even

more sorrowful. "Actually, prostitutes are stoned. Traditionally, at any rate,'twas the chosen punishment."

"Stoned?"

"Maybe I should tie ye to the front porch railings and send out notices to all the sinless, so they might come to throw rocks at ye."

Cassandra blinked. "Rocks?"

"Big, sharp ones. It takes a while to die. A nice, slow, very painful death. Ye'd be sure to pay for yer sins that way to pave yer way to heaven."

"You're teasing, right?"

Father cocked an eyebrow. "Teasing? Not a bit of it. 'Tis a terrible thin' ye've done, lass. Ye've committed a mortal sin."

"But I confessed."

"That, ye did." He rubbed his chin. "I momentarily forgot." He sighed and shook his head again. "Technically speaking, then, ye wiped the slate clean, and what ye did after the weddin' was no sin, but the partakin' of a sacrament. Of course, a smart girl like ye knows all of that is hogwash."

Cassandra was starting to feel a litle lost in this conversation. Father was talking in circles, and strange ones at that. "Hogwash?" she asked carefully.

"The sacraments. Hogwash, all of 'em. Confessin' yer sins, bein' sincerely sorry, receivin' absolution, doin' penance. Marriage vows makin' physical intimacy a sacrament. All of it hogwash." He hooked a finger under his white clerical collar, gave a hard jerk, and pulled it off. After gazing at the collar for a moment, he threw it on the floor. "Good-bye to that, and good riddance."

"Father, what are you doing?" Cassandra straddled the tub, pushed up from the chair, and bent to retrieve his collar. "What are you—? Why did you—? Have you lost your mind?"

"I'm quittin'."

"Quitting what?"

"Me job, lass. After listenin' to ye, I've realized I'm no' fit to be a priest."

Panic raced through her. What had she said to make Father behave like this? "Oh, no, Father. I never meant to make you feel that way!"

He waved the collar away when she tried to press it on him. "Don't ever be tellin' anyone this," he said, lowering his voice to a whisper, "but I once fornicated meself."

Cassandra felt her eyes go round. "You didn't!" she whispered back.

"Oh, yes. With a young miss in her father's hayloft. Ah, but she was a pretty girl. That was way back when, of course, when I was still young and foolish and hadn't yet realized 'twas me callin' to be a priest."

"You, Father? I didn't think priests *ever* did such things."

"There, ye see? I'm no' fit to wear the cloth."

Horrified, Cassandra looked down at the starched band of white in her hand, thinking of all it represented. "Oh, but, Father. Surely you went to confession and—and did your penance?"

"Aye, I did at that. But as ye pointed out, none of that matters. Like ye, I committed a terrible act."

She gaped at him. "But you can't mean to quit your job. Not over something you did years ago!"

"Time is to God but the twinkling of an eye. Me 'way back when' is like a second ago to Him. So, ye see? I'm as guilty as ye are." He leaned back in the chair and crossed his arms. "We're a sorry pair, are we no'? Sinners, both of us. Lost souls, with no hope of salvation. I'm quittin' the priesthood. Ye're hangin' yer head. Ah, but I suppose there's no help fer it, the two of us doomed sinners as we are."

Father Tully was one of the sweetest men Cassandra had ever known. "You're not doomed. You're a—a *priest*!"

He winked at her. "And ye're a good, sweet girl who had stars in her eyes fer a wee bit of time."

She sat back down, the collar still clutched in her hand. "You've been having me on."

"A wee bit."

She touched a hand to her heart. "Thank goodness. You scared me to death!"

"Good. I always like to return a favor."

"I'm scaring you?"

"Out of me skin, lassie. Clear out of me skin." He settled a kindly gaze on her. "'Tis no sin to love, Cassandra. Nor wrong to trust someone. And when we're truly sorry, it *does* wipe the slate clean. What went before yer marriage? 'Tis o'er. God forgives ye. Now ye've only to forgive yerself."

He tugged the white collar from her fingers. "I think I'll be takin' this back now, if ye don't mind. I feel a little naked without it."

Cassandra felt tears welling in her eyes. "Oh, Father, if what went before doesn't matter, why does it hurt so much?"

"Sometimes lovin' hurts." He shrugged. "And sometimes 'tis glorious. One never knows how it'll go, from one day to the next. Ye just trudge along, takin' the good wi' the bad."

"In this case, lots of bad."

"Ye'll recover, and ye'll go on. There's no question of that. I only ask that ye do so with yer head held high. Luke is the one who has trespassed against ye, not the other way 'round. He's the one who should feel ashamed. He took somethin' very precious—yer love— and dragged it through the dirt."

At the back of the rectory, Cassandra heard voices approaching. "Papa's coming," she whispered.

Father Tully glanced back over his shoulder, then fixed her with his gaze again. "Cassandra, one more thin' before yer papa comes stormin' in, talkin' a mile a minute." He leaned closer, so as not to be overheard. "I know ye need time to lick yer wounds, lass. And maybe a lot more time to heal. But remember one thin', please?"

"What's that, Father?"

"We Catholics don't have a corner on forgiveness." His mouth kicked up at one corner. "Ye told me Luke said he was sorry, and by that, ye condemned him. Is that what ye learned in yer catechism, child?" He reached out to pat her hand. "I'm not sayin' ye must face him right now or go back to him. Only yer heart can tell ye to do that. But ye absolutely must forgive him. If ye don't, the person ye'll hurt the most will be yerself."

TWENTY-THREE

The drapes were drawn, and the lamp had long been extinguished. The study was cloaked in shadows that deepened to an icy darkness in the corners of the room. Sprawled in his big leather chair, his booted feet crossed at the ankle and propped carelessly on the edge of his desk, Luke leaned his head back and took another long pull from the whiskey bottle. Though the liquor had long since lost most of its bite, his throat still burned after he swallowed—more from shame, he suspected, than from the drink.

But what the hell. He'd lived with shame for most of his life, from that awful moment when he'd been five and gone running outside to play ball with two other boys in the street in front of the brothel. He hadn't understood the names they'd called him, but he had felt the sting of rejection. He still felt it, no matter how rich he became or how many men he hired to do his bidding.

Distantly aware of voices coming from the foyer, he wiped his mouth with his knuckles and exhaled with a whistle. He was drunk, all right, he decided after a moment's careful reflection. But not drunk enough.

Soon, he knew, the sting of the whiskey would vanish, replaced by a stuporous oblivion. Oh, yes. He wanted to guzzle so much skull-popper, he couldn't think, let alone feel. So much that he forgot 'Little Miss Sunshine's' name and had trouble recollecting what she looked like.

To hell with her. To hell with all of them. So he was a lying, conscienceless bastard. What else was new?

The study door creaked open. Luke narrowed an eye. "I said not to disturb me, goddammit!"

The figure silhouetted in the doorway was short and plump, the outline of clothing too refined for that of Milo Zerek, the first person who came to Luke's mind. It definitely wasn't Pipps, who was skinny as a scarecrow and bean-pole-tall.

"Who the hell is it?" Luke inquired with a growl calculated to send faint hearts scurrying.

The door swung closed, snuffing out the daylight that had spilled briefly into the room. Luke watched his shadowy visitor walk toward his desk. "Ah," said a familiar voice he couldn't quite place, "imbibin' a wee bit, are ye? Care to share wi' a friend?"

Luke squinted to see, and Father Tully's round face came into focus. Leveling the priest a glare, he took another long gulp of whiskey. "I prefer to drink alone, thanks."

"Well, now. I'm thinkin' mayhap we should have a wee talk, if it's all the same to ye."

431

"If you've come to tell me my marriage is going to be annulled, save your breath. Frankly, I don't give a shit."

"I can see ye don't." The chair at the opposite side of the desk groaned in protest as the priest settled his considerable bulk onto the leather cushions. "Back to yer old habits, I see."

"Damn straight, and fine habits they were, too. I haven't felt this good in a month." Luke plunked the bottle down at the center of the desk. "Help yourself, if you aren't afraid you'll burn in hell."

"Fer havin' a wee snort?" Tully chuckled. "I'll pint with ye, Luke Taggart, the devil take his flames. Jesus turned water into wine at the wedding at Cana. 'Twas His first miracle, ye know. I've always taken that to mean He would no' hold a wee snort again' a man."

"Protestants will tell you the 'wine' referred to in the Scriptures was actually only grape juice," Luke replied with a sneer.

The Father took a hearty belt from the bottle, then wiped his mouth with his sleeve as he gasped for breath. "God forbid I should ever listen to a Protestant!" He shuddered. "'Tis good stuff ye've got here. Mighty good stuff, indeed!"

Ordinarily Luke might have laughed. He liked the old fart, starched collar and all. "How'd you ever wind up a priest?"

Tully laughed softly. "'Tis a question I've asked meself a few times. Some days I've a good mind to quit."

"Why don't you, then?"

Father took another generous slug of

whiskey, then returned the bottle to the blotter. "Ah, now, there's a question." He seemed to consider his answer for a moment. In the shadows, his eyes appeared to twinkle uncommonly brightly when he met Luke's bleary gaze. "I reckon 'tis because I occasionally stumble across some damned fool who needs me help, and lending a hand makes it all seem worthwhile."

Luke shook his head and grabbed the bottle by its neck, sloshing a little liquor as he dragged it across the blotter toward him. "Seems a high price to pay. No gambling, no skull-popper, no snatch. Jesus, Father. Why not just shoot yourself?"

Tully chuckled again. Then he settled back, kicked his stout legs up to settle his feet on Luke's desk, and folded his lily-white hands over his black shirtfront. "Is that all Cassandra meant to ye—a wee bit of snatch?"

Luke strangled on the whiskey, fought to get his breath, then bit down hard on his back teeth and blinked, refusing to dignify that question with an answer.

"Well?" the priest pressed. "No' a bit of snatch, then? A swatch of calico, perhaps? A piece of ass?" He lifted one hand to rub his chin. "It's been so long, I'm forgettin' all the vile little names and phrases men use to describe a woman, so forgive me if I stumble about, tryin' to hit on the right one. Does 'beaver' apply? How about 'honey pot'?"

Luke lurched forward in his chair, his feet hitting the floor with a resounding thud, the base of the whiskey bottle crashing down on

433

the desktop. "Go get yourself screwed!" he grated.

Apparently unalarmed, the priest steepled his fingers over his plump belly. "Sorry, but me vows of celibacy prohibit such activities."

Luke narrowed his eyes. "Then go screw yourself."

"Ah...that, too, is forbidden, I'm afraid," the priest replied with a calm smile that made Luke want to ram his teeth down his throat. "Besides, I've heard from several reliable sources that such occupations can make a man go blind. I've no personal experience, of course. Is it true, do ye think?"

"You're pressing your luck, Tully. I've asked you politely to leave. If you're smart, you'll do it."

"Politely?" The priest cocked an eyebrow. "Ye're roarin' at me, more like. And, mayhap I'm wrong, but I believe ye're threatenin' me person."

"And coming goddamned close to carrying through on the threat."

"May I take yer angry reaction to me inquiry to mean ye don't regard the young lady in such base terms?"

"You can take it to mean whatever the hell you want. Just remove yourself from my house!"

"Not until I'm clear on one thing. Purchased whore or cherished wife? Which was she to ye?"

Luke shot up from the chair, reeling for a moment before he could get his balance.

"When you're talking about that girl, keep a civil tongue in your head," he said raggedly. "Or so help me God, Father, I'll make you eat that collar you're wearing."

The priest cackled. "I've chewed on it a few times before, believe me. 'Tis to be expected, I guess, when I go stickin' me nose in other people's business. Sit down, Luke, before ye fall down. I meant no insult to yer lady. I was merely seekin' an answer."

"To what?"

"An extremely important question. A test, if ye will. Which ye've passed. Ye love her, don't ye?"

Luke's gut twisted, and he brushed a hand over his eyes. "I don't love anyone. I'm incapable of the emotion."

"Horseshit." Father reached out to slap the desktop. "Sit yer ass down, Luke Taggart. I'll not be havin' yer face in mine while I'm tryin' to talk sense into ye."

Luke had little choice but to obey. His knees gave out, and he folded like a hinged chair onto the leather cushion behind him. Propping his elbows on his thighs, he buried his face in his hands. "Are you sure you're a priest?" he finally managed to croak. "You talk like a damned sailor from the docks."

"I once *was* a sailor from the docks. As fer me speech, I've learned o'er the years that wi' certain blockheaded addle-brains, talkin' polite is like tryin' to drive a spike with a tack hammer."

"Are you implying that I'm a blockheaded addle-brain?"

435

"Did I stammer, or are ye deaf as well?"

Luke gave a choked laugh. After a long moment, he asked, "How did a sailor from the docks end up celibate? That must be one hell of a story."

"A longer one than we have time fer, to be sure. Suffice it to say that durin' the great famine, I left home to get any job I could find, hopin' to send coin back to Ireland to feed me mother, brothers, and sisters. They all died while I was aboard ship, some from starvation, some from a contagion that struck the area. 'Twas a black time in me life, and afterward I stayed wi' the sea fer a time until I realized I had a callin' to the priesthood."

"How could you bring yourself to devote your life to God?" Luke sighed and sank back in his chair. "Pardon me for saying so, Father, but that doesn't make a lot of sense. If there were a God, how do you explain the tragedy that befell your family?"

"I suppose it never occurred to me that God might be in the potato business. Did He make the spuds rot, do ye think?"

"He didn't stop it."

"No. So let's blame Him, shall we? And in the doin', blame Him fer all else as well. Sunshine, flowers in spring, the existence of one wee lass named Cassandra."

Luke closed his eyes. "You're a merciless bastard, aren't you?"

"I leave it to God to be merciful. But a bastard, I'm not. Me mum was a good, God-fearin' woman, much like the wee lass ye married. Stars in her eyes, and a smile to light up a room."

"Is Cassie…is she all right?" Luke asked in a raspy voice. "She left here in her night-clothes and bare feet, with that lunatic father of hers. It was raining, for Christ's sake."

Father Tully dragged in a weary breath. "If ye mean, did I get her some clothes and see to it she'd have some food, yes, she's all right. But that does no' mean the heart has no' been ripped from her breast. They went off to take shelter in their mine, God bless 'em."

"Oh, Christ."

"I said His blessed name meself a few times as I watched 'em straggle away. Not a nickel to their names. All they had was a few ragged blankets that I gave 'em and some pots to cook in. It's a fine mess ye've made of things with yer schemin', Luke. A fine mess, indeed."

With an audible swallow, Luke whispered, "I'd cut off my right arm to undo it all, to have her back!"

"Milo might settle for yer balls."

Luke flopped a shirtsleeve over his eyes. "Hell, why not? I'll probably never get it up again anyway."

"And why might that be?"

"Because every goddamned time I look at another woman, I'm going to see her face. You should've seen her eyes, Father. When Milo told her…you should have seen her eyes."

"Oh, I saw 'em, right enough. All the light snuffed out, her face as pale as wax."

Luke couldn't breathe for a second. The muscles along his throat snapped taut, grew distended, and choked off all his air. "I—I never meant to—to hurt her."

437

"I know ye didna, lad. It goes wi'out sayin'. The question, as I see it, is how can ye go about fixin' things."

"I'll do anything."

"Yet ye do no' love her?"

"Love! It's nothing but a word. I'd give up everything I own, buy her the world, set her family up in high cotton for life. Anything...just to have her back. Isn't that enough?"

"Must it always come back to yer money, Luke Taggart? Is it so difficult fer ye to see that there are some things ye canno' buy or take?"

Luke turned his head to see that the priest had risen to his feet. "How, then? Tell me how to get her back, Father. I'll do it in a heartbeat. Just tell me!"

Filled with sadness, the priest's gaze settled on Luke. "I will no' lead ye by the hand to get her back, lad. Ye'd only break her heart ag'in. Ye must find the way yerself and learn it well, so ye ne'er repeat the same mistakes. But I will tell ye this much: the secret does no' lie in this grand house or wi' all yer money."

"What, then?"

"Ye must learn to give of yerself."

"How?"

"That is for me to know and ye to find out."

Tully picked up the whiskey bottle to take one last swig. He shuddered as the liquor burned a path to his stomach. Then he turned and moved back to the door. At the threshold, he paused.

"'Tis oft said that there's nothin' like a bit o' good Irish whiskey to cure what ails ye. I caution ye not to take that old adage too much to heart. Ye'll not be findin' what ye seek at the bottom of that jug, lad. No answers, fer sure, and definitely no lass."

"Thank goodness I ain't got a chair," Khristos said cheerfully. "If I did, the legs'd sink in the mud!"

Forcing a smile, Cassandra glanced over at her little brother, who sat huddled on a rock she'd moved near the fire for him. As rocks went, it was reasonably suitable as a seat, save for the jagged edge right in its center, which apparently jabbed Khristos in the bum no matter where he chose to sit. Her own rock wasn't any better, but unlike Khristos, she didn't mind the discomfort. It took her mind off other hurts.

Waving a hand to clear away the smoke, which trailed up from the small fire and hovered like a fog bank at the ceiling of the tunnel, Cassandra said, "Thank goodness I'm not wearing a fine silk gown. It would be ruined by the smoke smell."

Khristos drew his frayed wool blanket more snugly around his narrow shoulders, his small body shuddering. "Thank goodness it ain't hot," he said. "We'd be thirsty, and it's a fair walk to haul water."

"Thank goodness we've got a bucket," she replied distractedly, "for otherwise, we'd be walking back and forth to the creek with a cup."

Khristos, warming to the game, dreamed

up another reason to be thankful, but Cassandra scarcely heard him. Her mind drifted away with the smoke as she gazed into the feeble flames. Without an ax for cutting firewood, they'd gathered the wet bits of wood from the hillside, and the warmth, meager though it was, truly was a blessing.

One hand fisted tightly around her beautiful diamond wedding ring, Cassandra couldn't help but think of the man who'd given it to her. *Luke.* His name had once moved through her thoughts like a lilting song. Now it had the ring of admonishment.

She couldn't recall a single word that had passed between her and Luke that didn't seem humiliating now. *I had more intimate games than chess in mind.* Oh, God, he'd paid for the use of her body, she realized with quivering shame. *Do you understand the term "wifely duties"? Those are the sort of duties I've hired you to perform.* In the end, he'd actually made her his wife, all simply to have her in his bed. Her cheeks burned when she thought back and realized how dumb she'd been, believing that their first night of intimacy might have made her pregnant. Luke hadn't completed the act that night, but he'd played her along, like a trout he was hauling in on a line, so she would marry him before she learned the truth about him from her papa and Ambrose.

The clothes. His unfailing kindness. The money he'd spent on Khristos. His care of Lycodomes. Even her wages. She'd sold herself to him and hadn't even realized it. *I love you, Luke. I love you so much.* Never once had he said the words back to her, not even during their wedding ceremony. Every time he'd touched her, he'd thought of her as a costly possession, a plaything, according to her papa.

Even so, pictures of Luke kept flashing in her mind, and a part of her yearned to run back down the mountain, to return to his house and fling herself into his arms, to beg him to tell her it was all a horrible misunderstanding, that he'd never intended to shame her like this. She couldn't help but remember the tender look in his eyes, the gentleness of his hands when he made love to her. How could all of that have been a lie? And, if it had been, why had Luke married her? According to the terms of the contract she signed, he needn't have bothered.

Her papa claimed Luke saw marriage as yet another way to own her, that that was how a man like Luke saw things. To him, women meant little more than a piece of horseflesh and were accorded even less respect. Luke Taggart was a conscienceless rake, plain and simple. He'd wanted her, so he took her.

"What do you think, Cassandra?"

Jerking back to the moment, she stared blankly at her little brother, the diamond slicing cruelly into her palm as her fingers closed more tightly around it. "About what, Khristos?"

Her brother gave her an impatient look. "About supper. What kind of food do you think Papa will buy?"

"Something fine, I'm sure." Cassandra

stared out the mouth of the tunnel at the dreary, wet hillside. Rain slashed at the mud and pelted the leaves of the bushes. Soon that rain would turn to snow, and the drifts would mount taller than a man. With all their possessions in a storage shed somewhere, Papa had not even a rifle for hunting, and soon whatever deer still remained in the mountains would head for low country. "Some salt pork, I'll bet, and probably some beans." She flashed her younger sibling another stiff smile. "We'll make corn patties, too."

"Mmm. I like corn patties."

Cassandra focused on Khristos's pale face. "Are you hungry, Khristos?"

"A little."

Slipping the ring into her skirt pocket, she pushed up from the rock. Gathering the gray wool blanket close around her shoulders like a cloak, she went to rummage in the gunny-sack of items Father Tully had given them that morning. "There are more biscuits," she said, striving to sound cheerful.

"Only one."

"Well? There is only one of you."

"What about you?"

As she clutched the edges of the blanket, Cassandra suddenly remembered her mama's shawl, which she'd left behind at Luke's. The loss of it filled her with grief, yet she couldn't contemplate returning to Luke's for it. The thought of facing him was more than she could bear. "I'm not hungry, Khristos."

"I'll split it with you."

"No," Cassandra said lightly as she thrust

the biscuit into her brother's grubby little hand. "You eat it. I'm still full from breakfast."

Khristos broke off a bit of the bread and stuffed it into his mouth, his blue eyes getting the contented look of a kitten suckling. Cassandra's heart broke a little, watching him savor the taste as if he were partaking of fine food. When the biscuit was gone, what then? Her little brother's belly would begin to gnaw, and she would have Luke Taggart to thank for it. Perhaps her family hadn't had much before Luke had entered their world, but at least her papa had seen to it that they seldom felt hungry.

What if Papa and Ambrose found no work? Thanks to Luke, the Zereks were no longer exactly well-thought-of in Black Jack. Indeed, some of the miners undoubtedly hated them, believing them to be low-life claim jumpers, another circumstance Cassandra could lay directly at Luke's door. Unless Luke made a public retraction, which she doubted he'd do, the shopkeepers who needed odd jobs done might turn her relatives away in favor of others begging for work.

Cassandra's gaze became fixed on the biscuit Khristos held. The boy broke off another morsel and deposited it carefully on his tongue, careful not to drop a single crumb. In that moment, she knew she wouldn't be able to bear watching him go hungry. Pressing a palm over her skirt pocket, she considered selling her wedding ring. The price she might get for it would keep them in food for a year. But no...if she were to do that, it would be the same as taking money from Luke, and that she would not do. Tainted money, that's what it was. If she took anything from him, he would have succeeded in making her his whore, in essence paying her for services she'd rendered.

Lycodomes suddenly pushed up from where he'd been lying by the fire, his muddy plume of a tail swinging wildly. His splint, Cassandra noticed, was smeared with grime. The poor dog. No more comfortable, warm pallet by the Taggart kitchen stove for him.

"Papa and Ambrose must be coming back," she told Khristos, indicating the dog's welcoming wag with a nod of her head. "Lycodomes seems to think so, anyway."

Khristos closed his small fingers over the biscuit. "I bet they're hungry, and I'm starting to feel full. I'll just save the rest of this for them."

Knowing well that Khristos wanted the rest of the bread for himself, that his tummy probably ached for more, Cassandra blinked away sudden tears. *This* was love, she thought sadly. Not pretty dresses and lovely rooms that sparkled, but going without for others. *Love.* Luke Taggart didn't comprehend the meaning of the word, which undoubtedly explained why he never said it.

"Cassie! Oh, God, Cassie!"

Raw with urgency, Ambrose's voice floated up into the tunnel. Cassandra stepped to the mouth of the man-made cave to scan the hillside in search of her brother. When he finally staggered into view from behind a stand of brush, she saw that his ragged tweed coat was stained across the front with something blackish-red. "Hey, there, Ambrose!" she called, lifting a hand to wave. "Did you find work, then?"

His steaming breath forming clouds around his face, Ambrose staggered closer, then finally reeled to a stop some twenty feet from her. With one look at his features, Cassandra knew something was terribly wrong. She'd never seen her older brother so pale. His mouth worked, but for a second no sound came forth. He spread his hands, his blue eyes filling with tears. Cassandra glanced in mounting horror at his splayed fingers. They were covered with what looked like blood.

"It's Papa," he finally managed to say between panting breaths. "He's dying, Cassandra. You must come quick!"

Suddenly Cassandra couldn't feel her legs. "Wh-what?"

"Shot! A drunk. Came out of one of the saloons. Saw Papa. Started cursing him, saying he was a claim jumper. Shot him! From just a few feet away, he—shot him. Right in the chest. Doc-doctor Mosley—working on him now."

Ambrose staggered, hugging an arm to his waist and bending forward slightly to fight for breath. "Hurry, lass. He's dying, I think."

Khristos came running from the tunnel. He stopped between Cassandra and Ambrose, whirling to stare up at first one of them, then the other, his eyes crawling with fear. "Papa?" he squeaked. "Our papa is dyin'?"

A broken, hoarse sound shuddered up from Ambrose's chest. His face twisted, and his lips drew back to bare his clenched teeth. Then his broad shoulders began to jerk. "I-I couldn't st-stop it. Saw wh-what was gonna happen, but I couldn't stop it."

Khristos started to sob—soft, barely audible sounds. "No! Not my papa!"

The prized biscuit, their last scrap of food, slipped from the boy's fingers and landed in the mud.

TWENTY-FOUR

Stone-sober from shock, Luke paused for a moment outside Doctor Mosley's office, his trembling hand on the brass door handle, thumb poised to press down on the latch lever. Rain pelted the back of his head, the water falling in droplets from his hair to trickle in icy rivulets down his spine. Milo Zerek, shot. Pipps's voice, as it had sounded when he'd delivered the news, kept whispering in Luke's mind, the words too awful to comprehend. Cassandra's beloved papa, a kindly man whose only real fault was to have chased a dream—that of finding gold and striking it rich.

It was a dream Luke, himself, had once chased, only he'd been one of the fortunate few to have actually captured it. Milo Zerek had stumbled upon something far less appealing than gold: a lying, cheating, conscienceless man who'd brought about his downfall.

This was Luke's fault. All his fault. Luke Taggart, the mining magnate, was a heartless son of a bitch. He'd proved it well, taking Cassandra Zerek from the protective arms of her father. Now Milo Zerek lay dying, shot in the chest for a claim jumper.

Milo would die. Luke held no hope that the man might miraculously survive; that wasn't in God's giant scheme of things. Oh, yes...Luke finally believed in God. After living his whole life as an atheist, after all his sneering at Christians and their ludicrous, bleeding-heart moral ethics, he'd finally become a staunch believer himself. No doubts lingered in his mind, not even a niggling uncertainty. There was indeed a God, and just as Luke had feared the night of Lycodomes's accident, that divinity had been hovering over his shoulder these twenty-nine years past, watching everything he did and keeping a tally. Now, as surely as the clouds wept precipitation, God was raining punishment on Luke's head.

The worst punishment of all was going to be opening this door. Luke stared at the brass handle, cursing himself for a coward. He imagined the accusation he would see in Cassandra's eyes, the unmitigated hatred. She would never forgive him for this.

He would never forgive himself.

When he finally gathered the courage to step inside, the waiting room was dim, just as he remembered. Only now the three worn, metal-framed chairs were occupied. Cassandra, Ambrose, and Khristos. Luke pushed the door closed and stared at them. They stared back. Three sets of blue eyes, all the same shade of cobalt and glassy with grief. Faces as bluish-white as new-fallen snow in the dawn's dusky light. Mouths pressed into thin lines. A silence that screamed.

Luke simply stood there, a condemned man facing his accusers. God, how he wished they'd say something—curse him, spit on him, anything but this awful quiet, so cold it felt frozen.

Luke was finally the one to break eye contact. Dropping his gaze to the floor, he groped for something he might say. There was nothing. "I am so sorry," he finally whispered. "You'll never know how sorry."

No response, not even the creak of leather cushions to tell him one of them had moved—or even that they were breathing. Maybe they weren't, he thought crazily. Maybe God had frozen this moment in time, and it was going to last forever. Luke Taggart's own private hell.

"I...um..." Luke forced his head up, made himself meet their gazes. Even little Khristos looked back at Luke as if he despised him. "I know you don't have any money. I'll pay the doctor bill. What happened is—well, it's my fault. And I should be the one to pay."

"We Zereks don't want your money," Ambrose replied softly. "We want nothing from you. Now, please, if there is any shred of decency in you at all, Mr. Taggart, leave us to our grief."

Luke's muscles jerked involuntarily when Cassandra suddenly pushed to her feet. His heart caught when she walked slowly toward him with one hand outstretched. He reached out to her. As their fingertips touched, the years that yawned between Luke and his childhood seemed to dissolve, and he was once again a beggar boy. One morsel of affection, one whisper of forgiveness. He'd have dropped to his knees for either one.

"Cassie, girl," he said on a shuddering breath, "forgive me. Please, forgive me."

Those blue eyes he cherished—eyes that had once been sparkly with an inner glow—met his with blank hardness. No light, no laughter, no life. Just a curious nothingness, as if the girl he'd known and adored had vanished.

Something hard and cold touched his palm. She brought up her other hand to curl his fingers around it, her touch as frigid as her gaze. Then she turned her back on him and moved across the floor to resume her vigil beside her brothers. Luke opened his hand to stare down at what she'd given him.

Her wedding ring rested against his palm, glittering and cold.

Luke left Doctor Mosley's and headed for the Golden Slipper, his legs numb, his chest hollow. As he shoved open the bat-wing doors of the saloon and stepped inside, he froze for a moment to stare. At the people. At their hopeless faces. The sounds reverberated against his eardrums: harsh, almost desperate laughter; tinkling piano music that seemed to have no tune. The rancid smells of perfume, liquor, and humanity at its worst closed in around him.

His shoes felt stuck to the floor where men had spit phlegm and wads of tobacco gone slimy with saliva. *His birthplace*, he thought vaguely. This was the kind of filth from which he'd sprung, the spawn of some unknown, foul-mouthed drunkard who'd spilled his seed between a woman's thighs, then walked away, never looking back. And why should he have? The night of Luke's conception, his mother had undoubtedly serviced a long line of men, and knowing her, she probably hadn't even bothered to wash up between customers.

When Khristos Zerek grew up, he'd think of sweet things when he recalled his sister's affectionate hugs. Love and laughter, a caring touch. All Luke remembered when he thought of his mother was the rank odor of a woman in need of a bath. That and the feel of her hand striking his cheek.

This was Luke's heritage, a place like the Golden Slipper, where men came to satisfy their perverted lusts, and women were paid coin to satisfy them. He'd suckled as a babe at a whore's breast and was still suckling at the breasts of whores as a man. There was no way out and never would be. His blood ran thick with the taint.

"Listen up!" Luke yelled.

The piano player froze and glanced back over his shoulder. Men at the gaming tables lowered their cards to stare. The kohl-lined eyes of whores Luke had once romped in bed with became fixed on him. The rich and powerful Luke Taggart was about to speak, and woe to the poor devil, male or female, who didn't pay attention. As a kid, Luke had hungered for respect, for just one person to look at him as if he were somebody. Well, now they were looking, and he felt nothing—certainly no sense of pride or accomplishment.

"Today," Luke said loudly, "Milo Zerek was shot down in the street only a few paces away from this establishment by a drunk who believed Zerek was a claim jumper. The reason everyone believes that is because I lied. I won't compound the terrible wrong I've done Milo Zerek by giving you details about why I wanted him arrested. Let's just say I'm a conniving bastard, and leave it at that. I hired a man to deceive Milo Zerek and convince him to sign a partnership agreement to dig on one of my claims—a claim that Milo Zerek was led to believe was legally filed upon by the man I hired. A rich claim on the back side of Taggart Mountain, where Milo knew there was probably gold. He fell for the trick, and I escorted the marshal up there to catch Milo red-handed, digging on my land. I wanted Zerek and his son Ambrose arrested so they'd be out of my way."

The expressions on the faces of Luke's audience didn't change. The same reverent attendance, the same respectful homage. It occurred to Luke in that moment that he could tell these people he'd brutally murdered a half dozen people, and they'd still just sit there, fearful of judging him, not even with so much as a look.

"As many of you are aware, I'm sure," Luke went on, "I married Cassandra Zerek,

451

and from that moment, I came to think of her family as my own. Now that Milo Zerek has been shot because of my actions, I'm sure the Zereks won't lay claim to me, but I do lay claim to them." Luke paused to directly meet the gazes of several people. "Put the word out. If anyone in this town harms the Zereks, that person will answer to me. If they ask for credit, they'd better get it. I'll guarantee payment on their charges. If one of them asks for work, create a job, and it'd better be a damned good one. I'll cover the wages. In short, if you encounter anyone in the Zerek family, treat them as you would me or be prepared to suffer the consequences."

The ensuing silence was brittle. Luke stood there for several seconds, looking from one person to the next. Then, before turning to leave, he said, "I'll remember all your faces, and I'm commissioning each of you to deliver the message to everyone in this town. If one damned thing happens to Cassandra Zerek or any of her family, the people in this room will be the ones to suffer for it. I promise you that."

After departing from the gambling establishment, Luke headed directly for St. Mary's. Father Tully answered Luke's urgent knock on the rectory door. The plump priest, whose black shirt and pants were streaked with flour, wore two white linen towels knotted together and tied about his thick waist to serve as an apron. He wiped his doughy hands on the cloth as he ran a kindly gaze over Luke.

"Milo Zerek has been shot," Luke blurted out.

Father nodded, his eyes darkening with sadness. "I know, lad. I was called directly after to administer last rites."

Luke's eyes burned. He averted his gaze for a moment. "I was surprised not to see you over there when I stopped in."

"Yes, well, I stayed with 'em fer a bit, then decided me time could be better spent. Forgive me appearance," the priest said warmly, gesturing down at himself. "Makin' biscuits, I am, for me dinner. Thought I'd bake up a few extra fer the family." He chuckled. "Me largest mixin' bowl has proved to be not quite large enough."

Of course, Luke thought. How like Father Tully to be making biscuits—probably enough for a regiment—which he would claim were leftovers that would go moldy if the Zereks didn't help eat them.

After wiping the interior doorknob clean with his makeshift apron, the priest bumped the door farther open with an elbow, which happened to be one of the few clean spots on him. "Come in, Luke. Come in and feel welcome." When Luke stepped inside, the priest added, "If ye'd shut the door, I'd be grateful. Me hands are a bit of a mess."

Luke closed the door and leaned against it, his legs feeling oddly weak. "Father, I need to talk."

Tully motioned with a dough-covered hand for Luke to follow him down a dimly lighted hallway that spilled into a brilliantly white kitchen. White walls, white cupboards, even a white tablecloth over the mahogany table. Oddly enough, instead of seeming stark, the brick-floored room seemed cheery, the monotonous sameness lending it a feeling of spaciousness it might otherwise have lacked. The single wall ornament was a wooden cross. No figure of Christ hung upon it, which Luke appreciated. As firm a believer as he'd recently become, that didn't necessarily mean he considered himself to be on good terms with the Almighty.

"Talk away," Father Tully said as he resumed his chore of rolling out biscuit dough on a flour-sprinkled oilcloth. "Ye'll excuse me if I cut out me biscuits and stick 'em in t'oven. 'Tis hungry they'll be, whether they realize it or not. Especially the little fellow. I've got a weddin' scheduled fer this evenin', I do. No rest fer the wicked, as they say." The priest swung his head toward a cupboard. "Ye'll find a mug in there. Help yerself to some coffee. 'Tis freshly brewed."

Luke glanced at the well-scrubbed coffeepot set away from the heat atop the iron cookstove. "No, thank you, Father. I'm having trouble swallowing my own spit right now."

Tully chuckled. "Ye were havin' no trouble guzzlin' earlier today, if ye don't mind me makin' the observation. So, what is it ye wish to talk to me about?"

Luke sighed and raked a hand through his hair. "About the Zereks. They won't accept any help from me, and I know that if any family on earth ever needed it, they do."

454

"Yes, well, ye can't hardly be blamin' 'em, now can ye?"

"No, Father. All the same, I'd like to help them. I was thinking that—well, if some anonymous person were to make a sizable donation to the church, and you were to pass on that money to them, a little bit here, and a little bit there, to see them over this rough spot..." Luke's voice trailed away. "They'd accept help from you, Father, where they won't from me."

"Yes," the priest said thoughtfully, "I reckon they would, at that."

"Well?"

Tully kept rolling and patting his dough. "What ye're askin' me to do is lie to 'em, Luke, about where the money is comin' from."

"A white lie, Father." Luke swallowed and closed his eyes for a second. "They've got no money. Not a cent. Cassandra could have sold her wedding ring, but instead she gave it back to me. How will they eat? Or stay warm? Right now, Ambrose is glued to his father's bedside. He can't be counted on to provide for them."

"'Tis a serious situation, to be sure."

"Then you'll do it?"

"I did no' say that, now did I? I can't be lyin' to the people, lad. 'Tis another of those little luxuries denied me, the tellin' of white lies, now that I'm a priest." He smiled at Luke over his shoulder. "In me experience, 'tis just as well. I'm a terrible liar, ye see. Ne'er did get it down to a fine art, if ye know what I mean."

"Then what if I just gave you a bunch of

money for the church? You could take from that to give to them. Simply tell them the gifts came from church funds."

Father Tully heaved a weary sigh and punched the dough with his fist. When he turned his back to the counter and fixed his gaze on Luke, his expression was filled with sadness. "Luke, me boy, ye just ne'er learn, do ye? A lie is a lie. Ye can twist it and turn it. Ye can dress it up, or ye can dress it down. But in the end, 'tis still a lie." He held up a hand. "Understand, please, that I know yer heart is in the right place. 'Tis fair bleeding out of yer eyes right now, fer all to see. Ye adore that wee lass as well, deny it though ye may. But ye've got to learn, lad, that yer money is no' the answer to everythin' that happens!"

Luke threw up his arms in sheer frustration. "It's all I've got, damn it! How else can I help them, Father? You tell me that, goddammit, and I'll go do it! You tell me!" He waited, but the priest wasn't forthcoming with any answers. "I caused this mess. I've got to fix it somehow. At least help them a little. The doctor bill alone will be far more than they can pay."

"Forget yer money," Father said softly. "That is me advice to ye, lad. Forget ye've got it."

Luke gaped at him. "And?" he asked loudly. "What then? For the sake of argument, let's pretend for a moment that I haven't a cent!" Luke held out his hands. "I'm broke. Not a penny to my name. A whore's bastard. How can I help them? Trust me, I've been there, Father, and I couldn't even help myself."

Father smiled slightly. "Be on yer way." He nodded at the doorway. "Go on, lad, and just keep on pretendin', will ye? That yer a penniless whore's bastard whose heart is fair breakin' o'er what ye've done."

"And then what?" Luke asked, so frustrated he wanted to grab the priest and shake him.

"Follow yer nose," Father Tully said solemnly.

It was nearly dark when Luke left the rectory, and the clouds overhead that had spilled occasional bursts of rain all day had finally opened up to deliver a deluge. He stood on the porch, eyes closed, face lifted to the pummeling raindrops. *A penniless whore's bastard.* He tried to clear his mind and fill it with that reality, an easy enough thing to do since he'd lived more than half his life under just those circumstances. Now what?

A rueful smile touched his mouth. Ten years ago, on a rainy night like this, with not a penny in his pocket, he would have headed downtown to pick some poor sot's pocket. That definitely wasn't what Father Tully had had in mind, Luke felt sure. Nonetheless, he decided to pick a pocket anyway, this time his own. He wrapped the money in his handkerchief and placed the bundle as close to the rectory door as he could to protect it from the rain. *A small anonymous gift.*

As Luke walked away into the twilight, his tightly woven jacket repelling rain like the feathers on a duck's back, he smiled humorlessly. Father Tully would know where the money had come from, of course. Knowing that old fart, Luke imagined the priest would hem and haw, but in the end, he'd give the money to the Zereks, telling them, in all honesty, that he didn't know for sure who had left it.

There was more than one way to skin a cat, and Luke knew most of them.

He hauled in a deep breath, feeling better, if only marginally so. At least he'd know Cassandra and Khristos weren't going to go hungry. His money was the only clean thing he had to offer them, for Christ's sake. He'd come by his original fortune honestly, and he'd invested wisely since. Though shrewd and heartless in his business negotiations, he'd never actually stolen from or lied to anyone to make an advantageous financial deal since he'd struck it rich. It wasn't *how* he'd made his money that had been so wrong, but the way he'd chosen to spend a large share of it, mostly on gambling, drink, and women. As wrong as that may have been, it didn't make the rest of his money dirty, dammit. And since he had so much to spare, why not put it to good use for a change?

His pockets completely empty for the first time in a decade, Luke headed for Mosley's office. When he arrived, he found Lycodomes curled up in front of the door. The huge dog slapped his soggy tail against the cobblestones, his canine grin the only truly understanding greeting Luke had received all day.

"Hello, Lycodomes," Luke said softly.

The dog whined and rose up on his forelegs

as Luke sat down. The close proximity to Lycodomes's tongue earned Luke several wet kisses along his jaw. He looped an arm around the animal's neck and pressed his face against rain-soaked fur. Odd, that. The dog smell seemed pleasant to him now—a comforting familiarity in a world that had turned topsy-turvy.

"At least you're still my friend," Luke murmured, ruffling the dog's ears and scratching his broad head. "Isn't that a hell of a note? In the beginning, you were the one who saw straight through me and hated my guts."

Lycodomes nudged Luke's neck with a cold, wet nose.

"Now, you're the only one in the whole Zerek bunch who can abide me."

Luke had the strange feeling that the canine was the only creature on earth who truly understood him. He remembered Cassandra's saying once that Lycodomes was an excellent judge of character. A burning sensation washed over Luke's eyes. He guessed she wouldn't believe that now.

Giving the dog a final pat, Luke leaned his head against the clapboard and closed his eyes, prepared to wait for news of Milo's condition, even if he had to sit there in the rain all night. The downpour soon soaked his trouser legs where they extended beyond the shelter of the eave, calling to his mind the fact that Lycodomes's splint was supposed to be kept dry. Luke peeled off his jacket and spread it over the dog.

The canine whined, the sound conveying

what sounded to Luke like gratitude. He smiled slightly. "Don't start thinking I'm a soft-hearted animal lover," he warned. "It's just that you're the only friend I've got left. Don't you go getting sick on me, you mangy mongrel. Then where the hell will I be?"

TWENTY-FIVE

Cassandra perched woodenly on the waiting room chair between her brothers, her chest aching with pent-up tears and her face numb. For hours, they had sat thus, like studies for a family portrait, missing the most important member. Cassandra guessed it was well after midnight by now. Outside the window of the waiting room, rain pattered steadily against the cobblestones, like the weeping of angels holding vigil on high, shedding tears for her papa.

Father Tully had visited several times, the last a few hours before. He'd brought them a package of biscuits large enough to sustain them for several days and offered yet another heartfelt prayer for her papa's recovery. Before taking his leave, Father had divulged the welcome news that the drunkard who'd shot their papa had been arrested and was in jail. Though Cassandra knew it wasn't very charitable, she was glad to know the man would be punished. She only wished another certain individual she knew would get his comeuppance as well.

Weary of sitting, Cassandra longed to leave

her chair and pace, yet she remained frozen, locked in a torturous suspense. Each of her brothers held one of her hands, Ambrose clamping down on her fingers with a bone-shattering force that conveyed his agony, Khristos clinging to her with both hands, a frightened little boy who'd already lost his mama long ago and now might lose his papa.

For both their sakes, Cassandra knew she had to be strong, that she couldn't let herself fall apart, but exhaustion and heartache had taken their toll. Her body ached, her legs and arms felt as if they weighed a thousand pounds, acidic flames licked up from her stomach to burn her throat and send pain dancing along her ribs. One second, she wanted to leap up and scream, her heart hurt so much, and the next second, all she could think to do was pray—disjointed prayers that circled endlessly in her mind, little snatches of the Hail Mary and Our Father and self-composed entreaties. *Please, God, please, God.*

She tried her best not to think about Luke. When images of his face came into her head, it was all she could do to remain sitting still. *Rage.* She wanted to walk over to his house, storm through the front door, and scratch his eyes out. If not for Luke Taggart's lies, her sweet papa wouldn't be lying inside the surgery, fighting for his life with every breath. For that, Cassandra could never forgive Luke, no matter what Father Tully said. Never, not as long as she lived.

Yet Father Tully was right about one thing. The helpless fury she felt toward Luke was a piercing agony, like a pick being driven straight through her heart. *Why?* That was the question that bludgeoned her weary brain. Why had Luke done this to them? She had loved him so much, so very much. Still loved him, God help her, which was why thinking of him and picturing his face made her feel as if she were dying inside, inch by torturous inch.

"Cassie?"

Khristos's voice snapped Cassandra erect. Disengaging her fingers from Ambrose's grip, she twisted on her chair to loop her arms around her little brother. "What is it, Khristos?"

"I'm scared. Is Doctor Mosley cutting open Papa's chest to fix him inside?"

The thought made Cassandra nearly vomit. "Oh, no, sweeting. He just has to remove the bullet, that's all. It's way deep inside Papa, you see. I think he'll pluck it out with tweezers, sort of like we do your slivers."

"Why's it takin' so long, then?" Khristos asked.

"Well, I think because he has to wait until he thinks Papa is strong enough."

Khristos shuddered and clung more frantically to her. "I want to see him."

"We can't, love. Not right now. Papa's lost a lot of blood, and that has made him go to sleep. It's the body's way of conserving its strength." She ran a hand over her brother's hair, thinking rather nonsensically that it was time for a shampoo. Between washings, Khristos's hair felt silky at first, then began to feel coarse as the grime accumulated. She pressed her face against the strands, inhaling the smell of him, a curious blend of soap, wool, wood smoke, little-boy sweat, and dog. A smile curved her mouth, a smile that made her chest twist with pain. "Oh, Khristos, I love you so. Do you know how much? You mustn't be afraid. No matter what happens, you'll still have me and Ambrose and Lycodomes."

"And Luke?"

She stiffened. "No, not Luke, sweeting. He hasn't turned out to be as grand a friend as we thought he was, I'm afraid. He's done some very bad things, told lies about Papa and Ambrose. That's why that drunken man shot Papa, you see...because he believed the lies Luke told about our papa."

"Luke said he was sorry."

"I know," Cassandra whispered hollowly. "But sorry is as sorry does. Sometimes the words are useless, like a candle flame in a high wind. Do you understand?"

Khristos rubbed his nose clean on the front of Cassandra's hand-me-down dress, a drab gray thing that hung loose around her waist and stretched so taut across her bosom that the buttons strained. "I don't think Luke meant for Papa to get shot," he said.

A denial lodged in Cassandra's throat. Remembering Father Tully's lecture, though, and hoping to spare her little brother at least some of the pain that she was feeling by helping him to put the bitterness behind him, she murmured, "No, probably not."

"He bought me new clothes and shoes."

"Yes, he did do that."

"And he saved Lycodomes by takin' him to

the doctor. He even brought home cuts of meat from the butcher for Lycodomes to eat, so he'd get well quicker."

"Yes, I know."

Khristos drew back a little to look up, his blue eyes pleading with her. "You know what I think? I think Luke got caught in a whopper."

"A 'whopper'? How so, Khristos?"

"Papa told me never to tell a whopper, because it could get me in a pickle and I'd wind up tellin' more whoppers to keep from gettin' in trouble for tellin' the first one. And pretty soon, the whoppers would pile up and up, until they was like a mountain. That's why Papa says we should never lie—'cause tellin' one makes you have to tell another one, and pretty soon, you're lyin' more than you're tellin' the truth."

"Yeah, well, your *friend*, Mr. Taggart, sure as sand did that," Ambrose inserted bitterly. "Lie after lie after lie."

Cassandra shot her older brother a warning glance, then returned her attention to Khristos. She ruffled the little boy's hair. "You know, Khristos? I think Papa would be very proud of you for trying to understand why Luke did the things he did, instead of simply feeling angry at him." She only wished she could do the same. "I know I'm proud of you, anyway. I think you're growing up, and not only that, but into a very fine young man."

"As fine as Papa, do you think?" the child asked shakily.

Cassandra blinked away tears. "That's a mighty tall order to fill, but if anyone can do it, you can."

"I want Papa to be here to see me all grown-up," Khristos cried. "I don't want him to die, Cassandra. Don't let him go away, please?"

She caught Khristos close and held him while he wept, her own unshed tears welling in a gigantic lump at the back of her throat.

When the boy had finally fallen quiet and lay in an exhausted slump against Cassandra's chest, Ambrose whispered, "I think you should get the biscuits Father Tully brought us and take him home, Cassie. He's worn plumb out. I'll stay here. If there's any change, I'll come get you."

Home. Cassandra pictured the cold, dank tunnel and nearly shuddered. She was ashamed to admit it, but the thought of going up there alone in the dark scared her half to death. The cave would be black as pitch until she got a fire started. Even more frightening was the realization that she'd be nearly three miles from town, without even a gun for protection. She tucked in her chin to gaze down at Khristos's pale little face and chided herself for being silly. The dark had never hurt anyone, and her little brother needed to rest.

"I guess you're right," she agreed. "He *is* tuckered. I just hate to leave when Papa is so fragile. What if he—" she broke off and swallowed. "I want to be here if—well, you know."

Ambrose pressed a big, strong hand over her shoulder. "I know. But, Cassandra, he could linger for days. We have to take care of Khristos meanwhile. That's the way Papa would want it."

Cassandra nodded and gave Khristos a little shake. "Khristos? Let's go home, shall we?"

The words had no sooner passed her lips than the surgery door opened, and Doctor Mosley stepped out. The rolled-up sleeves and the front of his white shirt were smeared with crimson. He sighed and pulled off his spectacles to pinch the bridge of his nose. "I got the slug out of him, and the bleeding has finally stopped."

"Oh, praise God!" Cassandra cried.

Doctor Mosley smiled wearily as he put his eyeglasses back on. "It's early on to be making any promises, but if a bad infection doesn't set in, I believe he may pull through."

Cassandra felt like a tightly wound ball of twine that someone had suddenly slashed through with a knife, the severed ends flying in all directions. Letting go of Khristos, she hugged her waist and bent sharply forward over her knees, unable to breathe, scarcely able to form a thought, tears blinding her. When at last she could drag a breath into her lungs, she wailed like some crazed creature, then began to sob. The next instant, her brothers were hugging her, and their sobs joined with hers, an awful sound, a mixture of joy and pain held at bay for too long.

The three of them clung together and wept until exhaustion made them limp. They leaned into one another like a trio of saplings uprooted by high wind, their arms like frail limbs intertwined, the counter-support of their weights all that held them erect.

Doctor Mosley, no stranger to grief for a patient he'd lost or joy for one he'd saved, stood to one side, not speaking until the worst of the storm had passed. "His heart sounds strong and steady," he told them. "If I were a betting man, I'd put my money on his making it. Just pray with all you've got that he doesn't get an infection. As weak as he is, that could finish him."

Ambrose scrubbed at his wet cheeks, his tanned face beaming, his blue eyes gazing out at the world from under swollen eyelids. "Thank you, Doctor Mosley. If not for you, he'd be lost to us already. I know you must be exhausted."

The doctor smiled. "Well, there's no point in all of us staying up the entire night." He inclined his head at Khristos. "That boy should be fed some supper and tucked in for a rest."

Cassandra pushed shakily to her feet. "We were just heading home when you came out." She stepped over to give the doctor a fierce hug. "It seems you're always saving my loved ones. Thank you so much for all you've done!"

Doctor Mosley returned her hug. "Go get some sleep, honey. He'll still be here in the morning. Maybe by then, he'll be awake so you can go in to see him, hmm?"

Ambrose rose as well. "I'll be staying, if that's okay. Just in case there's any change."

The doctor looked relieved to hear it. "That'll be fine. Move the chairs around, if you like, to fashion yourself a bed. I'll come out, now and again, to give you a report."

• • •

When Cassandra led Khristos from the doctor's office, the night was even darker than she'd imagined, the blackness up and down the deserted street slicked with sleeting rain. The only lighted windows were those of the saloons, which seemed to make the darkness everywhere else seem all the more sinister. Looking up at the sky, Cassandra couldn't even make out the silhouette of the mountains beyond the shadowy roofs of the buildings. The thought of traipsing three miles into that void of lightlessness without so much as a torch made a shiver crawl up her spine.

Because of his injured leg, she'd left Lycodomes up at the digs so he might stay dry. Now she almost wished she'd brought the dog along. Even with a splint to encumber him, Lycodomes would fight to the death to protect her and Khristos. Of that, she had no doubt. What if she and Khristos fell along the way? Or encountered a wild creature?

"How is he?"

Cassandra nearly leaped out of her skin at the sound of Luke's voice. Khristos still clamped to her side, she whirled and peered through the shadows to see her husband sitting on the cobblestones, his back braced against the exterior of the building. Stripes of light came through the Venetian blinds at the window above his head to lie in golden lines over his tawny hair. His face was obscured in shadow—not that it mattered. She knew every feature by heart. The imperious arch of his brows, a shade darker gold than his hair. The strong, squared line of his jaw. The firm yet full shape of his mouth. The stubborn thrust of his chin.

"Luke..." she whispered.

An indistinct movement next to him drew her gaze. She bent her head closer to see. Lycodomes? The unmistakable outline of the dog's head came into view, but from the shoulders down, the animal looked like a large, dark lump. After squinting for a moment, she finally determined that Luke had thrown his jacket over Lycodomes, to keep the canine's leg dry, no doubt.

Her gaze shot to her husband, concern welling within her despite her attempts to tamp it down. The fool. He was sitting there in nothing but his shirtsleeves. "What are you trying to do, catch your death?"

"That depends. How is your papa?"

"The doctor says he's gonna make it!" Khristos piped in.

Cassandra thought she saw Luke's shoulders slump. With relief? She gave herself a hard mental shake and called herself a hundred kinds of fool. How could she have a single good thought about this man, whose lies had nearly cost her papa his life?

She bent to jerk the jacket off Lycodomes and tossed the garment to its owner. "Thank you for keeping Lycodomes dry." She snapped her fingers. "Come along, Lye-Lye. It's time to go."

The dog lumbered to his feet, his splint going *kerthump, kerthump* on the stones as he fell in behind Cassandra and Khristos.

"Time to go where?" Luke called after them.

Several steps up the street already, Cassandra called back, "Home!"

"Home? Up to that mine, you mean? Cassandra, don't be a fool."

Cassandra quickened her pace. Her heart kicked against her ribs when Luke spoke again, somewhere close behind them. "Honey, please. Go to my house. I swear, I'll stay away. You and Khristos can stay warm and dry there. Cook will fix you a nice breakfast as well. And you'll be a lot closer, that way, if your papa takes a turn for the worse."

Staring straight ahead at the endless blackness of the mountain she knew she'd have to climb, Cassandra yearned to take him up on the offer. Lord help her, she was pathetic. Even now, still shaky from the heartache he'd caused and knowing all that he'd done, something deep within her responded to that wheedling, tender tone in his voice.

"Go away!" she cried shrilly. "Stop bothering us! We don't want your help. We want nothing to do with you!"

"So you'll risk life and limb to go up that mountain in the dark? To do what, sit there by a sputter of fire, wet to the skin? Use the brains God gave you."

"Don't speak to me about God! You aren't fit to utter His name."

Khristos balked, straining to look back. Cassandra jerked him into step with her.

"Bye, Luke!" he called.

"Good-bye, Khristos. Watch after your sister for me."

Sheer rage got Cassandra halfway up the mountain to the mining tunnel. After that, she was on her own, with only exhausted legs and flagging determination to keep her moving. Khristos huddled against her, so weary he needed to be pulled along half the time, and Lycodomes trailed behind, the ascent even more difficult for him because of his injury.

Once at the tunnel, it took all Cassandra's courage to enter a hole that was blacker than black. Inside, she stumbled about, patting the air to find the rock Khristos had been sitting on earlier that day. "You stay right here, Khristos," she said shakily when her hand made contact with the jagged granite, "while I build us a fire. All right?"

"I'm scared," her brother squeaked as she pressed him down onto the rock.

Cassandra's skin felt as if it were turning inside out. She thought she heard something outside the tunnel. She stared through the blackness, her heart pounding into her throat, her eyes feeling as if they were grapes popping out of their skins. "Don't be silly, Khristos. There's nothing to be scared of."

Then she heard it again. A *plunk* just beyond the mouth of the tunnel. She groped to relocate her brother.

"Th-there's somebody out there," Khristos whispered.

Cassandra was so frightened, she couldn't reply. She quickly dismissed all thought that the noise might have been caused by mischievous leprechauns or evil goblins. But the possibility that a drunk might have followed them wasn't so easy to thrust aside. What on earth could she do to protect them? The cave was so black, she couldn't even see to find a stick to use as a club. She strained her ears, listening for Lycodomes to growl, which he would surely do if he sensed an intruder.

Just as she was about to whisper the dog's name, light suddenly flared. She threw up a hand to shield her eyes. "Who is it?"

"You didn't really believe I'd let you traipse up here all alone and try to build a fire in the dark?"

Cassandra squinted against the glare of a torch as it bobbed toward them, the dark hulk of a man behind it. "Luke?"

"Of course, it's Luke," he replied, his deep, masculine voice ringing with impatience. "Do you know any other damned fool who'd be up here on a night like this?"

With a mighty thrust, he drove the unlighted end of the tree limb into the earth so it would stand erect. A pitch bole about three-fourths of the way up from its base hissed and sputtered as flames licked over its surface. The light was most welcome; Luke Taggart was not.

"I told you to stay away from us!" she cried.

"I will! Just give me a few minutes to gather you some wood. Then I promise, you won't see hide nor hair of me."

472

He disappeared back into the darkness beyond the mouth of the tunnel.

"We don't want your wood!" she yelled after him. "We don't want anything from you! Why can't you understand that?"

No response. Cassandra stood there, shivering beside her brother, for a moment. Then she glanced around for Lycodomes. He lay nearby, his plumed tail whacking the earth, a flag of welcome to their visitor. "Traitor," she said bitterly.

She gathered what remained of the limbs and twigs they'd found on the hillside earlier that day, arranging the meager amount of wood for a fire. She nearly wept with frustration when the stick matches refused to ignite. Their heads had drawn moisture. She looked bleakly at Khristos. He was wet from walking up there in the rain. A night spent here without warmth wouldn't be good for him.

She wrapped her arms around her knees, too weary to stand back up. "Oh, Khristos."

"Now what'll we do?" her brother asked.

Cassandra bit her lip. All day, she'd managed not to fold, but the urge was getting more and more difficult to resist. "Well, I guess we'll cuddle together for warmth," she suggested. "Won't that be fun? Just like when you were little."

With shaking hands, she tried again and again to get one of the matches to light. None of them responded. She was trying frantically to strike the last one when Luke's voice came from out of the darkness.

"You could have used the torch to light it."

She jumped and looked up. Arms loaded with odds and ends of wood, he strode up to the unlighted fire and dumped his burden, the limbs and twigs clattering upon impact.

"Not that you're so tired you can't think, or anything like that," he added with a sharp glance toward her. "Maybe that explains why you're up here, soaked to the skin, instead of at home, in a nice warm bed. Your brains have turned to mush."

Heat scalded her cheeks. She looked toward the torch, not quite able to believe she'd become almost frantic trying to light a fire when she'd had a blazing pitch bole at her disposal only a few feet away. Luke was right, she realized. She *was* so tired she couldn't think, and she was growing more exhausted by the moment.

He crouched and reached into his trousers pocket, withdrawing a corked vial of the sort usually used for gold dust. Inside were matches, which had been protected from the dampness by the airtight container. "I'll leave these with you," he said, his tone going husky. "Unless, of course, you don't want my lucifers either."

Cassandra swallowed, imagining her little brother shivering with the cold. To a point, stubborn pride could be commendable. After that, it bordered on sheer stupidity. "To keep Khristos warm, I'll take them and be grateful. Thank you for thinking to bring them."

"Actually, it wasn't thoughtfulness on my part. I'm a man who likes his vices," he said as he rasped the end of a match against a rock and cupped his hand around the spurt of flame. "I usually carry matches in my pocket in case I want a cigar or cigarette."

"I didn't know you used tobacco," she said stiffly.

He leaned forward to coax the twigs and pine needles to burn. "There's a lot you don't know about me, as I'm sure you're beginning to realize. I wasn't raised like you were, with pretty stories and prayers filling my head. Until I met you, I didn't even believe in God."

Cassandra couldn't bear to look at him, so instead, she stared at the flames that licked feebly to life, hissing and sputtering in slender tongues over the wet wood. Luke had located bits of pitch, she realized. Otherwise, even God and all his angels probably couldn't have gotten those drenched lengths of wood to burn.

"Never having learned a moral code," Luke went on, "I grew up not knowing any limits. If it felt good, I did it. If I wanted it, I took it."

She bit down hard on the inside of her cheek.

"I drank. I smoked. I chewed snuff. I gambled." His voice trailed away as he waved out the match. "If I started to lose, I cheated to get the odds back in my favor."

Cassandra thought to herself that he'd left out two of his most important transgressions: fornicating and lying. But she held her tongue.

"You name it, I've done it," he said softly. "And until you came into my life, I was damned proud of it. I used to say, 'I'll try anything once.' It never occurred to me that was wrong. Because no one ever *taught* me it was wrong. Don't misunderstand; I'm not making excuses for myself. But at least try to understand how I came to this pass, and believe that I never meant to hurt anyone."

Silence…a long, horrible silence, during which she dug her fingernails into her palms, cutting crescents in the tender flesh.

"Cassandra, are you even listening to me?"

"No, I'm ignoring you."

He snorted with disgust. "Another thing you seem determined to ignore is that I'm damned sorry about all of this."

Damned sorry? She stared across the feeble beginnings of a fire at his darkly burnished face. Her father lay hovering at death's door, and Luke was "damned sorry about all of this."

"Sometimes being sorry isn't enough, is it?"

He straightened from blowing at the flames. "What *will* be enough, Cassandra?"

She felt the tug of his gaze, wanted to throw herself into his arms. But then she remembered her papa—how he'd looked the one time Doctor Mosley had allowed her to see him, like a corpse that was still breathing. It was disloyal of her to even *think* about forgiving this man.

"Go away, Luke. Please."

"I'll do anything," he whispered. "How about a mine for your papa and brother? A rich one. I've got several. I'll sign one over to them. I'll even hire the men to work it for them. They'll be set for life."

Cassandra felt as if a hand were squeezing her throat. "Is that the new price you're willing to pay me to be your whore, Luke? A mine for my papa and brother?"

His jaw began to twitch. He glanced toward Khristos. "Watch what you say in front of the boy."

She gave a bitter laugh. "Trust me, he knows what *whore* means now. Both of us learned it in our vocabulary lesson today."

His amber gaze took on glittering depths. "How could you think I *ever* intended to make you my whore?"

Straining to speak around the shame that had crawled up her throat, she said, "I believe I read it somewhere." She scratched her temple, pretending to ponder. "Let me see...where was it I read that? Oh, that's right. In the contract *you* had drawn up! Only, of course, the wording was a bit more polite. 'Paid companion' was the term I believe you used."

"Forget the damned contract," he retorted. "I admit my intentions were less than honorable at first."

"Less than honorable?"

"Cassandra, please—"

"Go away," she cried vehemently. "Just, please, go away! And stay away! I can't bear to *look* at you."

"Forgive me, please," he whispered. "I'm sorry. Tell me how to prove it to you. Please."

She stared at him through blinding tears. "By going away," she said in a hoarse voice. "By leaving me alone."

He rose to his feet. After gazing down at her for a long moment, he turned and walked away, disappearing into the blackness that lay beyond the nimbus of light and warmth he had created for them.

Believing him gone, Cassandra remained hunkered down by the fire, her head pressed to her knees, her arms looped around her shins. Then she heard Lycodomes's tail thumping. She glanced up to see that the dog was gazing out at the darkness beyond the tunnel. She turned to study the night as well.

"He's still out there, ain't he?" Khristos whispered. "Sittin' in the rain and watchin' over us."

TWENTY-SIX

When Cassandra and Khristos returned to the doctor's office the next morning, Milo had been moved from the surgery into a back room. He lay on a narrow cot, his gaunt face nearly as white as the pillowcase upon which his head rested. Holding her little brother's hand, Cassandra knelt beside the bed and rested her other palm on the gray, coarse wool blanket that covered her father from the chest down.

His dark lashes fluttered, and his eyes slowly opened, as though he were fighting to waken. Finally, apparently with great difficulty, his unfocused gaze settled on her face. After staring at her for a long moment, recognition

478

flitted across his pallid features, and he moved his parched lips.

"Don't try to talk, Papa," she whispered, moving her hand lightly over the blanket to clasp his limp fingers. "Save your strength and concentrate on getting well."

"Yes, Papa. You gotta get well," Khristos seconded in a quavery voice.

Cassandra could feel her younger brother trembling, and she tightened her hold on his small hand, wondering if she should have forbidden him to see their papa just yet. This wasn't a pretty sight, and it was difficult, even for her. Ambrose, who stood behind her, seemed to sense her tension and moved closer to rest a comforting hand on her shoulder.

Milo closed his eyes. "Don't worry...about me," he rasped out. "It's the three...of you I'm concerned about. Ambrose says..." He fell quiet for a moment, as if the effort of speaking had completely drained him. "He says you and Khristos slept at the...digs. Did you...stay warm, lass?"

"Sure we did!" Khristos piped up. "Luke built us a great fire and gathered us lots of wood besides. We was warm as bugs in a rug."

Milo's eyes flew open. He fixed a suddenly alert and unmistakably accusing gaze on Cassandra.

"Luke?" he grated weakly. The name fell from his lips like a curse and seemed to sap the little remaining strength he had. In that moment, Cassandra knew that her papa, who'd spent his whole life abiding by Christian codes and turning the other cheek, had finally been sinned against so gravely he would never be able to forgive it. The hatred he felt for Luke burned in his eyes like banked embers. "No, lass. Tell me you didn't."

Cassandra squeezed her father's hand more tightly, acutely conscious that it was Luke Taggart's fault her papa lay there, fighting for his life. If she had anything to do with her husband now, Milo Zerek would see it as the worst kind of betrayal.

In a twinkling, Cassandra saw scenes from her life flitting through her mind. As a young child, being scooped up in her papa's strong arms and giggling when he tickled her neck with his whiskers. At twelve, being held against his broad chest and weeping because she'd already gotten big bubbies, and none of the other girls her age had any. At fourteen, watching him drag in from an eighteen-hour day at the mine and realizing for the first time how terribly hard he worked for the meager wage that fed his family. At fifteen, seeing him walk through the door carrying a puppy that he could ill afford to feed, a father's birthday gift to his only daughter.

Tears stung her eyes. To her knowledge, her papa had never lied to her or deceived her, unless she counted the times he'd told her how pretty she was, and those little fibs didn't count because he'd only told them to spare her pain. He'd been her rock, this man, for as long as she could remember. He'd taught her all the necessary lessons of her life, how to love, how to laugh, how to hold her head high. But most importantly, he'd taught her how vital it was to be loyal. She could no more betray him than she could herself.

"I sent Luke away, Papa," she whispered. "He followed us up to the mine without my realizing it."

Milo lifted his gaze. "Ambrose, take Khristos out of...here, please. I want...a moment alone with your...sister."

Khristos tugged his hand from Cassandra's grasp. "I love you, Papa! Get well quick, please!"

Milo smiled slightly. "I know you...love me, Khristos. Never a doubt. Now go...with your brother."

Cassandra heard her brothers' receding footsteps. Then the door behind her opened and closed. Still on her knees, she resisted the urge to avert her gaze from her father's. All her life, he'd looked at her with tenderness in his eyes, as if she were a little angel who had dropped in from heaven to bless him with a visit.

Cherished, that was how he'd always made her feel.

A woman now, who'd been intimate with a man, she understood so many things she hadn't before, particularly the innumerable ways in which her papa had protected her from the depravity of men, as if her innocence had been some sacred sort of trust bestowed upon him by God.

The tenderness was no longer in his eyes...in its stead, there was pain. When she'd seen it yesterday, she'd believed he was ashamed of her. Now she realized how wrong she'd been. The reason he looked at her thus was because his heart was breaking for her.

He disengaged his hand from hers and reached up to touch her cheek, his fingertips as cold as death—a jarring reminder to her of how close they'd come to losing him and that they still could lose him yet. "Do you know, Cassie girl, how very...much I love you? More even than my boys. You...have always been my...special one. The one...I love the most."

Cassandra smiled through blinding tears. She'd never tell her papa, but she and Ambrose had compared notes, and their father had told both of them this exact same thing, many a time. Oddly enough, Cassandra knew it wasn't really a lie. Her papa truly did love her most of all...in one special corner of his heart.

Her papa reached down to squeeze her hand, his frigid fingers trembling with weakness. A ghost of a smile touched his mouth. "I'm...so sorry, little girl," he whispered raggedly.

"For what, Papa?"

"For..." His voice trailed away, and he closed his eyes for a brief moment. When he looked at her again, his gaze was once more dark with pain. "For letting you down. Thought I was doing...the right thing, protecting you like I did...never letting you see the ugliness in...people."

"Oh, Papa, don't!" Cassandra cried, lightly

touching her fingertips to his mouth. "Please, don't. None of what happened was your fault."

"Yes." That single word held a world of regret. "Didn't...teach you. Never let you...see how bad people can...be to each other. It was...like sendin' you into a...den of lions without a gun."

The lump of tears in Cassandra's throat made it impossible for her to speak.

"Luke Taggart...he's one of the bad ones," Milo croaked. "Silver-tongued and evil-hearted. You can't trust him, honey. I know you...care for him. Can see it in your...eyes. But you gotta be strong and harden yourself. Promise me, lass."

A cold hand seemed to grab at her heart. How could she promise to rip her feelings for Luke from her very soul? And yet, how could she refuse to honor her papa's plea? A plea made when he might still be dying?

Please, God, make me strong! she prayed with a desperate anguish.

"I promise, Papa," she managed to whisper. "Please, don't upset yourself like this. I promise! I promise." Her father's increasing pallor, which now held a tinge of gray, terrified her.

He squeezed her hand again, his once-powerful grip now without strength. "You're too sweet inside, Cassie, love. Too sweet for your...own good. It'd break my heart to watch him take you...down with him. Swear to me...you'll have nothing...to do with him. Swear it!"

A picture of Luke's eyes, pleading with her for forgiveness, flashed through her head. "I swear it, Papa," she said in a shaky voice.

Over the next few days, while her father teetered precariously on a narrow ledge between life and death, delirious with fever, his body raging against infection, Cassandra remembered his last words to her more than once, usually when she glimpsed Luke—either at the doctor's office, where he stopped daily to check on her father's condition, or out on the street, where he seemed to be walking, always aimlessly, his broad shoulders slumped as though he carried the weight of the world.

Even from a distance, Cassandra could feel the pull of his amber eyes, always delving deeply into her, always voicing a silent plea. At those times, she felt that same cold, brutal fist squeezing her heart. *One of the bad ones*, her papa had called him. Cassandra knew her father had never been harsh in his judgment of anyone. Milo Zerek was a kindly man with a big heart and limitless patience; he'd always taught her to believe the best of others until they proved her wrong.

Luke had done just that. She'd believed in him with all her heart, and he'd ground her trust under the heel of his boot.

Be strong and harden yourself, her papa had whispered to her. Cassandra fought desperately to follow his advice. Every time she remembered something sweet Luke had done, every time she thought of the tenderness in his touch when he'd made love to her, every time she recalled the husky affection in his voice when he'd said her name, she chided herself for having been a fool—a stupid, gullible fool who'd worn her heart on her sleeve and believed in fairy tales instead of facing reality. His whore, that was all she'd been. A plaything he'd purchased to entertain him for a year.

Well, maybe she was a poor girl from the mining district, but she also had her pride. She wasn't a thing to be bought and used by any man, no matter how rich he was. In short, she wasn't for sale.

What she was, she soon realized, was pregnant.

She realized it the day her father's fever finally broke, and Doctor Mosley came out to the waiting room to tell them Milo was going to live. After their initial rejoicing, Ambrose had stepped over to the calendar hanging by the surgery door. According to the doctor, it would take their papa at least six weeks to completely recover from the gunshot wound, which was going to take them into late November.

"We'll have to stay the winter," Ambrose said solemnly. "The passes will be knee-deep with snow by then. Even if we could save enough out of what wages I can earn, we could never travel anywhere under those conditions."

Cassandra was about to say that their papa would not be happy about staying in Black Jack until spring when a cold dread skipped down her spine. She stared at the calendar, remembering the one that had hung on the wall of their little house down in the mining district and how she'd always marked off the days of her "curse" with little *x*s. She hadn't done that in the last part of September or the first of October when she'd been staying with Luke. She'd never even thought about it—because her curse had never come.

For an awful moment, Cassandra was afraid she might faint. All she could think about was the clause in the contract Luke had gotten her to sign—the one in which she'd relinquished all rights to any issue that arose from their relationship.

"Cassandra? What is it?" Ambrose asked softly, his gaze moving over her face. "You look like you just saw a ghost."

More like the devil himself, she thought a little hysterically. And she'd sold more than her soul to him. She pressed a hand over her waist, not entirely sure her legs would hold her up.

A baby...*her* baby. And if Luke ever found out about it, he'd take it away from her.

Suddenly Ambrose's prediction that they would have to stay in Black Jack until spring took on new significance and filled her with rising panic. She couldn't stay here that long. She'd grow large with child before spring, and Luke would know the instant he clapped eyes on her.

"Cassie?"

She jerked her gaze to her older brother. The question in his eyes made her look quickly away again. "It's nothing, Ambrose," she whispered, not wanting to add to his burden of worry, which was already mountain-high. The responsibility of having to feed their family rested entirely on his shoulders now, and she knew he felt overwhelmed by the prospect. "I was just thinking how unhappy Papa will be when we tell him."

"Well, unhappy or no, I don't see a way around it," Ambrose said absently.

No way around it, no way around it, no way around it. Cassandra crossed the room and sank weakly onto a chair. Maybe she'd just miscalculated, she told herself. Or perhaps her curse was just late.

Even as the thoughts crossed her mind, she knew she was lying to herself. She'd never been late. Her female affliction came as regularly as clockwork, every twenty-eight days.

"Let's look on the bright side," Ambrose said with determined cheerfulness. "In three days, we can take Papa home. We'll make him a nice bed, and you can wait on him and fuss over him to your heart's content."

Cassandra nodded, trying her best to feel joyful. They'd nearly lost Papa, and she should be on her knees thanking God that he'd been spared. It was just so terribly hard to be grateful when she was suddenly faced with the possibility of losing another loved one—her very own baby.

The day Milo Zerek was released from Doctor Mosley's clinic, Luke Taggart showed up at the mine carrying a pick and shovel in one hand, a wedge and sledge in the other. Cassandra glanced up from where she knelt beside her father's makeshift pallet, scarcely able to believe her eyes when she saw that it was Luke standing there in the sunlight just beyond the mouth of the tunnel. Indeed, if not for his face, she might not have recognized him.

Gone was the wealthy-looking man in the expensive silk shirt and tailored suit. Dressed like a common laborer, he stood with his booted feet spread wide, a pair of well-worn and faded blue Levi jeans riding low on his narrow hips and hugging his long, muscular legs. His blue chambray work shirt was open at the throat, the unstarched front plackets drawn limply back by the turn of his collar to reveal a broad swath of darkly burnished, powerfully padded chest, the light furring of hair glistening against his skin as if the fairies had sprinkled him with gold dust.

Since Ambrose had gone into town to look for work and her papa was so weak, Cassandra was the one who had to face him. She rose on trembling legs, one hand pressed protectively to her waist. She had the horrible feeling that Luke would guess her secret the second he looked into her eyes.

He inclined his tawny head, squinting against the light to see her. A muscle along his darkly tanned jaw twitched as his gaze shot past her to rest on Milo.

"Hi, Luke!" Khristos called.

Luke glanced toward the boy, who sat on a rock by the fire. "Hello, Khristos. It's good to see you."

Her papa pushed up on an elbow. "What're you doing here, Taggart? We've issued you no invitation, and you're not welcome."

Luke's mouth twisted up at one corner. "I didn't expect to receive a welcome, Milo. But I'm here, all the same. As for my reason, I've come to work."

"Work?" Milo repeated hoarsely. "At what?"

"Busting rock." Luke hefted the tools in one hand. "The way I see it, you and Ambrose worked at my silver mine for three weeks, and you refused to take the pay you had coming to you. That means I owe you six weeks' labor." He sauntered into the tunnel. "You can say what you like about me, but I pay my debts."

Milo snorted. "You won't last half a day, swinging a pick. Those baby-soft hands you used to defile my daughter will be blistered and oozing blood in two hours, maybe less."

"They've been blistered before," Luke said, and kept coming. "Believe it or not, I could once swing a pick with the best of them."

"Yeah? Well, go prove your manhood some-place else. As I said, you're not welcome here."

Luke never missed a step, just kept moving toward them.

"I mean it, Taggart! Stop right there and get out of here!"

As he came abreast of them, Luke turned to face them. He glanced only briefly at Cassandra before meeting her father's fiery gaze. "I came here to work off my debt, Milo, and that's exactly what I'm going to do." He glanced around the tunnel, his gaze narrowing as he assessed the jags of rock along its walls. "So, you think there's some gold in this hole, do you?"

489

"That's none of your damned business. Get out, I said!"

Luke smiled slightly. "The only way I'll leave this tunnel is if I get carried out feet-first."

"You know I can't best you in a fight, you son of a bitch."

Cassandra had never heard her papa use such language. That he did so now conveyed the depth of his rage.

"No," Luke agreed solemnly. "And it's my fault you're lying there, isn't it?"

"And you think busting rock in my mine will make up for it?" Milo cried.

Luke shook his head, his gaze moving to Cassandra's. He looked into her eyes for an endlessly long moment. "No, I don't think anything can ever make up for it," he finally replied, returning his attention to her papa. "Some things can't ever be undone, no matter how you try or how much you might wish they could be."

He turned and headed toward the darkness that lay like a pit behind them, tugging a miner's light from his belt as he walked.

"I may be flat on my back," Milo yelled after him, "a weak old man who can barely stand! But, by God, Ambrose isn't! He'll beat the ever-loving hell right out of you when he gets here!"

Luke missed a step, then drew to a slow stop. Looking back over his shoulder, he softly said, "If he does, I'll just bandage myself up and be back tomorrow so he can beat the hell out of me again. And again the next day,

I'll be back. Sooner or later, he'll get tired of barking his knuckles."

"Goddamn you!" Milo cried as Luke resumed his pace. "You'll stop at nothing, will you? First you try to buy my daughter with your money. Now with your sweat! Well, Mr. High-and-Mighty Taggart! My girl isn't for sale, not for any price!"

TWENTY-SEVEN

With the first ring of steel striking rock from deep within the bowels of the mining tunnel, Cassandra wanted to run. The thought of listening to Luke swing a pick all day was almost more than she could bear. She threw a frantic glance at her father, who'd fallen back against his pallet, pale from expending his strength in the argument with Luke.

She couldn't leave, she realized. She was trapped here because her papa needed her to care for him. Biting the inside of her cheek, Cassandra tried to block out the sound of Luke's pick, which struck the stone with forceful and rhythmic precision, testimony to the hard, sharp-edged muscle that corded his lofty build. Was this just another attempt on Luke's part to buy her, as her papa had determined? Or was it a bid for her forgiveness, a last-ditch effort to show her what he seemed unable to say with words: that he loved her?

"Don't even think it, lass," Milo said weakly. Swinging his head toward the tunnel behind him, he added, "The man's a master, isn't he?"

Cassandra flinched, realizing her thoughts must have been showing on her face. Her papa looked deeply into her eyes, his own aching with sadness.

"You mustn't let yourself fall for it, Cassie, love. He knows how to tug on your heartstrings. I'll give him that. But love is as love does. He's a shallow, empty man, with nothing to offer you but heartbreak. Trust me on that."

Cassandra nodded and rose to her feet. Grabbing up the bucket, she said, "I think I'll go fetch some water before the afternoon rains hit."

Her father held her gaze for a long moment. "You do that. And maybe sit for a while by the stream in the sunshine, lass. By the time you have a nice long rest and get some color back in your cheeks, that no-account yonder will have given up and gone home."

Relieved to escape the tunnel, where the ring of Luke's pick was a constant reminder of his proximity, Cassandra nearly ran down the hill to the creek, her feet flying so fast the bucket clanked against her leg with every step. Once at the stream, she sank onto a rock and let the pail tumble from her hand to roll over the rocks. Hugging her waist, she bent forward over her knees, her heart twisting with a pain so acute she wasn't sure how she might survive it.

Luke. Oh, God, she wanted to feel his arms around her again, so badly it was like a ravenous hunger eating away at the lining of her stomach. She wanted to feel his big hands running firmly over her body again, feel his silken lips against her skin, lose herself in the passion that had flared so easily to an inferno between them.

Oh, God, she wanted him so—an awful, terrible wanting that lurked deep inside her, someplace where Papa's words of wisdom couldn't reach. A place where dreams and yearnings dug in and lay low, like an army under siege, to survive the ceaseless riddling of facts and reality Papa kept drilling into her head like a furious volley of hot lead.

Luke. As she rocked back and forth, her heart racing, his name kept going through her mind until she felt nearly demented. She pressed one hand against her belly, thinking of the babe nestled somewhere inside her. Luke's baby. Her baby. *Their* baby. Dear Lord, had she created life with a man who cared nothing for her, who thought her no better than a whore?

What a pitiful legacy to pass on to an innocent child.

Though she'd lost her mother at a young age, Cassandra could still remember her mama's warm hugs and the lilting sound of her voice. Never once had Cassandra doubted that she was loved.

Would her own child grow up and be able to say the same?

Don't be a fool, Cassandra, a voice inside her head chided. *Made to look the fool once, shame on Luke. Made to look the fool twice, shame on you.*

For her baby's sake, she had to set aside all her tangled feelings and look at the facts.

And they weren't pretty. Luke was in the mine, trying to play on her sympathy, acting the part of martyr. And to what aim? To convince her that he was sincerely remorseful, that he'd changed. That he was willing even to punish himself physically to prove it. And here she sat, rocking and weeping, her heart fairly breaking because of it.

Who was she going to believe? she asked herself harshly. Luke, who'd almost never told her the truth since she'd known him? Or her papa, who'd never lied to her in her entire life? Setting aside her feelings for Luke, which had been born in a treacherous web of deception, Cassandra figured it was a fairly easy decision to reach. She had to believe her papa, who was a lot older and a lot wiser than she.

Luke Taggart was a master of manipulation. Even now, he was attempting to work his wiles on her, acting as though he really intended to swing a pick for weeks on end in the black bowels of the Zerek mine because he cared for her. How long would he stick it out? A couple of hours? Maybe several days? Even if he lasted it out the entire six weeks, was she going to let that sway her?

Once he realized she was no longer the gullible, gushing fool he'd found in a leaky miner's shack, he would cut his losses and move on. There were plenty of women in Black Jack who'd give their eyeteeth to be Luke Taggart's lady.

Her heart ached at the thought, but she made herself square her shoulders and lift her chin. Papa was right. Luke was the lowest of the low, a man without heart. Without honor. A man she dared not trust ever again.

When Ambrose returned to the mine, he was white-lipped, glassy-eyed, and holding his arms rigidly at his sides, his massive hands knotted into fists. Cassandra turned from the fire, where she was simmering a stew made from a rabbit Khristos had killed with a makeshift slingshot and some vegetables Father Tully had given them. When she looked up at her older brother, she thought she'd never seen him look so angry—a cold, shaking anger that frightened her.

"Ambrose? What is it?" she asked faintly. "Couldn't you find any work?"

Ambrose gave a harsh laugh. "Oh, yes. I found eight jobs, all of them full-time and offering better wages than I've ever made in my life."

Cassandra frowned, certain she must have misunderstood him. Her papa, who'd pushed up from the pallet on his elbows, looked equally bewildered.

"Eight jobs?" Milo repeated. "And all for good wages? Ambrose, that's wonderful."

Ambrose just stood there, gazing down at his father for an interminably long while, his hands still clenched into fists. "No, Papa, it isn't wonderful. Not unless you want to take Luke Taggart's money."

"Taggart's money?" Milo's dark brows drew together. "What d'you mean, lad?"

Ambrose shifted his weight from one booted foot to the other. He glanced around their makeshift living quarters. "Where is Khristos?"

"Off hunting with his slingshot," Cassandra replied. "Lycodomes went with him."

Ambrose drew in a ragged breath and slowly exhaled. He returned his gaze to his father. "After I landed the first job, I was so excited and happy, I almost did a jig in the street, Papa. Then, as I started home, it occurred to me I'd come by it too easily, and that the wages were way too good for a stock boy at the dry goods store. Better than the hourly rate paid a miner who swings a pick all day." He gave a bitter laugh and shook his head. "I hated to look a gift horse in the mouth, but something about it didn't ring true. So I headed back for town. Everywhere I stopped and asked for work, I had a good-paying job offered to me so fast it almost made my head swim."

Fingers of dread clutched at Cassandra's throat. She didn't want to hear the rest of what Ambrose was going to say.

"Finally, at the livery stable, when I landed a job as a groomer for better pay than that of a shabby woman who works on Sundays, I knew for sure what was happening. Just to be positive, though, I slammed the livery owner up against the wall and demanded the truth. It seems Luke Taggart put the word out. Anyplace I go and ask for a job, I'd better get one, and a damned good-paying one at that. And why the hell not, when he'd be the one paying my wages?" Ambrose dragged in a lungful of air, his frown thunderous. "It's blood money, that's what it is. And I'll be damned if I'll take it."

Milo fell back against his pallet and closed his eyes. "Well, then, and I don't know why I'm surprised. We've always known he owns the whole town, or nigh close to it." He licked his parched lips. "It's a long reach that Luke Taggart has...a very long reach, indeed. When we first came here, I was told he had political clout all over the state. Now I'm beginning to believe it."

Cassandra's legs had begun to tremble. All over the state? She curled an arm around her waist, wondering how far she would have to run to get safely beyond Luke's reach. More specifically, to get her child safely beyond his reach. She looked down at Papa, knowing she had to tell him of her pregnancy soon. Somehow, they had to figure out a way to leave Black Jack. Maybe by wagon—they could make Papa a bed in the back. If they took it slow, maybe he could withstand the trip.

"Anyway, I didn't take any of the jobs," Ambrose finally finished. "I can chip rock here and keep us alive with the bits of gold dust I can scrounge. We'll make it through the winter without Luke Taggart's money, dammit, or my name isn't Ambrose Zerek."

As Ambrose finished speaking, the sound of steel striking rock rang up from the depths of the tunnel. Ambrose jerked his head around and stared into the darkness. "What was that?"

"Just what it sounded like," Milo said, and then recounted to his older son the events of the morning. "It seems Mr. Taggart doesn't stop with trying to buy people with his money. Now he's going to try bribing us with a little of his sweat."

A cold, hate-filled hardness came over Ambrose's features. His teeth flashed white behind snarling lips as he whispered, "Like hell he is. Not in our mine."

He started past Cassandra with his fists already raised to fight.

"Ambrose!" Milo said sharply. "Stop right there, lad."

Trained since childhood to obey his father, Ambrose halted in mid-stride, his stocky body vibrating with rage. Cassandra could see that her brother was itching to go into the mine to find Luke, that he was relishing the thought of crunching his knuckles against the bones of the other man's face.

"The man had us thrown in jail," he said softly. "Then he bought my little sister as his whore. When that didn't earn him a place between her spread thighs, he married her. And you tell me to stop? It's about time that piece of slime got what's coming to him! We'll see how much good his money does him when I beat the bloody hell out of him."

Milo shook his head. "He's getting his comeuppance at the business end of a pick. He hasn't done an honest day's work in years, and he's been swinging that pick or sledge steadily for four hours, without so much as a break."

Ambrose's body relaxed slightly. He glanced from his father down into the tunnel with a speculative frown.

"We've been there," Milo said with a humorless chuckle. "I'll bet his hands are raw with blisters by now, and every muscle in his body is screaming. Let him go, Ambrose. It'll be far harder on him than a good, quick licking would be. Besides, the man isn't worth you breaking a sweat to kick his ass."

When dusk fell several hours later and Luke came staggering from the depths of the mine, Cassandra didn't even look up. She continued to dish stew, her heart enclosed in a hard, cold wall of numbness.

"I'll be back at daybreak," Luke told her father, his voice heavy with exhaustion.

"That's your choice," Milo said smugly. "If you can walk, that is."

Luke didn't respond to the jibe. He simply turned and headed out into the rain-swept darkness. Cassandra turned to hand Khristos a tin cup of stew.

"Mind that you don't slop any on your jacket," she warned.

"He tried to hide them," Ambrose said with a snort of laughter, "but did you see his hands?"

Milo chuckled. "Down to raw meat," he said with satisfaction. "We'll not be seeing him up here again, mark my words. It'd take a better man than he is, by far, to swing a pick with hands covered with bloody blisters."

Cassandra winced but refused to let herself think about the pain Luke must be suffering. Her papa had suffered worse. All of them had.

Because of Luke.

Yes, she thought as she stooped to dish up a bowl of stew for her papa and brother. Papa was dead right. They'd not be seeing Luke at the digs again.

Milo Zerek was dead wrong. Right before dawn the next morning, Cassandra jerked awake at the sound of footsteps and metal softly clanking. She pushed up from her pallet, rubbing the sleep from her eyes and squinting to see. In the eerie twilight of the newborn morning, Luke stood at the mouth of the tunnel, the rising wind whipping his tawny hair and molding his faded chambray shirt to his ruggedly lean torso. Lycodomes, who lay at the foot of her bed, whined in welcome and gave a glad thump with his tail. *Traitorous dog.*

Her defenses momentarily crumbled by sleepiness, Cassandra simply sat there staring at Luke. He stared back, his whiskey-and-smoke eyes emitting a heat that curled around her like smoldering tendrils. Bathed in the multihued iridescence of dawn, he appeared to be surrounded by a nimbus of rosy light, making him seem unreal—the embodiment of the phantom lover who now haunted her dreams. His firm mouth kicked up slightly at one corner, his jaw muscle bunching as he returned her regard.

"I'll just tiptoe through," he said softly, his darting gaze taking in the sleeping members of her family who lay around a fire long since burned down to ash. "No need to get up."

Last night, he'd left his mining tools in the tunnel. This morning, he carried a dented lunch box in one hand and a brown paper package tucked under his other arm. As he drew abreast of her, Cassandra saw that his palms were bound with white strips of linen—bandaging to protect the blisters he'd gotten from swinging the pick all the previous day.

"You're stupid to do this," she couldn't stop herself from whispering. "It won't work. All your suffering will go for naught."

He drew to a stop, his gaze holding hers and cutting off her breath. "Will it? Six weeks is a long while. Every time you hear that pick hit rock, remember this: I'm doing it for you."

He bent and laid the package on her lap. "Open it," he whispered.

Cassandra lowered her gaze to the package. "What is it?"

"Look and see for yourself."

She tugged at the twine and peeled away the paper. Inside lay a pair of patent leather slippers, like those she'd once admired in Miss Dryden's dress shop window. Tears blurred her vision as she stared down at them.

"If I didn't care about you," he said softly, "would I remember the things you wished for, Cassandra? Would I even have bothered to find out?"

Cassandra shoved the slippers off her lap and made fists in the wool blanket. "I'm not for sale, Luke. Not for any price."

He smiled slightly. Then he turned and disappeared into the blackness.

"Crazy son of a bitch," Milo Zerek muttered under his breath after lunch later that day. He pushed up from his bed on one arm, shaking his head. "Crazy, mule-headed, stubborn son of a bitch!"

Startled to hear her papa swear, Cassandra glanced up from the bucket where she was busy washing dishes. Her father was looking over at Ambrose.

"Did you see those rags on his hands?" Milo asked his older son softly. "Soaked through with blood."

Ambrose, who'd been sipping coffee from a tin cup, emptied the mug with an angry fling of his arm. "Don't go letting him get to you, Papa. The bastard came up here to eat his lunch in the hopes we'd notice. Don't you see? He wanted you to look at that blood and feel guilty. And it's working."

Milo sighed and looked over at Cassandra. "What drives a man to punish himself like that?"

Cassandra met her father's gaze evenly. "The man bleeds like any other, Papa. So, what? It changes nothing."

"She's right," Ambrose seconded. "Remember that paper he made her sign. And the shame."

Milo grunted as he sat up, a hand splayed over his chest. Concern for him made Cassandra's heart jump about like a confused toad in a frog-leaping contest. "Papa, are you all right?"

"I'm fine, lass. Healing good. Just a little sore."

Unconvinced because of the deep lines pleating his forehead and the shadowy expression in his eyes, Cassandra gazed at him, her hands frozen in mid-motion. "We're supposed to change your bandages today. Maybe I should have a look."

"I said I'm fine, and that's the end of it!" Milo retorted with a snappishness that was uncharacteristic of him. He grimaced as he sought a comfortable sitting position. Khristos leaped up from his rock by the fire to run over and support his papa's back. "Leave off, lad. Let me be."

Khristos moved back, dropping to his knees on Milo's pallet. "But, Papa, you look all sick-like," the boy said, echoing Cassandra's thoughts.

Milo sighed and turned his head to gaze down into the tunnel. The steady ring of steel hitting rock drifted up from the dig to them. "Damn him," he finally said softly. "Every time I hear that pick drive home, I can almost feel the pain of it."

"That's exactly his aim," Ambrose reminded him. "Just block it out, Papa. He won't come back tomorrow. I've seen better men than him unable to work on the third day when they're unaccustomed to swinging a pick. He'll be lucky to roll out of bed and even luckier if he can walk."

Milo's mouth tightened. "That's just it," he said. "I've experienced it. You've experienced it. The pain in your back and shoulders and arms taking your breath every time you move. Yet he keeps swinging. He hasn't done this kind of labor in a long, long time, Ambrose. You can't tell me he isn't suffering the agonies of the damned right now."

Ambrose, who was occupying the rock Cassandra often sat on, bent his dark head, arms propped on his knees, hands dangling between them. "You aren't starting to feel sorry for that bastard, are you?"

Milo hauled in a deep, shaky breath, the effort clearly causing him discomfort, for he once again grabbed for his chest. "I'm just wondering if maybe I wasn't a little too quick to judge him, that's all. Why? That's the question I keep asking myself. What man in his right mind would put himself through this for what lies between a woman's—"

Milo broke off, his face flushing scarlet. He glanced apologetically at Cassandra. She averted her gaze, a suffocating sensation filling her chest.

"I'm sorry, lass. I didn't mean to talk foul," her father said hoarsely. "It's just that I'm starting to question my own good sense."

"No, Papa!" Ambrose put in, the thunder back in his frown.

"This is between me and your sister, Ambrose. I'll thank you to let me say what needs saying." Milo shifted his gaze to Cassandra's face, his own frightfully pale. "Hear me, girl. I've been lying here thinking maybe I was a little too quick to snatch you away from him and talk so hard against him. A man doesn't swing a sledge with hands that are nothing but raw, bleeding meat unless he cares for a woman, and cares deeply. Maybe you should—"

Cassandra cut him off by springing to her feet and throwing the rag she'd been using to wash dishes onto the ground. The sodden cloth hit the earth with a wet *splish* that seemed to echo in the tunnel.

"Stop it, both of you!" she cried, her hands clenched at her sides. "All this talk, like I'm nothing more than a brainless child." She held up her hands. "You were right about Luke Taggart. He's nothing but a conniving rake, a man without a conscience. You asked me to harden my heart toward him, and I have! Don't be changing your mind now!"

Wheeling, Cassandra ran from the mine, shame scalding her cheeks. Though her father had cut himself short, he'd nearly said Luke wouldn't swing a pick with bleeding, sore hands if all he wanted was what lay between her legs. It was humiliating to be discussed in such terms, especially in her presence. As if a woman's greatest worth and most important function in men's eyes was the physical pleasure she could provide.

At the creek, Cassandra sought refuge in a thick copse and sank down on a log. Mindless of the rain, she singled out a leaf to stare at, feeling a certain kinship with the triangle of green as it was pounded and buffeted by the wind and rain. Luke, her papa, the circumstances she suddenly found herself in—like that leaf, she felt pummeled and wind-tossed, unable to control her life.

Pregnant. She kept remembering the clause in the contract she'd signed that had stripped her of any legal right to her baby. Her papa was a good, kindly man with a heart as big as these Colorado mountains, and always before, she'd trusted his judgment implicitly. But not this time. If he began to waffle about his feelings toward Luke, it would be up to her to remain steadfast.

The bottom line was, she knew Luke Taggart better than anyone. She'd looked into his twinkling, expressive, convincing gaze while he lied to her through his teeth. She'd been completely taken in by his charm. Oh, yes, she knew better than anyone else how treacherously sincere he could seem.

TWENTY-EIGHT

For two weeks, Luke showed up at the Zerek mine shortly before dawn every morning and worked like a slave until nearly dark, stopping only to eat lunch. After the third day, Ambrose finally relented and went down to work beside Luke. Over the course of the next week, the two of them unearthed enough bits of gold to buy supplies to feed the Zerek family for the next month.

"By gum, there *is* some gold in that hole," Milo said with unconcealed delight when Ambrose held up a vial of sparkling dust for his father to appraise. "I guess my nose wasn't so far wrong, after all."

Luke, who for the first time had joined the Zereks at their evening campfire, stood with his feet spread, his arms hanging loosely at his sides, his hands wrapped in crimson-stained bandages. Exhaustion slumped his broad shoulders, and lines of weariness etched his bronzed face. It looked to Cassandra as if he'd also dropped weight—not that she cared. Maybe he'd made her papa and Ambrose start to doubt their own judgment, but her own convictions still stood firm.

"I'd like your permission to tunnel east, Mr. Zerek," Luke said softly.

Milo squinted up at him from where he sat cross-legged on his pallet. These last few days, much of his strength had started to return, and his craggy face had lost its sickly pallor, taking on a more ruddy glow. "Why east?"

Luke rubbed at his jaw with the back of his wrist, undoubtedly to make sure everyone in her family saw how badly his hands had been bleeding, Cassandra thought testily. She fixed her gaze on the fire, refusing to reward his fine theatrical performance with so much as a second of her notice.

"I could be wrong, but I think that's where the gold is," Luke finally replied.

"Another tunnel? It'd take new timbers," Milo pointed out. "That means money'd have to be spent."

Cassandra braced herself, convinced Luke would offer to become an investor. Instead, he surprised her by saying, "You've got the capital in those bottles. It takes spending money to make it."

Cassandra shot a look at the vial Ambrose held. That gold dust wasn't going to buy any tunneling timbers. They were going to need the money it brought to get a wagon, so they could get out of these mountains before the first heavy snow.

She fixed a worried gaze on her papa. Milo's eyes were glinting, which was a bad sign. Cassandra knew that look: Gold fever. Her papa had had a bad case of it for years, and once he got on the trail of what he called "a big find," she'd be hard put convincing him to leave here. She would have to talk to him soon, she decided, to tell him about the baby. Once he realized the urgency, he'd be as anxious as she was to get away from Black Jack. He wouldn't want any grandchild of his to be raised by a man as heartless as Luke Taggart.

Like a portent of doom, snow was falling when Cassandra awakened the next morning. Shuddering with the cold, she huddled under the cloak of her wool blanket and stood at the mouth of the tunnel to gaze out at the drifting flakes of white, a sight she'd always delighted in. Only now, she didn't envision carolers trudging through pristine drifts to sing Christmas songs to their neighbors. No thoughts of flickering Christmas tree candles or gaily wrapped packages or sugarplums danced through her mind. All she could think about was the mountains, and how quickly they would become impassable once the snow-storms of winter finally struck.

Directly after breakfast, when Khristos had gone off to play in the fluffy white stuff and Ambrose had disappeared into the tunnel with Luke to start the day's work, Cassandra approached her father.

"Papa, I have to talk to you," she whispered as she sat down beside him on his pallet of cast-off quilts they'd been given by Father Tully.

Her father settled a loving gaze on her. "I'm glad, for I've been wanting to talk with you as well."

"What about?"

He smiled slightly. "You go first."

Beneath the blanket she had draped around her, Cassandra pressed a protective hand over her waist. "Prepare yourself for a bit of a shock, Papa."

He inclined his head. "I'm braced."

She sucked in breath. "I'm pregnant."

"Ah…I suspected as much."

She shot him a startled look. "Am I showing, do you mean?" The thought that Luke might have guessed as well nearly made her heart stop. "Oh, no!"

"You're not showing, Cassie, love. But there have been other signs." He reached up to smooth her hair. "I've fathered three children, you know. And that's not counting the four wee babes your mama lost. I know what an expectant mother goes through, especially early on. You've not been eating much. And you take so many trips out yonder to douse the bushes, I'd swear you were working fire brigade. I've also heard you retching a couple of times."

Cassandra bent her head, relieved she wasn't showing, yet embarrassed even so. After a long moment, she said, "You have to get me away from here. I know you aren't up to traveling yet, and I'm sorry to burden you with such a worry right now. But I was

509

thinking. Maybe if we bought a wagon, we could make you a nice soft bed in the back of it, and we could take it real easy, so as not to jostle you. We could winter in Denver if we had to. Boulder would be better, probably, it being farther away. But—"

"Hold it!" Her papa held up a hand. "Who says we're going anywhere?"

"Papa," she whispered urgently, "we have to. If Luke learns about the baby, he'll take it away from me." Tears filled her eyes. "I can't give up my baby. I just can't."

Milo sighed and looped an arm around her shoulders to draw her against his chest. "Ah, Cassie, love, what have I done to you? God forgive me."

Mindful of his wound, which wasn't yet completely healed, Cassandra clung to him, remembering all the times as a child that he'd held her this way. "Oh, Papa, please, get me away from here. Please don't let him get my baby. I'd die."

Milo stroked her hair, then patted her back, much as he always had, his touch comforting her as nothing else could. "Luke isn't going to take your baby, honey. Trust me on that."

He suddenly grasped her by the shoulders and forced her to sit upright so he could see her face. His mouth twisted in a sad smile as he wiped the tears from her cheeks. "Just look at you, so pale and with shadows under your eyes. And thin, Cassie, love. You're starting to look like a scarecrow with bubbies."

She blushed and ducked her chin. "I could

be a rack of bones and still be cursed with those."

"Cursed or blessed?" He winked at her. "I'd say Luke's vote would be for the latter."

Cassandra opened her mouth to protest, but he laid a finger over her lips.

"Cassandra Zerek, you listen to your papa. Until now, God bless you, you've always been a good girl and heeded my every word. Now, suddenly, you're turning mule-headed on me. Am I going to have to turn you over my knee to get your attention?"

She blinked. Her papa had never laid a hand on her in all her life. "My attention? How can you say that, Papa? I've never ignored you."

"No, and more's the pity. Maybe you should have." He cupped her chin in his hand. "I'm only a man, Cassie, love. I try to be a good one, but sometimes I make mistakes. My faith tells me to forgive, and I didn't when I should have. My faith tells me to turn the other cheek, and instead, I struck back." A suspicious brightness misted his eyes as he ran his gaze over her face. "And, God forgive me, the weapon I used was my daughter. I retaliated against Luke through you, child, and dealt him a fell blow by turning you against him and making you hate and fear him." He leaned forward to press a kiss against her forehead. "I was wrong to do that."

Cassandra gulped. "What are you saying? That I should go back to him? Papa, are you forgetting the baby? He could take it!"

Milo chucked her under the chin. "Cassandra, would you say I'm a stupid man?"

"Of course not!"

"Would you say I've given you bad advice your whole life long?"

"No."

"Then listen to me. Luke won't take your baby from you. I'd stake my life on it. He'd be more likely to lay the world before you and then kiss your feet. The man loves you, sweetheart. It's there in his eyes, every time he looks at you."

Cassandra closed her eyes. An awful pain welled up inside her. "Don't do this to me, Papa. You're asking me to gamble with my baby!"

"There is no gamble." He sighed and rested his arms on his bent knees. "I'll tell you what. Let's strike a little bargain. Tonight, after Luke goes home, you go down the mountain to talk to him." He held up a hand to forestall her words. "Hear me out! You go with your heart open and ready to forgive. You tell him about the baby, and that you're afraid he'll take it away from you. If he doesn't tell you then that he loves you, we'll buy that wagon and make me a bed in the back of it, and we'll hightail it for Denver tomorrow, weather allowing."

"He won't say he loves me. He's *never* said he loves me. Not even when we were getting married would he say the word. He said *cherish* instead. Don't you see, Papa? He isn't capable of the emotion! If I tell him I'm pregnant, he'll have all the power. He'll hold that contract over my head. To be with my child, I'll have to stay the rest of my life with a man who doesn't love me—if he doesn't grow bored with me and toss me out on my ear! Think what you're asking!"

"I already have." Her papa turned a solemn gaze on her. "You go home to your husband tonight, lass. You have this out with him. Let Luke do his own talking; see what he has to say. If it isn't that he loves you, I won't let you be forced to stay with him. I swear it." He paused a moment, his expression conveying his conviction. "Think about this until you go to see him. He isn't holding the contract over your head now, is he? If he were, you'd be a prisoner in his home and sharing his bed every night."

By nightfall, the snow lay ankle deep and fluffed like icy cotton. Cassandra slipped and scrambled for balance beside Ambrose as they descended the mountainside, heading for town. Clinging to her brother's arm, Cassandra fought desperately to quash the dread that rose within her like bile. Never in all her life had she been as frightened to confront anyone as she was when she contemplated facing Luke.

"Are you mad at Papa for asking you to talk to Luke?" Ambrose asked, his words oddly muffled in the chill night air, as though the drifting snowflakes absorbed some of the sound.

Cassandra considered the question, acutely conscious of the muscle that flexed in Ambrose's arm when he tensed to support her weight. It didn't seem all that long ago that they'd been children, romping in the snow like wild little hooligans, their voices and laughter ringing in the air. Ambrose—her older brother, her constant tormentor, yet always her friend. Now, it seemed, he wanted to assume the role of her confidant as well.

She glanced back over her shoulder. "I sure hope Papa doesn't forget to watch Lycodomes. If that silly dog tries to come down this hill, he'll slip and hurt his splinted leg, for sure."

"Papa won't forget to watch him," Ambrose assured her. Then he said, "Cassie, are you feeling embarrassed?"

"About what?"

"About me knowing you've got a bun in your oven."

She'd never heard pregnancy referred to in quite that way. "A bun in my *oven*? Ambrose, don't be crude. And, yes, I feel sort of embarrassed."

He gave her a heavy-lidded glance. "I suppose you thought I never noticed you were female from the neck down...and a mighty pretty female, at that. Sex and babies are natural things. Your being pregnant isn't any big thing that we've got to be secretive about."

Cassandra slanted him a look of sisterly teasing. "I can't believe you just said the word *sex* to me."

He chuckled and rested a hand over hers where she clutched his jacket sleeve. "I'm sorry. I guess I should've said fiddlin' and diddlin'."

She swung her free hand around to sock him on the shoulder. The sudden movement caused her to lose her footing, and she nearly upended herself. Laughing, Ambrose kept her from falling. "You need your mouth washed with lye soap!" she cried, clutching the front of his rough wool coat to keep her balance.

"And you'd better stop acting like a two-year-old," he said, grappling to keep her standing on the slick-soled hand-me-down shoes that kept skating out from under her. "If you fall, Papa will have my head. Thunderation! That's why I'm escorting you down the mountain, to make sure you reach Luke's house in one piece. You're pregnant, for cripe's sake!" His words cracked like a whip in the brittle air.

"Just yell it out, why don't you, for God and everyone else to hear!" she whispered.

"I think God already knows. And when you start to look like you swallowed a pumpkin, everyone else will, too. You're a married woman, Stump. It's not an awful thing to be with child. It's what married folks do, you know. Fiddle and diddle and make babies."

"Don't call me 'Stump'!"

He slipped a brawny arm around her waist to ensure she stayed upright. "Why not? In a few months, you'll look like one that has a very large and round pitch bole poking out its front." He chuckled when she elbowed him in the ribs. "Just between you and me, you're the cutest little stump I've ever seen."

Cassandra flashed him a smile, but her heart wasn't in it. They had nearly reached the bottom of the mountain, and every step they took led them closer to Luke's house.

At the corner of his street, she tugged Ambrose to a halt and drew in a breath of frigid air. "I can go the rest of the way alone."

"But you won't."

"Ambrose—"

"It's too slick, Cassie." His expression was suddenly somber. "That's my niece or nephew you're workin' on, you know."

Taking a tighter grip on her arm, Ambrose escorted her clear to the Taggart front gate before he finally released his hold on her. Cassandra gazed nervously at the house. Golden light illuminated some of the windows, casting an amber glow over the blanket of snow that covered the shrubs around the foundation.

"Scared?" Ambrose asked, all note of teasing gone from his voice.

Cassandra nibbled her bottom lip. "If I denied it, I'd be lying."

Ambrose regarded the house for a moment. "Nobody's perfect, Cassie, Luke least of all. And we all make mistakes. The way he went about getting you was wrong, very wrong. But I truly do believe he loves you."

She glanced up at him, astonished. "You what?"

Her brother, who so seldom treated her with anything more than teasing disregard, suddenly bent forward to kiss her forehead. "I've been working beside the man for almost two weeks. He's been sweating blood down there in that tunnel. Not for me. Not for Papa. But for you."

"That's not what you said that first day when he showed up with his pick."

"I was wrong." He gave her a rueful look. "Funny, isn't it? The person he's done it all for has refused to notice, and it's Papa and me he's managed to impress, the ones who started all the trouble between you in the first place."

She shook her head. "No, Ambrose. Luke started it all with his lies. You and Papa just finished it."

"Papa says that loving a woman can change a man." He turned his gaze toward the house. "I think it's changed Luke Taggart. For the better. Much, much better." He flashed her a slow smile, his eyes soft with understanding. "Gather up your courage, little sister, and go in there. See if I'm not right. I'll wait for you down at the corner."

TWENTY-NINE

After an amazingly informal greeting from Pipps, who grabbed her up and gave her a fierce hug the instant she stepped into the foyer, Cassandra asked if she could see Luke.

Pipps eyes lighted. "Of course, my dear. Let me announce you."

Feeling a sudden flare of panic, she forestalled him with a hand on his arm. "No, but thank you, Mr. Pipps. If you'd just tell me where he is."

Pipps's sigh was heavy. "In the study. Where he always goes when he comes home."

Cassandra repeated her thanks and moved along the hall. At the study door, she paused, heart thudding, to wet her lips and straighten her spine before she entered. For good measure, she pressed gentle fingers to her tummy before slowly turning the knob.

The door opened soundlessly on well-oiled hinges. Frozen on the threshold, she stood staring at the man seated in a circle of light from the lamp flickering on the desktop.

Luke sat leaning back in his chair, his muddy boots propped on his desk. Still garbed in work clothes, his tawny hair lying in untidy waves over his forehead, he looked exhausted, dirty, and very out of place in the elegantly appointed room.

Having entered unannounced, Cassandra shut the door quietly and simply stood there gazing at him. The oddest thought came to her as she studied him, that *this* was the real Luke Taggart, a man of sweat and steel, who'd survived poverty and God knew what else, only because he'd had a will of iron.

Memories. They came over her like tumbling debris carried forth on a gigantic wave. *I'm a toad pretending to be a prince.* That had been true, she realized now; the wealthy, polished man she'd believed him to be had been an imposter, a very clever, manipulative fraud who'd broken her heart into a million pieces.

Only now, with the advantage of hindsight, was she beginning to realize that maybe she'd hurt Luke as well—not deliberately, but by failing to see him for what he really was. Not a prince, and not a toad, but a man made up of both good and bad.

She'd looked at him through a shimmering

layer of unreality, wanting to believe he was almost perfect. That was an impossible order for anyone to fill. Yet, in his way, Luke had taken a stab at it, desperately trying to be someone he wasn't. Then when he finally fell from the pedestal she'd placed him on, she'd turned her back on him.

Don't leave me, Cassie. Swear you'll never leave me. And she'd promised she never would.

Maybe, if she'd been more mature, she wouldn't have broken that promise. But deep in her heart of hearts, she doubted it. If she lived to be a hundred and became as wise as Solomon, she would still want the one thing from Luke that he seemed unable to give, his love. To her, a good marriage couldn't exist without that, and she refused to settle for less.

Cassandra looked desperately around the room for something that might insulate her from the pain. Her gaze landed on the whiskey bottle at center stage on his desk. He had been drinking, she decided, evidently straight from the jug, for there was no fancy crystal brandy snifter in sight. Some "big change" his feelings for her had wrought in him, she thought with disdain. He obviously still liked to guzzle his whiskey, and if he hadn't foregone that particular habit, how could she be sure he didn't still indulge in others, falsehoods being at the top of the list? For all she knew, he might have stopped by the Golden Slipper on his way home for a casual romp with one of his shabby women.

His pale blue work shirt, unfastened halfway down the front, lay open to reveal the bronze chest and midriff she remembered so well, only now the mounds of muscle and corrugated tendon had been honed to steel by swinging a pick these last two weeks. Folded back to reveal thick, darkly burnished forearms lightly dusted with golden hair, his shirtsleeves stretched tautly over the powerful contours of his upper arms.

Doing something with his hands, which she couldn't see because they lay in his lap behind the desk, he had his head slightly bent, a preoccupied frown pleating his high forehead. He seemed completely unaware of her presence, his expression so bleak that he once again put her in mind of Khristos when he'd awakened from a bad dream, lost and in need of a hug.

Growing impatient with herself and her silly, gullible heart, Cassandra took her tangled emotions firmly in hand. She'd walked this path before, and the heartbreak at the end of it had nearly killed her. Luke wasn't a little boy; he was very much a man, and completely in control of his world. Completely in control of *her* as well. She'd be wise to remember that.

"Luke?" she said softly.

At the sound of her voice, he shot up from the chair as if someone had jabbed him with a red-hot poker. A green tin of salve fell from his lap and bounced across the floor; the clanking sound nearly made her leap. Now that he was standing, she saw that he'd removed the bandages from his hands. Apparently, he'd been applying salve to the raw and bleeding patches where the blisters had burst and festered.

Hesitant, her heart slamming, she avoided his gaze as she took a step farther into the room, the lies and the hurt forming a chasm between them that could never be bridged.

Her attention fell to his hands again. The flesh of his palms resembled the meat she'd run through a grinder for Khristos when he was a baby. For the life of her, she couldn't imagine how Luke could stand to flex his fingers, let alone swing a pick, hour after endless hour. Her stomach knotted, and she glanced quickly away, searching for something, anything, to focus her gaze on besides his poor, injured hands.

"Cassandra…" He said her name so softly, so…reverently, that her gaze jerked up as if drawn to him by a magnetic force. Was it hope that she saw in his eyes? An almost desperate hope? After searching her face for a long moment, he asked, "What brings you here this time of night?"

"I, um…I need to talk to you about…something."

The tendons along his throat worked as he swallowed, his Adam's apple bobbing. He gestured toward the chair at the opposite side of his desk. "Do you have time to sit down?"

She approached warily. As she perched on the leather cushion, an awful smell assailed her nostrils. Wrinkling her nose, she blurted, "What on earth *is* that?"

One corner of his mouth twitched as he sat

back down. Inclining his head toward the whiskey bottle, he said, "A special remedy of Cook's for blistered hands. Cider vinegar, brine, tincture of iodine, and whatever else it struck her to pour in, I think. Burns like a son of gun, but it seems to be toughening my hands up. Sorry it smells so bad."

"I thought it was whiskey."

He leaned back in his chair to regard her with eyes that seemed to miss nothing and twinkled faintly with amusement. "I've backed off quite a bit on my drinking."

"Why?" she couldn't resist asking.

"I was told by someone I greatly admire that I wasn't going to find any answers to my troubles at the bottom of a jug. Since he was right, and all I found down there was a headache, I decided to drink a little less and think a whole lot more."

"And?"

His gaze dropped to where her hands lay in her lap, the knuckles white with tension. "I think you're very nervous." That bleak, lost look came back into his whiskey-and-smoke eyes. "I know I've done some unforgivable things, sweetheart, but surely nothing to make you afraid of me."

"There are all different kinds of fear, Luke, and so many different ways to inflict hurt. You never hit me or treated me mean, I'll give you that. But didn't it ever occur to you that perhaps you drew blood in places you couldn't see?"

He sat there, gazing at her, his face stony and expressionless.

She disentangled her fingers and made fists on her skirt. "Luke...I didn't come here to quarrel with you, or to dwell on what's already done."

"Then why have you come?"

"I, um...want to ask a favor."

"What is that?"

She forced herself to meet his gaze. "You remember the contract you had me sign?"

His mouth tipped up at one corner in a rueful grin. "If you're talking about *the* contract—every confounded word of which is emblazoned on my brain—yes, I remember it."

She dragged in a bracing breath. "There's one clause in there—the one about my relinquishing all right to any issue that arose from our relationship—that I was, um...wondering if you'd consider waiving."

His whiskey-colored eyes darkened to misty gray around the irises, and a muscle along his jaw began to twitch. "You're having my child," he whispered.

It wasn't a question. Cassandra sat there, her gaze held relentlessly by his. The tension that crackled in the air between them was almost electrical. Finally, she said, "I'll die if you take my baby away from me, Luke. Please, say that you won't."

He said nothing. The silence pounded against her eardrums, the rhythm slow and ponderous at first, then escalating to a rapid and deafening thrum.

"I-I'm willing to strike a bargain with you, if I must," she finally said in a shrill, shaky voice that sounded nothing like her own.

"What kind of bargain?" he asked in a dangerously silken voice.

"Wh-whatever you ask, in return for custody of my baby." She leaned slightly forward, entreating him with her eyes. "Please, Luke? I'm even willing to be your paid companion again for a specified period of time if, at the end of it, you'll let me take my baby and leave." She waved a hand toward the window. "You've seen the snow. The mountain passes will be knee-deep." She gnawed her lip for a moment. "I'll be honest. I made Papa promise he'd take me away from here so you'd never know. But with this turn of the weather, that'll be impossible. I'm left with no choice but to try and reach an understanding with you."

Power. Gazing across his desk at her, Luke realized that he once again had it within his grasp, the proverbial high trump card. *His paid companion for a specified period of time.* Having her here with him again, in his home and in his bed. It would give him a chance to make her fall back in love with him.

He was about to take her up on her offer. Hell, scotch that. He was about to leap at the chance. But then he looked into those big, blue eyes. Innocence and complete trust had once shone in those cobalt depths. Now all he saw was crawling fear and a desperate urgency. His gullible little angel had become a cynical, distrustful, frightened young woman. And why the hell not? She'd been tutored in the realities of life by an expert. He had taught her every lesson, brutally and without compassion, so self-centered that his only thought had been for his own self-gratification. He'd pursued pleasures of the flesh relentlessly, and in the chase he'd captured a blue-eyed seraph who'd stolen his heart.

Now her shimmering halo and spiritual wings had been stripped away. No more glow in her eyes. No more uplifting dreams to buoy her. He'd single-handedly destroyed everything about her that he'd adored and taught her to watch her back, lest the people she trusted most come at her with a knife. Lies and deceptions and treacherous plots. Oh, yes, he'd drawn blood in places he couldn't see, inflicted wounds that might never heal. And as his punishment, he might lose her. But better that than to hold her here against her will, snuffing out what little light still burned within her.

As Luke pushed to his feet, he felt old beyond his years. He walked slowly toward his wall safe, knowing with every step that it was a desperate gamble he was about to take. But while teaching Cassandra so many brutal lessons, he'd learned a few himself—namely that love couldn't be grabbed or stolen or bought. If she stayed with him, he wanted her there of her own free will, not because he held their child over her head as leverage.

As Luke worked the combination lock to his safe, he silently started to pray. It wasn't the first time, for over the course of these last few weeks, he'd implored God for His intervention more than once. But this was the most heartfelt prayer he'd ever said, eloquent in its simplicity. *Please, God, don't let her leave me. Please, God, don't let me lose her.*

This was, without question, the biggest risk Luke had ever taken. He could only hope she realized how dearly this gesture was costing him, and that she'd decide to stay with him, after all.

After drawing both his and her copy of the contract from the safe, Luke stood there, holding them in his hands and staring down at them. Power. Sucking in a hard breath, he grasped the documents more firmly in his hands and, as he turned back toward his desk, began ripping them to shreds. There was another copy in his attorney's possession, of course, but Luke promised himself he'd destroy it as well.

Cassandra's eyes went wide and bewildered as she watched him tear the contracts to pieces. Once back at the desk, Luke let the bits of paper drift from his fingers to rain on his blotter. Blood from his hands now spotted the thick vellum, and he hoped with every fiber of his being that she'd notice it and that it would remind her of the punishment he'd inflicted on himself.

Cassandra sat stiff and motionless on the edge of her chair as he resumed his seat. He opened a drawer to locate paper and then reached for his fountain pen. His sore, raw hand screamed with pain as he crimped his unwilling fingers around the writing tool.

Given the condition of his hands, he wrote only a few lines, in which he not only gave Cassandra custody of their unborn child, but took financial responsibility for any legal costs she might incur while seeking and attaining a divorce.

As Luke slid the paper across the desk to her, he gruffly said, "I do make two requests, Cassandra. That I be allowed to see my child occasionally, and that you accept financial help from me for its support."

Her eyes wide and wary, she took the paper, then bent her head to read what he'd written. When she looked back up at him, there were tears swimming in her eyes. Luke couldn't breathe. God help him, he could scarcely think. If she got up and walked out, he didn't know what he'd do. To let her go would kill him.

"You're setting me free?" she finally whispered.

"Yes," he managed to grate out.

She simply sat there, staring at him, as if she were waiting for him to say something more, her big blue eyes sparkling with tears and dark with a desperate yearning. For a wild instant, Luke thought he'd won, that the yearning in her eyes had to mean that she still felt something for him—if not love, then at least fondness.

Then, in a shaky voice, she shattered that illusion. "You won't do anything to try and stop me? You'll just let me get up and walk out?"

Luke's throat felt as if someone were stretching his neck on a rack. He couldn't drag breath into his lungs. "Yes," he rasped.

She bent her head again. When she looked back up at him, the desperate yearning in her eyes was gone, replaced by a glassy hardness. She pushed unsteadily to her feet, and Luke steeled himself against the urge to jump up and grab her. Not breathing, his heart laboring like an unoiled piston in his chest, he watched her turn and walk toward the door. She paused with one small hand on the doorknob to look back at him.

"Thank you, Luke," she said softly.

And just like that, she walked out.

As the door swung closed, Luke shot to his feet. Only sheer force of will prevented him from bolting after her. He stood there, shaking like a palsied old man, his throat and chest aching. From out in the foyer, he heard the front door softly swing shut.

She was walking out of his life....

You won't do anything to try and stop me? Luke curled his hands into throbbing fists, trying desperately to resist the compelling urge to run after her. Only it was bigger than he was—a mind-numbing desperation he couldn't control. His life wouldn't be worth shit without that girl. He couldn't just let her walk away without putting up a fight.

Luke launched himself across the room, then out the door into the foyer. He was scarcely aware of Pipps as he raced the length of the hall. "Cassandra! Cassie, please, wait!"

She was about to let herself out the front gate when he stumbled onto the porch. Snowflakes drifted around her, dotting the upsweep of sable curls atop her head with white, swiftly melting flecks. In the threadbare gray wool dress, with a tattered wool blanket drawn around her shoulders to serve as a cape, she looked like a little waif standing there, her eyes huge splashes of darkness in the pale oval of her face. One hand resting on the gate latch, she looked back at him, her expression unreadable.

"Please...don't go just yet," Luke managed to say as he descended the three front steps in a leap. The soles of his boots lost traction on the snow-covered walk, and only the execution of some fancy footwork saved him from falling on his ass. *Christ!* Why was it that he bungled everything around this girl, the one person in the world he wanted to impress? "Let's talk about this."

She tucked the paper he'd given her under the edge of her blanket, almost as if she feared he might snatch it away from her. Luke's throat tightened as he walked toward her. He was the one who'd taught her to be so wary, God forgive him. He alone was responsible for those dark circles under her eyes. And, oh, God, those glorious eyes...

"What is there to talk about, Luke?" she asked in a thin voice.

It was a damned good question, and he suddenly realized he had no answer. He didn't have a clue what he meant to say, only that he couldn't just let her leave. With shaking hands, Luke reached for her, vaguely aware as he curled his grip over her small shoulders that the pain in his palms seemed oddly distant, as if he'd somehow become removed from everything but her.

How long had it been since he'd touched

her? Dear God, she felt so good. He wanted to jerk her against him and cinch her tight in an unbreakable hold. To hug her and keep hugging her, until she ceased to resist him. To keep her here with him, no matter what the cost.

It seemed to Luke that a whole minute slipped past, each painful second measured off by the slamming beats of his heart. She looked up at him expectantly, her eyes no longer expressionless and glassy, but still aching with hurt.

Luke hadn't begged anyone for anything since he was a boy. He'd clawed and kicked and scrambled his way up from the gutter to a life of wealth and superficial respectability, and he'd sworn, once he got there, that he'd never demean himself again. Not for anything, or for anyone. But he'd beg for this girl. Crawl, if he had to. To hell with dignity.

"I know I've done a lot of bad things," he told her raggedly. "But can't we start over fresh, Cassie girl? Won't you give me just one more chance to prove to you that I'm sincerely sorry for everything and that I really have changed?"

In the eerie light of the snow-brightened and moon-touched darkness, her eyes became luminous with wetness that sparkled and spilled over her lush lower lashes like diamond teardrops. "Oh, Luke, don't you see? There's only one thing I want from you. Only one thing that could convince me you've really changed."

"What?" he asked with raspy desperation. "Name it, Cassandra, and it's yours. What?"

An infinite sadness came over her pale

face, and she slowly shook her head. "You really don't know, do you? And the fact that you don't makes it impossible for us."

She pulled free of his grasp to unlatch the gate.

"Cassandra, tell me what you want from me," he urged. "I meant it about the mine for your papa and brothers. I'll see to it they live in the lap of luxury for the rest of their lives."

She drew the gate open, her skirt snagging on the pickets, then pulling free as she swept out onto the sidewalk. Luke walked abreast of her along the opposite side of the fence, his boots crunching in the snow.

"What?" he cried, lifting his hands in bewildered supplication. "At least give a man a fair chance! Tell me what you want from me! I made a public retraction, exonerating your papa and brother! I'm working off the wages I owe them! I've made sure they can get work any goddamned place in town! What else? Tell me, and it's yours."

She just kept walking, her small chin held high. In the moonlight, Luke could see that tears were still streaming down her cheeks.

"Are you still angry because they served time in jail?" he demanded. "Dammit, I'll have myself locked up. And I'll serve double the time they did to make up for what I did to the both of them!"

She hugged the blanket more snugly around her shoulders and quickened her pace. That same, chest-squeezing panic rose within Luke again, nearly cutting off his breath. Up ahead,

531

he saw Ambrose Zerek standing on the street corner, his hands shoved deeply into the pockets of his worn tweed jacket. Luke knew the younger man could probably hear every word he said, which went beyond humiliating, but at this point keeping his pride intact had sunk to the bottom of Luke's list of priorities.

"Jewelry? Clothes?" He lengthened his stride to keep up with her, acutely conscious that the section of fence that bordered the side of his front yard stood only a few feet ahead of him. He was running out of room to follow her—and running out of offers as well. "I'll build you a new house. How about that? The grandest house you can imagine, Cassie. A mansion! And you can reign in it like a queen. A new carriage with a matched team of horses. Beautiful clothes and jewelry beyond your wildest dreams. Silks and furs!" He threw up his hands. "Goddammit, stop walking! Aren't you hearing anything I'm saying to you?"

She never missed a step. As she reached the corner of the fence, she called softly, "Good-bye, Luke. God be with you."

He jerked to a stop, the suffocating panic within him quickly turning to rage. A blinding, red rage. He reared back and planted the heel of his boot against the decorative picket fence, nearly uprooting two of the posts.

"'*God be with me*?' That's a hell of a thing to say to a man who's practically on his knees, begging you to stay with him!" he yelled after her. "If I wanted God's company, I'd go to the frigging church!"

She didn't look back. If anything, she hurried her footsteps.

"Fine!" Luke roared, the distended muscles and veins in his neck aching with the distorted pitch of his voice. "Go, then, if you're so goddamned high and mighty! Turn your back on me and everything I've got to offer you! Mark my words, you'll wind up married to some penniless ne'er-do-well, with a dozen snot-nosed brats clinging to your skirts, all of them squalling with hunger. Go, and see if I try to stop you!"

Realizing she was doing exactly that, Luke gazed after her with tears burning at the backs of his eyes.

"Good luck!" he fairly snarled as a parting shot. "Happy husband-hunting! I may be a whore's bastard. And, raised in a brothel like I was, maybe I'm not a sanctimonious church-goer who knows which hand to dunk in the holy water and what knee to genuflect on! But let me tell you this! You can look for a thousand years, and you're *never* going to find a man who'll love you more than I do!"

Cassandra reeled to a stop so suddenly, she nearly pitched forward on her face. She spun on the sidewalk to stare back at him. "What did you say?" she asked in a shaky voice.

Luke sucked in a sharp breath, the icy night air slicing a path to his lungs. "I said you'll never find another man who'll"—he broke off and gulped for breath, that one word he found so difficult to say snagging crosswise behind his larynx—"who'll *love* you as much as I do." He dragged in another deep draft of air. "I love you, Cassie girl. I love you so much it's—it's about to kill me."

She gave a broken little cry and came flying back along the sidewalk toward him. Gawking at her, Luke just stood there, one foot still drawn back to kick the fence again. *I love you*, the words he'd vowed a lifetime ago never to say again. Evidently they were magical, for as she reached the fence, she launched herself at him as if the pickets weren't even there.

Luke caught her against his chest and lifted her over the fence, scarcely able to believe those three words had been what brought her back to him. He'd offered her the world, and she'd waved it all away, as if it meant nothing.

"Say it again," she cried with a sob, hugging his neck so hard he could scarcely breathe. "Say it again, Luke, please!"

He tightened his embrace around her, knowing as he did that he held the whole world in his arms. "Oh, God, Cassie...I love you." He bent his head to bury his face against the sweet curve of her neck, his favorite spot because the scent of her surrounded him. "I love you."

"Oh, Luke, I love you, too. And all I've ever wanted was to be loved back!"

Love. For so many years, Luke had regarded that word as a vile curse he'd never utter. Now he realized it was a gift, the very sweetest and most precious of gifts.

The paper he'd drawn up and signed, making it possible for her to leave him, slipped from her fingers and fluttered to the snow-covered ground. From the corner of his eye, Luke saw it land, the ink immediately starting to bleed as the pelting snowflakes melted over it.

It didn't matter...from here on out, theirs was a verbal contract, based solely on trust, the wording quite simple, to the point, and equitable to both of them. *I love you.*

Luke whispered those words, over and over, as he carried his wife into the house, up the stairs, and into his bedchamber. As he laid her on his bed, where he had dreamed of having her since the first instant he'd seen her smile, he knew he had finally discovered Cassandra Zerek's asking price.

His heart.